Luna

Luna

Sharon Butala

HarperPerennial
HarperCollins*PublishersLtd*

First published in by Fifth House: 1988
First HarperPerennial edition: 1994

Canadian Cataloguing in Publication Data

Butala, Sharon, 1940–
Luna

"1st HarperPerennial ed."
ISBN 0-00-647491-8

I. Title.

PS8553.U6967L85 1994   C813'.54   C94-931585-0
PR9199.3.B87L85 1994

94 95 96 97 98 99 ❖ HC 10 9 8 7 6 5 4 3 2 1

Printed and bound in the United States

for my sisters:

Cynthia
Sheila
Deanna
Kathleen

Diana in the leavës green,
Luna that so bright doth sheen
Persephone in Hell.

Skelton

Luna

UNDER THE MOON

Rhea is sitting in her armchair at the end of the living room in the house she has occupied for sixty years. She is drifting. Her eyes may be open or they may be closed. It no longer makes much difference to her. My two worlds have met at last, she thinks, the inside and the outside. The feeling is a comfortable one, even a glorious one, the world either grey and ordinary, or bizarre and gorgeous, or both at the same time. She never knows when the ordinary will expand, intensify and become, as she watches, the extraordinary, and the extraordinary, as it blossoms around her, will suddenly reveal its ordinariness. Either way, she thinks, I can only laugh, and she chuckles, deeply, in her chest and full round abdomen, and listens to the sound and feels it with complacent pleasure.

She is remembering other springs, or perhaps this spring, or next spring, at twilight, visiting the pen of colts down by the barn. No matter how dark the winter, how deep the snow, how bitter the cold—the men chopping the frozen feed out of the stacks, coming in after dark, cold, exhausted, the cattle still hungry, all of us suffering, the men, the cattle, me—the earth would turn. I grew to feel it underfoot, spring would come again. I, who never saw another woman from one week's end to the

1

next, year after blessed year, had friends. Ah, friends. The pen of colts are my friends—were, she tells herself, remembering how they kicked their heels, tossed their bright heads, touched their delicate muzzles to her arm, snuffed outward with their hot, moist breath onto her wrist.

She sees herself. I, she thinks, a heavy woman even then, old already at forty, yes, that's true, she tells herself. An apron still on over my house-dress, Jasper's old jacket thrown over my shoulders against the evening cold, standing, brooding in the setting sun, watching a pen of colts. She feels herself smile at the image, or perhaps it is not an image, perhaps she is really there again, the evening breeze blowing around her bare legs, making the hem of her cotton housedress flutter, the pigeons in the barn flying out, cooing wildly overhead against the darkening sky. She can smell the warm flesh of the colts, feel their coarse manes brushing the back of her hand. And all the birds, big and small, setting up that evening chatter, their last busy gossip before night descends.

Christmas concerts and playing cards with the neighbours, coming home in the moonlight, the sleigh runners squeaking on the hard-packed snow of the trail, the horses blowing steam, their harness covered with frost, the children asleep under the horsehide blankets and Jasper nodding over the reins. All of them, come and gone before I knew it . . .

JUNE

Selena banged the truck door shut once, twice. Her palms were wet with impatience, her heart beating a little too quickly, so that she had to pause to catch her breath. She turned the key, pulling the choke out slowly till the motor caught, cautiously slid it back in part way, then listened to the motor's uneven rumble, her head cocked, her foot playing the gas pedal.

Late as usual, she was impatient to go, to get out of the yard before some minor disaster kept her, Kent needing her for one last chore. But if she pushed the motor too hard, she would only kill it. And God knew when it would start again, or what Kent would say if she had to find him to help her get it going. Nothing, she knew. He would say nothing, but she would read his amiable superiority in the tendons of his hands as he turned the key for her, or in the shape of his lips as he raised the hood, and in his eyes when the motor was running again.

Satisfied by the rough but steady purr, she put the truck in gear, backed around, and drove out of the yard, keeping her foot as hard as she dared on the gas till she knew the house behind her was out of sight at the other end of the road. Every time she left it felt like an escape.

She slowed a little then, and took a deep, shaky breath. How she hated this in herself, this persistent feeling of guilt, as if she hadn't the right to leave, as if she had to steal away. Though she refused to think about it, she hated it anyway, yet couldn't imagine not feeling it.

Afternoon sun poured in the windows, the day too bright to look at. Long patches of buffalo beans blazed down the ditches on each side of the road, strips of tiny scarlet mallow at the very edge. She could smell the hay, the sweet smell of alfalfa and clover wafting in the open window. Oh damn, she muttered and rapidly rolled it up, but not before a cloud of fine beige dust and a few grasshoppers found their way in. The grasshoppers skipped from her arm and shoulder to the floor at her feet, the dust settled on the dash and on her fresh makeup. She could taste it on her lipstick and feel it on her powdered forehead.

As she turned onto the grid road, the cake in the pan beside her began to slide off the seat and she caught it by the far rim, getting her thumb in the icing where the cellophane wrap had come loose. Without looking away from the road, she straightened the wrap, then sucked the icing off her thumb. She glanced at her watch. Ah well, if Rhea was ready, she'd be only five or ten minutes late.

She stepped on the gas again, but this time without that pull of haste, or was it anger? Or fear? No, not fear. Never fear, she scoffed at herself. She drew another long breath, blew it out slowly, and looked through the now dusty windshield at a flock of horned larks dipping and weaving above the ditch on her left. Grasshoppers hit the windshield and bounced off, or caught in the wipers by a wing or a leg and lay there flapping in the wind. One splattered, a gob of sticky yellow, just above her line of vision. She thought of stopping the truck to wipe it off while it was still wet, but another one splattered to the right of the first so she gave up without bothering.

She turned left again and bumped down a narrow, potholed track, worse even than the one into their yard. The house she was approaching, little more than a shack really, looked deserted but for the flowers of every colour that bloomed between, around and in front of the healthy green shrubs and bushes in front of the low house.

For some reason, Rhea, who hadn't kept cattle for twenty-five years, had shut the barbed-wire gate to the houseyard. Selena hit the brake in time, jumped out of the truck into the cloud of dust it had made and which caught up with her, wrestled the gate open, got back into the truck, tried to brush off a long streak of dust on her pale yellow dress, drove into the yard, and pulled to a stop at the edge of a bed of purple, blue and yellow pansies.

Nothing stirred, the kitchen door didn't fly open and slam shut behind Rhea as she hurried out. Only insects buzzing above raspberry bushes and butterflies darting among the pink and white hollyhocks lining the rickety fence. Irritated, Selena got out of the truck, and instead of using the kitchen door immediately ahead of her, she followed the half-buried old stone path around the west side of the house to the side door, the one that had, all the years she was growing up, been the main door. She knocked. There was no answer, so she pushed the door open and called, "Auntie Rhea? Are you here?"

The living room was dark and cool, the blinds all pulled. A grasshopper found its way in past her legs and landed on the edge of the faded rag rug in the little bar of sunlight that had sneaked in too, and she quickly put her foot out and brushed the grasshopper back behind her so that it hopped outside again. She stepped in and closed the door.

For a moment she could see nothing but the velvety darkness. She blinked and waited, the coolness settling beautifully on her bare arms. Slowly she made out Rhea sitting at the end of the room in her armchair. her eyes wide open, staring directly at Selena.

"Auntie!" Selena said, exasperated. "Why didn't you say you were there?" Then, concern suddenly striking her. "Are you all right?"

"I've been all right more or less." Rhea said, "for eighty years. I should think I'll be all right this afternoon, too." Irritated again, Selena, without replying, lifted the windowblind nearest her a foot or so, letting in the sunlight, so she could see Rhea more clearly.

Rhea was wearing her good dress, a shiny, wine-coloured material that looked black in the dimness. It had a row of spherical buttons down the front, like candies, with a rhinestone in the centre of each which winked at Selena. She was wearing her brown orthopedic shoes, the ones which had taken Selena three trips to Swift Current to acquire for her, and which Rhea had then refused to wear. The shoes were a good sign.

"Good," Selena said, with a firmness she never felt in Rhea's presence, "you're ready. Let's go then." She opened the door and stood back as if this gesture alone would be enough to bring Rhea to her feet and across the room.

"I've changed my mind," Rhea said. Selena closed the door, but not before a breeze crept in and stirred the skirt of the stained, red-flowered tablecloth on the round table against the opposite wall.

"Oh come on, Rhea," Selena said, trying to sound merely reasonable, hiding her annoyance. Flies buzzed on the window above the table, beat against it, climbed above one another trying to get out. And if we let you out, Selena thought, all you do is try to get back in again. Surprised, she laughed out loud, a short quick sound, which she immediately stifled. That was the kind of thing Rhea said. Every time I come here I catch myself thinking like her, she thought, and grew even more irritated.

Rhea paid no attention to the noise she'd made, or behaved as if it were normal to laugh like a fool for no reason in somebody's house over nothing, and then to stop in mid-noise, like a motor shut off.

"Is it your arthritis?" Selena asked. "Is it bothering you? Are you in too much pain to go?"

"I've had enough of women," Rhea said.

"What?" Selena said. Even from Rhea, who constantly surprised, an astounding thing to say.

"I've had enough of women's company," she said. Selena abruptly let go of the warm porcelain doorknob and sat down on the blanket-covered couch by the door. Exasperation mixed with incredulity flooded her.

"For years and years and years—you told me yourself, Auntia Rhea—you said you *died* for the want of women's company, and now, when you have the chance . . ." Rhea drew in a long breath.

"I no longer require the company of women," she said, and folded her fat and wrinkled brown hands on her ample lap.

"I could get Kent to take you to a Kinsmen meeting," Selena said, teasing.

Rhea didn't reply, nor did she take her eyes away from Selena's face, although she didn't seem really to be looking at her. Baffled, Selena cast about for something to say to persuade her. "I can't just leave you here alone day after day. It isn't good for you, Rhea. You don't have to be alone anymore. Why won't you come with me?" She paused, then added, "There'll be lunch—it's at Helen's—you know what a good lunch she always serves. Everybody'll be there . . ."

"You have no idea why you want me to come," Rhea said. "You clearly have never thought about it."

"I want you to come . . . so you won't be . . . lonesome." At this, Rhea let out a long peal of high-pitched laughter. It went on and on, a variegated stream of sound, a wordless humourless message to the universe. Eventually, the sound stopped, she closed her mouth, re-settled her hands on her lap, the fingernails were stained as if she were a smoker, although she was not, and she fixed her eyes on Selena's face again.

"Stop looking at me like that," Selena said, and was again surprised at herself. Rhea gave no reply, nor seemed to notice the strangeness of Selena's remark, its abruptness from one who was always gentle, its rudeness from one who was unfailingly polite. Neither did she take her eyes away. She's going blind, Selena suddenly thought, and rose quickly, making a short aahing sound of sympathy, which she cut off at once, and turned it into a throat-clearing.

"Listen, Selena" Rhea said. Now it was her normal everyday time-to-do-the-dishes voice, time-to-make-the-pickles, time-to-hoe-the-potatoes. Selena sat down again. "I'm not lonely . . ." Rhea began, then stopped, the purpose in her voice leaving it as quickly as it had come. Now she turned her head away and looked at the blank wall behind the table which was covered with potted plants: geraniums, a Christmas cactus; they bloomed and bloomed in the darkened room as if they had all the light they needed, as if the air was not so dry it made you cough. Selena stood quietly.

"I have to go!" she said, suddenly remembering her meeting. Her tension had returned, the pull in her stomach was there again. "I really have to go. If you won't come . . . well, there's nothing I can do about it." She was angry, but she stood still, waiting to see if Rhea would, at this last second, struggle to her feet and without another word, come. It wouldn't be the first time. But Rhea didn't move.

Selena took a few quick steps into the centre of the room and looked to her right, into the kitchen. Everything seemed normal, bunches of dried weeds, lumpy things, Lord knew what they were, hanging down from hooks screwed into the old wooden ceiling, and in the centre of the room, the old round oak table with the lion's paw feet and the matching chairs with the sunburst carved into the back, and beyond that, by the door leading into the flower garden, the big, battered blue granite bread-making bowl that had hung there as long as Selena could recall.

Rhea spoke.

"The world devoid of humans is hardly an empty place. I've told you that." She paused. "How are the children? And Kent?" The first sentence spoken in a deep, vibrant voice, the rest of it in a quavery, old lady's voice, a sociable smile that was almost grotesque suddenly appearing on her creased brown face. Selena sighed. No wonder people think she's crazy.

"Everybody's fine," she said. "We'll be haying before we know it." She moved back and put her hand on the doorknob, turning it slowly.

"I'll do some baking to help out," Rhea said, her tone growing more distant, as if she had moved away.

"Thanks," Selena said, but she was no longer paying attention to her aunt, as her aunt had stopped paying attention to her. She opened the door and took a step out, so that she was half in the cool, dusky room, and half out in the hot and brilliant June afternoon. "I have to run. I'll drop in again tomorrow or the next day." She hesitated. "Can I bring you anything from town? I have to pick Phoebe up after the meeting. She's playing ball in Chinook."

"Nothing, thanks," Rhea said. She still had not moved.

When she was back in the truck again, and had wrestled the gate shut behind her and was rolling down the grid, a long cloud of dust billowing out behind her, Selena, still struggling to shake off that new and unwanted way of seeing things that always overtook her in Rhea's presence, thought again: she's going blind, and frowning, tried to think what she ought to do about it.

The yard at Harry and Helen's was full of trucks and cars parked this way and that, and their little dog, beside himself with wonderful, yapping excitement at her approach, ran in front of the truck. She braked, the ball of white fur rushed away again, she parked the truck where it had stopped, rescued her cake as it slid toward the floor, knocked a big grasshopper off the cellophane wrap, brushed again at the long smudge of dust on her dress, failed to dislodge it, and hurried to the house.

"No Rhea?" Helen asked, as she opened the screen door with one hand and took the cake with the other. "Thanks."

"It's a little the worse for wear," Selena said, as she handed the cake to Helen. "Rhea's in one of her moods. You know how she gets." Helen laughed and shook her head, carrying the cake to the counter where she set it down among the cherry squares, the lemon loaf, brownies, butter tarts, iced sugar cookies, and one dish of homemade candy.

"The best thing you can do when she's like that is go away," Helen said firmly, her back to Selena. "She always gets over it. The next time you drop in on her, she's perfectly fine." A ripple of female voices came from the living room and occasional bursts of laughter, mixed with the piping voices of small children.

Selena paused, straightened her dress, and went into the living room, Helen following close behind, muttering, "Time's a passing. Let's get started."

The living room was a big, rectangular room with a large front window that let in so much light that Helen always kept the white undercurtains pulled shut, even in winter, to soften the unbearable brilliance that faded furniture and rugs, set teeth on edge, and gave piercing headaches that only a cool, dark room and silence could cure. Women were seated on the long sofa that faced the window, on single chairs and a rocking chair, and in the one armchair, all set in a circle around the room. Behind the circle sat the dining room table surrounded by matching chairs, the dark wood polished till it glowed, the table covered with a thick, white crocheted tablecloth, the centrepiece a vase of artificial flowers Selena knew Helen had made in a community college class. Selena had taken the class too, only her daisies and lilies were failures, she had long since thrown them out. She sat down in an empty chair in front of the window and arranged her skirt so that the dusty streak wouldn't show too much.

"No Rhea?" Ella asked from her corner on the couch. Selena shook her head no.

"I couldn't get her to come." Beside Ella, seated in the armchair, Margaret shook her head, tsk-tsking brusquely.

"You can't talk to her when she's like that," she said disapprovingly. Margaret was close to Rhea's age, the only old woman in the room, most of the women had retired from the club by the time they were that old, and she seemed to need to deny to everybody the possibility that she might ever be like Rhea.

"She's her own worst enemy," Helen said, still standing in the doorway, and Lola said, shaking her head wisely, "Some old people, honestly. My Aunt Jean was like that."

"I think . . . I wonder if maybe she's losing her vision?" Selena swung her head toward her younger sister, Diane, who sat in the rocking chair on her right, wearing a bright red dress, her long legs crossed at the knees, her head resting as if she were exhausted against the patterned wooden back of the chair.

"It's like a plague," Margaret said. "But I seen it before," and sighed, pursing her lips.

"We sprayed for them three times last summer and we've got more this year than last, Lola said, and the spray killed our dog."

"Not that big black one? Paddy? Oh, no," somebody commiserated, while Lola nodded, and murmurs of dismay and sympathy spread around the room.

"It's in our drinking water, it's in the air, it's everywhere," Margaret said, a touch smugly.

Ruth said, her voice tinged with a sadness that seemed to go deeper than the conversation warranted, "I don't know where it will all end."

"The end of the world, eh?" Selena's sister-in-law, Rhoda, said, laughing, as if all of this were only more old wives' tales. Selena noticed Rhoda was wearing new glasses, stylish ones, with elaborate arms, curlicued and shiny, and with glittering things in the top corner of each eyepiece. Very nice, she thought, and planned to compliment her when she got the chance.

"Between the dust and the grasshoppers and the spray," Ella said, "it's a wonder any of us are left out here."

"I hope you're staying locked inside when the municipality sprays the ditches," Margaret said sternly to Joanne, nodding toward Joanne's smock-covered rounded stomach.

"Under the bed," Joanne said, and when nobody laughed, "I've heard about the miscarriages. I asked the doctor about them, but he said there's nothing to worry about."

There were several hahs, and Rhoda said, her glasses glinting cheerfully, "You'd be better to let Rhea look after you," and then everybody laughed, although not too hard, and sobered quickly, so that Selena wondered if they had half-meant the laughter or the advice, or if it was just that they had remembered too late that she and Diane were Rhea's nieces.

Diane barely hears the women chatter all around her. *This* is my life, she thinks, this women's society. This is what fate has set me into the midst of. She allows herself one slow, cautious look around the room, barely moving her head. No one seems to see her, no one returns her glance. This confirms for her the unreality of this moment, here in Helen's living room. As she looks at each of them one by one, she is surprised at how they seem set apart each from the other, even though their eyes meet and their voices bounce and touch. She closes her eyes then, and feels her youngest, Cathy, leaning against her feet as she sits, diapered, on the floor in front of her. She has moments when she cannot believe she has become the mother of two children.

"Ladies," Helen called. She was seated now at the far end of the dining room table with Enid on her left. Immediately, hearing the authority in her voice, Selena and the other women rose and pulled their chairs around to face the table.

Phyllis helped Margaret turn the heavy armchair. "If we don't get started right away, we'll all be late with supper," she said.

"Let them make their own supper," Rhoda said, and everybody burst out laughing. Beside Helen, Enid took the cap off her pen, spread her notebook open in front of her, and assumed a solemn expression.

"Queenie's not here," Selena said.

"She phoned to say Ross needed her for something or other." Helen peered over the women's heads, searching for Diane. "Aren't you coming up here?" she asked. Everyone turned to look at Diane, who sat rocking slowly, her thick, dark brown hair spread out against the chairback.

"I can give my report from here," Diane answered, still not lifting her head.

Two little girls suddenly emerged from under the table where they had been crouching, their cotton slacks creased at the knees. One of them perched silently on the arm of Margaret's chair. Joanne called, "Lana, come here," to the other. Helen paused again, her lips pursed, while Lana went to Joanne and stood in front of her mother, one finger in her mouth, her knees locked and her small stomach jutting out, watching the other women with a wide-eyed, speculative gaze, while Joanne replaced the barrette in her smooth yellow hair.

"She's got knowing eyes, that one," Margaret remarked, nodding wisely.

"She's cute," Ella said, smiling at Lana. "Just like her brother." She sighed. "Before you know it, she'll be helping serve at the Fowl Supper."

"And we'll be putting on her wedding supper . . ."

Helen opened her mouth to speak, but there was a scream from the kitchen followed by a wail in a different key. Two children, then. Lola leaned forward, past the television set, and looked around the room. Not seeing her child, she got up and disappeared into the kitchen. In a second she was back in the doorway.

"Phyllis?" Phyllis rose quickly and went into the kitchen with her. In the lull Selena noticed that Diane had begun silently picking at the fabric of her full red skirt, where it smoothed itself over her knees. She wanted to reach out and cover Diane's busy hands with her own, to quiet them, as she would have done if Diane had been her daughter. She forced her eyes away and turned back to the meeting with a surge of exasperation. How she hated these meetings, boring and long-winded and inconsequential, with all their petty quarrelling and back-biting. She had to laugh at herself, remembering how eager she always was to come to them. We do good work, she reminded herself. What we do is needed here. If it wasn't for us, the community would fall apart. Still, she preferred doing the actual work to attending the long meetings about it. Probably all of them did, she thought.

"The agenda today," Helen began again. "We have to make plans for Louise and Barclay's twenty-fifth . . ."

"When is it?" A chorus of voices.

"The end of July."

"And we have to set a date now for the Fowl Supper so we can get a good time when there aren't fifty other things going on."

"Yeah, like rock concerts and dances and everybody else's Fowl Suppers . . ."

"Shshsh." Rhoda was hushed by several women at once. She dropped her head, flushing.

"And we have to look over the bills for the spring Dine and Dance and get authorization to pay them. Then . . . there are a few more items." She consulted a sheet of paper in front of her. "Classes for community college this winter, some fund-raising, and . . . so on."

Lola returned, carrying a small boy still in diapers in her arms. Phyllis followed, steering ahead of her a toddler munching on a cookie. They tiptoed to their chairs and sat down, Lola still holding her son on her lap, while Phyllis's little boy folded his plump legs and landed with a soft bump on the carpet, his cookie still in his mouth. The little girl perched on the arm of Margaret's chair suddenly abandoned her and went to Diane.

"Mommy . . ."

"Shsh," Diane hushed her. She leaned then, up against her mother's legs, watching the women seated at the table. Selena watched Diane, who was staring at her daughter's back without reaching out to touch her. She wanted to say, forget whatever it is, just for a minute. Forget it, Diane. But she knew this was not the moment and she stopped herself from leaning over and whispering in Diane's ear. She turned back to Helen.

Diane cannot comprehend how it is that this child, this little girl, grew out of that baby she once was, the baby she brought out of her own body. This little girl, ready for school in the fall, already, when it seems she was just born. Diane feels her own life slipping away from her, fears it will be gone in a smear of empty, busy years. She wants her life to slow down, give her a chance to see it, to figure out what it means, what she should be doing. She studies Tammy's narrow back, the way the tendons of her neck, so thin and delicate, swell faintly under the exquisite skin of her neck. She feels such tenderness for her daughter, it breaks her heart to think that this small girl will be a woman soon.

Helen forged on.

"Enid, the minutes of the last meeting, please."

Enid rose and began to read. Selena noted the new pink dress with the heavy, padded shoulders. Ah, she's young, she can wear it, she thought. A young girl can wear anything. She glanced across the row to Phyllis in last year's lightweight, flowered cotton, noticing how it was all wrong for Phyllis's long, muscled body. Phyllis's hands were clasped on her knees and against the tiny pink and blue flowers they looked painfully rough and red. Enid's voice quavered with nervousness and Selena brought her attention back to the young woman. Enid had become a member only the fall before, after her wedding to Malcolm. That stupid Malcolm, Selena thought, but she'll make him grow up.

Diane moves her eyes to Enid, watches how she flushes prettily now and then, trying to say the right thing, trying to be womanly, yet modest, as befits the young. Diane sees Enid's eyes going soft as she looks across the room and through those annoying curtains to the long, hazy field beyond. So Diane knows it is Malcolm she is thinking of, her new husband, the one she loves, the one she can barely believe loves her too, knows Enid is remembering the joy of their nights after the door is closed and the day's work forgotten.

13

"Treasurer's report. Diane?" Helen's voice was steady, business-like, as if she didn't disapprove of Diane's refusal to sit with the rest of the executive at the table. Diane turned her head slowly, cleared her throat in a soft, tentative way, but didn't stand. Tammy, leaning against her knees, stared back at all the women who were staring at her mother with expressions ranging from puzzlement to stern disapproval. Abruptly, she turned and buried her face in Diane's lap. Diane's hand crept out to rest on Tammy's head. Cathy, sitting on the floor by her feet, threw one fat arm upward, then brought it down gaily.

"I forgot the account book," Diane said. Again Helen pursed her lips, then released them.

"Could you maybe give us a quick rundown of our position? Whatever you can remember." Helen had begun brusquely, but in mid-sentence had smoothed all the irritation out of her tone, so that Selena dropped her eyes and blushed for Diane. No secrets here. Anyone who had eyes to see could tell that something was wrong with Diane. The women sat motionless; the children, sensing the emotion in the air, were for once silent.

"I think," Diane said, "that we have about four hundred and fifty left in the bank. We just broke even on the Dine and Dance." She stopped, and it was apparent she had said all she could be bothered to say. A cat meowed plaintively on the deck just outside the screen door, and a truck could be heard passing down the grid. Tammy suddenly lifted her head from her mother's knee, pushed herself away, and ran into the kitchen, giving two little skips as she reached the door.

"Oh, no." Phyllis sniffed, then bent forward, scooped up her cookie-smeared son, made her way past the women and disappeared into the hallway that led to the bedrooms and bathroom.

"One day you're changing their diapers, and the next day, they're telling you what to do," Margaret said. There was an amused silence, a few giggles.

"Now, Louise and Barclay's twenty-fifth. Floor is open for discussion." Helen laboured on.

"Well," Ruth said. Everyone turned to look at her, faintly surprised. She had been a member of the club for thirty years, yet she rarely spoke at the meetings, except privately, in conversations. "I'm not so sure they'll want one." There was a puzzled silence.

"Why not?" Helen asked. Nobody spoke, and in the silence the coffee urn in the kitchen bubbled, reminding them all of the passage of time. The odour of perked coffee drifted into the too warm room and Cathy clapped her little hands together and crowed, so that all the women smiled at her.

"Because," Ruth said, "the situation over there is pretty serious. That's probably why she isn't there today." She paused, them murmured as if to herself, "You kinda lose heart." There was another long silence. "She was over yesterday afternoon. That's how I know."

"The bank?" Joanne asked, faltering a little. Ruth nodded.

"That was her father's place," Margaret scolded.

"Can we have some cookies?" Lana asked, standing in front of Lola. Lola hushed her, nodding and shifting her head to see around her daughter.

"How bad is it?" she asked Ruth.

"Buck said he was in Antelope on Wednesday and he saw them both coming out of the bank there. They looked pretty worried, he said. And then he drove on over to Chinook to see about some fertilizer at the Pool there and who should he see coming out of the Credit Union but Louise and Barc." There were murmurs of dismay around the room. You only went around from bank to bank like that if you were looking for money and nobody would give it to you."

"How much land have they got?" Joanne asked.

"Six, eight quarters," Rhoda said. "Not enough."

"I don't see how we can not give them a twenty-fifth," Helen said. "They might not feel much like celebrating, but how would they feel if we just let their anniversary pass and didn't do anything?"

"We could always freeze the baking," Ella pointed out, "if something happens and we have to call it off." Phyllis sniffed the air again.

"Oh, no." She rose, picking up her son, and carried him out of the room.

"Has he got diarrhea?" Ella asked.

"Just started," Phyllis called, out of sight in the hallway.

Selena found herself again watching Diane. She was looking through the curtain to the yard beyond, at the row of steel bins which

15

was almost too bright to look at in the full sun. A breeze crept through the screen door beside her and stirred the curtain so that it floated up against her head.

She raised one hand absently and brushed it down, then folded both hands across her abdomen. Seeing this gesture, Selena wondered, is she pregnant again? No, that's not possible, she thought, Diane had sworn that she would die before she'd have another child, two were more than enough, she had said, two were too many. Selena had been deeply shocked when Diane had said that, and even now, remembering, the same emotion stirred deep inside her. She couldn't understand how any woman could feel that way.

Diane knows Selena is studying her, but she doesn't turn her head to meet her sister's eyes. Poor Selena, she thinks, how little it takes to satisfy her, as if she is only partly alive. Like Margaret. To wind up like Margaret, a shadow of a woman—old and shallow and empty. Diane would like to let herself sink irrevocably into this sucking lethargy she feels, but when she holds her baby in her arms, she thinks, not yet. Still, she cannot understand, in the face of everything, why her love for Tony, her love for her children, is not enough.

"We'll set up a lunch committee right now," Helen said. "Who's going to write them a song? You, Selena? Will Phoebe play the piano for us? Diane, you always do the best skits, can you think up one for Louise and Barc?"

The meeting moved on to other subjects while the children played around the room, giggled or whined, nagged their mothers and each other, kissed the babies to everybody's delight and pinched them when nobody was looking, though everybody knew it by the wide-eyed look on the offender's face and the surprise in the baby's howl. At last it was time for lunch.

Women rose, changed seats, went to the bathroom, settled children, went to the kitchen to help with lunch and serve it. Selena bent down and picked up Cathy. The child was getting sleepy and she leaned back against Selena's chest. Selena smoothed her fine, curly hair with her palm, enjoying the warmth of her body and the silkiness of her hair. Before she had time to suppress the impulse, she found herself longing for another baby of her own.

She turned to Diane and said, with more intensity than she had meant, "Are you okay?"

"Yeah," Diane said. Selena could see her making an effort to collect herself. "The crop's looking really poor. If it would just rain."

"Maybe you and Tony should take a holiday," Selena suggested. "Spring work's done, and I'd be glad to take the kids for you." Diane made a noise that might have been a laugh, or a smothered sob.

"Tell me what's the matter," Selena pleaded.

"Rhea has a remedy for diarrhea that never fails," Ella called across the room to Phyllis.

"I don't know," Diane said, after a pause, looking away from Selena. She sounded almost angry.

"I'd appreciate it if anybody who has any ideas for community college classes for the fall would let me know," Phyllis called over the chatter. "We have to get in our requests pretty soon."

"Microwave cooking," Rena suggested. Again Diane made that peculiar sound in her throat.

"What about that class they had last year in Antelope?" Lola asked. "The one everybody was talking about. Farm stress, or something."

"Stress management," Helen corrected her.

"You have good ideas," Phyllis said, turning to Diane. "What do you think?" For a moment Selena thought Diane was not going to answer. She drew in her breath slowly.

"What's the point?" she asked, and the room grew quiet. "Crocheting, embroidery, wheat-weaving, sewing mukluks . . ." Tentatively, Ella spoke.

"It's just . . . entertainment. It passes the winter."

"But is that all it's for?" Diane asked. She sat up abruptly and looked around the room as if she were angry at all of them.

"I think they're darn good," Lola said, bristling at the implied criticism. "I've learned lots in those classes."

"Flower arranging, cake decorating." Diane's voice was filled with scorn.

"You tell us what we ought to have, then," Phyllis said, too vehemently. "You've been on the committee. You know nobody will come to academic classes."

Diane searches for the words that will explain to them what it is that makes her ache so, with a yearning that feels as though it will never be stopped. She wants to tell them something, she wants to use words they will recognize, identify what each of them knows secretly, but will never acknowledge out loud. But all she can think of is Rhea telling her: sometimes I would cry for days at a time. I looked after the children, I cooked the meals, weeded and hoed the garden, carried water to it, made cheese and canned beef, washed the clothes and hung them on the line to dry. And all the while—all that spring or all that fall—tears ran out of my eyes and down my cheeks, dripped off my chin into the dishwater or washwater, or onto the cabbage leaves I was hoeing, or the clean clothes I was ironing. I never willed them to start. I couldn't make them stop. One morning I'd wake and they'd be seeping out of me, and they would seep for days.

Unexpectedly Ruth said, "I know what she means." Her voice was too loud in the sunbright, crowded room. "You go on day after day, year after year. The kids grow up. You find yourself thinking, there must be something more. There must be." She stared from woman to woman. "Do you know what I mean?" Nobody answered her.

Selena thought, ah well, she'd be the one to say that. Buck drinking too much all the time, mean with her when he's drunk, they say.

"Well," Phyllis said, her brightness a new note in air heavy with unspoken words. "I don't know what the college can do about that."

"Lord, when I first came here," Margaret intervened, "when I was young as you," she indicated Phyllis with her chin, "we'd have given anything just to get together once in a while." She shook her head, reflecting. "It was so lonesome. You can't imagine how lonesome it was. How do you think Rhea got the way she is?" She lifted her head at this, her eyes suddenly fierce, then laughed, a little embarrassed. "Just to get together every once in a while for a class still seems like a miracle to me."

The conversation went on around them, but Selena had stopped listening. She would have to talk with Diane, see if she could find some way to help. Soon Lola was rising, packing the cracked vinyl diaper bag Selena remembered giving her at her baby shower when Lana was born. Phyllis was gathering her baby's things and Joanne was rising clumsily from her chair.

"Heavens," Selena said, looking at her watch. "I've still got to get Phoebe. She'll be having a fit."

"Where is she?" Diane asked, lifting Cathy onto her hip.

"Playing softball in Chinook. The bus is only coming as far as Mallard, so I said I'd drive in and pick her up. Here, I'll carry Cathy out to the car."

They went out together in the midst of the crowd of women, all calling good-byes, reminding one another of this and that, exclaiming about the heat and the dust and one more time about the grasshoppers. Selena settled Cathy into her car seat, kissed her, then stood back so that Tammy could climb in beside her little sister. Diane got in behind the wheel and turned the key.

"Diane?" Selena asked, leaning in the window.

"What?" Diane asked, turning her head toward Selena too quickly, frowning, then hurriedly turning back again, as if she were embarrassed by her own bad temper.

"Come over tomorrow morning. Kent's going to Swift Current for baler parts. We can talk."

Diane stared ahead out the windshield, a faint flush rising in her thin cheeks. Selena thought she would burst out in anger again, or not answer at all, or cry, but after a moment, Diane said simply, "Okay." She shifted into gear and began to inch the car away. Hastily Selena withdrew her hand.

The yard was filling up with dust as one by one the vehicles drove away. A grasshopper landed on Selena's shoulder, then leaped away before she could brush at it. The crops will be burning up, she thought, peering through the haze at the long, pale fields, and it's only June. She got into her truck and drove through the dust out of the yard, turned right at the end of the approach, and headed toward Chinook, twenty-five miles to the north.

Phoebe was leaning by herself against the brick wall of the high school when Selena pulled up. The schoolyard was deserted, but it seemed for a moment that Phoebe, lost in thought, had not noticed her mother's arrival. Selena leaned over, a little puzzled since Phoebe had never been given to periods of deep thought, and opened the door on the passenger side. Phoebe jumped then, smiled at Selena, then as quickly wiped the smile away.

"It took you long enough," she said.

"I got held up," Selena apologized, then annoyed, said, "You're lucky I came at all. You could have taken the bus as far as Mallard." Phoebe didn't answer. As Selena turned the truck out of town, she set her schoolbooks down on the seat between them.

"How was the meeting?" she asked humbly, as if to make up for her rudeness.

"Oh, you know," Selena said, although Phoebe had never been to one of the meetings, not since she was a preschooler. "Pretty boring, but we're starting to plan for Louise's twenty-fifth. They want you to play the piano. Okay?" Phoebe shrugged.

"Sure." She sighed and sat back, looking out the passenger's window. "Can we shorten my dress tonight?" Selena nodded without speaking. "Grad's next week," Phoebe pointed out in a sulky tone, as if Selena had refused.

"Tonight's lots of time," Selena said in a soothing voice, then remembering how Phoebe hated her to use that tone, she said quickly, "When do the boys pick up their suits?"

"They're not wearing rented suits," Phoebe said, her surprise changing to annoyance. "It isn't a wedding."

Has Brian got his yet?" Selena asked, willing herself to keep her voice friendly.

"He got it last weekend," Phoebe said. "I told you. It's a pale sort of blue-grey tweed. It looks really nice on him."

"Oh, that should really look nice with your dress," Selena said.

"I gave him and his mother a little piece of cloth from my dress so they could make sure they'd go together. There's a deeper blue fleck in the tweed that's exactly the same colour as my dress."

"Queenie's good about things like that."

"It's no big deal," Phoebe said, offended now. "It didn't hurt her, and anyway, Brian said he wanted to."

This last couple of months talking with Phoebe was like going for a stroll in a minefield. Phoebe read mistrust, or accusation, or laughter at her expense, into every remark. Selena tried to remember if she had been like that at seventeen. But her own mother was dead by then, and she had been a mother herself, trying to raise her little sister.

"What about corsages?" she asked, just to keep Phoebe talking to her.

"Oh, Mom, I told you," Phoebe wailed. "It's either pink or yellow carnations. I decided to have yellow." It was all Selena could do not to snap at Phoebe now. She reminded herself, it's a hard time in her life, it's scary—graduation from high school, the end of her childhood. Thinking about it, she felt overwhelmed by all the things Phoebe was facing, including what would happen to her relationship with her boyfriend once she left for university in the fall. They had turned onto the black-top road now where there was not dust, and she rolled down her window to let in the fresh air.

"The windshield's sure a mess," Phoebe remarked. She forgot her little flareups as fast as they happened. Selena relaxed. She had been thinking for some time that she should have a talk with Phoebe about grad night. She had told Kent she would, had made him promise he would say nothing if she would talk to Phoebe.

"Phoebe," she said, then stopped, frowning.

"What?" Phoebe asked, not looking at her mother, as if she had, that quickly, sensed that the conversation would turn serious. Selena had slowed down without realizing it, and the air rushing through the cab turned softer. A meadowlark sitting on a fencepost called to them as they passed, and the notes had a melancholy tone that Selena had never noticed before. She turned her head to look at her daughter. Phoebe sat quietly, her hands clasped between her thighs, looking ahead, out the grasshopper-smeared window."

"I was thinking," Selena said, slowly.

"About what?" Phoebe asked, her tone wary.

"About grad night," Selena said. "You'll be out all night . . ."

"Sure," Phoebe said, confident now that if there was to be an argument about this, she would win easily. "That's the way it is. It was that way when you graduated, wasn't it?" Selena didn't say anything. "You mean, will there be drinking? Sure, some. You can't stop that, not even with that Safe Grad stuff." She turned her head away with what might have been stubbornness or even triumph, but the gesture seemed to Selena to hold a touch of fear. So it worries her, too, she thought. They were driving past dry fields covered with mats of short, dusty crops that were just beginning to turn green. "Lorna May's pregnant," Phoebe said suddenly.

For an instant Selena couldn't respond. What is she telling me? she wondered, and then thought, Mary and Bill's oldest, the pretty one with the dark red hair.

"Oh, no," she said, a soft sound, filled involuntarily with dismay.

"She'll probably have an abortion," Phoebe said, as if it was nothing. "She's only seventeen and she was planning to go into nursing in the fall."

"Who's the father?" Selena asked, a little timidly. Phoebe shrugged.

"Paul, I suppose. He's been her boyfriend since grade ten."

"How's she taking it?" Phoebe shrugged again, refusing to look at her mother.

"She doesn't act any different." She paused. "Nobody's supposed to know." They both laughed a little at this.

"But you'd think in this day and age . . ." Selena began.

"What?" Belligerence again.

"Nothing. It's just that—it doesn't have to happen anymore, and still it does . . ." But never to you, Phoebe, oh God, never to you, Selena prayed. Her hands tightened on the steering wheel.

"Most of the girls sleep with their boyfriends," Phoebe said. She tossed this out casually, in a dreamy voice, as if she were talking to herself. Selena turned her head quickly again to look at her daughter. Why had Phoebe said this of all things to her? And why now? She was overwhelmed with things she wanted to say, but uppermost was: Do you? but as quickly as she wondered this, she knew the answer. No, not yet. There was still something in her manner. . . . Selena could see the childishness in the plump curve of her cheeks, and in the way she still slept at night, deeply, innocently, like a five-year-old. Even though she had developed the full figure of a woman, even though she had bled now every month for almost five years, Phoebe was still a child.

"I could . . . get you the pill, if you want it," she said. She was surprised at herself for saying this, she hadn't planned to. Her face felt hot, and she wondered, what am I offering her? The thought frightened her.

"I don't like talking about this," Phoebe said into the silence, growing angrier as she spoke, and somehow this relieved Selena. "I *hate* talking about this. If I want the stupid pill, I can get it myself. And anyway . . ."

Any anyway what? Selena wondered. But she didn't dare ask, she could feel Phoebe withdrawing, rapidly and inexplicably retreating from her. And Diane, too, she thought sadly, I can't find Diane anymore either. Surely it will all pass, she thought, it's just a bad time right now, and glanced at Phoebe again. But Phoebe sat motionless, staring into space. When I was seventeen, she reminded herself, I was sleeping with Kent. Yes, she answered herself, and look where it got you. But this surprised her, too, because where it had gotten her was a home of her own and a family of her own, and that, surely, was all she had ever wanted.

JUNE

It seemed to her that this was not her husband, not the man she had known as a child and a youth, the one who sat across from her at the table three times every day, every inch of whose body she knew as well as her own, but only heat and weight, thrusting her into that infinite blackness she had come to know so well, the place where she floated bodiless, which had no landmarks, only sometimes a pinpoint of light, or a flash, red or blue. It was a darkness, but with depth and resonance, and it was beautiful. It filled her with boundless joy to be going there, to be there. It was so alien a place, so beautiful, so complete, that she forgot it was her husband who took her there, Kent, a man who had no idea where she had gone. She supposed that to him she was warm, familiar flesh against his body, something he can touch and hold. She imagined though, that in this act he, too, forgot her, Selena, his wife, but only in his moment of climax, while she had long since left him, his caresses sending her to that black and vibrant other place from which she came back always reluctantly, always surprised to have found it again.

"Jesus Christ, Selena," Kent said, into her hair. Her repositioned one arm and leg and lifted himself to one side while she slid out from under him.

"What?" she murmured, thinking of rearranging her pillow, finding her nightgown, but still too spent to move. Above his shadowed profile the night sky, washed silver with moonlight, glowed and in the trees a pair of owls were questioning the moon. The Indians say owls are the souls of dead people. Beside her she could hear Kent swallow, draw his breath in deeply, sniff. He put one arm up and rested his forearm on his forehead, throwing his face into impenetrable shadow.

"The goddamn moon's too bright," he said. "You better pull the curtain." She got up, naked, and standing in the white light of the moon, pulled the curtains so that the room fell into a homey darkness. She found her nightgown where she had dropped it on the floor by the bed, pulled it on, and got back in beside him.

When she was settled, she said, "What were you going to say?" He put his arm down and turned his head away from her, then back again. She could see none of this, knew it all by sound and memory in the darkness.

"I don't know what the hell it is," he said. She waited. "You scare me," he said finally. For a second she was alarmed, her heart speeding up, fluttering against the thin cloth of her nightgown. "You never used to be this way," he said.

"What way?" she asked, although she was smiling to herself now in the safety of the darkened room. Again he was silent for a moment.

"You get right away from me," he said. This time when she laughed ever so gently, he turned his head toward her angrily. "It don't seem right," he said rapidly, fiercely. She felt herself retreating from his anger, searching for a way to respond that would give him nothing to use against her later.

"Oh, come on, Kent," she replied, choosing to make light of what he had said. "Remember when we first started sleeping together? Even up until after Jason was born? Would you want it to be like that again?" She could feel him remembering, the silence filled with their shared memories: her tears, her shame and her fear; his hurt, his frustration, and finally, his tense, silent anger. He snorted.

"No way," he said. They lay beside each other, not touching, closer now than they had been in sex, and then the said, half to himself, "I wonder if all the women get this way."

Selena thought of Lola and Phyllis, young mothers as she had been once herself, of Enid, really still a child, of Diane, and Margaret who was old. And then of Phoebe.

"No," Kent said. "They couldn't all be like you are, or the boys wouldn't do so much complaining." He laughed, growing sleepy. But Selena thought of the time she had complained to the doctor that she was tired all the time, Jason was a year old then, and he had asked her if she had a regular sex life. You'd be surprised how many of the men around here are dead from the neck down, he said, and laughed. Seeing her embarrassment, he added quickly, the older ones, I mean.

She closed her eyes, wondering again who they could be, still only able to half-believe what the doctor had said. Kent heaved himself onto his side, his back to her, and began to breathe deeply. When she was sure he was asleep, she crept out of bed, opened the curtains a crack so that a little moonlight shone in the room, then got back into bed.

I'm going to try to get back in time to check the cattle late this afternoon, at least before dark," Kent said. "You drive out and see where they are. Save us a couple of hours riding looking for them." Selena, who was making sandwiches for the kids' lunch kits and had her back to him, didn't answer. "Where's Phoebe?" he asked Jason, who had just come into the kitchen and sat down at the table beside him.

"I dunno," Jason said, reaching for a piece of toast. "Studying."

"She'll miss the bus," Kent said. "I suppose I could drop her off on my way to Swift Current." He sounded indifferent, but Selena turned to Jason.

"Did you wake up Mark?"

"He's coming," Jason said, his mouth full.

"He got any exams today?" Kent asked.

"History," Selena replied. "I drilled him last night when you were out in the shop. He knows it. He should do okay."

Kent pushed back his chair, went out into the hall and called up the stairs, "Mark, Phoebe, hurry up. Get down here. You'll miss the bus!" In a moment Selena heard them thumping down the stairs, Mark, two steps at a time, and Phoebe's light, even step behind him.

"My last exam today," she announced in a voice so breathless and high-pitched that Selena turned to look at her. She was wearing her usual tight jeans, even Kent had given up arguing with her about them, but today she had put on a new white blouse which brought out the freshness of her complexion and made her blue eyes look even bluer. Her father's expression changed slightly when he looked at her.

"Last one," he repeated, and shook his head disbelievingly. "Till next year, anyway." He glanced at Selena proudly, smiling.

"I'm not even going to think about that," Phoebe said, pulling out her chair. "Everybody says university is really hard." Mark had sat down silently in his place.

"No way you'll catch me at university," he said.

"Me neither," Jason echoed. Mark drank his orange juice in one gulp, while Selena set the three lunch kits on the floor by the kitchen door, then sat down in her place.

"More coffee?" Kent said, holding up his cup. She got up quickly, apologizing, and got the coffee pot.

"So, you write history today," Kent said to Mark. Mark nodded.

"Grade ten history's easy," Phoebe said.

"Phoebe," Selena warned her. "It wasn't so easy when you were in grade ten."

"Did you study?" Kent turned abruptly to look at Mark, his voice suddenly harsh. Mark nodded again without looking at his father. He reached for Selena's homemade raspberry jam.

"I said I quizzed him last night," Selena said, keeping her voice neutral. "He'll do all right." Kent grunted, then sipped his coffee.

"We shortened my dress last night," Phoebe announced.

"Nobody cares," Jason said, and Mark laughed. Phoebe flushed.

"Boys!" Selena said. "Wait till your grad and we have to go looking for new suits for you. You'll care then."

"Leave them alone, Selena," Kent said, without emotion, so that Selena felt herself flushing, too. Phoebe sprang up, pushing back her chair, then stopped by the door for her lunch kit.

"No more stupid lunch kit after this week," she said, and went into the hall where they heard her opening the outside door.

"Hurry up, you two," Selena said, unaware that she had been saying this to the two of them every morning since they'd started school. Jason jumped up and Mark unwound his long legs and rose as they heard the school bus rolling in on the gravel to the front door. The horn honked, once, Phoebe had probably told Basil to do it, and in a rush of activity the two boys were gone, the door slamming behind them.

Then it opened again and Mark called down the hall, "I got a ball game after school and Jason wants to stay to watch. I'll phone if we can't get a ride back with Jerry." The door slammed again before either of them could answer.

"Damn!" Kent said. "Well, that means you'll have to ride with me." Selena nodded. Now that the boys were old enough to help they did most of the riding, but Selena found that if she didn't get out every week or ten days, she began to miss it.

Kent rose then and went out into the hall with Selena following him. It was cramped there, and dark, since the front of the house faced north and never got the direct sun. They could hear the whine of the bus as it turned onto the grid and began to pick up speed. Sparrows were chirping in the trees beside the house and red-winged blackbirds whistled, then trilled cheerfully. Kent set his cap onto his head, felt his back pocket for his wallet, then opened the door.

"Hey," Selena said softly. He turned, looked down at her.

"Don't forget to check where the cows are. It'll save us some riding later. I'll get back as early as I can." He bent and brushed her forehead with his lips and then was gone. She stood in the doorway and watched the half-ton pull out of the yard.

He was not the same man during the day that he was at night. At night he seemed vulnerable, she could reach him. During the day she was just another person who worked around the place, who ran to him when he called, like the kids did. Watching the billowing dust swallow his truck she thought she could feel his kiss, too, vanishing from her forehead, and she felt a lassitude creeping through her so that she had to lean on the door-frame. Oh well, she thought, finally, that's the way it is for everybody, I guess, and pushed herself away.

She went to the back door, kicked off her shoes, and began to pull on the old, muddy pair she wore for gardening, then, remembering, kicked them off again and went to the phone. She dialled and waited.

"Diane? Are you coming over? We really need to talk." She could hear Cathy crying.

"I don't know," Diane said, sounding exasperated.

"Where's Tony?"

"Gone to see the Pool man in Mallard."

"Put the kids in the truck and come over then." Diane was silent. "Come on," Selena said, coaxing. "Don't think about it, just do it."

"Where's Kent?"

"Gone to Swift Current, he won't be back before four, and the school bus just left." Cathy was still crying.

"Tammy!" Diane's voice was a muffled shout as if she had put her hand over the receiver. "See what's the matter with her!" There was something, some new recklessness in Diane's voice that alarmed Selena.

"Diane," she said, "I am your older sister. Our mother's dead. I'm telling you to put those kids in the truck and get over here. Now do it." Diane laughed.

"Oh, Selena," she said. "I had noticed that our mother is dead."

"Diane," Selena's determination was turning to a kind of impotent, fearful anger, "I . . ."

"Oh, okay," Diane interrupted. "I'll be over as soon as I can get Cathy settled down and pack some diapers and a bottle."

Selena hung up, then thought, good heavens, there's no reason why I couldn't have gone over there.

Hurriedly she tidied the kitchen, put the dishes into the sink, wiped the table, then took the left-over toast to the back door, where she stepped into her gardening shoes, opened the door, and tossed the toast into the carragana hedge. Without waiting for the birds she had disturbed to fly back to the toast, she went down the steps, took the hoe from where it leaned against the corner of the house, crossed the grass to the garden, which was directly behind the house, and stopped by the rows of corn.

She loved her garden. Each year she began to think about it in February, by March she had ordered and received her seeds, in April she was watching the still snow-covered patch impatiently, until finally, in late May, Kent worked it for her and manured it and worked it again, and then she could at last seed it. She spent part of every day in it, sometimes only making work for herself, tying things up, pulling off dead leaves, or just studying the plants, touching a pea blossom here, or kneeling to smell the scent of a squash there.

It was nine o'clock, and the inevitable wind had risen, rustling the knee-high corn and making the powerline overhead hum. Already the sun was hot, it would be unbearable if the wind died down, fat chance of that, and she noticed how brown her hands and arms were already. She sighed, thinking of the even hotter months to come, of the hard, dry heat of August.

At first she hoed too hard, chopping at the dry ground, the grasshoppers whirling away with every stroke, but gradually she slowed, found a working rhythm, and began to cut at the ground with lighter strokes and more care, even with a certain precision. She concentrated on what she was doing, watching the ground, occasionally going down on one knee to pull a weed she was afraid to chop at with her hoe for fear of damaging a plant. It needs water, she thought, testing the ground with her hoe, but it was no use watering the wind. The water only blew away or evaporated and it was too scarce to waste. She would water in the evening, if the wind went down. She finished the four rows of corn and moved to the beets, letting the hoe rest in the grass at the edge of the garden, as she worked on her knees among the red-veined, dark green leaves.

The wind was blowing harder now, but crouched low and sheltered by the corn and the row of lilacs that ran down the side opposite the carraganas, she didn't notice it. Forgetting her presence, the magpies came nearer, and a robin caught grasshoppers on the lawn. As she thinned the row, her fingers became stained a wine colour from the beet stems. She rested, squatting on her haunches, and squinted up at the sky. The inevitable hawk, only a speck against the pale blue, circled slowly. She thought she could hear its sharp cry carried to her on the wind. Behind it, the faint, white outline of the half-moon hung eerily, a shadow in the sky. There's a killdeer, she thought, surprised at hearing the "killdeer, killdeer, killdeer" cry so far from water. Then she heard the sound of truck tires on the gravel at the front of the house. She rose hastily, regretful, and brushed the dirt from her knees and off her hands. At the front of the house, Diane's truck had rolled to a halt.

Cathy was asleep in the car seat beside Tammy, her head lolling to one side. Tammy opened the passenger door carefully, got out, and shut it quietly without being told to. Selena could see that Tammy had been crying, too. She put her arm around the little girl and said to Diane, who was still sitting in the driver's seat, "Why don't you leave Cathy here till she wakes up." Diane nodded and got out quietly. The three of them went inside the house and down the hall to the kitchen. Tammy stood in the doorway looking uncertainly toward her mother as if she didn't quite know what to expect from her, and was a little afraid to ask.

"Tammy," Selena said gently, "you go up to Phoebe's room and get that box of toys from her closet. You know where it is?" Tammy broke into a smile, nodded, and ran out of the room. They could hear her awkwardly climbing the stairs.

"Good old Auntie Selena," Diane said.

"Oh, shut up, Diane," Selena said, running water into the sink. "I'll make some more coffee." She felt better, less concerned now that she had Diane in her own kitchen. She busied herself filling the coffee pot, taking down clean mugs, and looking in the fridge. Suddenly she shut the fridge door and turned to her sister. Diane raised her head and their eyes met.

"Are you pregnant?" Selena asked. Diane flinched, then her face resumed its closed, disinterested expression.

"No."

"Is Tony running around?"

"No!" This time she sounded angry.

"Well," Selena defended herself, "something's sure bothering you, and he was quite a lady's man before you married him. You can't blame me . . ."

"I know, I know," Diane interrupted. "He isn't running around as far as I know. Not that I'd care if he did."

"You don't mean that!" Selena said, shocked.

"No," Diane said, sighing. "I don't mean that," although she did, in a way. Tammy was coming down the stairs now, dragging the box behind her.

One of them should help her before she fell, Selena thought, but neither of them moved. She reached the bottom of the stairs and began dragging it down the hall toward them. Selena went to the doorway and said, "Good girl, now take it into the front room. You can spread the toys around, there's nobody home to bother you." Selena turned, as Tammy dragged the box away, and said to Diane, "She's so good about playing by herself." Diane had leaned her head back so that it rested against the wall, and that deep, inward-turning look that Selena found so disquieting had returned to her eyes. It was as if Selena wasn't even there.

"Is it money?" Selena probed. Diane moved her eyes slowly to her sister. She took a moment to answer.

"We're no worse off than anybody else. If this drought keeps up there'll be no crop this year, but . . ." She shrugged and lowered her eyes. Selena sat down across from her. Studying her, she noticed that Diane's skin had a sallow, unhealthy tinge to it. She remembered her as a teenager, full of life, daring in a way Selena could never have been. It had been a relief when Diane had married Tony, young as she was.

"Something's sure wrong," she said, knowing she must have said this before, perhaps more than once, "you're grouchy with the kids, you act like you couldn't care less about Tony, and you were crazy to marry him not even seven years ago. You don't want to do anything."

Diane said nothing. She bent her head so that her dark hair fell on each side of it, hiding her expression. Selena realized she was crying. Good, she thought, now we're getting somewhere, and at the same time, look, her hair doesn't even shine anymore. Pity swept through her, but she dampened it at once. She just needs a good talking to, she told herself, and opened her mouth to speak. But before she could get out any words Diane spoke.

"I'm sick of this place. I'm sick of this life." There was a noise in the hall and Tammy's small voice came to them in the bright, quiet kitchen.

"Mommy? Cathy's crying."

"I'll get her," Selena said, and jumped up before Diane could respond.

Diane wants to say, something terrifying is happening to me, Selena. She wants desperately to say to her sister, sometimes I wake in the night and I know I've been somewhere, somewhere huge and dark that's inside me. It's not a bad place. It's beautiful, I think, it's . . . right . . . somehow, it's trying to tell me something and I don't know what it is and I'm so afraid that I won't be able to come back. I fight, I struggle back to consciousness and find myself lying awake in our bedroom with Tony, my beautiful, long-boned Tony asleep beside me and I think, no, no, I'll never leave him. Never. And I know that wherever he is in his sleep, it's not that dark and rich place, that lies beneath or inside the ordinary world, where I go. And I don't know what any of this means. Am I losing my mind?

But she says nothing, only watches Selena hurry down the crowded hall and out the front door.

Cathy was screaming, flailing with her fists at the chair that confined her. Selena, angry with herself for forgetting her, hastily lifted her out and carried her into the house. By the time she got to the kitchen, Cathy had stopped shrieking and was hiccoughing into Selena's blouse. Diane was at the stove, wiping it where the coffee had boiled over.

"She's okay, she's just scared," Selena said. "Did you think we forgot you?" she asked the baby, kissing her damp cheeks. Diane reached out to take her, but Selena said, "No, let me hold her for a bit." So Diane filled their coffee mugs and admired the way Tammy had dressed Phoebe's old doll, while Selena rocked Cathy in her arms.

Diane sits down and watches Selena cradling her daughter, rocking her as she sits across the table from her. My baby, she thinks. My little girl. She looks around the kitchen, at the taps above the sink glinting in the morning sun, at the shiny toaster, at the dish towel hanging on the stove door. My life, she thinks—this is what it is to be a woman—and the clarity of this understanding, which both repels and appeals to her, is new. Her emotion crystallizes in the baby Selena is holding, the child she both wants to take and press to her breasts and at the same time to refuse to ever hold again. This confusion of desire is almost too much to bear.

"The cat's brought her kittens to sun on the back step," Selena told Tammy. Tammy set the doll on the table and ran out the back door. Diane and Selena could see her bend down and between gusts of wind, could hear her high, light voice crooning to the kittens. Cathy had grown quiet so Selena set her on the floor and put a cracker into her plump fingers.

"Are you tired of being a wife?" Selena asked. "Of being a mother?" Diane was leaning back in her chair again, her head resting against the wall. Selena noticed that her cheeks were wet.

"I love my kids," Diane said.

"I know that," Selena said, chastened. Yelling at your kids, having no patience with them didn't mean you didn't love them. Sometimes kids were too much, that was all, every mother knew that. Even the kids knew it. "What about Tony?" she asked, a little timidly now. Diane moved her head, blinked, and finally spoke.

"He's so much more than this life lets him be."

"What do you mean?" Selena asked, not sure whether to be angry or not. What is 'this life?' What is 'more?'"

"Life on the farm," Diane said, bitterness creeping into her voice, although she didn't mean it to. "You can't imagine anything else, can you?" Selena was silenced. It was true. She tried, but city life—how could you live it, except running, running all the time, in the traffic and the bad smells, never feeling safe . . .

"Tony's a bookkeeper, you know. He did two years at university. I'd like to see him without that filthy cap on his head and grease under his fingernails."

"Tony's a good-looking man, all right," Selena said. Out on the steps Tammy gave a little scream and Selena half-rose from her seat to peer out the screen. "Be careful, dear," she called.

"I'm not talking about his good looks," Diane said, annoyed. "I mean, he could get a job. He doesn't have to stay here beating his brains out for nothing."

"But," Selena said, hesitating. "He's a country man," then, translating this into something more manageable, "he wants to farm."

"He's been at it long enough to see the writing on the wall."

"What writing?" Selena retorted, even though she knew perfectly well what Diane meant.

Diane didn't even look at her and there was no answering rise of anger in her voice. She recited, "Costs are going up all the time, prices are dropping, all over the world competition is getting stiffer and stiffer. You don't have to be too bright to see there's no future out here on the farm. And this damn drought is the finishing touch."

This much Diane can say. This much Selena can understand. How can I tell her the rest, she wonders, when I don't know myself what it is, or what it means? Selena doesn't know that I'm hanging onto my sanity by the tips of my fingers, that I know if I stay here I'll go crazy, I really will, because in this tiny, smug little world no woman can ever matter, she can never be taken seriously, and I can't stand it. I've got to get away from here—even though I am terrified that for me there may be no escape anywhere.

Selena was thinking, if this is all that's wrong with her . . . and she had to remind Diane, "You know Tony quit university so he could come back and live this good life here on the land."

"What good life?" Diane asked, her voice suddenly fierce, light appearing in her dark eyes for the first time since she had arrived in Selena's kitchen. "What good life?" Tammy rose and pressed her face against the screen, trying to see into the kitchen. After a moment, she stepped away again. Cathy toddled into the hall and the women let her go.

"What do you mean?" Selena's voice was low, she had never expected to hear a member of her own family question the creed that all of them lived by.

"Tell me what you did last night," Diane said. Caught by surprise, Selena tried to remember.

"Hemmed Phoebe's grad dress, helped Mark study history, watched a little tv."

"And the night before? And the night before that? What do you do to pass the time around here? What do you *do* with your life?" She was sitting up straight now, staring angrily at Selena.

"Raise your kids," Selena said, angry too now. "Raise them where you don't have to be scared every minute for their lives—that they'll get beaten up, or that your daughter will get raped. Where there aren't so many things going on that you can't even be a family . . ."

"Oh, yeah," Diane said, looking away, her voice heavy with sarcasm. "Family." She was silent a moment, looking restlessly around the room, her eyes bright and hard now. "Family. Twenty-four hours a day, year after year." She rose and went to the screen door, then turned back to Selena, who watched her, knowing her shock was showing on her face, but unable to conceal it. "I've got two daughters, Diane said. "Two little girls. They're *people*, not just future baby-havers and housekeepers and dress-hemmers! I can see already that if we stay around here they're going to wind up in exactly the same fix I'm in." Selena could feel the colour rising up her neck and flushing her cheeks.

"You're not thinking of leaving Tony!" Diane didn't reply. She walked to the sink, then went back to her chair and sat down. Selena kept talking, as though it were normal for Diane to be so agitated. "Where would you go? How would you support the kids?"

"I'd go to Calgary, or Winnipeg, maybe. Maybe even . . . Vancouver?"

"Are you crazy?" Selena was appalled. "Don't you realize what it would be like? They'd both have to go into daycare, you'd have some kind of awful job that wouldn't pay anything—you'd never see the kids, you wouldn't know who was looking after them, or what was happening to them. You'd have nobody to come home to. You wouldn't even have a house to live in. You'd have to live in an apartment, and they're awful."

"How would you know?" Diane asked. "You've never been off this stupid farm."

"It's not a farm, it's a ranch," Selena pointed out, and was immediately annoyed with herself. "Anyway, everybody knows what the city's like."

Diane hates herself for getting into what feels to her like a stupid argument, but she hears the words falling out of her mouth, some part of her spinning them and spitting them out, while the rest of her sits in silence, listening and wondering and crying no, no, no—this isn't it, this isn't what it's about. But what's true is that I'm dying here, and Selena, isn't that enough? I don't know what it is that's driving me, I don't understand it and I don't know what will satisfy this thing that's tearing at me, but you don't either, it's laughable that you should be advising me, reciting your homely truths to me. Oh God to escape, if only from the platitudes that are piled up around here like barriers everywhere I turn.

"Selena," she said, sighing. "Look at me. I'm young. I'm only twenty-five." But Selena saw instead the fine lines at the corners of her sister's eyes, and the rigid tendons in her long neck, and that bright, deep light in her eyes that so dismayed her that she dropped her eyes from Diane's. This was too much. She had never seen such intensity, she didn't know how to deal with it.

But Diane, looking at Selena, remembers instead the story Rhea had told her about how, when she was reaching middle age at her home on the ranch, she had cried for days and days at a time. How Rhea had said, not looking at Diane, but out across the distant prairie, there was some tragedy going on inside me, some loss so deep there were no words for it. I must have known what it was at night. I must have known it in my sleep, in my dreams, because that was always when the crying would start.

Diane, filled with awe and sorrow at this picture, had ventured, what about Uncle Jasper? What did he say? What did he do?

Rhea had replied, Jasper would turn away from me, angry and afraid. He'd go out and work twice as hard, hitch the team and wagon and go twice as far for a load of feed, be away twice as long, because to work harder was the only answer he knew in life, and it had to suffice for every problem.

No, Diane thinks sadly, I won't turn to Tony for help with this.

Somewhere a cow was bellowing. Had it lost its calf? Selena remembered she was supposed to check on the cattle. She thought of the plants growing in her garden, could feel them brushing against her legs as she walked among them, she thought of her own dress for Phoebe's graduation lying upstairs on the sewing machine, unfinished, its tiny, cream-coloured flowers slipping by under her fingers as she guided the silky fabric under the needle. In the hallway Cathy had pulled down one of the coats hanging on the wall and had fallen asleep on it, and on the back lawn Tammy was chasing a magpie that had been tormenting the mother cat.

"I want . . . more in my life," Diane said, and to Selena her voice sounded more puzzled than sure. "I don't want my little girls to grow up sad, and not know why. I want them to . . . know . . . things. I . . . Oh, Selena, life here is so . . . mindless!".

"Mindless!" Selena exploded, but Diane ignored her.

"I want them to get out into the world, to see . . . life . . ." Her voice trailed off. "You still don't have a new stove," she said, fastening on this, as if it would explain everything. "Look at the floor. The vinyl's worn out. It's been worn out for the last five years. When was the last time you bought yourself a new dress? I bet you're making your dress to wear to Phoebe's grad, aren't you? You won't even allow yourself that much."

"I don't do it because I don't have the money . . ." Selena began, embarrassed.

"Oh, I know that," Diane said, standing again. "I know that perfectly well. It's just that every penny you make goes back into this ranch. You go without holidays year after year, you do without any kind of frills, you don't even have a stove to cook on that works right. Selena, what do you think the money you and Kent make is for? What do you think you're alive for?"

There was a long silence.

"You don't even know what you want," Selena said, her voice quieter now than it had been during the whole argument. "You want some kind of a life like you see on tv, like on 'Dallas.' You want fancy clothes and cars and . . . affairs with other men. That's all you want. And for that you'd leave your husband and ruin your kids' lives. I really think you must be losing your mind."

The coffee pot on the stove bubbled sporadically. The voice of a meadowlark, carried on the wind, came to them, from a fencepost by the barn.

"Thanks a lot, Selena," Diane said. Selena winced at the bitterness in her sister's voice.

They remained like that, Selena sitting at the table, looking down at the patterned plastic top she had been looking at for fifteen years or more, Diane standing with her back to the sink, staring at the clock on the wall above the table. It ticked quietly, year after year. It had hung in their parents' house, above their kitchen table. It had been their grandparents'. The phone rang, a long and a short, the neighbour's ring. Tammy came in, letting the screen door slam.

"I'm hungry." In the hallway Cathy woke and cried sleepily. While Diane went to her, Selena rose slowly and went to the cupboard, then turned to Tammy.

"I forgot to feed the chickens. Come on, we'll go feed the silly old chickens, okay?" She went outside with Tammy, through the hot, dust-laden air into the coolness of the barn. Tammy stopped at the first pen, stricken at the sight of two sick calves. They stood and watched Selena and Tammy with dull eyes, their ears drooping, as Selena opened the door into the box stall. Years ago it had housed a stallion and the wood was scarred from the stallion's hooves, even high up on the walls. Selena left the door open and Tammy came in beside her and helped her fill the pail by dipping the prepared feed out of the sack with an old dipper. Years ago, the dipper had been used in the kitchen, before they piped water into the house. It had always sat by the water pail, next to the nicked enamel basin, when the kitchen was still Kent's mother's. It comforted Selena to use the old dipper, to feel herself following in the paths of the women who had come before her. When the feed pail was full, Tammy and Selena went out, shutting the door on the scent of manure, old hay, and horse, and stood blinking in the sunlight before they started walking to the chicken coop next to the barn.

"Here," Selena said. She took a handful of feed and scattered it on the bare, hard-packed ground beside the henhouse. "Here, chick-chick-chick."

Tammy took a handful, too, and imitating Selena, called, "Here chicken-chicken, here chicken-chicken." Chickens began to appear from under the corral railings and around the corner of the bar. Selena saw Diane come out of the house, leading Cathy, and sit down in the sun on the steps. Selena glanced down at Tammy, who had taken her hand, and thought how much she was beginning to look like Diane.

It's a shame Diane doesn't keep chickens, she thought. How is Tammy supposed to learn. She watched the chickens pecking and ducking in that self-important, funny way they had. I like my chickens, she thought. The women in my family have always kept chickens, and sometimes ducks and geese and even turkeys. A place doesn't look like home without some birds pecking around, a rooster crowing now and then. It didn't seem possible to her that Diane would really leave.

When they had finished throwing the feed, she and Tammy put the pail away and went back toward the house.

But surely, Selena was thinking, watching Diane playing with Cathy in the sunshine, surely this is what a woman's life is? Feeding the chickens, playing with your babies, weeding the garden, just enjoying the summer weather. Diane said, as if she had been rehearsing this, "I wish I *could* be like you, Selena. Please don't think I don't appreciate what you are. But somehow . . . all of this just isn't enough for me." She frowned at Selena, searching her sister's face for something Selena knew somehow she couldn't find. "Don't you start hating me."

Before Selena could reply, she had been frozen by surprise at this last comment, Diane had stood up, picked up Cathy, and was going back inside. By the time Selena entered the kitchen with Tammy close behind her, Diane had gathered the diaper bag and was in the hall, going toward the truck parked at the front door. Selena and Tammy followed Diane from the sunshine, through the dark house, and out into the sunshine again. She helped Tammy open the truck door and get in next to her sister.

"Diane," Selena pleaded. "Think about going away with Tony for a week or two, won't you?" Diane didn't reply. For a moment she stared straight ahead, her jaw set, then slowly she turned to Selena. For a moment Selena couldn't look away, Diane's large, dark eyes held hers. There was an expression Selena hadn't seen before and that she didn't understand, as if Diane were asking her something, only Selena didn't understand the question, never mind what the answer might be, or if there was an answer. Finally she jerked her eyes away and looked down, putting both hands on the truck door as if for support. "At least go see Rhea," she said, and then wondered why she had said Rhea.

"All right, Selena," Diane said, and she drove away with Tammy waving a frantic good-bye out the window.

Selena was upstairs working at her sewing machine in the bedroom when she heard Kent drive in and stop the truck at the front door. She shut the machine off and hurried down the stairs. He was hanging up his good hat, and turned to look up at her as she descended.

"Did you check those cows?" He sounded a little tired, she thought.

"I forgot," she admitted, dismayed. He lifted his beat-up straw hat off the peg, set it on his head, and went into the kitchen. "But I did get the horses in," she offered, hurrying down the rest of the stairs and following him into the kitchen. "They're in the barn."

"Good," he said. He went to the sink and ran water into a glass and drank it. "How come you forgot to check on the cows?" he asked amiably, turning to her.

"After I watered the horses and filled the mangers, I came in to sew for a few minutes while they ate, and I just forgot." She shrugged ruefully. "I had things on my mind."

"What things?" he asked, grinning up at her, as if she could never have anything serious on her mind. He was sitting down by the back door now, pulling off his good boots.

"Diane," she said.

"Poor Tony," he said. "Never marry a pretty girl, I always say." He set his good boots neatly side by side next to the chair.

"Thanks a lot," Selena said. He looked up, surprised, and laughed. "Get me my boots, okay?" She went into the hall and brought back his worn riding boots.

"So, what's new with Diane?"

"I think she might really be going to leave him."

Kent bent and began to pull on his old boots. After a moment's silence, he said, his voice muffled, "He'd be better off without her, if she won't settle down and pull her weight." Selena felt heat rising in her face.

She wanted to say, this is my sister we're talking about, but she didn't, remembering how Kent had allowed her to keep Diane with them for years, how he had fed and clothed her as if he were his own child, never complaining about the expense.

"It's never all one person's fault," Selena said. "It takes two to tango, you know." She kept her voice casual.

"She's lazy," he said. "It must have something to do with losing her mother when she was so young. And let's face it, your old man wasn't that hard a worker. I know you did your best, but she don't do nothing to help Tony." He stood up, went to the hall and came back carrying his light summer jacket while she stood silently, leaning against the counter, watching his lean back, remembering, too, that it was Kent who paid for Diane's wedding, when her dad was so sick that they couldn't even tell him Diane was getting married.

"Come on, then," he said, putting his arm across her shoulders. Their eyes met and for a second she thought he was going to kiss her. But no, they walked outside together, she catching her straw hat from its peg and setting it on her head as they went by the door. They curried their horses and saddled them, let them out of the barn, through a gate which Kent opened and closed behind them. They mounted then, still not speaking, and Selena waited while Kent, holding his horse steady, looked off into the distance ahead of them, to the right, and to the left.

They rode north, stopping while Kent opened another gate, leaving this one open behind them. It was late afternoon and the wind was still fairly strong. It made the horses nervous and hard to manage. Selena was anxious to get into the hills near the northern edge of their lease where they would settle down. She had been as big a daredevil on horseback as anybody until she was pregnant with Phoebe and then all the years when her children were young she was nervous about riding, and did only as much as was required of her. All the women, at least most of them, were that way, they laughed about it among themselves, and yet they were faintly ashamed. It was only in the last couple of years that Selena had begun to enjoy riding again. Still, she knew her days of riding only half-broken horses and of taking chances on horseback without even noticing it were over. In a way she regretted it, but she accepted what seemed inevitable.

Selena liked riding with Kent beside her. He talked to her when they were riding in a way he rarely did otherwise. It was as if, out on the prairie on a horse, in the wind and under the sun, he lost some of his reserve, and for once the words flowed freely.

"I been thinking," he called to her, and she turned her head to hear him over the wind. "Our hay crop looks really bad, there won't be nearly enough feed to last the winter, and the way things are, the calves are gonna be pretty light this fall. I been thinking I'd like to try to feedlot a liner load of 'em—just try it out, you know." Selena listened, thinking. This had been her father's business, too. She knew it pretty well.

"That won't leave us much income to get through the winter." He nodded, riding on through the short, dry grass. She called again, "How are we going to pay the feed bill if we do that?" They rode on, calling to one another, or not speaking, listening to the prairie noises they could hear during a lull in the wind: the whistle of the occasional gopher, the cry of a hawk. The day was still, the sun cast a burning heat over the land that even the wind could barely dull.

At the waterhole they found cows grazing, or lying motionless, except for their moving jaws, while their calves ran and played in the grass around them. They stopped and Selena began counting.

"How many?" Kent asked.

"I get eighteen cows, eighteen calves," she said.

"Me too."

They began to ride again at a walk, no longer talking, both of them watching and listening. Horned larks hopped out of their way, Selena saw a duck's nest hidden in the grass, and once Kent stopped, dismounted, and bent to pick up a buffalo horn, which he stuffed into his saddlebag. They crested a hill and then another one. They were riding down it when Kent abruptly pulled up his horse and pointed toward a cow standing a hundred yards apart from the cluster of cattle they were approaching. Her head was down, her ears drooped, and her tail was a dark green, dripping mess.

"She's the one lost her calf after that last February blizzard," he said, and Selena relaxed. One lost calf they wouldn't have to look for. "She's pretty sick," he said, after watching her a moment. "We'll have to take her back with us."

Off to the east a calf was bleating, its voice fading, lost in the wind, then growing louder. Without speaking, they touched their horses and rode in the direction the sound was coming from, passing through a deep draw where the grass was tall and thick, and emerging into a dried-up slough bottom. On the far side of the slough a young coyote raised its head, then disappeared at a slow lope around a hill. A calf approached them, walking slowly, raising its head every few steps to bleat beseechingly.

"Goddamnit!" Kent said, more concerned than angry. He rose in his stirrups to search the surrounding landscape, but there wasn't a stray cow in sight anywhere. Selena sighed.

"I think that coyote has a couple of pups," she remarked. "There must be a den around here somewhere."

"It's over there," Kent said, pointing, but not looking in that direction, his eyes still on the calf that had stopped and was staring up at them in what appeared to be wonder, so that Selena began to laugh, which made it jump and turn away. Kent rode around the calf, studying it. "Doesn't look like it's been lost too long." He sat still again, looking around them. The calf walked away, quickly disappearing down the draw they had just come through. "Well," Kent said. "You go that way," pointing to the southeast, "and I'll check over this way. Maybe we'll get lucky and she'll be close by."

Selena set off at once in the direction he had pointed out to her. It still felt strange to be able to ride freely, without having to worry about time, about getting back to the house knowing that her kids didn't need her anymore to cook their meals, or look after them. The boys would grab a bite at the cafe in town and Phoebe could take care of herself, too. She might even have a hot meal ready for them when they got home. She didn't know whether she felt relief knowing the kids could look after themselves, or chagrin.

A little of both, I guess, she told herself.

She had reached the hills on the far side of the slough and she started up one of the highest ones, zigzagging her horse and holding onto her saddle blanket just ahead of the saddle horn so that it wouldn't work its way out behind the saddle and fall off. At the top of the hill, holding onto her hat against the wind, she paused and looked out over the lease. Far off to the east, low on the horizon, the blue of the sky had turned to a brownish haze. The blowing dust even hid the elevators ten miles away at Mallard. She lowered her eyes to the field below where she sat and scanned the grazing cattle, counting them, searching the field for strays off by themselves. She counted the calves, too, and then spotted a lone cow far off to the east. Hurriedly she descended the hill. Near the bottom she urged her horse to a lope, then eased off after a minute to a trot, and headed in the direction of the solitary cow.

Passing through a draw she skirted a patch of cinquefoil blooming yellow against the grey-green grass, and for no reason, thought of Rhea. At the opening of a shallow, sloping coulee, she stopped, then began the descent, following a cowpath that wandered among the wild rosebushes, past low, stunted saskatoons and greasewood. Little patches of antelope droppings were scattered along the path. She climbed the other side and rounded a patch of vetches not yet opened to the light.

She saw that look in Diane's eyes again. It made her shiver just to think of it. It reminded her of the look she had seen in her mother's eyes in those last days before she died. She knew that none of the things she had said to Diane had made any difference to her, and she was sorry now that she had been so harsh. But she had thought Diane needed to hear those things. She had thought she could convince her that she was being foolish. But now, alone, she had to admit to herself that she really didn't understand what it was that Diane wanted, or what was going on in her mind. All I ever wanted was to be a wife and mother, Selena thought. No nursing for me, like my mother wanted. She thought about the first time Kent made love to her that weekend in the fall of their grade twelve year. A bunch of them had gone to a dance at Antelope, and then gone from there to another dance they had heard about in the park. Her mother had been furious with her because she didn't get home till five in the morning. She remembered how she had endured the questioning, the accusations, the punishment, without really noticing. What could her mother say that would matter after what had happened last night? From that moment when he entered her, Selena realized, the world never looked the same again. And then they had married.

A long-eared jackrabbit burst out of a clump of sage and bounded away with long, lazy steps. She lifted her head to watch him go, then noticed that while she had been daydreaming, she had ridden up on the cow. I might have ridden right past her, she thought, disgusted with herself and glad that Kent wasn't there to see it.

She stopped her horse and turned in the saddle to search the clumps of sage and the rocks for a lost calf curled up beside them, but there was none to be seen. Checking the cow again, she saw that her bag was uncomfortably full. Good. This must be the cow that belonged to the lost calf. She settled down in her saddle and nudged her horse to a trot. It was getting late, six at least, judging by the sun. She began to chase the cow back in the direction she had come from, concentrating hard on what she was doing now, anxious not to lose the cow, and thinking of what Kent would say if she did.

But the cow was willing to go and offered little resistance. In fifteen minutes they were back at the waterhole. As she neared it, Selena saw Kent on the far side, his rope unfurled and dangling, using it to persuade, with gentle touches, the lost calf to go around the waterhole toward Selena and the cow she had brought with her.

The calf began to bleat again and the cow lifted her head, bellowed an anxious reply and began to run toward the calf. When they met each other, Selena and Kent on opposite sides of them, watching, the cow smelled the calf all over and, satisfied that it was her own, stood to let it nurse, which it did eagerly and fiercely, butting her firmly with its head as it searched for a teat.

They watched for a moment. Then Kent called to her, "You start back with the sick cow. It's going to be awful slow going. I'll do the rest of the checking myself."

"Okay," she called back, ready to say something more, but he had already turned his horse and was heading west, riding fast. She turned too, then, found the sick cow over the next hill, and started back to the corrals two miles to the south, with the cow stumbling slowly ahead of her.

The wind at last had died away, and all the delicate prairie noises were clear in the stillness: the quack of a couple of ducks half a mile away at the waterhole, the musical chatter of the larks, and the sound of her own horse's feet swishing through the grass. Even the laboured breathing of the sick cow ahead of her was loud in the evening hush, and Selena rode slowly, not to make the cow's suffering worse. Kent or any of the other men, busy and harassed with their interminable work and financial worries, would have pushed the cow much harder, but there was enough daylight left, and Selena had no other job pressuring her, so she took her time.

"You have to go home, girl," she said to the cow. "We can't look after you out here." The cow lumbered on through the grass, its head down each step an effort, stopping every few feet. After a while they settled into a steady, slow walk, leaving a crooked path in the grass behind them.

They passed another duck's nest, hidden in a patch of tall grass, she noticed it only because the duck flew up as they drew near and she caught a glimpse of a handful of beige eggs, barely visible in the nest. Coming around a hill they startled a few antelope, a buck and three does. The does disappeared at once over the hill but the buck stopped to watch Selena and the cow draw a little nearer before it, too, dashed away, its hooves not appearing to touch the ground as it ran. Selena and the cow plodded on and soon were out of the hills and onto the flat land that began a mile or so from the buildings. A few minutes later the house, barn and corrals appeared, specks against the grass.

When they were about a half mile from the yard, Selena dismounted and walked, leading her horse, behind the cow, which had slowed even more. In this way, at last, she brought the cow into the corral, penned her, and closed the gate.

She turned away then, still leading her horse, and stared out toward the west, the direction she had just come from. Darkness was falling, the last glow of red was fading from behind the hills, which had flattened and merged with the evening purple. She could no longer make out any details, but she knew that somewhere out there, in those shadows, Kent was riding toward her.

Melancholy pierced her, the lateness of the hour, the sun gone down, the land disappearing all around her into the night shadows. Her horse drew near and nudged her shoulder, then brushed his soft nose to her cheek and hair. A shiver ran through her. The dark sky, the low, distant hills, the land itself were pressing into her, claiming her, and she felt as if there was nothing left of her own, her private soul.

To the west the coyotes began their nightly wailing. Her horse, hungry and thirsty, stopped its restless moving and lifted its head as its ears went up. She wanted her heart to close, she wanted the gaping hollow that had opened in her gut to suck in, she felt as though she might fall, weighted as she was with the world.

She led her horse into the barn, unsaddled him and turned him out into the corral. He went straight to the waterer and she went back to the barn and came out with an armload of hay from a broken bale and threw it over the fence to him.

The moon had risen. It hung low in the sky over her garden, eerie and white. She shut the barn door and crossed the corral. As she opened the gate, she could hear hoofbeats coming across the field and she knew that in a minute Kent would be there. She shut the gate and went toward the house, not waiting for him.

JULY

"They're starting to come in," Helen called over her shoulder from the doorway between the kitchen and the hall. She had to raise her voice to be heard over the hissing of the big pots on the two stoves, the clattering of dishes being washed in the sink, and the voices of the other women hurrying around the kitchen. Selena leaned past her to look down the hall. It was filled with rows of long tables covered with white paper tablecloths and set with cutlery, salt and pepper shakers and cream and sugar sets. Rena was moving among the tables, setting small vases, each holding a pink and a blue artificial daisy and a sprig of artificial fern, two to a table. She was moving quickly, straightening the chairs and benches arranged on each side of the tables, while her daughter Tracey followed, carefully carrying the tray of vases, her expression serious, both of them intent on their work.

At the far end of the hall, by the main entrance, Selena saw Phoebe and Melissa sitting at the reception table. As she watched, Phoebe stood up, accepted a shining, silver-wrapped parcel from the couple who were bending to sign the guest book, and carried it to the table behind them, which was beginning to be piled with gifts. Selena smiled without meaning to, because Phoebe looked so pretty in her white cotton dress with the pink belt, her shoulder-length, light brown hair carefully brushed and shining. Then she scoffed at herself—an ordinary teenager, like all the rest of them here, she thought. Yes, but my own little girl. She threw the tea towel she was holding over her shoulder, then hastily took it off again: don't put your tea towel over your shoulder, your hair will touch it, it's a messy habit, her mother's voice still echoing in her ears after all these years. Sometimes she thought she would never shake her mother's teachings. It both angered her and pleased her to think that she was what her mother had made her.

Phoebe was seated again, laughing with Melissa about something, and more people were coming in, smiling and calling to each other. And Phoebe? she wondered, watching her, what have I made her? Phoebe was standing again, moving quickly, several parcels piled up in her arms. She tried to think of what she had taught her: don't let the boys touch you, was the first admonition that sprang into her mind, seeing her now, so womanly and pretty. But no, earlier than that. She frowned, trying to remember. Wash your hands often, it's important to be clean. Be neat, comb your hair whenever you think of it during the day. Don't make a lot of noise, nobody likes a roughneck girl. Be polite . . . more admonitions came crowding into her mind.

No, she thought, as Phoebe returned to her chair. Surely those weren't the things that would make a woman of Phoebe. It wasn't that they weren't important, it was just that something seemed to be missing. What was it that was missing? It seemed to her that there was some core to what it meant to be a woman that she had never had the words to talk about. Was it God? Phoebe had asked her about God more than once over the years. Yes, there is a God, Selena had told her; ask the minister, ask your Sunday School teacher. Maybe she should have tried harder to answer Phoebe herself. But what answers do I have? she wondered.

"Excuse me," Joanne sang in her ear. She had to turn sideways to squeeze through the door past Selena. She was carrying a dish of pickles in each hand and her cheeks were flushed with the heat in the kitchen, her eyes too bright. The ties of her apron barely met at the back.

"Let me take those," Selena said, reaching for the thick glass dishes without waiting for Joanne to answer her. She took one in each hand, and nodded toward the only chair in the kitchen, pushed back into a corner in front of the cupboards. "You better go sit down."

"I'm fine," Joanne protested, not smiling.

"Do what she tells you," Ruth called from behind them. "You'll work hard enough once the baby comes." Ruth was a cousin of Joanne's so she could boss her around. Joanne went slowly to the chair and sat down, then began to fan herself with a paper napkin.

"If it weren't so hot, it wouldn't be so bad," Enid remarked to Selena. "I'll take those." Before Selena could move, she had taken the two dishes of pickles from her and had hurried out into the hall with them. Selena made a little face at her back.

"These potatoes are ready," Ruth said. Selena hurried to the stove. Together they lifted the steaming pot and drained the boiling water off into one of the sinks. Phyllis and Lola had begun cutting the pies and were setting the pieces onto rows of dessert plates. Phoebe came into the kitchen, asked Helen something, then went out again. Ruth and Selena set the big pot of potatoes onto a backless chair and began to take turns mashing them with a long-handled potato masher.

"It's so hot," Ruth said, "but you can't open the blamed door for the flies and grasshoppers. Did Phoebe make her dress?"

"In Home Ec." Ruth mashed vigorously for a moment, then lifted her head and straightened, panting, her face red, her temples glossy with sweat.

"Let 'em have pretty dresses while they can," she said. "Lord knows, it don't last." Selena thought of Ruth's husband, Buck, and shuddered inwardly, thinking of Phoebe. At least Brian was a decent kid, drank only a little, if Phoebe could be believed, had no reputation for being hard on vehicles or mouthy with the older men. Didn't touch drugs, Phoebe swore. Still, you never knew. Marry a man, then find out what you've gotten yourself into.

She took the masher from Ruth and bent, raising and lowering it, thrusting hard, holding it with both hands. It took all her strength to push it through the mound of potatoes.

"Okay, no more lumps," she said. At the table in the centre of the kitchen Enid and Ella were mashing another big pot of potatoes. The milk and butter sat on the table beside them and Selena reached for them, poured in a quantity of milk, then cut of a piece of butter which she broke into smaller pieces and added to the potatoes which Ruth had already begun to whip, using the masher. Selena grasped the pot and held it steady for her.

"Look out everybody!" Lola had opened one of the oven doors and was pulling out a roaster, which she set on the oven door. She lifted off the lid and a cloud of steam and the smell of roasting beef swept through the sweltering room. Ruth's husband, Buck, detached himself from a group of men he'd been standing with near the doorway and put his head into the kitchen.

"Give me a hand in here," Lola called to him and he hurried in, took the oven mitts from her and lifted the roaster onto the table. Ruth lifted her head from the potatoes, and Selena saw her send a sharp glance toward her husband's back, her lips tightening. Lola, after two children, still had her figure; she was still young and attractive. And there was Buck, grey-haired, gnarled, with a lined, reddish face from hard work and drink, being jovial and overly helpful.

"Does he do that at home, too?" Selena muttered to Ruth, half-grinning, and laughed at Ruth's sarcastic "Hah!" Selena took the masher from her and began to whip while Ruth held the pot.

"Where's Diane tonight?" Ruth asked. Her head bent, working hard to move the masher swiftly through the potatoes so they would cream and whip up, Selena hardly had the breath to answer. She hadn't even noticed that Diane wasn't there to help. Diane had never been as faithful as many of the members. Some women were like that. Sally Macklin was another one, although sometimes Selena suspected she didn't come too often because the women didn't really accept her. She had always been a little bit different anyway, but when she started writing poetry and getting it published, it was worse, nobody knew how to talk to her. But Diane—maybe Kent was right, maybe Diane was just a little bit lazy.

"I think that's enough," she said, standing back, panting. "Diane must have gone to get Rhea." She turned toward the second pot to help, but Ella was already working at it, talking to Enid as she mashed.

"For a pot this size, it takes about a pint, sometimes more, depends on the potatoes, what kind you use and how old they are and so on."

"I've never cooked such a big potful," Enid said, apologetically. She came from a town seventy-five miles down the road. They must do things differently there, Selena thought.

"You young ones'll have to take over when us older ones give up," Ella said, puffing as she whipped.

"I'll do that," Enid offered, and Selena had to smile at how the young ones always think they're stronger than the ones who've been at it for years. Enid would play out long before Ella would, she thought.

Rhoda had begun to fill two big serving bowls with the creamy potatoes. Lola and Ruth were slicing the big roasts of beef and Phyllis was standing at the stove, sweating, and stirring the gravy. Selena stood back out of the way and looked around the busy, crowded kitchen in search of another job that needed doing. The commotion out in the hall was growing louder by the minute and people kept spilling into the kitchen, looking for a drink of water or a damp cloth to wipe a child's face, or to gossip, or to offer help.

Selena thought of all the times since she was a girl, since she was Phoebe's age, she had come into this kitchen carrying a salad, or three dozen buns, or two pies, or some combination of these, and then had worked here for hours getting a meal ready for the community. Aware of the ache in her legs now, she thought, I wonder what would happen if we all quit. She saw the hall, deserted, weeds growing up through the steps, the windows broken or boarded up. Why, the community would fall apart. Nobody but us women would do this. There'd be no more community if we quit celebrating people's anniversaries and weddings, births and deaths, departures and arrivals.

"Imagine," she said to Ruth, who had come to lean against the counter beside her, things were coming together now, the buffet tables were ready, the people were lining up and beginning to fill their plates, "if we all quit the club, if we all stopped working like this." Ruth turned her head quickly to look at Selena, a surprised expression on her face. She laughed, a short, stout, older woman in a cheap, neat dress, looking up at Selena with wide amused eyes.

"I wouldn't have varicose veins, maybe," she said. "My God, the hours I've put in here on my feet. I've baked enough buns over the years to stretch from here to Swift Current and back again." They relaxed, and watched their neighbours file by, filling their plates with the food they had prepared. "That'd be the end of the community," Ruth said.

"Some of the towns are getting men's service clubs," Selena remarked.

"They think they can take our place?" Ruth asked. "Let them try. Did you ever know a man who could even remember his own anniversary, never mind anybody else's? And who'd do the cooking?"

"They sure know how to make money," Selena said. "Not like us, working our feet off just to break even."

"Well, we don't do it for the money," Ruth pointed out.

"There's not many young ones coming up to take over," said Margaret, who had been listening to their conversation. "What with the kids getting away to the cities to school nowadays, and all them farms going down, people moving away." She shook her head reflectively. "Heaven knows where it'll all end."

You could always depend on Margaret for doom and gloom, Selena thought. There'll always be farms. Or will there? She risked a quick glance at Margaret, who after all had been here a lot longer than she had, and therefore ought to know more. But Margaret was smiling serenely at the people filing by, as if she herself hadn't heard what she had just said.

Selena squeezed past everybody and looked out into the hall again. Louise and Barclay were seated at the head table, Louise wearing a corsage of pink carnations and smiling happily, Barclay solemn, wearing his seldom-worn grey suit and navy tie. Phoebe was still sitting at the table by the door. Diane, Tony, and their two little girls had just entered. Tony was bent over, signing the guest book, and Diane was shooing the girls ahead of her, straightening their dresses, then looking down the length of the hall. She saw Selena standing in the doorway, smiled, then bent her head again to her children as if she were smiling over some wonderful secret. It had been so long since Selena had seen Diane really smile that she felt a lightening of some burden she hadn't realized she'd been carrying, and she turned back to the kitchen half-smiling herself, wondering, what's she so happy about?

At last, when all the adults were seated at the tables, the small children already dodging chairs, tables and people's legs, congregating at the back door and in the cloakroom with the door shut, or racing up and down any open spaces they could find, unabashedly screaming, the women in the kitchen filled their own plates and moved out into the hall to find places to eat beside their own families or with each other. Selena saw Tammy leave her place beside Diane. Quickly she filled her plate and went to squeeze in the empty spot Tammy had left.

"Where's Rhea?" she asked Diane.

"She said she was too tired to come, that it was too much for her," Diane replied, picking up a bite of raisin pie with her fork.

"That'd be the day an thing was too much for Rhea," Selena said, laughing, and Diane laughed with her.

"She gets stranger all the time." Diane shook her head. Cathy sat on her right, next to Tony, who was occupied talking to Gus, Kent's older brother. The weather, Selena thought, the hoppers, grain prices. They never got sick of it. She noticed that Diane was wearing her favourite dress again, the red one with the low neck, and that her long, dark hair caught the light and shone. Remembering how distraught Diane had been a month before, she was pleased, then wondered what this meant.

"What are you so happy about?" she asked. The teenage girls were making their way among the tables now, filling the cups with coffee or tea. Diane had to lean forward so that Tracey could squeeze past behind her.

"I don't know how to tell you this, Selena," she said, laughing, moving close to Selena to be heard above the noise. "But, I'm leaving this place." The forkful of food Selena had just swallowed seemed to stick in her throat. Diane was still looking at her with delight in her eyes. "Don't look so horrified," she said, laughing. "Tony's coming with me."

Without really noticing what she was doing, Selena reached for her glass of water and took a sip. She forgot the long tables crowded with people, the noise, the heat. She was seeing Tony and Diane at their wedding in the church at Mallard, the one that was boarded up now. She remembered how they had kissed. Something about it had startled and upset her. A surge of envy had swept through her, and something else, something strange, an opening up, so powerful that her knees had almost given way right there by the church in her blue matron-of-honour dress.

She knew it was important. Funny, she thought, remembering the feeling. Once she had flipped on the radio and caught a singer in the middle of a song, and something, some note in his voice had done the same thing to her, had struck a sadness in her that was far beyond tears, that had nothing to do with tears. And once somebody had brought to a meeting a magazine that had one of Sally Macklin's incomprehensible poems in it, and there was a line in that poem that had done the same thing to her as when Tony and Diane had kissed. And frightening as it was, she recognized it as something that was necessary to know, even though she didn't understand what it meant. There was a part of her, some part buried deep inside, that knew what it meant, and she was satisfied by this, had never struggled to know more. If she thought about it at all, she thought that full understanding of its meaning would probably come to her one day, as naturally as giving birth to her children had, and until then, she was content just to know it was there.

But, she thought, looking back at Diane, there is some restraint bred into me that is as natural to me as breathing. Diane doesn't have it. With Diane, anything was possible, she was like a man in that—while for

Selena, she knew it—there were no real choices. Her life had been all set out for her and she accepted it. She suddenly felt closed and tight beside her sister, and it made her angry with Diane.

"You don't seem very excited," Diane said, teasing.

"I don't know what to say," Selena said slowly, staring down at the food that was growing cold on her plate.

"I talked Tony into selling the farm before we lose all our equity, what little we have."

"Oh, Diane . . ." Selena began, her voice filled with the dismay that was rapidly overwhelming her.

"I told you, Selena," Diane said, "I want more out of life than this."

"If you could just tell me . . ." Selena began, aware of the futile repetitiveness of her pleading. "What is it? What is it you want? I mean, really?" Diane lifted her coffee cup, then set it down again. "You've got family here," Selena said, feeling helpless because this was not really what she wanted to say, but unable to find the words that would shape what she was feeling. Diane snorted, and Selena said hotly, "You'll see if that matters or not. You've got friends in this community—people who care what happens to you. They won't care in the city." Diane turned her head sharply to Selena, and her cheeks flushed red.

"Oh, sure," she said, her voice heavy with sarcasm. "Safe in your mother's womb forever." Selena blinked and looked away. "There's a whole enormous world out there . . ."

Selena raised her head and looked around the hall at all the chewing, talking people, at their wind and sun-reddened faces, at the women's large, rough hands that gave them away, no matter what they wore or said. She wanted to cry. How many times had she seen them here—their children, their grandparents, their high school sweethearts, their neighbours, their enemies, their secret liaisons—all together in this hall, eating and talking, smiling and laughing, as if this could go on forever just the way it always had, as if there were no hardship, no injustice, no ugliness, no evil.

"There's things out there neither one of us has dreamt of . . ." Diane said, her voice reflective.

"Like what?" Selena retorted. Diane's eyes shifted out beyond the heads of all the people in the hall, beyond, it seemed, the hall itself. What was she seeing? Her eyes so bright, her face smoothing, changing somehow. Suddenly Selena was angry, she wanted to jolt that look off her face.

"You're wrong," she said tightly. "If you think life's any better out there, just because there's more people and more things to do. They're just as unhappy out there. Maybe more. You'll find that out." Selena's face felt hot and her throat was quivering.

"So you do admit that not everybody is happy," Diane teased, laughing.

Later, when they were both in the kitchen doing dishes, Selena tried again to talk to her. But after listening to her for a moment in silence, Diane finally turned to her and give her that same long, searching look, with an expression on her face that was almost tender, as if she were the older sister. It so embarrassed and disconcerted Selena that she fell silent.

As she was taking the wet dishes from the draining rack and drying them, Selena found herself thinking again of that feeling she had had when Tony and Diane kissed outside the church after their wedding. Had Diane had such a moment somewhere, sometime herself? Was that what impelled Diane? If it was, did that mean that Diane understood it and that it had something to do with her leaving? But if your world seems complete to you where you are, she wondered, why do you need to go someplace else? Especially a woman, when we carry all our possibilities around inside ourselves, in our wombs.

Helen came hurrying into the kitchen.

"Hurry up, everybody, it's time to start the program." Everyone left the kitchen then, filed out into the hall and found places to sit.

First Phoebe played two pieces on the piano, losing her place only once and having to start a passage again. The three of the younger girls, eleven and twelve-year-olds, sang a song. At last it was time for the part of the program everybody had been waiting for. Selena, Diane, Helen, Ella, Ruth and Rhoda made their way through the crowd to the stage and arranged themselves in a group. Helen nodded to Phoebe, she began to play "Clementine," and the women began to sing the song that Selena and Rhoda had composed.

"In a ranchhouse, in a valley,
Baking apple pies,
Lived the daughter of a rancher,
Louise Olnyk was her name."

Then the chorus, which had been the easy part to write:

"Oh my darling, oh my darling,
Oh my darling Louise,
Marry me and live forever,
On my farm in Antelope."

Selena had produced the next verse by herself:

"I'm a farmer, thirteen quarters
to my name,
Got no horses, got no cattle,
Growing wheat is my fame."

Then back to the chorus. The song went on to tell about their courtship and marriage, their four children. The audience laughed or chuckled now and then, and Louise and Barclay, sitting at the centre of the head table, surrounded by their children and grandchildren, turned in their chairs to see the singers better. Barclay laughed, but everybody could see the tears shining in Louise's eyes. Louise, famous for her wonderful pies, a rancher's daughter who had deserted her family's way of life to marry a grain farmer, her oldest son killed in a car accident when he was seventeen, drunk, driving too fast.

When their song was finished, the singers went back to their chairs amidst furious applause and laughter. There was a long break in the program while the people in the skit disappeared out of the chattering crowds, and the children began to move around again, a few of them running, sliding on the freshly polished floor. Then the skit was announced, the audience grew quiet, people hushed the children and took them on their laps, and the actors filed onstage, holding papers with their lines written on them. Everybody tried to guess who each of them was.

Helen always organized these things, but Diane had written most of the skit, she was acknowledged to be the best at it, and everybody laughed especially hard when they realized she was playing Barclay. They had persuaded one of the teenage boys to play Louise; he was quite a bit shorter than Diane, who seemed even taller because of the straw hat she was wearing. It was immediately recognized as Barclay's work hat. He was famous for it. It was so beaten up, dusty and stained, that there was a bet on to see when he would get a new one. One of their kids must have smuggled it out of the house, Selena thought, laughing.

Diane read her lines with gusto, making everybody laugh. The skit was a mock wedding between a ranch family and a farm family, with each side so mad at the other they were barely willing to go along with the wedding. It ended with a brawl, and Barclay and Louise escaping out a mock window.

Everybody in the audience knew it hadn't happened that way, but they all knew, too, that it might have, that there was no love lost, when it came right down to it, between farmers and cattlemen and never had been, but that only made them laugh harder. As they wiped their eyes and grinned at each other, they said, "It's a wonder it don't" and "Isn't that the truth!"

Helen's husband, Harry, rose to make the presentation of the gift of money collected at the door. Then Louise and Barclay begun to unwrap gifts which Phoebe and several of the other girls carried to the head table. The men began to stand up, to move about the hall and to collect in groups here and there. Cathy crawled up onto the stage and began to bang on the piano until Lana, Lola's oldest, came and pulled her away. Tammy wandered over to where Selena was sitting and leaned against her legs. Selena leaned forward and smoothed her fine hair and replaced her barrette. Soon she'll be gone, she thought, and already she missed her.

She looked around the crowd for her own boys. Jason was just going out the door with a group of boys his own age. They would probably play scrub on the ball diamond until dark. She couldn't see Mark anywhere. Probably he had gone somewhere for the hour or so before the dance started. To Simca's with Jerry, most likely. Kent and Tony were standing talking together, their heads close. They were almost the same height.

Kent, his fair hair glinting in the overhead light . . . tonight when they went to bed together, he would want her. She had felt it all day, when he had come to help with the old square baler because it was balking and wouldn't knot the string right, and in the way he had carefully not looked at her whenever she had passed him and the kids were in the room. Tonight she felt herself wanting him, it was the one thing that was sure still, in the midst of so much that was changing. In a few years they would celebrate their twenty-fifth anniversary. Or would they? The question jolted her. It had never occurred to her that they might not.

The women were rising, going back to the kitchen to finish the cleaning up, crumbling the long paper tablecloths, soiled now with gravy stains, bits of spilled food and coffee rings, while behind them the men had begun to stack the chairs and move them, to collapse the tables and store away the ones that wouldn't be needed for the dance. Reluctantly, Selena got up and began to help remove the tablecloths, to crush them and throw them away.

The musicians moved onto the stage and started up their sound system. Out of the corner of her eye Selena saw Brian come in from outside and stand alone in the doorway. Phoebe saw him, had probably been waiting for him to arrive, and walked over to him. They stood together talking, not touching. The hall was clearing fast as the tables were rearranged or removed to make a dance floor. As Selena finished and went toward the bathroom she saw Kent arranging the tables along the far wall, then draping his jacket over a chair at one end of the tables near the middle of the room.

When she came out again, her feet and legs aching, but with fresh makeup on and her hair combed, she sat beside him. He had brought her a rye and Coke from the bar and she took a sip, relaxing at last. She had been at the hall since four, had hardly sat down in all that time.

The tempo in the hall had slowed down, the air had changed, the mood was less filled with humour. The musicians were tuning their instruments now, the tables were filling, and through the open outer door the summer night hung, vast and friendly. Phoebe came up to them with Brian following her.

"Is it okay if I go to Chinook with Brian? There's a dance there, too, for his mom and dad's friends."

Kent said, although Phoebe had spoken to Selena, "I want you back here by one in time to go home with us."

"Oh, Daddy . . ." she began, but Kent was looking past her to Brian, who stood back deferentially. He came forward now and leaned toward Kent to hear what he was saying.

"Okay," Brian said, and he took Phoebe's hand and led her away, Phoebe smiling up at him.

Mark had returned and was lounging in the doorway with Jerry and a few other boys. Jason, his shirt-tail untucked, came blinking into the light with his friends and went into the kitchen, probably to get a drink of water. The band began to play "The Anniversary Waltz" and everyone at the tables stood and watched Louise and Barclay circle the floor a few times, an embarrassed, solitary pair on the wide dance floor. After everyone had clapped, they all began to dance too. Soon the floor was full of waltzing couples.

Selena felt the hard muscle of Kent's back under her hand, remembering how, when she had been only Phoebe's age, they had gone out to his truck and spent half the night necking, and later, making love. How her body had been then, like Phoebe's, soft, yet tough, and how Kent had buried himself in her, as if she were everything.

She could feel the heat of his body radiating into her palm. She wished they could go home, go to bed. A wave of tenderness for him rose up in her and she lifted her hand and rested it on the back of his neck. He gave her a warning glance and twirled her fast around a corner.

Then it was almost midnight, the band had stopped playing and gone outside for a smoke. On one side of the dance floor, four or five little boys were stacking white plastic cups into pyramids. They had apparently gone all around the hall and gathered the empty cups. They had so many that there were three separate piles of them, and a couple of little boys concentrating over each pile. Adults at nearby tables watched them, calling out good-natured advice.

"Want another drink?" Kent asked. Selena shook her head no, watching the children. "Careful," Kent called, laughing, to the nearest boy, who was trying to set just one more glass onto his pyramid, which now reached above his head. He was too little and, stretching to reach, he swayed a little, lost his balance, the pyramid wavered, and then all the cups came tumbling down. All around the hall the people who hadn't noticed the children turned to see what was going on, while those who had, laughed and made a collective "Ohhh," of regret.

Diane had come to sit beside Selena. She held a sleeping Cathy on her lap and she rocked her now and then and smoothed her hair.

"Why don't you spread out her blankets and put her to sleep under the table in the kitchen?" Selena suggested. Her last words were drowned out in a second long, "Ohhh," of commiseration as another pyramid fell, the plastic cups bouncing across the dance floor. On her other side Jason rose and found a chair closer to the last child who was still building his pyramid, his brow furrowed with concentration. Jason pulled his chair forward to offer advice to the smaller boy, who glanced shyly toward him, then turned back to his project. From across the hall, his face lost in shadows, a man called out encouragement, then another male voice, and a woman's. The pyramid wavered, a chorus of "Uh-ohs" came from around the hall, followed by friendly laughter. The pyramid righted itself and the boy lifted another cup from the pile on the floor beside him. Even the members of the band, who had returned to the stage, were watching now.

A movement in the knot of men standing around the open entrance caught Selena's attention. Phoebe was working her way through the crowd, her shoulder turned sideways, the men moving aside for her when they realized she was trying to get past them. Brian wasn't with her. Selena waved so that Phoebe would spot her in the dim, warm room and the crowd, but Phoebe's head was down and she didn't see Selena's gesture. Instead, skirting the edges of the table and the people standing around watching the boy's pyramid, she hurried down the length of the hall to the bathroom, clutching one side of her full skirt in folds against her hip. Selena was puzzled by this and by the tight way she moved—and where was Brian? Phoebe disappeared into the bathroom and Selena looked back to the entrance.

Brian had just entered and was standing easily, spread-legged, a little apart from the other men, one hand dangling in front of his crotch, the other hand clasping it at the wrist. His face looked pale, but, she thought, it must be the light.

"That's the way, Terry! You got it there!" Barclay called.

"Careful!" from Rhoda. The boy stood up, a cup in his hand, his arm stretched as high as he could reach over his head, preparing to set the last cup on the pyramid. People clapped and called to him. The child touched the top of the pyramid with the bottom of the cup, it swayed, he waited, drawing back his hand, then bringing it down to rest his arm for a moment while the pyramid tottered, then steadied. More calls, more laughter and advice from the ring of children that had gathered around him, and from the adults seated at the tables.

The musicians were picking up their instruments again, talking to one another, glancing now and then to see how the boy was making out. Diane came back from putting Cathy to sleep in the kitchen and Tammy and Lana came running up. Tammy put her head down in her mother's lap, yawned and rubbed her eyes. Lana wandered away.

"Has Tony got a job?" Selena asked Diane.

"Not yet," Diane said. "He phoned his old company and they're supposed to call him back." The little boy set the last cup on top, the pyramid wavered, appeared to settle, then faltered again, and down came all the cups, a shower of white plastic. They rolled and bounced, scattering out over the dance floor. The band began to play a polka, a dozen little kids ran onto the dance floor and began to gather the cups, waving and jostling each other to see who could gather the most, while the grownups, still laughing, turned back to their drinks, or moved out onto the dance floor.

Suddenly Phoebe was beside Selena, sliding into Jason's vacated chair. She was out of breath, as though she'd been running .

"What's the matter?" Selena asked, alarmed.

Phoebe shook her head, said, "Nothing," but without that spurt of anger Selena had come to expect. Had she been crying? Then Selena noticed a wet patch on her skirt.

"My period started," Phoebe said into her ear. She let her skirt hang down between their two chairs so that the wet patch could dry but not be seen by anyone else. "I wasn't expecting it," she said, not looking at Selena.

"Did somebody give you a tampon?" Selena reached for her purse, which she found under the table in a puddle of spilled beer. Phoebe nodded.

"I'm okay," she said, still not angry. Puzzled, Selena glanced back to the doorway. Brian was still standing there, his legs planted firmly apart. He was looking out over the room at nothing. There was a tightness around his mouth, Selena knew she was really seeing it, that it wasn't just a trick of the light.

"What's the matter with Brian?" she asked, nodding toward him. Phoebe turned her head, looked at him, closed her eyes, and turned away. A fight? Selena wondered. "How was the dance at Chinook? Was there a good crowd?" Phoebe shrugged.

She was sitting on the chair Diane had left turned so that it was facing the dance floor, but she wasn't watching the dancers. Her legs were pressed together, crossed at the ankles and she kept twisting her feet. Her arms were crossed in front of her, her right arm resting on her left shoulder and her left hand holding onto her right forearm next to Selena. As she watched this tight, uncharacteristic posture, Selena's uneasiness grew. She leaned toward her and said into her ear, "Are you all right?"

For a second she thought Phoebe was going to cry. Phoebe lowered her head even more, shook it no, a slight, almost imperceptible motion. "Did you have a fight?" Selena whispered gently, directly into Phoebe's ear, holding back her light, sweet-smelling hair.

Phoebe said nothing for a second, then nodded miserably, blinking, yes. Selena put her arm around Phoebe's shoulders and turned her gently so that she was in shadow, facing the table. Phoebe lifted and slid her chair around. This way no one would see how upset she was.

"It'll be all right," Selena whispered into her ear again. Phoebe said nothing. Selena brushed Phoebe's hair back from her face and set it so that it hung down her back. She thought to herself, I'm not so sure I liked Brian anyway. Phoebe took a deep breath, her throat quivering, as if she might be fighting back tears.

Selena noticed then that the bodice of her dress and the full skirt had come apart at the seam just below her belt. Selena pushed the seam together and tugged the belt down to hide it. Phoebe didn't move. Bent forward that way, her arms on her lap, Selena, leaning close to her, couldn't help but notice how round and full Phoebe's young breasts were. How desirable she must be to men, she thought, so young and yet so womanly, and a pang of pity for Phoebe's innocent beauty went through Selena. That's why Kent is so hard on her. To keep her safe, she thought, as if that were possible. She looked back to the doorway, but Brian had disappeared, or at least she couldn't pick him out of the crowd standing in the doorway. Phoebe hadn't moved, but since everybody who had been sitting on the opposite side of the table was up dancing, Selena didn't bother trying to cheer Phoebe up. Let her feel badly for a little while, she thought. She just needs a little time. Kent was dancing with Rhoda; she was glad he wasn't there to disapprove or to cross-examine Phoebe.

She thought of her own father, but in the noise and confusion, couldn't get a grip on her memories. Funny how she still sometimes found herself expecting him to come into the kitchen on a gust of wind, slamming the door, and shouting at her, what's for supper, girl? as if by shouting at her he could fill the void left by her mother.

"I have to help serve lunch," Selena said to Phoebe, seeing the other women going to the kitchen. "Do you want to help?" Phoebe shook her head no, and pointed to the wet patch on her skirt. Selena patted her arm, and was startled to find it cool, almost cold in the hot room, and glancing once more at her, rose and went into the kitchen. At the door, she turned and looked back. Lola was just depositing her little boy in Phoebe's arms for Phoebe to hold while she helped with the lunch. Phoebe was cradling him and looking down at him with a serious, tender expression. Selena remembered how eagerly she herself had been to hold the other women's children when she was a girl, sometimes even secretly pretending they were her own. At one time or another, she thought, glancing quickly around the room, she had held and rocked nearly every child in the hall.

When the buffet table was set with food again and people were lined up and serving themselves, Selena went looking for Diane. She found her in the kitchen checking Cathy, where she lay asleep on the floor in the corner.

"Too bad Rhea couldn't come," Selena said, as Diane got up and brushed off her skirt.

"I think we should get her to a doctor," Diane said. "She's getting awfully funny."

"She always has been funny," Selena said. "As long as I can remember. It's all those years alone."

"Yeah, I guess so," Diane said, sighing. "When I'm gone, can you handle her yourself?" It was true, Selena realized, she would be the last close relative.

"I'll have to, I guess," she said. She thought of Diane gone, living somewhere in the city. Tony trading in his workclothes for white shirts and a suit. She thought of Rhea, sixty years a ranch wife, most of those years without electricity or plumbing or telephone, now a half-crazy old woman, unable to enjoy the amenities she once would have given anything for. "It's funny, isn't it," she said. Suddenly she was so tired she thought she might never move again. Rhea, alone in her shack, her husband dead, her children gone or dead. Would they all wind up that way? Was that what happened to your life?

"What?" Diane asked, watching the lineup of people across the kitchen from them.

"I just keep thinking . . ."

"What?"

"That our lives would turn out . . . differently . . ." Diane laughed.

"Nothing ever changes out here," she said. But that's not true, Selena wanted to say. Everything was changing.

They were silent, leaning side by side against the counter. Selena yawned, then covered her mouth. She thought of her bed at home, Kent's weight on her, his breath in her hair. When she didn't understand things, when the world moved too quickly for her, there was always that retreat. How glad she was to have it.

"Have you found a buyer for your farm?" she asked.

"Probably Doyle. His land borders ours and he's about as land-hungry as they come. He won't be able to pass it up."

"Just as long as he can pay for it," Selena warned. Diane seemed not to hear.

Mark was passing them in the line now. He tossed Selena a quick, wordless half-smile, a little embarrassed, it seemed, at having a mother. She saw again his bony wrists sticking out of his too-short shirtsleeves. He would be a big man someday, bigger than Kent. Already he had left her behind, as if what she thought and knew were no longer of any consequence.

It was two o'clock when all five of them got into the car and started for home. Jason fell asleep in the back seat, his head bouncing against the window, which didn't seem to disturb his sleep. Mark sat against the other window, with Phoebe in the middle. Mark leaned forward.

"Rick says his old man is going to buy Tony out." Kent, leaning back to hear Mark, merely nodded.

"You'd think he had enough land," he said. "Some people are never satisfied."

"Did Tony talk to you about it?" Selena asked.

"Yeah. He said he can probably go back with that company he used to work for summers when he was in college." He was silent for a moment, thinking. "I hope to hell he can. I haven't got the money to help him if he gets into trouble. And I don't think that family of his will lift a hand."

"Well, if it comes to that," Selena said slowly. "Phoebe's room will be empty this fall, and I always grow plenty of garden, and there's always lots of beef." Kent laughed.

"Let's cross that bridge when we come to it. That sister of yours . . ."

"Who knows," Selena said, her tone dreamy as she yawned. "Maybe she's right."

"Right?" he said. "Are you crazy?" But Kent, too, seemed to have lost interest in the argument, and when she didn't reply, said nothing more. The car hummed softly, carrying them through the starlit summer night, toward their home. Selena thought again about Phoebe's strange behaviour. Phoebe hadn't gone to say good-night to Brian, but as they were leaving, he had come toward her and caught her arm as she passed him. Selena pretended not to notice. He had said something in an undertone to Phoebe. Phoebe had answered him, but had not stopped for long, so they hadn't had to wait for her like they usually did.

Then there was that grad night business, Selena remembered. When all the kids were returning to the hall after changing into jeans for their all-night barbecue, Phoebe had come toward Selena looking angry, hurrying across the empty floor, Brian trailing behind, an exasperated look on his face, trying to catch up with her.

Phoebe had only wanted Selena to take her grad dress and good shoes home with her, why Brian should be annoyed about that, Selena didn't know. As Phoebe handed her the dress, Selena noticed that the blouse Phoebe had changed into had a button missing. Irritated that Phoebe hadn't seen it, she searched through her purse for a safety pin. Brian stood there like a forty-year-old husband waiting impatiently for his wife. Selena had deliberately taken her time fastening the blouse.

"You okay, dear?" she asked into the back seat.

"Yeah," Phoebe said.

"Why wouldn't she be okay?" Kent asked. Selena patted his wrist.

"Never mind," she said playfully Phoebe made a sound, it might have been of disgust or agreement, and Selena twisted around to look at her. But it was dark in the back seat and she couldn't make out Phoebe's face.

AUGUST

At first Rhea can't make out what lies below. She is aware only of being high, high above . . . above what? Nothing of importance. She doesn't think this, it is simply there. She is detached, indifferent. She turns her attention to the things below, observing without warmth or anxiety, as though all her human emotions had been stripped from her. She sees a group of women. They are doing something. They talk to one another, they turn to and away from one another, their hands are busy, their bodies are moving. She hears their voices, but their conversation, their activities are so trivial, so irrelevant seen from this new plane of consciousness that she does not even bother to try to understand what they are saying or what they are doing.

Gradually it comes to her that she is no longer one of them, that she is elevated, on a higher plane than they are. But this is not possible, some other part of her tells her new, detached consciousness. No, I don't want this, it says. I'm just an ordinary woman. And at once she feels herself growing smaller, dwindling, her fleshly warmth returning, she sweeps through layers of blackness, with great effort returning from that calm detachment to the safety and comfort of her own flesh.

It is as though she is two selves. One is the self of the body, the heart-driven, vein-filled, blood-rushing, breathing body, and the other a creature that lives inside and sees out the eyes of the flesh-and-bone self. The creature inside looking out the eyes of the body sees . . . the yellow mass of wild sunflowers she gathered on impulse the evening before and thrust into a quart sealer.

Sunflowers. Flowers of the sun. The sun's flowers. She feels her fingers, fat and warm on the crocheted doilies of her chair arms. She flexes them. Her wedding ring is worn to a thin, tarnished thread that cuts into the flesh of her third finger. I'll have to have that ring cut off one of these days, she tells herself again. Filed off, torn off, wrenched off. She laughs, listening to the sound, long, ringing peals of sound like bells, or water over polished stones in the bottom of a coulee. She laughs again, to hear herself.

She is sorry she picked the sunflowers. They are too big and garish, they have none of the delicacy of so much that grows on the prairie, and no scent worth mentioning. Better to gather the wild roses, or the sage itself, dusty and silvered, to scent the house. A momentary aberration, she tells herself, and repeats the phrase several times, pleased with the sound of it.

Slowly she begins to feel all one person, the two selves melding as they always do after one of these visions. She waits, calmly sitting in her chair in her living room. She waits. How well I wait, she compliments herself. I always could wait. Learned young, she thinks, learned it when I was still a child. Sitting in the truck, the wagon, the buggy, the model T—over by the sale ring or next to the elevators or in front of the beer parlour or on the main street in town on Saturday night—hour after hour, waiting on the men. Who do they think they are, that we should have to wait for them, always be waiting on them—blowing children's noses, singing them songs till they fall asleep. Waiting, knitting, waiting . . . A woman has to know how to wait.

When she feels herself securely back in her own skin, she waits a moment longer, knowing that what is to be done next will come to her, her body will tell her. Ridiculous, she says to herself, there's diapers to be changed, hoeing to be done, and the men will be wanting dinner. She almost heaves herself up out of her chair, but the very silence of the place settles into her and she knows she is alone and time has passed. Years, she thinks, years.

Gradually the feeling she has been waiting for steals through her. She is alert now, all her senses attuned to it, straining to read its message. A hollow feeling, yes, it flows upward, engulfing her, a wanting.

Bread. Bread! That's it. She can smell the yeast already, feel the cool moist dough, its texture like the silken flesh of infants under her palms. She heaves herself up and scurries to the kitchen.

She takes her bread-making bowl from the nail where it hangs on the wall. It is a large blue granite basin with sloping sides and many nicks along the rim where the shiny, blue-speckled surface is missing and the black undercoat shows through. She tests the curved inner surface of the bowl with the flat of her hand, running her palm around it while she surveys the kitchen busily, planning her next move. Sometimes she finds she has hung the pan without cleaning it first. She's forgetful, she knows it, but this time it's clean. There is not a knot or a grain of dried dough on the smooth, inner surface.

She sets the bowl on her kitchen table and begins to gather her ingredients and set them on the table: lard, yeast, salt, sugar. She fills the kettle and sets it on the electric stove, then rolls her flour barrel over to stand beside the table. She is still strong, stronger than either Selena or Diane, and she's glad of it. A good life well-lived, she thinks smugly.

She will have to chop wood for the baking, but there's plenty of time for that. To this day she hasn't baked bread in her electric oven. Well, once, for an experiment, but the bread seemed tasteless to her and the colour wasn't right. So she continues to use her cookstove, which stands across one corner of the room, raised on a brick platform which her son Harold insisted on building for her, it had taken four men to move the stove onto it, over her protests and muttered imprecations—it's safer, Mother, these things are real fire hazards, now you'll be glad when we're done. She keeps the stove polished so that its nickel-plated trim gleams, its black surface shines dully. The children all stare and stare at it when they come to visit. She reaches out a hand to touch its coolness. A beautiful thing.

The kettle has begun to sing. She has let the water get too hot, and forgotten to set the yeast. Annoyed with herself, she stands for a moment, then shuts off the burner under the kettle and goes to the kitchen door, where she stands looking out over her garden through the screen. After a moment she pushes the door open and steps outside, letting the door slam shut behind her. She bends and pulls a dead blossom off the pink and yellow snapdragons at the door, and then off a mauve and purple pansy. A ladybug crawls onto her hand, and she flicks her wrist to shake it off. It flies away to land in the raspberries.

It is mid-morning, the sun is high, spreading its heat over the land. She never could stand the heat. She has to laugh at this, and a couple of wrens leap, startled, out of the lilacs in the corner of the garden. Five children to feed and care for, a husband, two, often three hired men, the house to run—ironing, baking, meal preparation—all in the blazing summer heat—she who couldn't stand the heat. Well, I stood it well enough, she tells herself grimly. That blessed sun! She shades her eyes from it, thinking how the gardens will be burning up.

Red-winged blackbirds, sparrows, a robin or two, finches, swallows, all sing in her oasis. She wonders idly, listening to them, if it was right for her to build this garden in the middle of the prairie, or if she should have left it the way it was. It'll go back soon enough, she reminds herself somberly, when I'm gone. Go-back land, she says, remembering the phrase the people used to say. Go-back land. The corn whispers to her, far off the prairie runs in the heat, and she can't help but laugh again. She shakes her head, as though someone who ought to know better has just said something ridiculous, and goes back inside.

This time she sets the yeast, puts the lard and some salt and sugar into the warm water she has poured into the basin and stands, one hand on her hip, while the yeast slowly rises in its dish beside the basin. She is reminded of when she was a girl and the threshing crew was at her father's place, she used to rise with her mother at four every morning to set the buns for breakfast. Once they got the first batch of buns or bread started, they never used yeast again, just saved a small piece of dough from the previous morning and mixed it into the fresh dough. It was enough to leaven the whole batch. Then around seven the crew had fresh, hot buns for breakfast. She and her mother and the hired girl sweating in the kitchen for weeks on end.

Then later, a grown woman in her own kitchen, baking twenty loaves of bread at a time to sell to the bachelors of the district—old Appleby, Jake Johns, Shorty Small, old Rhyhorchuck, and that blessed Loewen who never would pay her, till she wouldn't give him any more bread. And every week baking another twelve loaves for her own family. Oh, I've made enough bread in my day, she thinks.

The yeast is ready and she stirs it carefully, then tests the temperature of the mixture in the big basin by dropping it onto her wrist. Just right. And Selena wanting a recipe. A recipe! You do it till you get it right, and then that's the way you do it from then on, she had told her. She pours the yeast slowly into the big basin, then stirs carefully. She made Selena and Diane do it over and over again in her kitchen, when they were still girls, after Maude died. Selena never did get it quite right, but good enough, she supposed, Diane never could do it at all. She shakes her head. Buying her bread. Women don't know anymore, she thinks, don't know what bread-making is for, what it means to make your own bread.

She lifts the lid off the flour barrel and sets it carefully against the table leg. She puts her cup in and lifts out the first cup of flour. Its smell fills her nostrils, faint, not describable, but real. When she dumps the cupful into the bowl of yeasty liquid, a fine white powder rises and settles on her wrists and fat forearms. She works more briskly now, dipping, shaking, pouring flour into the big bowl. When she judges the amount to be right, she begins to mix it in, first using a big wooden spoon, then wiping the sticky dough off it and setting it in the sink. She begins to use her hands. The wet dough rises up between her fingers, sticking to them.

When all the flour is mixed in to her satisfaction, she cleans her hands off and adds several more cups of flour. Then she shoves the basin back from her, sprinkles flour by hand over the oilcloth surface of her table, turns the basin upside down over the sprinkled area, so that the dough falls out, rights the basin, and cleans out the dough left sticking to the inside of the basin.

She begins to knead, standing back a bit from the table, her legs set apart, knees locked, and pushes hard, but slowly, from the shoulder, not the elbows, so that she leans into the dough with her weight and the strength of her back: a quarter-turn, knead, flip; a quarter-turn, knead, flip; a quarter-turn, knead, flip. The dough feels heavy, stiff. She isn't worried, it will come.

Diane had sat across from her, watching her while she kneaded, holding the little one, what was her name? Some foolish modern name, no, Catherine. It was the other one with the silly name. Got it out of a movie, I suppose. Fold, quarter-turn, knead. The dough is beginning to respond, no longer warm, the flour working in well now.

Crying. I can't stand it, Auntie Rhea. Diane sitting at her table, crying. I'm going crazy.

Crazy! Hah! She doesn't know what crazy is. Old Mary Andras, now, there was crazy. Six sons, no daughters, all hard-working, which meant *she* had to work twice as hard as they did, twice as fast, to keep them all fed and clothed. And old Miklos, so strong he could lift a bull, but too stupid to see she was losing her mind. Carrying water to her dried-up garden day after day, the grasshoppers eating what the drought hadn't taken.

What are you going crazy about? she had asked Diane, trying not to laugh, or was it cry? I've had my own crazy days, she thinks, and as she remembers, she stops kneading, she is so surprised.

I started to pay attention to each living thing growing on the prairie: the plants, the lichen, the rocks . . . I wandered out on the prairie at night, it was the only time I had . . . I studied the rocks, one especially, I remember . . . a handsome rock, flat-topped, almost the size of my table. It was flesh-coloured . . . I thought it was my lover . . . under the moon . . . I knew it was madness. I didn't care. Out there things spoke to me . . . not with voices, but deep inside me, they drew me to them, or they pushed me away. And the wind blew, hot or cold, was silent or raged at me, told me where to go, where not to go, where to stay and wait. I knew then that I was first of all a woman, one that no man could satisfy . . . I wanted more, or was it less? Why should I have wanted anything at all . . . the rocks, hard, ancient, flushed with colour, cracked, shat upon by small birds, used as altars for the sacrifices of hawks and eagles. Many times I found the perfect, minute paws of gophers on them, and their bloody bowels . . . I sat in the centre of the tipi rings, silent, facing north, east, south, west. In that time I learned to listen to what welled up inside me. . . .

So what are you going crazy about, Diane?

I want . . . Diane said, and Rhea had felt herself nodding.

Don't we all, she had said, don't we all.

Not Selena, Diane had said, her voice full of anger. Rhea gives the bread a final turn and pat and leaves it to rest, going back to the door again to stare out, listening to the songbirds perched in the bushes.

You think Selena doesn't want? she had asked.

She's satisfied, Diane said, running after Kent and the boys, watching Phoebe grow up into the same thing.

So you're leaving.

I suppose you think that's wrong.

Hah! Rhea had snorted. What's wrong, what's right.

Well, if you don't know, you're the only one in the whole world who doesn't think she does, Diane said.

What do you think you'll find in the blessed city?

Life! Diane had shouted, so loud that the baby on her lap had wakened and cried.

What's that you're holding? Rhea had said, and remembering now, she has to chuckle. Tsk, tsk, her tongue goes. She goes back and pokes gently at her bread with her finger. A long enough rest.

Oh, Rhea, don't you see? I'm not stuck here like you were. I've got a choice. I can leave, I can get a job. Tony doesn't own me the way it was in your day. I'm a free person.

Free, Rhea had said and laughed again.

I bake cookies, I make the beds, I hoe the garden, I look after the kids, I sleep with Tony. And when everything's done, when the beds are all made, the floors swept, the dishes washed, the clothes ironed and the kids are asleep I look around and I think, is this it? Is this all there is? Her dark eyes had fastened on Rhea, a deep, black light shining in them.

Electricity, refrigeration, running water, vacuum cleaners, Rhea had recited.

Happiness. Happiness, Diane echoed softly, after a minute. Something in me insists that there is more, there has to be more.

Happiness, freedom, Rhea said the words back to Diane, or perhaps to herself.

In the same soft voice Rhea had just used, Diane asked, do you know what I want?

I see the energy churning in you, Rhea said. It comes out your eyes and the tips of your fingers.

She begins to knead the dough again, falling into the rhythm. She feels it growing lighter at last under the palms and heels of her hands. The muscles in her lower back and her shoulders begin to ache.

Diane had dropped her eyes abruptly and Rhea had known she was thinking, Rhea's madness has crept up on her again, she's not sane now. So Rhea hadn't said, you make me think of a young goddess—your slenderness and grace, your beauty, your long, glossy hair—a huntress, a priestess, a . . . She kneads her bread.

All the young women, she muses as she kneads, are sweet and slender at thirteen, their young breasts round and light, their skins fine-grained and easily flushed, their eyes have that quick sparkle. At sixteen their bodies have grown heavier, lost their buoyancy, their breasts have weight, their thighs and hips have thickened, their eyes have deepened and already that glow is fading from their complexions. At eighteen . . .

Well, right or wrong, I have to go, Diane said.

It's not wrong, Rhea had replied, hearing her own voice deepen and grow strong. You go.

Now her shoulders are aching. The dough has developed the smooth elasticity she has been waiting for, she can feel its lightness under her fingers and in the heels, the palms, the fingers of her hands. She puts her face close to it to smell it, she draws in a long breath of it, so cool, so sweet. Yet the wonder of it is how it rises and doubles itself and grows light as air itself. I wonder who invented bread? she thinks. God, maybe, but no, it had to be a woman. A goddess.

As she cleans the basin she remembers how she protested when Eli insisted she have water pumped into the house. I don't need it, she said. I've pumped water at the well for over fifty years and I can do it till I die. I like the sound of it, she said. I like how cold it is straight from the well. Now, Mother, Eli said. It's too hard for you now that you're older.

Then they were digging trenches to lay the pipe, and fiddling on her step with a pump. It's a jet pump, Eli said to her. What do I care? she replied. A well-witcher witched that well, she told them. It's the same well, Mother, Eli said. It's the same water. If you won't move to town . . .

And they were in her kitchen, tearing things out, sawdust everywhere, noise from morning till night, men lying on their backs on her floor with their heads vanished inside the cupboards. As if that wasn't bad enough, Martin had come home, too, with his wife and kids in a camper, parked outside on the prairie for two weeks while he built a bathroom onto the side of the house. It was pointless to protest, none of her sons paid any attention to her.

When the basin is clean she polishes it dry, then sets it back on the table beside the round of dough. She takes a wad of butter in the palm of her hand and slaps it back and forth till both hands are amply buttered, then butters the inside of the bowl with long streaks of yellow butter. She lifts the dough and sets it in the bottom of the basin, turning it a few times to round the edges. She butters the top delicately with a thin, shining coating of grease. Next she takes a clean cloth and drapes it over the bowl, moves the bowl to the centre of the table and stands back.

Her hands tingle from the flow of blood stimulated by the kneading. They feel large, swollen, and very warm. Sometimes she thinks she makes bread just to feel that heat and power in her hands. But her shoulders and back ache, reminding her that she has been making bread for more than sixty years. It is a thing of pride, she thinks to herself, to have sixty years of bread-making behind you.

She washes her hands in the warm running water her sons have given her, thinking, men dig wells and run pumps, and women make bread. Then she goes outside to the old woodpile near the back of the yard.

The sun is so hot it strikes her like a blow. I never could stand the heat, she observes again, and shades her eyes with her hand while she scurries back into the kitchen, takes her big straw sunhat from the hook by the door, ties it under her chin, and goes back outside.

She finds some kindling, a few sticks of wood left from her last bread-making. The axe waits in the chopping block. Jasper always kept the wood chopped, she has to give him that. After supper every evening, the familiar thud and crack, rhythmic, the silence, the thud-crack, the silence between the blows. She especially liked the sound of the dried sticks cracking as he twisted them on the axe. She rarely watched him, but could see with her mind's eye how his shirt wrinkled over his shoulders and stretched tight over his biceps, when he raised the axe, and how, when the axe began its long fall, the muscles in his back would swell and move. He was a strong man, Jasper was, she tells herself. But I'm stronger.

She lifts the axe and lets it fall. A flock of horned larks swoops past on the other side of the pole fence and then they are gone. I always liked horned larks, she says to herself, letting the axe fall again. They don't bother nobody, and they're pretty little birds.

She wonders if Diane is gone. She thinks Selena told her, but she can't remember. Oh, she went all right, I knew she would the moment she was born. Maude holding her up for me to see. Another girl, Maude said. A girl, and Archie so wanted a boy. Let him have the next one then, I told her, but poor Maude only burst into tears. This one's a seeker, I said, when I saw how she squirmed, her eyes already looking all around.

Suddenly Rhea's energy deserts her and she sets the axe heavily into the chopping block, turns, goes around the house and back inside. She is grateful for the cool, dim interior of her house and she takes off her hat and hangs it wearily back on its hook. She sits down again in her armchair at the end of the room and lets her head fall back against its padding. Jasper sat here. For years it was Jasper's chair. Now it's mine. She closes her eyes.

Darkness. Only pitch darkness behind her eyelids. She relaxes, sinks deeper into it. Slowly it begins to lighten, and she finds herself back in her own kitchen, many years before.

Blood. Blood everywhere. On the kitchen floor, the table leg. Sprayed out across the washstand, a trail from the door. All over his hands and face and his belly, too, soaking the clean shirt she had finished making only the day before. I'll never get it all out, she thought, flustered.

Jasper was white. The hired man supporting him by holding one arm at the elbow. There was blood all over his clothes, too. Jasper took his hand away from his calf, raising his head to look beseechingly at her. Do something, his look said, and she pressed her hands against her thighs, bending to see better.

Blood surged suddenly through the tear in his pant leg. He pulled up the cloth so she could see the wound better. It spurted again, three feet it must have shot out, splattering against the washstand, this time brushing her own calf as it shot past. It started another surge, but Jasper clamped his hand over it, and the blood leaked around his fingers. The hired man pushed a chair behind Jasper and he dropped into it. He was growing paler. She straightened, frantically searching the room with her eyes. Do something—stop the blood! Outside, the cows in the corral were bellowing, searching for the calves that had been taken from them for branding and castrating. The noise was too loud, the blood too red, she couldn't think. Then calm descended over her. Her eyes rested on the flour barrel, she strode toward it, bumping against the hired man, who stepped back out of the way. She wrenched the lid off the flour barrel, she could hear Jasper behind her taking short, quick breaths. She reached inside the barrel and scooped out a double handful of flour and carried it to him. He held his pant leg up, the wound clear, so small, a puncture he must have done with his castrating knife. She pressed the mass of flour against the wound, cupping her hands over it, pressing. Hold it, she told Jasper. He put his big hands where hers had been.

She rushed to the bedroom, found an old sheet she had been meaning to make into dish towels, ripped off a rectangle and hurried back to the flour barrel with it. She folded the rectangle double, then scooped flour onto it, folded it again and then again, so that the flour was sealed inside. She took the flour-filled cloth to where Jasper still sat, pressing the loose flour against the cut, pushed his hands aside, scraped away most of the blood-soaked flour, then quickly pressed the cloth against the wound. She pulled it tight. Hold it, she said again, and Jasper held it while she ran back to the bedroom and tore off another long strip with which to bind the cloth against the leg.

The hired man went back outside. She began to clean the blood off the floor. Tea? she asked Jasper.

The dream deteriorated into a shifting sequence of pictures, most of which made no sense. Then she was alone and it was night, coyotes moaning in the winter blackness beyond the windows. She was bleeding, the warm blood running down between her legs, her gut cramping, the pain growing, then releasing. No telephone in those days. Jasper away selling cattle. She would have to go out and hitch the team and drive the thirty miles to the nearest hospital if she wanted help. The baby asleep in its basket beside her.

She folded a flannel sheet over and over again and wrapped it around herself, the heaviest thickness between her legs. She made herself a cup of tea and went back to bed.

All night she had bled, bled and bled, and hurt, till finally it was over. One long, wrenching cramp that had forced, at last, a groan from her, and the baby she had not been sure she was carrying was gone. She had fallen asleep then, or lost consciousness, and when she woke again, the bleeding had dwindled to a manageable flow. She had heated water in the kitchen, filled a basin, taken some rags and scrubbed the inside of her legs. Then she had burned the sheet and the rags in the burning barrel in the yard, before Jasper returned.

It seemed to her now, musing, in some realm between sleep and wakefulness, that a woman's life was filled with blood. That its sticky texture, its odour, its blue-red colour filled her life, was always with her.

Menstruation, miscarriages, births—I even bled when Jasper went into me that first time, on our wedding night. There was no woman without that intimate knowledge of blood. Trickling down your legs, smearing itself on all the things you own, your hands, reminding you of yourself, the self you don't talk about. The self that seems most real to you, no matter how you try to pretend it isn't.

My bread. She opens her eyes. The light has grown yellower while she was resting. The day is waning. She rises and returns to the kitchen.

The dough has mounded up above the pan. She washes her hands, butters them, punches the dough down, divides it into six equal sections and shapes each into a loaf. She butters six breadpans and sets the loaves into them. That done, she begins to carry in the wood she has chopped. It is time to start the fire in the stove.

When she came around to the kitchen door again, her arms full of wood, Selena was standing there. Rhea was so startled she almost dropped the wood.

"Well!" she said, and went inside. She set the wood down in the old woodbox Jasper had built years ago, which sat beside the cookstove. When she turned around, Selena was standing behind her. "Well!" she said again, and wiped her hands on her apron.

"Oh, Auntie Rhea," Selena said, her voice filled with dismay. "Why all this bread? You can't possibly use it, and you don't even have a deepfreeze."

"It's for you, of course," Rhea replied, "that family of yours." She turned back to the stove, lifted the lid, and began to crumple paper, stuff it into the burning chamber and set kindling on top of it.

"And in the cookstove! In this heat!" Rhea turned away from the stove without replying and went back outside to get another load. As she stooped at the woodpile, she heard Selena coming after her. Selena stooped too, and began to gather an armload. She wanted to tell her to stop, she didn't want another woman interfering in her breadmaking, but she refrained, remembering that she had after all taught Selena to make bread, that Selena was her acolyte. Acolyte, she repeated to herself, and said it out loud, "Acolyte," wondering where such a satisfying word had come from.

"What?" Selena asked.

"Hmmph!" Rhea replied, embarrassed. They carried all the split wood into the house; it filled the woodbox and an armful sat on the floor beside it.

"You split all this yourself?" Selena shook her head. "I'm fifty years younger than you, and don't know if I could do it."

"Forty," Rhea said. "Let's have some tea."

She set the kettle on the electric stove, turned the burner on, got down the teapot and cups and then stood waiting for the kettle to boil. Selena pulled out a chair and sat down at the kitchen table.

"I see you picked yourself some wild sunflowers," Selena remarked, looking through the doorway into the living room.

"Pesky things," Rhea replied, having forgotten about them.

"Wherever did you find them? They sure don't grow out there." She nodded her head toward the bald prairie around the house, on the other side of Rhea's garden. Rhea shrugged her shoulders.

"There's a place," she said, tossing her head vaguely to the north. "You take them. I don't want them."

"What's that?" Selena asked, pointing to a bunched plant hanging upside down from a nail in the old wooden ceiling. The flowers were still yellow although they were fading.

"Cinquefoil," Rhea said.

"Cinquefoil! Whatever for?"

"Hah!" Rhea replied. She lifted the kettle and poured the boiling water over the teabags in the teapot. While the tea steeped she checked the fire in the cookstove, opened the oven door and put her arm in, elbow first. She straightened, then bent to the woodbox.

"It'll have to be a lot hotter than that," she said, pushing more wood into the fire.

"I have to admit, that stove does make better bread," Selena said.

Rhea sighed, pulled out a chair and sat down at the table across from Selena.

"To what do I owe the pleasure of this visit?" she asked.

"You mean, what do I want?" Selena grinned. "Nothing. I was lonesome, so I thought I'd drop over for tea."

"Lonesome!" Rhea said, astonished.

"Well, I can't go over to see Di anymore."

"You're lonesome now," Rhea said, "what will you do when winter comes?"

"Oh, take a community college class, I guess."

"It used to take us two hours with a team to get to Mallard. And when you got there, you weren't anywhere," Rhea said.

"We should get you to teach the young ones how to make bread." Selena brightened at the thought. "That'd be a good class for this winter."

"Somebody should teach them," Rhea said. "Lord knows. Some of them had better be able to make bread the right way. It could be forgotten."

Rhea rose again and poked the fire. She put another stick in, tested the oven again, and then set three of the loaves inside. The oven would hold only three loaves at a time and she had to keep shifting them because it was hotter at the back than at the front, and the left side browned better than the right.

Behind her Selena sighed.

"Things aren't going so well for our community college committee," she said. "They make us have a minimum enrollment before we can offer a class, and most of the women are only interested in crafts and things like that. If you offer something like history, you can't get enough people to come." Rhea sat down again and sipped her tea.

"I don't know," Selena said. "It seems like people out here are satisfied with their lives, and they don't have much interest in the rest of the world."

"Satisfied," Rhea said. She thought of all the men and women who had come and then gone—neighbours, friends, relations. It seemed to her that the countryside had once been full of people, where now it was empty. "Except for Diane."

"Except for Diane," Selena said. "Now they're taking away our post offices, our branch lines, killing off the few little stores we had left scattered around the country."

"Soon there'll be nothing left out here but grasshoppers and gophers," Rhea said. They both laughed wryly, and sobered, looking out the window to the slowly sloping field of grass that rolled out to meet the sky. How it must have been, when there was no one here but the Indians and the animals, Selena thought.

"The bank took over Louise and Barclay's place," Selena said.

"No!" Rhea said, although everybody knew it was coming, she must have, too.

"Yeah, they had to move out. Helen says they've gone to Swift Current to live."

"Poor Louise," Selena said. "I wonder if they have enough equity to come out at least not owing."

"Should," Rhea said. "Barclay should have let Louise keep the cattle her dad gave her. They could fall back on cattle now. Everybody so anxious to modernize. Look where it gets them."

"He hates cattle," Selena said, pouring more tea into her cup. "It isn't fair!" she said, banging down the teapot. "She worked so hard, she worked far harder than he did. She looked after the house, raised the kids and drove a tractor, picked rocks, harvest time she hauled grain—Kent even says she has a better business head than Barc, but he won't listen to her." Rhea lifted her head and her teacup to look hard at Selena.

"She isn't the only one works harder than he does," she said, mildly enough. "You never noticed that?" Selena thought a moment. Ruth did, everybody knew that, even Buck. And maybe Ella. Does she mean me? she suddenly wondered, glancing sharply at Rhea. No, not me. Kent's one of the hardest workers around here, cattlemen all work harder than straight grain farmers any day of the week.

She thought of Caroline, little Caroline, as brown as a native, hard as nails. Running her own ranch back in the hills. She could ride and rope better than lots of the men. Broke broncs, even castrated studs herself, the men said. A head shorter than I am, she thought, and made an amused sound. Seeing Rhea looking questioningly at her, she said, "I was thinking of Caroline." Rhea nodded. "She carries it too far," Selena said. "I mean, it's okay to work hard, but she's just like a man." She shook her head. The men all stayed away from her, and when they talked about her, they laughed. Funny, she thought. "It seems like it's okay to work hard, I mean, you have to work hard or people think you're no good—look at all the things people say about Di, because she doesn't help Tony farm—but if you work too hard . . ."

"Men don't like women to try to take their place," Rhea said.

"It doesn't seem fair," Selena said, thinking at the same time, who would want to live like a man, the way Caroline did. "Cutting horses, yuck," she said.

But in her mind's eye she was trying to imagine herself clumping into her own kitchen like Kent did, asking, supper ready? After we eat I'm going to doctor that heifer—no, I think I'll ride for an hour or two first. Move the cattle out of that north field into Jake's.

She laughed aloud. Rhea said, "That wind's going to pick up. It's going to rain."

Selena glanced up at Rhea, then looked past her out the screen door. The sun was just as bright as it had been, the little patch of sky just as blue.

"Gosh, your snapdragons are pretty," she said, deciding to ignore Rhea's remark. "You've got such a green thumb."

"Green thumb!" Rhea said disparagingly. "You just have to pay a little attention."

"I do pay attention," Selena said ruefully, "for all the good it does."

"Give it time," Rhea said, a note of finality in her voice.

The light was turning golden now. The wind was rising. They could hear it soughing through the grass far out across the prairie. It drew closer as they listened and before long it was whistling its way through Rhea's garden, snapping the shrubs and rattling the corn. The snapdragons bumped their swollen heads against the door frame and a kingbird rose, chirping in protest, to swoop indignantly away.

"I'd better get going," Selena said, jumping up. "If it's actually going to rain I don't want to get caught in it." She stepped outside, holding her hair off her face in the wind, starting down the path to the gate. "Will you come over and help me butcher my chickens on Friday?" Rhea nodded, holding the screen door against the wind. "See you," Selena called over the whistle of the wind, her skirt pressed flat against her backside. Rhea turned inside.

As she shut the door she heard a booming clap of thunder. No rain, she told herself automatically, just thunder and lightning to kill a few cattle and split a few fenceposts. For a moment she thought the door she had just closed might open and Jasper would come stomping in, shaking himself like a dog, then peer out the kitchen window with his hands in his pockets, while she put the tea kettle on.

She went to the bedroom and looked out the window at the sky. Black thunderclouds were rising above the hills, rolling toward the house. As she watched, sheet lightning flooded the sky. Nothing but a windstorm, she muttered, a tinge of hope nonetheless colouring her prediction and she hurried around the small house closing windows.

In the kitchen she removed the first three loaves of bread, dumped them out of their pans onto the table, and put the last three in. This change in the weather wasn't good for the bread. The kitchen had grown even darker. A few splatters of rain hit the window, and she went to it to look out, leaning against the sink. The wind was rattling the old barn. One of these days, she said out loud, it'll blow down, and that'll be the end of that.

Still, she liked storms. They thrilled her, brought her some kind of peculiar comfort, the evidence that life was not as simple and dull as it often seemed, that there were forces no one understood, sky gods maybe, and a power that could transform the prairie. A flash of lightning turned the prairie momentarily white and then black again.

She watched for another moment, then went to the living room, took the bouquet of sunflowers from the sealer, opened the front door into the wind, and threw them as hard as she could. They arced through the bluish, heavy air, caught by the wind, so that they went sailing, end over end, to disappear out into the storm.

It had begun to rain now. I hope Selena makes it home before it breaks, she thought. That road can get pretty tough pretty fast. She sat down again in her big chair in the living room. The thunder crashed now and then with a satisfactory boom and the room flashed with lightning. All these years, she thought, listening and watching, making supper, always busy, always doing.

Women! she thought. We just wander on with our lives, going here, going there, wherever we're pushed, willy nilly. Busy, busy, busy. One day you look up and it's over, they're gone—the husband, the children—and you're left alone.

With each year that's passed, Rhea thought, I have grown more and more into myself. I am more solidly myself now than I've ever been. She was sinking back into that blackness again, but Selena and Diane hovered in her mind's eye, would not yet release her. No, she said to them, there's nothing I can do; you have to do it for yourself, and then she was plunging again through the layers of darkness into that place she went that held both the past and the future.

NIGHT MUSIC

Diane is already in bed, watching Tony as he takes off his clothes. She is sitting up, her pillows pushed behind her, her hands clasped on the blankets that cover her knees. She likes to watch Tony because he is so beautiful. Well, perhaps his face isn't quite perfect, his nose a little too big, his chin not quite sculptured enough. But, no, the whole effect is pleasing, really pleasing.

"Gee, you're a good-looking man!" she says to him as he comes and sits on the bed beside her. He grins at her over his shoulder, half-embarrassed, half-discounting what she says.

You're not so bad yourself," he says, and then they both laugh because they've both said these things before. He sighs, lifts the blankets and slides under them, pulling them up to his chest, as she lies down beside him.

"Well, here we are," he says, putting his arms comfortably under his head. Diane puts out the lamp that sits on the floor on her side of the bed. "In the big city at last. Babes in the woods."

"Speak for yourself," Diane says smugly. "It feels like home to me." In the light coming through the window they can see the suitcases still open on the floor by the bed and cardboard boxes stacked up and squeezed into the corner by the small closet. The mirror, which hasn't been attached to the dresser yet, leans against the wall, reflecting the streetlight.

"God, this room is hardly big enough to turn around in. We've got to get things unpacked so we can get those boxes out of here." She knows Tony is frowning now, but refuses to let this bother her.

"You know finding a job is more important right now. And I've got to spend time with the kids too, until they get settled. Unpacking boxes isn't on the top of my list of things to do." Tony is silent.

"We've been here ten, twelve days," he says, finally.

"It seems like five minutes," Diane replies. "Tomorrow I'm taking the kids onto the university campus. Everybody says it's beautiful this time of year. And I want to see what's inside those gorgeous stone buildings."

"Did you set the alarm?" Tony asks, yawning. "I think I should get up about fifteen minutes earlier. Then I won't have to rush so much. You should see the traffic on the bridge when I hit it just after eight. You wouldn't believe it."

"Here," Diane says, handing him the alarm clock from the floor by the lamp which she has turned on again. "Set it however you want it. Cathy always gets me up." He takes it, sighing, sits up, and begins to fiddle with it.

"Oh, for the days when the sun got me up," he says. Diane resists saying anything.

"Have you got any job interviews lined up for tomorrow?" Tony asks. He hands the clock back to her, she puts it on the floor and turns the light out again.

"No, I phoned those places we saw in the paper, but without training and no education beyond high school, they don't want anything to do with me. So it's back to knocking on doors. I just try to look hard-working and humble." Tony has to laugh at this.

"You! Humble!" He can't stop laughing. He laughs so hard that Diane starts to laugh, too.

"Okay, not humble," she says, and leans over him, trying to shake him to make him stop laughing. He reaches up suddenly and grabs her with both arms, pulls her hard against him.

"My God, I love you," he breathes into her ear, and for some reason she feels irritation at this.

So what? she wants to say. She intends to say it as soon as he stops kissing her, but that heat he makes in her is already spreading downward through her legs, all the way to the soles of her feet, and upward through her lungs and heart, into her neck, relaxing the tendons there, her cheeks and forehead are warm with it too, and then she is lost, whatever she wanted to say, whatever she was thinking gone too.

After he is asleep, she lies well over on her side of the bed, staring into the warm summer darkness. The small window is open and through it she can hear the muted, hollow roar of the city. She closes her eyes, listening, not trying to pick out individual sounds, but somehow trying to rise into that humming, to merge with it. Gradually, as she concentrates on it, it begins to creep through her, she feels herself vibrating minutely with it. She can no longer feel the warm, rumpled sheets under her or over her, nor hear Tony's steady breath beside her. She hears the canopy of sound covering her. She is rising with the sound, she is the sound.

Tires screech on the street nearby, she opens her eyes and she is back in bed again beside Tony, in the hot, stuffy room.

She thinks of that long moment with him when they were once again making love, how good it was, how complete in itself, how necessary to her life.

Necessary to my life? She wonders. She tries to imagine a life without Tony in bed beside her every night, asking her questions, telling her things, making suggestions, reaching for her. She tries to imagine herself alone in the bed, lying in the centre, listening to the roar of the city. She grimaces to herself in the darkness when she realizes that in the room in her imagination there are no unpacked boxes or open suitcases full of rumpled clothing, the sheets are smooth and cool around her.

So I'm lazy, she thinks. I guess I must be. Lazy and vain, and what else? Selfish. Don't forget selfish. Dragging Tony and the kids here when they didn't really want to come.

Now she is swept by that same, nameless longing, so powerful that it is near to pain, that reaches into the roots of her being and spreads through her as inexorably and as powerfully as her desire for Tony did earlier, or ever has, only this is worse, far worse; it spreads itself outward from her soul, it is a need, a compulsion to know, to be a part of the larger life of the universe, to understand it. It has her entirely in its grip. She knows that somehow it is not only her private pain, that it is something ancient and something that is much bigger than herself. It is something primeval; it has something to do with womanhood, and she is nothing more than a pebble on a beach swept by a cosmic wave. She feels as if she can't even breathe. She feels herself being pulled . . .

She pulls herself back with great effort, forcing her eyes open, rubbing the sheets with her palms to assure herself that she is real, that she hasn't gone anywhere.

I've made them suffer. I know it, I know I'm responsible for their suffering, and I'm afraid, oh God, I'm terrified that it has only begun.

But still she knows, growing calmer again, even a little sleepy, that she will not stop doing what she is doing, that she will not, no, never, turn back, that she is in the grip of something that is far stronger than any of the things she has been taught to be, and that it has forced her into actions she doesn't fully comprehend or entirely approve of, but that she must go with, or die.

SEPTEMBER

The breakfast dishes were still sitting on the table, one untouched glass of orange juice and plates sticky with jam, eggs, and crumbs. Selena had forgotten to turn off one burner and the air was heavy with the smell of it, above the lingering odour of toast and the last of the morning pot of coffee. The chairs stood back from the kitchen table where Jason and Mark had shoved them in their rush to catch the bus. It was the first day of school.

Selena was standing where she had cleared a space to work at the table. She was cutting kernels of corn off their cobs with a heavy, sharp knife. Her hands had kernels sticking to them, there were a few on the front of her blouse and by the feel of it, on one cheek, too. The pail on the floor beside her was full of denuded cobs, in front of her sat a basin filled with kernels, and to her left, a pile of cobs still to be husked.

The door opened and Kent hurried in, letting the door slam shut behind him. He glanced at the mess on the table, but said nothing.

"I have to get the corn done while it's fresh," Selena said over her shoulder, embarrassed that he had caught her with her work undone. "Phoebe will clean up the dishes."

"Where is she?" Kent asked. He was scrabbling through the mess in the cupboard drawer they used for keeping odds and ends.

"What are you looking for?" Selena asked. "She's sleeping late."

"Christ! It's almost ten o'clock," Kent said.

"I know," Selena replied. "But she'll be off to university in another week and this is her last chance to sleep in. After all, she just finished twelve years of school. She deserves a break."

"Where the hell are those extra needles?" Kent asked. She set her knife down, hastily wiping her hands on the damp cloth that lay on the table beside her, and went to the cupboard to help him look.

"You doing some branding or something?"

"Have to doctor that sick steer. You spoil that girl. What the hell kind of a wife is she going to make if she sleeps in till ten o'clock?"

"I don't spoil her!" Selena said, surprised by her own vehemence. "She works hard around here, she does her share, and she's still only a girl. Soon enough she'll be running after kids and catering to some man . . ." She stopped herself. "Here they are." She took the small box of needles for the syringe out of the drawer and set it hard on the counter instead of handing it to Kent. Then she turned her back on him and went to the table. She picked up the knife and wiped the blade with her damp cloth. She was surprised to see that her hand was trembling.

She knew Kent was standing uncertainly by the door, but she began to slice the corn again, balancing the cob against the tabletop. She knew Kent wanted to say something to her but didn't know how, and she didn't know why his remark had made her so angry. It was late after all, and there was a pile of work to be done with Diane and Tony and the kids coming for the long weekend—the corn to be finished, the cucumbers and tomatoes still to be done.

She set the knife down and turned to him. As they looked at each other across the distance of the kitchen, she saw how he had aged. He was the same age she was and yet he was beginning to look old. She suddenly wanted to hold him, to put his head against her breasts and stroke his light-coloured hair as if he were one of her children. To work so hard year after year, and never get anywhere.

"I'll get her up right away," she said. "There's lots to be done." She picked the knife up again, holding its wooden handle, warm from her touch, balanced in her palm. He half-smiled, dropping his gaze to the door frame as he turned away, opened the door and stepped out into the still, damp fall morning. The door shut behind him. He hadn't even asked her to come and help him get the steer into the squeeze.

Abruptly she set the knife down, hurried to the stairs and called up, "Phoebe, time to get up." She waited, listening. There was a faint sound from Phoebe's room. "I need your help," she called again. "Come on down. I'm on my way out to the corral."

Selena pulled her jacket from its peg, walked back to the kitchen, past the unfinished corn, the unwashed breakfast dishes, past the basket of ripening tomatoes and another of cucumbers, and out the back door. Phoebe is a good kid. She'll have the dishes done by the time I get back. She was proud of Phoebe, of how well she had turned out. And now she's actually going to be a university student, Selena thought, her spirits rising. Imagine that!

It had frozen the night before, the leaves of the squash in her garden were blackened and wilting and the yellow grass left dampness on her runners from the melted frost. Crows were flocking on the corrals by the barn, but the sky was a deep, even blue. By noon it would be too hot to wear a jacket. As she came up to the main corral, she saw that on the far side Kent was walking the steer up the alley toward the chute and squeeze. The dog was standing outside the fence, his legs braced, fiercely yapping at the steer, but from a safe distance.

"Shut up, Blackie!" Kent snapped. The dog gave a couple of disheartened barks, then lapsed into a trembling silence.

"I'll walk him up," Selena said. She climbed the pole fence and dropped into the alley, then started up the chute behind the steer while Kent leaped the fence and hurried up the side of the chute to the squeeze where, using a lever, he opened the headgate and waited.

"Okay," he called.

"Blackie," Selena commanded. The dog squeezed under the bottom rail and nipped the steer's heel. It kicked backward angrily, but then moved forward, the dog pursuing it, barking, nipping at the steer's leg, then quickly retreating to avoid being kicked. Selena picked up the heavy fencepost leaning against the outside of the chute, brought it in between the railings and quickly slid it across the chute, resting it there, between her and the steer, so that the steer couldn't back up.

"Blackie," she said again and the dog moved in to bite the steer one more time while she gave it a poke on the haunch with a stick she had picked up. It lunged forward to what looked like freedom at the other end of the squeeze, got its head through the headgate and before it could make the move that would free it, Kent slammed the headgate shut, the iron closing around the steer's neck, trapping it. Quickly he grabbed for another lever and pulled down hard. The side of the squeeze drew in, immobilizing the animal. Selena climbed back over the pole fence and walked around the squeeze to where Kent was filling his syringe with antibiotic from a small brown bottle.

"I'm pretty sure it's diptheria," he said. Selena studied the steer. There was a swelling under its chin and in its neck, and its eyes were runny. But it was the way that its breath whistled as it laboured to breathe, that told the tale. If it wasn't diptheria it was at least pneumonia, and maybe emphysema.

"I want this one to go with the load when we sell," he said. "He's not too sick. I think he'll be okay." They had only thirty yearlings and their calf crop to keep the family going for another year. And with Phoebe in university, money would be even tighter than usual. The steer moved in the squeeze so that the iron groaned and the wooden floor thudded under its hooves. "If this stupid bastard dies . . ." Kent said.

"He won't die," Selena said. A few goldenrod had grown up around the edges of the chute and she poked at their golden heads with her foot. They looked pretty there, a pleasant change from the ineradicable kochia weed they were all so sick of looking at. She watched Kent while he reached in between the squeeze bars and thumped the animal high on the hip, twice, not hard, with his fist, then inserted the needle in the same spot, and slowly pushed in the fluid. The steer tried to pull away, but was held too tightly. He moved his feet then, his hooves stamping on the floor, not catching, and almost fell.

"Okay, fella, that's all," Kent said, and gave the animal a couple of commiserating slaps on its dark red back.

Selena touched Kent on the shoulder, then, and looking toward the house, said, "I've got to get back to the house if you don't need me anymore." He nodded without speaking, pulling down on the lever that opened the headgate, standing back while the steer lunged out into the corral.

Selena crossed the yard again, noticing that the day still hadn't warmed enough for more than a few grasshoppers to have ventured out. She took off her jacket and hung it up and when she turned back to the table, yesterday's letter from Diane, which she had thrust into her back pocket, crackled and she couldn't help pulling it out and reading it again:

Hooray! I got a job! In a doughnut shop. I work the graveyard shift. That way I don't leave home till the kids are asleep and I'm home by the time they wake up in the morning. It's not the greatest job in the world, and the pay is lousy, but at least it's work, and I'm bringing home money. God knows, I was beginning to wonder if I'd ever get anything at all. I'm thinking that with a little job experience maybe I can get something better soon.

Selena felt herself frowning. Really, she thought. She could have gotten a terrible job with bad pay in Chinook, she didn't have to go to the city for that.

"Mom?" Phoebe's voice startled her, she hadn't even noticed her standing by the sink. Phoebe had already cleared away the dishes and wiped the table clean around Selena's mess. "Do you want me to start skinning the tomatoes?" Seeing Phoebe leaning against the sink wringing out the dishcloth, Selena felt a wave of love for her daughter, then she noticed for the first time that a little curve of plumpness was developing under Phoebe's chin and that her flat stomach was curving a little too.

"You're putting on a little weight there," she teased, before she'd thought. "It looks good on you."

Phoebe turned back toward the sink.

"Or I could just do the vacuuming and dusting," Phoebe offered, her voice muffled. Selena could hear her draw in a deep breath, her hands hanging in the dishwater, and for a moment Selena stood watching her, puzzled. But Phoebe didn't turn to took at her, nor did she say anything more, and the half-finished corn, the grit underfoot, the unmade beds upstairs, the unbaked pies, the thought of company coming all pulled at Selena, distracting her.

"Yeah," she said. "That'd be best. I'll finish this corn. I don't know what to do about the tomatoes. I suppose they can wait till Monday, and those cukes too."

"When are they coming?" Phoebe asked as Selena picked up the knife again and reached for another cob of corn.

"About noon tomorrow. Diane has to work tonight, so she'll be pretty tired, but Tony's anxious to get back and close the deal on the farm. I think they must need the money." Phoebe was rattling dishes in the sink, scrubbing at the egg stuck to the plates. "It costs a lot more to live in the city than it does out here." Phoebe didn't reply.

You should see the people who come in to the shop where I work! It seems like after midnight when good, ordinary people are all asleep, dreaming their dreams of apple pie and flowered curtains, the world changes and a whole different part of the life of this planet emerges, from where, I don't know. But the people who come in after midnight aren't wearing that mask we all wear to keep us safe from the prying eyes of others, and safe too, from knowing too much about ourselves—the masks that make the world understandable and bearable. It seems that after midnight the masks vanish, everybody is too tired to keep them up.

It worried her to think of her sister, alone in that shop at night, waiting on such people—people she could not imagine, so that all she could feel about it was a heavy, nameless dread. She threw the cob she was working on into the pail by her feet.

"What's Brian up to today?" she asked Phoebe.

"I think he's . . . doing something with his dad. I don't know what." Phoebe shrugged her shoulders, not turning around.

"You two have a fight?" Selena asked, after debating whether she should say anything or not. She sensed that something in their relationship had changed in the last month or two. There was nothing she could put her finger on, but Phoebe's attitude toward Brian seemed different. When she thought about it, Selena couldn't say she cared very much. Phoebe would find a husband, one way or another, sooner or later. She was the kind of girl who would marry. At least she'll get a year or two away before she settles down for good, Selena thought. That's more than I did. For an instant that loss opened before her, and it took a second before she could push it away.

"Would you be really mad if I didn't go to university?" Phoebe asked. Selena set down the knife and turned to Phoebe, who was draining the water out of the sink.

When she had finished, Phoebe stood looking at her mother, a kind of pleading in her expression. Staring at her in surprise, Selena saw something in her daughter's eyes that seemed new and deep, as though Phoebe had looked at something she had never seen before and the sight had changed her.

When did that happen? And how did it happen and I didn't notice it? she wondered. Seconds passed while Selena was seeing the little girl, her mouth smeared purple with the juice of the saskatoons they were picking, looking up at her, mutely asking for forgiveness for having eaten hers. She blinked.

"What?" Selena asked, dumbly. Phoebe flushed, her expression had turned both wary and intense, now there was no trace of girlishness in her eyes or around her full pink mouth. Selena could only stare.

"Are you . . . thinking of getting married?" she asked, finally. She was flushed by such a rush of emotion she could hardly control it. Married! She drew in a deep breath. Phoebe turned back to the sink and began to scrub at it with the dishcloth.

"Maybe," she said, her voice barely audible.

"Oh, Phoebe . . ." Selena began.

"I said maybe," Phoebe warned her. "I didn't say for sure." Selena's stomach tightened, she found she was a little nauseated and weak-kneed.

"We borrowed the money . . ." she began, "but that doesn't matter . . . but you'd better decide pretty quick. You're supposed to leave in ten days."

"Oh, forget I said anything." Phoebe kept her back to her mother. "I probably won't anyway." She kept scrubbing at the sink as if the conversation she and her mother were having wasn't important. Selena knew it would do no good to say anything more now, Phoebe would only get angry.

She turned slowly back to the corn. She began to scrape again, thoughtfully, then gathered the kernels into a pile with both hands and tossed them into the basin. She dropped that cob into the pail by her feet and picked up another. Behind her she could hear the clink of the dishes as Phoebe put them away, and then the sound of more water running into the sink.

Already I've come face to face with exhaustion and despair, I know that's what I saw on the face of a tired businessman. It wasn't only his face though, when I think about it. It was in his hands holding his coffee cup, in his eyes looking at the doughnut he didn't eat, in the curve of his back, and the way his knees bent under the flimsy table. I could even see it in his feet. I think he was too tired and too sad to even want to die.

Suddenly Selena wanted to go to Phoebe and hold her, to kiss her soft cheek and forehead, to hold her tight against her bosom. She thought of how earlier that morning she had wanted to hold Kent, too, in that way, to comfort him, and somehow this surprised her and made her uncertain. Still, wasn't that what she was supposed to do? To be a mother to them all? And who'll mother me? she found herself wondering.

She glanced over her shoulder at Phoebe, but Phoebe was sweeping the floor, moving chairs and putting them back around the table. Which one of them wants to get married right away and which one of them doesn't? she wondered. And why? Brian doesn't want her to leave, he doesn't want to lose her. I bet that's it. He doesn't want her to go. I suppose he thinks she'll find someone else in the city and she won't come back.

Why doesn't she tell me? Why doesn't she ask me to help her? Phoebe was bending now, sweeping a pile of crumbs and dirt into the dustpan. Selena wanted to speak to her, she almost did, but Phoebe straightened, emptied the dustpan, set the broom back in its place by the door and went straight out of the room and up the stairs to make the beds. That was another thing about Phoebe. She had developed a singlemindedness about work. She didn't like housework, but instead of trying to get out of doing it, or doing it badly, she would grit her teeth and dig into it, not stopping till it was done. Selena admired that about her daughter, and was proud of her for it. And for the same reason, she didn't press Phoebe because she knew that when Phoebe was ready, she would talk about what was bothering her, and it wasn't right to try to squeeze answers out of her before then.

I've seen some pretty ugly things too. Lost teenagers, lost to normal life I mean, pale and sickly-looking and sort of evil under all that paint and weird hair and bizarre clothes. And people I know were criminals, don't ask me how I knew. When I read over what I've written I know you'll think there's something wrong with me. Or at least you'll laugh.

No, Selena thought, I won't laugh.

Why did I never see these things before, at home I mean? There must be despair and evil at home too. But I never noticed it, and I can't understand why. You get so used to

seeing the same faces that you don't really look at them anymore. But I won't stop looking at these things, ugly or sad or
what. Because this is what I came to the city for, I think, and
I won't turn away.

It was Saturday of the Labour Day weekend, noon, and already one of
those unseasonably hot days that sometimes struck in the early fall. At this
time of year the countryside was usually at its palest—the grassland a
creamy yellow the sky palest blue, the two shimmering together in a haze
at the horizon. But today the landscape burned, golden and blue with
light, and that look and the heat confused all of them and lent the familiar land around them a peculiar, unreal air.

It hadn't rained more than a few drops the entire month of August
and the roads were crumbling to powder in the heat and the dryness
under the tires of the vehicles that ran up and down the roads. The dust
trailing the car as it approached the house caught up with it as Tony
stopped the car. He waited a second for it to settle before he opened his
door. Then he was climbing out, Diane was turning to unlock the kids'
back door and Kent, Jason and Mark were striding across the yard from
the corral where they had been treating cows for lice, the dog barking
frantically at their heels.

Selena watched eagerly as Diane climbed awkwardly out of the passenger side. As Diane straightened, slowly turning toward Selena, her arms
out, Selena could feel her own expression changing in surprise. Seeing this,
Diane laughed nervously, dropping her arms to brush at her jeans.

"I've slept all the way," she said. "I must look awful." Quickly Selena
recovered, reached out for Diane, feeling her sister's thin shoulders under
her fuzzy red sweater.

"You must have lost ten pounds!" she said. "And you've only been
gone six weeks."

"I've been too busy to eat," Diane replied, a little distractedly. She
bent, half-turning to reach into the car for her purse. Selena saw the
streak of blusher along her cheekbone and realized that Diane was wearing a lot of makeup, like city women did. But then Kent had come around

the car to embrace Diane perfunctorily and kiss her cheek. Tony was hugging Selena, while Diane turned to Phoebe. The little girls were being lifted and hugged, and only Jason and Mark were standing back.

In the hallway in the house they divided, the men going into the living room, the women into the kitchen.

"Tammy, can you put Cathy on the toilet?" Diane asked.

"I'll take her," Phoebe volunteered. She and Tammy led Cathy into the hall and up the stairs.

"She leaves pretty soon, doesn't she?" Diane asked.

"In about a week," Selena answered. "It's too bad she's going to Regina. She could have lived with you in Saskatoon, helped you with the kids." The deep murmur of the men's voices provided a background to their conversation. Upstairs the two little girls could be heard chattering away to Phoebe, their piping voices carrying clearly down the stairs.

"That Tammy, she'll talk your ear off," Diane said, laughing. "I don't have enough time for her." She looked across the room to the screen door. As she watched, a flock of crows, with a rushing of wings, gathered in the trees at the back of the yard.

"Soon be winter," Selena remarked sadly. "Although you'd never know it by this heat."

"I hardly noticed it till today," Diane said. "It seems like you don't notice it so much in the city. You know, you're sort of protected from the weather, and anyway, I'm so busy."

"You must be starved," Selena said. She rose and opened the oven door, and the smell of roasting beef filled the room. Using oven mitts, she took the roaster out of the oven and set it on the counter, then lifted the roast out onto the carving board. "What are you so busy at?" Diane stood, too, pushing back her long hair and began to take plates down out of the cupboard.

"Oh, my job," Diane said. She began to set the table.

"And I had to find daycare for Cathy, and a school for Tammy and get her registered, and teach her the way there . . ."

"Teach her the way?"

"Yeah," Diane said, giving a little laugh in Selena's direction. "There's no school bus in the city, you know." She turned back to Selena, taking cutlery from the drawer. It was as though she had never left, and to Selena, it was as though she had not truly felt the loss of Diane until now. "We've got this little rented house and the yard was such a mess I hated to have the kids play in it till we got it cleaned up—and Tony's busy too, getting settled into his job."

Selena put the roaster onto the stove and began to stir flour into the grease.

"And there's still all the regular housework to do. The washing and ironing—thank God Cathy's out of diapers— and the cooking, but I've been pretty slack about that. We've been going out to McDonald's a lot." She laughed a little ruefully. "But we're surviving." She did not look at Selena during all of this. The two of them moved from cupboard to stove to fridge to the table and back again, setting the table and filling serving bowls with food.

"Sounds like you like it then," Selena said, her voice tentative. Diane suddenly pulled out one of the chairs and sat down in it.

"I love it," she said. Selena looked at her then, saw that her eyes had changed, too, as Phoebe's had not long ago, so that Selena wondered again how such things could happen without her observing or understanding them. There was a liveliness in Diane's eyes that Selena hadn't seen there since Diane was in high school. And yet she couldn't seem to focus on anything for very long. They just kept moving restlessly from one thing to another, and the brightness in her face even under her makeup seemed unnatural to Selena.

"But," Selena said slowly, "you just work in a doughnut shop, don't you? You could have found a job like that in Chinook." This made Diane laugh. Selena felt herself flushing.

"Sure. Thirty miles each way, through mud or drifts or on ice. So I could hand doughnuts to the guys I went to school with. The ones I wouldn't marry. And have their wives come in for a dozen sugar-dipped, and look down their noses at me." Even Selena had to laugh at this, in acknowledgement of its truth. Diane shifted her eyes to the floor, then lifted them again to her sister, her face filled with wonder, although it seemed to Selena that behind or through that wonder the same dark longing hovered. "Selena, you wouldn't believe the things there are to do! All kinds of movies, the best, the newest ones, not old things nobody wanted to see anyway. And you don't have to drive for an hour to get to them. Concerts in the park by the river! Fashion shows. There's art galleries . . . and night life! And people! Everywhere! You wouldn't believe the people!"

"I've been to the city once or twice," Selena said. Mark and Jason were both talking at once in the living room, with Kent's deeper voice intervening now and then. She should call everybody for dinner before the food got cold.

"Next week I'm going to register for a night class at the university. I'm finally going to get an education, and there won't be blizzards or mud to stop me. It's ten minutes to the university." She snapped her fingers to show how easy it would be.

Selena said nothing. She went into the hall and called, "Dinner's ready."

Selena was just about asleep when Kent said into the darkness, "Things aren't so good for Tony." She was awake at once, tense, listening for his next words. And Diane so happy!

"He says it's hard to settle back into a nine-to-five job. The money's okay, but he says he didn't know how much he'd miss the farm. He expected to spend the rest of his life here you know. He says he misses being outside, things like that." They lay side by side, staring into the darkened room as if they could pierce the darkness if they looked hard enough.

"Oh, Kent," Selena said, "what's going to happen to them?"

"Diane'll never come back," Kent said. "You just have to look at her to know that."

"And Cathy and Tammy," Selena said. "They're so little, and Diane's working too, and there's no family to fall back on like here." She searched for Kent's hand under the blankets. She set hers into it and he curled his fingers around her palm, brought her hand up to rest on his flat, warm stomach.

"Lots of people in the city live like that," he said, but there was no certainty in his voice, "and they survive. Their kids grow up. They don't know no other way to live."

"She told me she was starting Tammy on ballet lessons as soon as they get back, and piano lessons too, as soon as they can afford a piano." She thought with a flicker of bitterness how she used to drive Phoebe thirty miles to her lessons, wait for her, then drive thirty miles back, and how many lessons Phoebe had missed because of bad weather or bad roads.

"My God," Kent said. There was such dismay in his voice that Selena had to laugh.

"Listen to us," she whispered, giggling. "You'd think they were locking them in closets and torturing them." She rolled over on her side close to Kent and he slid his arm under her neck. "They've still got both parents—parents who care about them and they're well fed and clothed. Why do they have to have Diane with them every second?" She put her face against his warm neck. Did she really mean what she had said? Or was she just trying to put a good face on a rotten situation? The latter, she thought. Kids need their mothers, who could doubt that?

"Maybe we should offer to take them till they get settled," Kent said. She lifted her head, her heart speeding up a little.

"The girls, you mean?" she asked, stalling.

"Yeah."

She sighed, lowering her head again. I don't want them. I don't want to raise another family, I hardly have a minute to myself as it is. Then, don't be so selfish. It would only be for a little while. "Maybe," she said, trying to make her voice sound light and hopeful.

"Ah, hell!" Kent said, taking away his arm. "Tony'd never let them go. He's crazy about those kids. And, anyway, he's too proud. He'll raise his own kids or die trying."

"Diane'd never let them come back here, anyway," Selena said. "She thinks there aren't any opportunities for them here." Her relief was mixed with disappointment. Already she was imagining combing Tammy's fine, light hair, and kissing Cathy's round little cheeks. I wish we'd had another baby, she almost said.

"Opportunities," he said, disgustedly. "What opportunities? Our kids grew up okay. It was good enough for them." But Selena was thinking, what if Phoebe had had ballet lessons? What if she had gone to concerts every week, had heard the classical music her teacher was always telling her about, and had seen ballet and gone to art galleries? Would she be a better person? Would her life be better? She remembered the French count who had settled seventy-five years before only twenty miles or so from their ranch. Presumably he had been accustomed to all those things in France, knew all about art and music and culture, yet his kids had been no more cultured than any homesteader's kids, to hear people tell it. So what good were centuries of breeding, if it could be washed away like that, in one generation? Or was that not the point? What was the point? she wondered. Haven't I been happy with only the radio and the tv?

Kent let out a deep sigh, blowing the air out through his lips, and she half-laughed at herself for wasting her energy thinking about questions which she knew she would never find answers to. She thought then of telling him about Phoebe's remark that she might be getting married. She opened her mouth to speak, then stopped. Better say nothing yet. Although he had never really said so, she knew Kent couldn't see much point in Phoebe's going to university. As far as he was concerned she was only going to get married anyway, and all that money would be wasted. If she told him now, Kent might use it as an excuse to stop Phoebe from going. She turned away from him, onto her shoulder, and pulled up the covers.

Tony and Kent had pushed their chairs back against the wall at each end of the table to get out of the way of Selena and Phoebe, who were hurriedly gathering the breakfast dishes. They had finished brushing and braiding Tammy's hair and had bathed Cathy and put a fresh, clean dress on her. Selena had hounded the boys, who never wanted to go to church, till they had finally finished breakfast and changed into dress pants and shirts and sportcoats. Now Mark was lounging in the doorway, his white shirt that she had bought for him only that spring, already too short in the sleeves.

"Are you coming to church?" she asked Kent.

"Nope," he said. "Tony and I have some running around to do. And the boys want us to go to their ball tournament in Chinook this afternoon, so we have to do it now." She wanted to protest, but could see it would be no use. "You take the kids," he said. Selena glanced at the clock.

"Maybe I should let Diane sleep," she said. "She looked worn out." Tony shifted positions so that he was facing Kent instead of her.

"I didn't make her take that job," he said. "She's determined. You know what she's like. There's nothing I can do."

"I didn't mean that," Selena said, dismayed. "I know she wants to work. It's just that she's lost weight and she looks so tired."

"Yeah, I know," he said, glancing at Selena now. "I'm hoping she'll slow down in a month or two. She's just so damn excited. You'd think the city was paradise." He shook his head, raising his coffee cup to his mouth. "It beats me, but, if she's happy . . ." He took a drink from his cup, but Selena saw the concern in his eyes, belying the assurance he had put into his voice. "If you don't mind taking the kids," he added, apologetically, "it'd be nice if you could let her sleep."

"Oh sure, Tony," Selena said, angry with herself for having been so thoughtless. "The boys can help Phoebe and me. After all, they'll be fathers themselves one of these days."

"Hah!" Mark said from the doorway. Kent laughed.

"Where's Jason?" Selena asked. "Jason!"

"What!" he called back from the living room, where she knew he was reading comic books with his feet up on the coffee table.

"Are you ready?" she called. There was silence.

"Jason, get in here," Kent said, barely raising his voice. Jason's feet hit the carpet with a thump and in a second he was in the kitchen, squeezing past Mark, who refused to move to let him pass.

"What?" he asked, less belligerently, looking from one to the other of them, with a child's quick, bright eyes. Selena looked at him, checking his clothes. He was too small for twelve, almost thirteen, she hoped he would begin to grow soon.

"Okay," she said. "You two go wait outside. I'll be out in a minute." She cast one last hopeful glance at Tony, but she knew by the way he met her eyes and immediately looked away that he wouldn't say anything more about Diane. Maybe because he didn't understand her either.

"Can I drive?" Mark called from the hallway. He had just gotten his learner's licence.

"Okay," she called back. To Kent she said, "Will you ask Diane to

keep an eye on the goose in the oven? It should be okay till I get back."
Kent nodded.

"We're going over to Doyle's right away," he said. "But if she's up
before we leave, I'll tell her." Distractedly Selena ran a hand through her
hair, trying to think where she could find a pencil and paper to leave
Diane a note. The screen door opened and Cathy, Tammy and Phoebe
entered, all of them looking bored and impatient.

"Everybody into the car," Selena said quickly, before one of them
could start to complain. Obediently the three of them trooped past her,
while Selena grabbed an envelope lying on the counter and scribbled on
the back of it.

Lying on the bed upstairs, Diane listens to the medley of voices and to
the sound of doors opening and closing. If only I could sleep. If only I
could sink into that blessed oblivion the way I used to, and wake in the
morning feeling relaxed and fresh. Her back aches, her leg muscles feel
tight and cramped, and her eyes sting from lack of sleep. She raises her
hands to her face with a slow, deliberate motion, and places one palm over
each eye. Her flesh is cool against her eyelids and the world goes deeply
black. I've got to calm down, she tells herself, I've got to slow down, I've
got to settle down. Or I'll go mad. Maybe I am mad. Is this madness? A
wave of panic sweeps over her and she quickly takes her hands down and
opens her eyes. This voice in my head talking to me, always talking to me,
telling me all the things I already know, reciting the day's events, the
night's events, criticizing me, calling me names, complaining about my
life, planning, hoping, driving me to someplace I can't find, I only know
I haven't found it yet.

In the yard, car doors slam, a motor starts, gravel crackles as a car pulls
away from the house. The hum of the engine fades as the car moves onto
the grid. Selena, taking the kids to church. I should have gone, I lie here
pretending to sleep when I know Selena wants me with her. And she's
stuck with my kids. I'm a lazy, lazy, lazy bitch. No. I'm not a bitch.

Below her, Tony and Kent are walking down the hall. The outer door
opens and closes again, then their boots are crunching on the driveway

gravel as they cross to the barn, where the truck is parked. Not a breath of wind stirs the curtains. The sounds coming in the open window are as clear as if she were walking beside the men. She can see Tony raise one hand to scratch his chin. This is it. What will Doyle say? The truck doors slam, the engine starts, they drive away, roaring down the approach, whining into the sound of wind up the grid.

Alone at last, she thinks, lying back, relaxing. She smiles at the ceiling, then sobers. You're changing their lives, she reminds herself. And you have no right.

She throws back the covers and in one fast, continuous motion lifts herself up and out of the bed. The linoleum floor is warm under the soles of her feet and at last a bird cries outside the window, and she hears the swift beating of wings, then a long chirruping call. I'm up, I'm up, she tells the bird.

At least I can get dinner ready for Selena, so she comes home once to all the work done and a meal on the table. Clean up the dishes. Hah! That'd be the day Selena would leave a mess behind. And Phoebe working like a little slave right beside her. As if a clean kitchen, a clean house, were the only things that matter in this world.

Selena sent Mark into the pew first, then Phoebe, then Cathy, then she went in, bringing Tammy behind her, and Jason last so that he and Mark couldn't bother each other. They filled the pew and she was relieved because this way the little girls' squirming wouldn't annoy anyone else. The church was only half-filled, although it was the special Labour Day service.

The minister emerged from behind the altar and the service began. Selena struggled to pay attention, but she couldn't stop thinking about the goose in the oven, and Diane, thin and exhausted-looking and too wound-up, asleep upstairs. She studied the minister, a small, young man with an English accent. His peculiar lack of appropriateness for the job, the fact that he was a city man who knew nothing about crops or cattle, and that he was a bit effeminate, accounted at least partly for the half-filled church. And mostly women at that. Selena remembered when she was a girl. The pews were always full in those days.

She stole a glance at Tammy. The child sat primly, her hands folded on her lap, her soft face with its small, perfect nose turned upward toward the altar, although, Selena suddenly realized, she was too small to see anything over the heads of the people in front of her. Such perfect obedience, she thought, and wondered how Tammy got that way. Diane wasn't hard on her, nor was Tony. Maybe it was because she had always helped with Cathy. Maybe that had taken the childishness out of her. But that's what you do, she thought, frowning, the older ones help with the younger ones, don't they? Phoebe had always helped her with the boys. Jason especially, because he was five years younger.

She glanced at Tammy again, and as she watched, the child raised one small hand to push her hair away from her face with a half-weary gesture. It was a perfect imitation of an adult, perhaps her mother, but Selena was stricken by the gesture. Poor little girl, she said to herself, only a child, and already a mother. And it seemed to her then that girls never had the perfect freedom in childhood that boys had. Could this be true?

She leaned toward her and put her arm around Tammy's back, lifting her onto her lap. Tammy looked up at her, surprised, and then acquiescent. Selena settled Tammy on her lap, holding her tightly, her cheek against Tammy's hair. She was so light and pliant.

A few flies buzzed against the windows and somewhere outside the small wooden building a hawk screamed. Selena could imagine the dive, the beating of wings, the triumphant lift-off, a gopher dangling from the hawk's claws.

The minister began his sermon.

"The text for today is Genesis 3, Verses 17-19." He began to read, his light voice floating through the warm morning, reaching the corners of the small building, while the sun poured in through the windows, lighting the particles of dust that sailed down the beams.

"And to Adam he said, 'Because you have listened to the voice of your wife, and have eaten of the tree of which I commanded you, "You shall not eat of it," cursed is the ground because of you; in toil you shall eat of it all the days of your life; thorns and thistles it shall bring forth to you; and you shall eat the plants of the field. In the sweat of your face you shall eat bread till you return to the ground, for out of it were you taken; you are dust, and to dust you shall return.'"

"And thus was man cast out of the Garden of Eden, because of Eve's sin. And the Lord decreed that 'in toil' shall you live out your life, 'in the sweat of your face,' shall you earn the bread that you and your wives and children eat. And it won't always be easy. 'Thorns and thistles' will the ground bring forth for you.

"On this Sunday, we gather to honour the men whose back-breaking labour built this country. Farmers and ranchers are not the least of these. Even today, you toil among 'thorns and thistles,' you labour in the midst of drought, with grasshoppers destroying the fruit of your work as quickly as the grain sprouts."

As she expected, except for two coffee cups and spoons on the table, the kitchen is spotless. Something in the oven, too. A goose. Doesn't even need basting, she notes, opening the oven door and peering in, turning the roaster around in the oven. Pies are made. Diane can't help but shake her head, admiring Selena's diligence.

She wanders out the back door to stand on the steps and look out over what's left of Selena's garden. Don't tell me she's got all her preserving done already. Diane sits down on the steps, her chin resting on her hands.

It's so beautiful here. My God, it's beautiful. And peaceful. There is no sound, not even wind, only birds flocking in the carraganas and the poplars. A faint thudding tells her there must be horses nearby. The sun is slightly to her left, fairly low on the horizon, reminding her that winter is coming. Beyond the garden the land rises in low grassy hills, beige and yellow. A bush rabbit hops cautiously from under the carragana hedge and pauses, his head turning nervously, then freezing. She holds perfectly still, watching. He hops through the garden, testing this, testing that, his nose twitching.

How could I want to leave such perfect beauty and peace, she asks herself. And for once, the voice in her head that won't shut up is stilled. The sun beats down on her, she breathes in the scent of grass and sage, and is slowly filled with peace.

But of course it doesn't last. It never does. She moves irritably and the rabbit leaps for cover. The hours Selena spends in her garden. Year after year. The work with the cattle, the riding, the haying, and all the house-work and the kids besides.

A chicken ventures out beyond the strip of grass and begins to peck in tumbled, yellowing and stripped pea vines.

And yet I think she's happy. She seems happy. I have to admit, I have to now, that the peace of nature, the beauty of nature, seems to be enough for some people.

Why can't this be enough for me? It can't be, when there's books full of things to know, I've seen them myself in the university library, floor after floor of books, whole worlds Selena's never even dreamt of, waiting to be entered. Music, art, drama, poetry, foreign lands and people, ways of looking at the world that could change everything we think.

All she knows is work. Work and family. Family and work.

Well, it's not enough for me. I wish it were, but it's not.

She rises to go in and peel the potatoes, get the vegetables ready.

"And so you labour. Some of you began when you were little boys, milk-ing the cow so your brothers and sisters could have milk to drink and to spare your mothers a little toil. You started riding with your fathers when you were perhaps as young as seven, learning the honourable trade of the cattleman, or you rode the tractor, summerfallowing by yourself when you were no more than twelve or fourteen. This after a full day in school. Sometimes you rose before the sun was up to water and feed the animals in the barn and in the pen, and during harvest now you are out on the combines till midnight or longer, sometimes the entire night. And unlike city folk, you don't get a day off each week. A cattleman said to me once when I inquired if he and his family would be going anywhere for Christmas, "'Nope, the cattle get hungry on Christmas Day, too.'"

Cathy had been squirming for some time and Phoebe had taken her onto her lap, but now she slid onto the floor, despite Phoebe's attempts to hold her, and began to cry. Mark cast Phoebe an angry, embarrassed look and Jason leaned around Selena to see what was going on. The minister was ignoring the noise, refusing to look in their direction. Tammy stirred, but Selena rocked her a little, and whispered to Phoebe, "Take her outside, it won't be long now." Phoebe gathered the protesting Cathy into her arms, squeezed past Mark and started down the aisle. Her footsteps and Cathy's cries receded as she went down the aisle and out the church door.

"Today we celebrate that labour, we celebrate that toil. Look around you and see what it has brought you: a way of life that is good, a closeness to nature, to God's green earth and to his wide, blue sky, and to the care of the animals of the fields. It has bought homes for your wives and your children, and put food on the table for them. Your toil, even in this time of drought and grasshoppers, has not gone unrewarded."

Selena wished Kent and Tony were here to hear this. She would tell the minister on the way out what a good sermon he had preached. And Rhea too. If only I could get that woman to come to church with me. She used to go, I'm sure she did. Mother told me. Yet imagining Rhea sitting in the pew beside her with her face turned up toward the small minister almost made her laugh. That would be the day.

"You toil all your days because Eve disobeyed the Lord and ate the forbidden fruit. But she, too, has paid for her sin, for she bears children in pain . . ."

Selena looked at Mark, but he plainly wasn't listening. His eyes were fixed on the back of Marcie Morrow's blonde head two rows in front of them. Oh, Lord, she thought, before I know it I'll have a daughter-in-law to worry about. Jason sighed loudly. She glanced warningly at him and he straightened reluctantly.

After church, Mark at the wheel, they drove to Rhea's to pick her up and take her home for dinner. They had rolled up all the windows to protect themselves from the dust and the grasshoppers, and it was stifling in the car, but nobody bothered to complain.

"Boy, was that ever boring," Jason said, referring apparently to the service.

"It's the Word of God," Selena said, more to herself than to Jason.

She wondered if it was really true that God had made women bear children in pain because they were responsible for driving everybody out of the Garden of Eden. She supposed it must be, if the Bible said so. She remembered her own three labours. Phoebe, the first, was the longest and the hardest. But worth every second of it, she reminded herself. Labour. Funny the minister didn't mention that having babies is called labour, that women labour doing that.

She turned to Phoebe to tell her what she had just thought, but the presence of her two sons, and the look on Phoebe's face, stopped her. Phoebe was staring at the back of Mark's seat. Her eyes were so distant that Selena was afraid. What could she be thinking of?

"Phoebe?" she asked gently.

"What?" Phoebe asked, her expression not changing.

"I . . . Nothing," Selena said, finally. Phoebe turned to look at her then, her head vibrating faintly with the motion of the car. "Thanks for helping me with Cathy," Selena said.

"That's okay."

They were driving up the lane into Rhea's place now. Everybody itching to get hold of her land, Selena thought, so they can plow it up and farm it, and Rhea won't sell. So it sits there. She wondered who Rhea would leave it to when she died. Maybe Mark, she thought hopefully, then remembered Rhea's three sons, her own uncles. God knows what'll happen to it, what'll happen to any of us.

Mark parked the car in front of the garden.

"Jason," Selena asked, "run in and tell her we're here, will you?" Jason got out of the car and disappeared through the raspberry and gooseberry bushes.

"I don't know how she does it," Selena said.

"What?" Tammy asked, looking up at her.

"See all the flowers and the shrubs? Nobody else can make them grow like your Great-auntie Rhea does." Tammy climbed onto her knees, rolled down the window and leaned on the frame to stare out at the garden. Bees buzzed in the noon sun, and birds warbled and skittered from shrub to shrub. Selena thought of the Garden of Eden. Only the older

110

women could make gardens like that. She wondered why.

"Hi, Grandma Rhea," Tammy called, seeing first Jason and then Rhea come around the corner of the house. She leaned out so far that Selena caught her by the dress and held on.

Climbing into the car, Rhea said, "Been to church, have you," and then let out one of those long, pointless peals of laughter that went on and on and on.

When it was time for the little girls to go to bed that night, the men had still not returned from the ball tournament.

"I suppose we should have gone with them," Selena remarked, sighing. They were upstairs, Phoebe sitting at her desk in her room with the door open, Diane putting the little girls to bed in the extra room across the hall from Phoebe, and Selena leaning in the doorway watching her. They could hear Rhea coming heavily up the stairs.

"Oh, for heaven's sake," Diane said calmly. "At their ages they shouldn't need you there every time they play ball. When are they going to grow up?" Selena shifted, pressing her spine against the cool wood of the door frame. It would be so nice, she thought suddenly, not to have them to worry about or feel guilty over, for all the ways she was surely failing them.

"I'll tell the children a story," Rhea said, suddenly beside Selena in the open doorway. "Then I want to go home. There's a harvest moon tonight." Selena glanced at her, puzzled, but Rhea was looking at Diane, a funny, determined look in her eyes, as if she would brook no objections or interference.

"Okay," Diane said, a little surprised. She came from between the two single beds to where Selena stood beside Rhea. Rhea went into the room and seated herself on the foot of Cathy's bed. Tammy squirmed happily, trying to get comfortable to listen. Diane watched for a moment, then snapped out the overhead light. The hall light spilled into the room, across the foot of the beds, lighting Rhea's broad back and her head with its crownlike roll of white hair, from which strands were escaping—how long her hair must be when she lets it down, Selena thought—giving her silhouette a powerful, almost frightening appearance.

"I'm going to tell you about the beginning of things," Rhea said, into the darkness.

"The beginning of what things?" Tammy asked.

"All things," Rhea said firmly, and Cathy repeated in a sing-song, "All fings, all fings, all fings . . ."

Selena and Diane moved into the hall and paused at Phoebe's door.

"I'm going downstairs to put some coffee on," Selena whispered across the room to Phoebe, but Rhea had started to speak and Selena's intention slowly weakened. Instead, she walked into Phoebe's room and sat down on Phoebe's bed. Lots of time for coffee, a voice said in her head, and she agreed drowsily. Diane followed her and sank into the rocking chair across the room from where Phoebe sat at the table that had served her as a desk for years. She leaned back and closed her eyes.

Rhea's voice had begun again, steady and distinct even though it came to them from another room, across the hall. They knew she was speaking to all of them.

"I am going to tell you this story," she said. "And when the time comes, you must tell it to your children."

"I could tell it to my dolls," Tammy suggested in a sleepy voice, "Or to the kitties . . " Her voice fell off in a deep yawn.

Listen to her, thought Selena, that's not the way to tell a story to children. But, although the words of the criticism formed themselves in her head, she couldn't seem to speak them, and her mind had already jumped forward to follow Rhea's story.

"In the beginning" Rhea began again, and a shiver ran down Selena's back. Her voice was not loud and yet it resonated through the whole house. Selena could imagine the animals in the field hearing it and the birds nested down for the night in the trees and the tall grass.

Phoebe hadn't pulled her blind. Her bedroom faced east and the moon was rising between and above the row of steel bins. It rose orange, a perfect circle in the dark sky. The old house was silent.

"There was Woman," Rhea said, and they waited, they didn't know for what. "And she had all the wisdom from time when there was no time gathered together in her body. It rested in the soles of her feet, and in her knees, it

112

flowed with her blood upward into the secret organs of her body, it waited in her full belly and her great breasts, it murmured in the muscles of her arms and made the palms of her hands tingle, and it rose to sing its song in her heart.

"Around her head and massive shoulders there was a noise like the buzzing of a thousand bees, and when she moved she gave off a smell that was so powerful that, had there been any living thing to come near her, it would have been stupefied by the heaviness and sweetness of the scent and would have fallen into infinite sleep.

"No one knows what there was before she came. Perhaps there was nothing at all."

Selena and Diane, and even Phoebe, listened. They forgot where they were, they forgot what day it was, they forgot each other and the small, ramshackle house in which they sat. Selena and Diane forgot their husbands, they forgot their children. Who knows what Phoebe forgot.

"She was, before there was the sea or the sky, the forests or the meadows, the rivers, lakes and streams, the desert and the mountains. Before there were creatures that run on four legs or swim or fly, she was there. Before there were women or men, she was there. And all these things she contained inside her, in her womb, for Woman is possibility, Woman is life, and out of this possibility, she drew forth the universe.

"First, she made the sea. It issued forth from her womb, and she thought how beautiful it was, and she blew on it and watched it dance. She danced, too, with it, and her long silvery hair floated over the sea and through it, like long drifting fishes or fireflies, and this made the wind. She spun and her hair followed, flowing, and out of it she fashioned the moon and the stars.

"Although the moon was her creation—she had made him—he became her lover. As the moon waxed and waned she began a companion cycle, she began to bleed, and she called that time from bleeding to bleeding a month, a mense.

"And that is how time was born.

"Out of her monthly bleeding, her menstrual fluid, she fashioned the earth, a daughter, and the sun, which she threw into the sky so there would be light. She breathed life into earth and her daughter began to grow grasses, trees and flowers to cover herself with. Out of her menstrual fluid Woman made human creatures, first a small one like herself, which she called woman, and another which she called man, to keep woman company. Woman placed in the man seeds and the desire to plant them in the woman's womb so that he would be a faithful companion.

"For a time women and men were happy, peopling the earth as Woman had told them to do. Earth was good to them, giving them fruits to eat from her trees, and nuts, and roots. Seeing that her creation was complete and fruitful, Woman lay down to rest.

"But gradually, men grew jealous of women, for out of them issued forth new life. The monthly bleeding that coincided with the waxing and waning of the moon frightened man. It seemed to men that all nature was in harmony with women, and they felt themselves left out of this great and beautiful rhythm.

"Men muttered among themselves. Why should we be servants to these creatures, they asked one another. Gathering roots and berries, fruits and nuts for them to eat. Retreating to our huts when the moon shines and the women dance outside. Why must we bow to their rhythm?

"Huddled in their huts at night, they told stories about a day when men would rule, when men would be the ones to give birth, and about a great male god they would create for themselves.

"Till it came to them that the strength Woman had given them to build fires and gather food was greater than the strength the women had. When they realized this, their mutterings grew louder, and the care they took of the women grew less and less.

"Slowly men overpowered women and made them slaves. Because they could not bleed in the way of women, and because they knew that bleeding was the secret of women's power, they shut women away when they bled. No man could go near them at that time, nor when they were giving birth, either. Bleeding is dirty, bleeding is evil, they told each other. Men are clean and good because their bodies do not bleed in such an indecent way.

"They were jealous of that blood though, of the power that it seemed to hold. So men began killing, they began to kill animals and to drink their blood and to devour their bloody flesh. Killing makes us more powerful than women, they said, because we can make blood flow in copious amounts whenever we choose, and then they invented rape, and wifehood.

"The women became terrified of the men. They began to try to please them, they pretended they were weaker than men were, and they acted as if they had been designed to be ornamental, pleasure-givers. They pierced their ears and noses, and hung ornaments in them, they starved themselves, or ate far more than they needed to please first one demand and then another, they painted themselves and wore garments that hobbled them, or hampered them, or hurt them.

"As time passed the women grew more and more confused. Each woman became split within herself: one half of her stayed in harmony with nature, bleeding and giving birth, while the other half of her became coy, seductive and servile.

"But still the men were afraid, especially of what the women might be fomenting in the birth huts. One day they declared that they would take over the births. The women were astonished. Did this mean that men could now give birth? But no, it meant that from that time forth men would take charge of births, drugging women or not, removing them from their relatives and friends, placing them in a ritual environment of their own fashioning.

"Eventually men invented science in order to try to control nature. They even discovered a way to make human life in test tubes without the need for a woman: they wanted to make women, whom they hated and feared, superfluous. In their struggle to take control of creation they destroyed natural things and their efforts produced disasters. They were in danger of destroying all human connection to the Great Swelling Mother who gives life to all things and to her daughter, earth. All human life was threatened with extinction.

"But listen! Woman is waking now. Disturbed in her dreaming by intimations of disharmony drifting from her creation, her beautiful, silver-toed feet are stirring, there is a twitching in her massive thighs and in her great shoulders. She moves her head, and her long, silvery hair lifts and floats. The buzzing around her head, shoulders and arms grows louder. Soon Woman will wake.

"Woman has never spoken with words, but now, in her dream, a sound is issuing from her that is different from the buzzing around her shoulders. It is a gentle, broken hum that comes from deep inside her body and that threatens to grow louder as it gathers strength, that promises to burst forth in words or in song.

"If we hold silent, if we retreat within ourselves and listen with reverence, with humility, we begin to hear this voice. It will grow louder, it will fill us, it will give us courage and purpose, it will transform the world.

"Listen!"

Selena found herself sitting at the foot of Phoebe's bed.

She felt as if she had been asleep. Diane was still sitting across from her and Phoebe, at her desk, sighed and stirred.

"I meant to put some coffee on," Selena said, and gave a short, puzzled laugh. "I wonder if Rhea wants to go home now." She rose from the bed, stretching and yawning, straightening her skirt. Diane rose, too, yawning and shaking her head so that her long, dark hair fell back behind her shoulders.

"I think I hear a car," Phoebe said. She got up, too, and went to the window, apparently forgetting that she couldn't see the road from that side of the house. The moon shone in on them, bigger than before, but a paler orange. Diane and Selena were at the door before they noticed Rhea, who seemed to have been standing in the hall. They went downstairs together.

The front door opened and Kent came in, followed by Tony, then Mark, then Jason.

"Hi," Selena said, and Diane, coming behind her, murmured hello.

"Hey!" Kent said, "we could use some coffee." There wasn't enough room for all of them in the small hall, so the women waited on the stairs while the men hung up their caps, smoothing their hair with their palms, and went into the living room.

"How did you do?" Selena asked Mark.

"Won one, lost one." He stood looking up at her with his hands on his hips, as Kent often did. "We came in second."

"Hey, good for you!" Diane said.

"That's great," Selena added, "the last tournament of the year."

"He got a home run!" Jason said, looking at his brother, his eyes bright even in the dimly-lit hall. "You shoulda been there!" Selena's heart went out to Jason, so proud of his big brother, and envious of him. She wanted to tell him that he would have his moment too.

"How did your team do?" she asked.

"Oh, we got beat out early," he said. "I don't care."

He turned to go into the living room, but stopped as Mark looked up at his mother on the stairs and said, "Jason's a good second baseman. He's one of the best players on his team." Selena smiled at him. Jason, grinning, pretended to thump his brother on the arm, then went into the living room.

"There's Coke in the basement," Selena offered. They kept pop around only on special occasins, holidays, when they had company.

"Hey, Jason," Mark said into the living room, "want some Coke?"

When the coffee was made and served and everyone was sitting around the living room, stirring and sipping their drinks, Diane asked, "Well? What did Doyle say?" Tony set his coffee mug down carefully on the coaster Selena had set out for him on the coffee table. He drew in a long breath, his eyes finally meeting Diane's across the room.

"The bank wouldn't give him the money," he said. There was a surprised silence.

"What?" Selena said. If they wouldn't give it to Doyle, who would they give it to? Rhea watched attentively from the rocking chair in the corner, but didn't speak.

"They're scared he'll overextend himself and his whole operation'll come crashing down," Kent said. "Leave them holding the bag for a million or so."

"But . . ." Diane said. The two boys, sitting side by side on the rug, watched the adults nervously, careful not to move or make a sound. Rhea's expression hadn't changed, her eyes moved from Tony to Kent and back again.

"Don't worry, Di," Tony said, although there wasn't much confidence in his voice.

"What will we do?" she interrupted, her voice tense. Without the money from the sale of their farm, they couldn't pay their debts; no salary was big enough to do that.

"Find another buyer," Tony said. "What else?" She stared at him, holding her coffee mug in front of her, just where it had been when he first answered her.

"Another buyer?" she said slowly, as if she didn't quite understand this.

Selena wondered if this meant they would have to come back and live on the farm, but Tony said, before she could ask, if she had been going to, "You won't have to stay here."

Tony and Diane seemed oblivious to everyone else in the room. Selena noticed that Phoebe hadn't come downstairs. As if she had said Phoebe's name out loud, Diane broke from Tony's gaze to set her mug down on the arm of the piano they had bought for Phoebe when she started piano lessons. The hours I spent sitting in the truck while she had her lessons, Selena thought irrelevantly, then jumped up, lifted Diane's mug and slid a coaster under it. Diane paid no attention to her.

"It'll be okay," Tony said, and Kent put in, "Land always sells, sooner or later." Jason used this reassurance to make his escape.

"I'm going to bed, Mom," he said, through a yawn. He rose from the rug, set his Coke glass on the tray on the coffee table, and left the room, turning at the door to say, "Good night." Mark got up too, then, and after mumbling good-night to everybody, went upstairs behind him.

"Who's driving me home?" Rhea demanded from her rocking chair. Kent rose at once, hastily putting down his half-full coffee mug. Selena had to smile to herself. Kent didn't move that fast for anybody.

Even as Selena was going to the door with her, saying good night standing, shivering in the chilly fall night, noisy with crickets, she was thinking with awe of that look of certainty in Rhea's eyes. Where does it come from, Selena wondered. Does she know things the rest of us don't know?

PHOEBE PLAYING THE PIANO

Tony and Diane's car was churning dust down the lane. It billowed up behind them, blotting out Tammy's frantic good-bye waves through the back window. It was as though they were being swallowed by the dust. Selena dropped her arm slowly—farewell, she thought, farewell, what a good-sounding word.

She turned to Kent. His eyes had shifted from the dust cloud to the stubble field in front and to the east of the house where their small crop sat in bales. Kent had decided that it wasn't worthwhile to hire somebody to combine it. There was barely any grain in the heads, so he had baled it for feed.

"Time I got those bales picked, I guess," he said, sighing, looking toward the shed beside the barn where they kept their few pieces of machinery. He turned to Mark, who stood a little apart from his parents, still watching Tony and Diane's car turn onto the grid. His longing to go too spread through the quiet air to Selena, she felt it in her gut and was surprised by this news. Surely Mark would never leave?

Jason bent down beside Kent, picked up a stone and threw it hard down the road. It skipped, throwing out puffs of dust. Phoebe said in an annoyed voice, "Jason," although it hadn't come anywhere near her. In reply, Jason threw another stone, harder this time.

"It's time you learned to pick bales, Mark," Kent said.

"You mean drive the bale wagon?" Mark asked. He couldn't keep the eagerness out of his voice. His father nodded, grinning.

"Okay," Mark said, casual now, as if it were nothing to him. He started toward the shed. Jason threw another stone. This one struck the dirt suspiciously close to Mark.

"Jason!" Kent said. "I want you to dig the potatoes today. All of them."

"Yeah," Jason said, a hint of surliness in his voice.

They could hear the faint hum of Tony's car, a long way off, vibrating on the still air. Phoebe stood with them, watching Jason till he disappeared around the house on his way go the potato patch on the far side of the trees. A horse whinnied in the pasture nearby and they could hear the dull hammering of its hooves as it broke into a gallop.

"I got his feet to attend to, too," Kent remarked, trying to catch sight of the horse pastured beyond the barn.

"Could I talk to you?" Phoebe asked, not indicating which one of them she was speaking to. Something in her voice made Selena swing her head quickly to look at her. Kent, too, seemed to sense something out of the ordinary. Phoebe glanced rapidly from one to the other, then abruptly dropped her eyes. Her cheeks and forehead flushed. Is she sick? Selena wondered, then: she isn't going to university.

"Come into the house," Kent said, with an easiness in his voice that Selena recognized as false. He looked past them to the bales out near the road, and far across the yard to the fields of grass lifting into the distant yellow hills. But then he opened the door and led the way down the hall and into the kitchen. He sat down quietly at the table and assumed a listening posture, his arms resting on the table, but instead of looking at Phoebe, he fixed his eyes on the square in the screen door that looked out over the backyard to where a huge flock of birds perched in the trees, on the power line and the clothesline.

Selena went around behind Phoebe, who had stopped in the middle of the room. As she passed, she touched Phoebe's upper arms encouragingly, then sat down gingerly, opposite Kent, facing Phoebe.

Phoebe backed away, her hands behind her, until she was touching the sink. She brought her hands around in front of her and as she pressed her palms together, Selena saw that she was trembling and the colour had left her face, revealing the pale transparency of her skin.

Something terrible was about to happen. The knowledge swept through Selena and she found herself gripping the edge of the table with both hands.

"I'm pregnant," Phoebe said quietly, as if she were asking a question. She dropped her arms, then immediately clasped her hands together again, so tightly that the blood drained from them, and Selena could see the sharp blue bones of her knuckles.

Selena glanced rapidly at Kent, but he was staring at Phoebe. Suddenly he hit the tabletop with his open hand.

"Brian!" he said. His voice was flat and hard, the name a truncated sound. Again inadvertently, Selena found herself wondering what he would say if it turned out to be somebody else. She shuddered, then opened her mouth to say something although she had no idea what. "Is it?" Kent insisted, his voice too loud in the small room. There was a massive swooping of wings, a great wind of sound, and all the birds outside on the lines and in the trees lifted off and whirled away. Phoebe shrank up against the cupboards.

"Yes," she said. She could hardly be heard. Kent let out a violent rush of breath, at the same time turning his head toward Selena, his expression at once angry and bewildered. Selena was afraid to speak until she could see him settle on one emotion. Finally he turned to her, she could see he was actually trying not to smile—but it would not be a happy smile, it would be a sour, ugly smile—"I suppose that money we borrowed is going to pay for a wedding now."

Selena tried to speak, but couldn't. Her own emotions, struggling with each other, rose and filled her chest and throat, blocking out words. Images filled her mind, the wrong things, stupid things—the new sweater she had just finished knitting for Phoebe to wear at university, the basket of tomatoes in the cool cellar, the kitchen floor that needed washing. The one image she did not want to see, Phoebe and Brian together, loomed behind all of them, a dark, unspecific cloud, like a thunderstorm blowing in from the mountains, far, far to the west.

"Does Brian know?" Kent asked, in that same harsh, too-loud voice, as if his vocal cords had inexplicably tightened. Phoebe shook her head, no. "Jesus!" Kent began, but she interrupted him.

"I . . . I . . . don't want to marry him," Phoebe said. Her eyes had filled with tears, tears began to run down her cheeks. She stared at the floor, sniffling, and let the tears fall without trying to wipe them away. Selena and Kent stared at her in astonishment.

"But," Selena began.

"Of course you'll marry him," Kent said, not shouting now, his tone reasonable. "You're going to have his baby." Then, "Jesus!" again. Phoebe began to sob, the sound surprisingly quiet in the shabby, familiar kitchen. Selena found herself searching in her pockets for a tissue, not taking her eyes off her daughter, not able to move from where she sat.

"He . . . raped . . . me!" Phoebe gasped, the phrase broken by her sobs. She lifted her head to say this, her voice was loud, her eyes burning now. She pulled in a hard, wheezing breath, it sounded as if she were choking. At that, Selena found her legs and jumped up, hurrying to

Phoebe, putting her arms around her, pulling her against her breast. Phoebe began to sob in earnest against her mother's shoulder, as if she were only now fully realizing what had happened to her, when? months before.

Kent was standing now, too, Selena heard the thump of his boots and his chair scrape the vinyl floor.

"Raped you!" he was shouting again. "What the hell are you talking about?"

Just then Selena caught sight of Jason's face at the back door. He stood there for a second, looking in, not opening the door, then went quickly away. Selena lifted Phoebe's head gently and wiped at her reddened, wet eyes with the tissue.

"Phoebe," she murmured, "Phoebe."

"He raped you." Kent repeated. He was striding the length of the kitchen, his boots making a hollow, hard sound on the creaky old floor. "He's your boyfriend for Christ's sake! How could he rape you?" Phoebe pulled away from Selena, and bent toward her father where he had stopped with his back to the kitchen door. His face was in shadow, Selena couldn't make it out.

"I didn't want to!" Phoebe shouted at her father, then began to cry again. "You told me not to!" She turned to her mother. "Mom?" she asked, in an unnatural, high tone.

"How the hell could he rape you?" Kent asked, as if she hadn't spoken. Selena, pushing Phoebe's damp hair away from her swollen, tear-stained face, heard what Kent said. She heard it with her ears, but she pushed it away, he couldn't have meant it.

"It'll be all right," she crooned to Phoebe, gathering her in her arms again. "It'll be okay." Although she couldn't see how it could be, ever again.

She turned to Kent, who was still standing there, his back to the door, the pale autumn sun shining in behind him, keeping his face in shadow. Selena peered into the darkness that was his face, trying to find his eyes. It felt as if he was looking out at her, or perhaps at Phoebe. There was a silence, lasting perhaps a full minute, while birds chirped outside, and far away a hawk screeched. So many hawks, Selena thought, this time of year, fall, the young ones learning to hunt.

"Well, you'll marry him, that's all," Kent said. He turned away and put his hand on the door. "The sooner the better, before the whole country-side knows about it." He pushed open the door. "Get Brian over here," he said, over his shoulder. Phoebe pulled away from Selena.

"Don't you care that he raped me?" she screamed. She went toward her father, her nose running, tears pouring down her face again, her body bent at the waist, and Selena was struck by the awkwardness and yet beauty of the movement. "He raped me!" Phoebe screamed again.

Kent hesitated, letting the door go, looking down at her, not speaking. Selena said, "Kent, wait, don't go." He looked at her, made a disgusted sound, then stepped out into the cool morning sunshine, letting the door slap shut behind him. For a second he blotted out the light, then he was gone, striding toward the barn, his bootheels striking up dirt.

Phoebe turned to her mother. Her eyes did not seem to be focusing, at least whatever she was seeing, it wasn't Selena, and her hands were fluttering in front of her. Selena had seen that once before, when a neighbour woman was told that her husband was dead, caught in a power take-off. Whole one minute, torn to bloody shreds the next. Selena had been a child at the time, watching her mother try to comfort the woman. And now she was the mother. She grasped Phoebe by the shoulders and shook her.

"Phoebe," she said, putting her face close to her daughter's, "Phoebe." Phoebe lifted her face to her mother's and her eyes seemed to focus again.

"He raped me," she said softly. He did."

They were sitting side by the side on the living room couch.

"I can't marry him," Phoebe said. "I couldn't . . ."

"It's all right," Selena said. "I understand," then found herself standing, walking around the room, touching things, and noticed her hands were shaking. "A nice boy." She spat the words out. "A decent boy." She felt she might be sick. She crossed the room and sat down again beside Phoebe, taking her hands in her own. "What happened?

You'd better tell me what happened." Although, God knew, she didn't want to hear.

Phoebe turned her face away from her mother so that she was speaking to the wall. She swallowed and when she began to speak, her voice was quiet and uninflected, as though someone else were speaking, or she was telling her mother someone else's story.

"We were in the truck, necking. Dad's right about that part. We were necking. But he kept on kissing me. He put his hands between . . . my legs. I tried to pull his hands away, but I couldn't. It was like . . . something took over in him, and it didn't have anything to do with me. Like he didn't even know who I was anymore." She paused, lifting her hands as if she were about to wipe her eyes or rearrange her hair, then setting them down quietly in her lap without touching anything. "I began to get frightened. I knew what he wanted. I might even have been able to . . . let him, if he hadn't turned . . . like that. If he'd . . . remembered . . . it was *me*." She paused, breathing quickly, but still not moving.

"Did he hurt you? Did he hit you? Or . . ."

Phoebe shook her head, no.

"I knew I couldn't stop him, though. And I kept thinking, you can't do this! Nobody can do this!" She was shaking, and when Selena put her arms out to hold her, she was amazed to find that Phoebe was shaking with rage—not sorrow, not fear. But then the trembling subsided, she sighed, like a child, and went on.

"I wanted to scream, but I couldn't stand the thought of anybody finding me like that. Helpless. Under him." All the times she must have gone over it in her mind, Selena thought. "And besides, I couldn't have called out even if I had wanted to. He put his arm here." Phoebe put her fingers against her throat.

There was no other sound in the house. Only the faint roar of the tractor pulling the bale wagon in the nearby field marred the silence.

"He had no right," Phoebe said. "Nobody has the right to do that to anybody else. To turn them into . . . an animal." Her voice had lost its composure. She turned to her mother. "Is that how it is, Mom? It can't be like that. It can't."

"No," Selena said. "No. That's not how it is."

"I didn't think it could be. I thought, the world would die if that's how it is." She was silent now, thinking. "You should have told me, Mom," she said, softly, not reproachfully.

"I thought I did," Selena said, helplessly. "I said, wait till you're married. I meant, then you'll know it's right." She could hear the uncertainty in her voice. What else could I have told her? she wondered, searching her mind, trying to think what she had missed, hadn't understood herself, perhaps. But no, she did understand, only she had thought that Phoebe was still a child, that she was protected, that nothing would ever happen to her. I could kill him, she thought.

"Brian doesn't know about the baby?"

"I don't think so. I didn't tell him."

"What do you think he'll say?"

"He'll want to get married, I guess."

"Have you talked about getting married?"

"No."

"You should have told us when it happened."

"I couldn't. I was ashamed. I . . . couldn't understand . . . what had happened. I couldn't believe that was the way the world is, and I had to . . . think about it." She was silent, her mouth working as she tried not to cry.

"I never dreamt I'd wind up pregnant. I never even thought about it." She gave a little laugh that was cut off by a sob. Selena was torn between her own sorrow, anger at Brian, and bewilderment at what Phoebe was saying, such peculiar, unnatural things to think, they baffled her.

"I won't marry him," Phoebe said. "Mom, what if he kept doing that to me? And we were married?" Her voice cracked with fear, or was it disgust? Selena put her hands on Phoebe's shoulders.

"No," she said. "You won't marry him." Although how she could persuade Kent otherwise she didn't know. "We'll go to Rhea."

"Why?" Phoebe asked, surprised.

"Because," Selena began, then paused, the idea having simply popped into her head without reflection. "Because . . . she's been around a long time; she's seen this before, I'm sure. She'll maybe know how to . . . help, what we should do."

After a minute Phoebe said, "You mean . . . an . . . abortion?" They looked at each other and Phoebe seemed to turn inward, frowning. Selena didn't answer her, realizing only now, herself, that this would be one of the things Rhea might say. "All right" Phoebe said, slowly. "But what will Dad say?"

"He doesn't need to know."

"But he'd know if I lost it."

"Women lose babies all the time," Selena replied. "I lost my first baby. I was six weeks pregnant and I just lost it." There was a silence.

"I like . . . . babies," Phoebe said.

"I do too."

"If I have it," she hesitated, "Dad will make me marry Brian. Brian will want me to marry him, if I'm having his baby." She put her hands over her face, then took them away again. "I don't suppose he'd let me have it without a husband." She picked at the worn threads on the couch between them.

"Go phone Brian," Selena said. "Tell him to come over tonight. By then we'll all have had time to calm down. Him too."

"I won't marry him," Phoebe repeated, as if she hadn't heard Selena's instructions. She scuffed the carpet with her running shoes so that Selena wondered if there was a stain there.

"One way or another we have to talk to him," Selena said. Phoebe rose and went into the kitchen. Selena could hear her dialling.

Selena stared at the rose-coloured mahogany piano, an old-fashioned, secondhand upright. They had been lucky to find such a good one so cheaply. They had bid on it at an auction sale. It was one of the household goods that belonged to an old piano teacher in Chinook who was going into a nursing home. She hadn't even been at the sale. Her daughter, who had come home to look after the sale, had said to Selena as her husband, Kent, and Kent's older brother, Gus, were loading the piano onto the pick-up, Mother loved that piano. I think she loved it more than us kids. She glanced at Selena guiltily, then scurried away, obviously surprised and embarrassed by what she had said. We'll take good care of it, Selena had called to her retreat-ing back. And she had, polishing and dusting it even more than it needed.

It must be ten years we've had that piano, Selena thought. She could hardly believe it. Ten years. Standing in the kitchen year after year listen-ing to Phoebe striking the keys, timidly at first, then more boldly, playing little tunes, exercises, working her way up to more complicated pieces. Starting, making a mistake, starting again.

What kind of a person is Phoebe? she wondered, staring at the piano. Making a mistake, starting again, speeding up, slowing down. I've known her since before she was born. I ought to know, but I don't. She could hear Phoebe's light voice in the kitchen, rising, now falling, mingling with the piano notes Selena was hearing in her head.

Phoebe sitting at the piano, playing. Her hair so fine, shiny as silk. Her shoulders softly rounded, the skin delicate and fine-grained, glowing. Her torso tapering inward to her slender girl's waist, then flaring outward to form the curve of her hips. Phoebe playing the piano. The notes rose, floated over her shoulders, coloured the light of the room. Notes pure and clear, each one beautiful. And Phoebe a part of that beauty.

"Mom?" Selena turned to the doorway and saw Phoebe standing there. She saw the stringiness of her shoulder-length hair, her skin blotchy with emotion, her new chubbiness, the vulgarity of her too-tight jeans, her ragged, faded blue sweater. Phoebe suddenly leaned against the door frame. She slid one hand half-way into her pocket, her toes in their scuffed runners turned clumsily inward. Her expression was despairing.

Who is Phoebe? Selena thought, and stared at her, bewildered.

Phoebe looked back at her. Her blue eyes had lost their colour, only blackness remained, and then, flushing, she lowered them to the thread-bare patch in the rug at her feet.

The day grew warmer. Selena debated, then sent Phoebe outside to help Jason dig the potatoes. As soon as she had gone, Selena put her jacket on too, and went to look for Kent.

She found him in the shop. He didn't seem to be doing anything in particular, just rearranging the hammers, screwdrivers, and other pieces of equipment and tools scattered over the worktable. She stood in the doorway with her hands in the pockets of her jacket, studying his back before she spoke.

"Kent?" He looked over his shoulder at her, then resumed whatever he had been doing. She walked in, avoiding Jason's bike, which was parked in the middle of the shop with a flat tire, a five gallon pail of oil and a tire leaning against it. She stood beside him. He stopped moving things and looked at her.

"We should talk about this." He turned away from her again.

"Is Brian coming?"

"Seven tonight," she said. "Phoebe didn't tell him why."

"He probably knows why," Kent said angrily. "Stupid kids." She leaned toward him, trying to get him to look at her.

"Kent," she pleaded, "remember us? It was just luck that we got away with it. How can we be hard on her?"

"It wasn't luck," he said. "We always took . . . precautions." She wanted to tell him that lots of times, everybody knew, precautions didn't help.

"I feel so sorry for her," she said. "Her plans wrecked, not knowing what's going to happen to her." He threw down the piece of metal he was holding and walked to the wide doorway and stood in it, leaning against the frame, one hand high against it. She watched, then walked the length of the shop to stand beside him.

"What will we do?" she asked him, wanting only that he should help her, help them plan something, anything.

"Brian will marry her," he said. "I'll see to that." She had thought at first that it was anger that clogged his voice, at Phoebe, at Brian, at the mess they had gotten themselves into. She looked at his profile, as he stared toward the front yard where even the lawn grass was turning yellow. She saw then that he didn't know yet how he felt or what to do. Marry him, that was all he could say. She thought that she should leave him for now, give him a few more hours.

"You'll tell Brian?" He nodded. "You'll stand by Phoebe?" not daring to say what she really meant. He turned his head quickly to look at her, a little surprised.

"Of course I will," he said. "She's still my daughter. I'll make him marry her."

"I mean . . ." she said, helplessly.

"What?"

"Kent, she said he raped her." He dropped his arm, then slammed his fist up against the door frame.

"Raped her," he muttered angrily. "That's stupid. It's just her excuse." Then he walked away, back to his worktable and began shoving boxes of machinery parts, and jars full of screws or nails, from place to place.

She watched him from the doorway, both astonishment and anger working in her. She wanted to follow him, to strike him on the back hard, to make him turn and listen to her. Rape! she wanted to scream at him. Rape! Why won't you listen? But she kept thinking, he needs time, that's all, it's hard for a father, he thought he could keep her safe, and he knows he's failed.

At seven-fifteen Brian drove into the yard in his new pick-up. He took his time getting out of the truck, shutting the door carefully, then wiping his palms on the seat of his pants. Selena was watching out the living room window and saw all this, saw how slowly he walked to their door, saw it with pleasure. Good, she thought, let him worry.

Kent had just gotten back from driving the boys over to Simca's and was sitting in the armchair, staring at a newspaper. Now, as Brian knocked, he got up, set the paper down on the piano bench beside him, went into the hall and called up the stairs, "Phoebe," then turned to open the door.

Phoebe and Selena sat side by side on the sofa and Kent motioned Brian to the chair he had just vacated. He came in himself and stood between them, facing the door, in front of the television set.

Brian glanced at Phoebe, but she kept her head down, refusing to look at him. Brian turned to look at Kent, and Selena took that moment to study Brian's face. She hadn't realized what seeing him would do to her. Her heart had begun to pound, it was all she could do to sit still. His bland, handsome face, his heavily muscled arms, his short, crisp hair. Who would know, to look at him? she wondered. Who would ever guess.

Kent did not seem to know how to start. He put his arms behind his back, then brought them around and crossed them over his chest.

"Phoebe here," he said, finally, loudly, directly to Brian, who flushed at the sound of his voice. "Phoebe's going to have a baby." Brian lifted one hand from his lap and grasped the arm of the chair, looking up at Kent. He swallowed.

"Is it yours?" Kent asked. He waited. Brian didn't say anything, and Kent said, "She says it's yours." He said it flatly, in a voice that brooked no disagreement.

Brian said, "I . . ." He cleared his throat, and Selena saw his lip quiver, ever so faintly. "I guess it is," he said. Phoebe didn't look up. What if he had denied it? Selena thought.

"If you don't take precautions," Kent said, his voice rising again, "this is what happens, for Christ sake." There was a silence, during which Kent put his arms down and shifted his feet. "What are you going to do about it?" Kent asked him.

Brian shifted his gaze quickly to Phoebe, but she stubbornly kept her head down. He glanced at Selena, then quickly away from her, back to Kent, as if Kent were the only one in the room whose reaction he could depend on. Brian cleared his throat again and said, "I suppose . . ." a tremor had invaded his voice and he started again. "I suppose . . . marriage."

"No," Selena said, immediately amazed at herself, then closing her mouth firmly. Both men looked at her with surprised expressions.

"Shut up, Selena," Kent said, in an undertone.

"She says you ra. . . ." Selena began.

"Selena!" Kent said, not even looking at her. "I'll handle this."

Yet his expression was more perplexed than angry. He knew what to do about an out-of-wedlock baby, Selena thought, but a rape? This kind of rape. If Phoebe had come home beaten and bruised, he would know how to act. She could see that Phoebe's insistence baffled him, that he could not understand this. "I want to know . . . what this is about, Brian," he said slowly.

Selena could feel Brian's anxiety reaching her in subtle waves from across the room. If she had ever had the smallest doubt about Phoebe's story, it vanished at that moment. She looked up at Kent again, expecting him to pounce on Brian, to shake him and throw him across the room, but Kent ran his hand through his hair, and shifted his feet again.

"She says you . . . forced yourself on her." Phoebe drew in a long, quavering breath. Selena quickly put her hand on Phoebe's arm. Neither of the men looked at Phoebe. "She says she tried to stop you, and you wouldn't stop." It was more a question that a statement, delivered without force, and Brian, after a second, gave a small shrug, then allowed his glance to shift to Phoebe, who still had not raised her head. He avoided looking at Selena.

"You know how it is," he said. "I . . . she . . . I didn't really *force* her."

"You did," Phoebe said, her voice quiet, but quivering with outrage. She might not have spoken at all.

"You . . . get so far," Brian said. "And . . . ah, hell. You know what I mean." Kent seemed to accept this. He studied Brian and Brian met his gaze, the two of them locked in some communication that excluded Phoebe and Selena.

"He raped me, Daddy," Phoebe said again. Kent broke his gaze with Brian and turned to face Phoebe. It was the first time he had looked directly at her since she had told him that morning. Selena wondered what he was seeing.

Kent drew in a long, audible breath, then expelled it slowly and turned back to Brian.

"She says she doesn't want to marry you," he said. Brian swung his head to Phoebe.

"If she's going to have my baby," he said, perplexed and surprised.

"There's abortion," Selena put in quickly. Both men looked at her as if they thought her remark extraordinary.

"Not my daughter . . ."

"Not my baby . . ."

This made Selena laugh. Tears sprang to her eyes.

"Look," Kent said to all of them. "I'm not about to raise an illegitimate child. It's too hard on everybody, the child too. But abortion is out." He turned to Phoebe. "Phoebe, look at me." Slowly she raised her head. "You and Brian have to work this out, somehow. You pretty well have to get married. What else can you do?"

"She could have it and give it up," Brian offered tentatively, looking at Kent again.

This time Selena jumped up.

"Never! You men have no idea what you're talking about. You have no idea at all! Women who give up their babies never, never get over it. I won't let that happen to Phoebe!" In the face of her pure rage, Brian shrank back against his chair as he had not done with Kent. Seeing this, Selena felt powerful, she felt glad that she had frightened him. Then Kent was beside her, putting his arm on her shoulder, pushing her down on the sofa.

"Take it easy, Selena," he said to her, as if she were ill. His words barely registered, she hated Brian with a pure hate, she would never let Phoebe marry him.

"Phoebe," Kent said, and his voice was gentle. "Don't you see?" They waited for Phoebe to speak. She looked from her mother to her piano, its polished wood gleaming richly in the evening light. She looked at it sadly. Then she looked at her father, and at Brian, who refused to meet her eyes.

"Yes," she said finally. "I see."

THE WOMEN CONFER

Selena opened the creaking gate with the paint peeling off it that led into Rhea's garden. Phoebe followed her. Except for the late-blooming zinnias and the last of the petunias and marigolds, the garden was stripped of blossoms, and as they passed, the hollyhock stocks along the sagging fence rustled and whispered to them.

As if she had been waiting for their arrival, Rhea stood at the kitchen door. When she saw them she didn't smile, but pushed the screen door open and stood back to let them come inside. She said, "Well, hello there. Sit down," and gestured toward the round oak table in the centre of the room.

Clear fall light spilled in the window over the sink and lit up the room, shrinking and fading any shadows. A small wild rose (at this time of the year?) bloomed in a vase in the centre of the table. They sat down, Rhea went to the electric stove, turned the burner on under the kettle, then sat down at the table, her back to the window, facing Selena with Phoebe on her left. She looked from one to the other, her palms flat on the table, while the kettle began to sizzle on the burner.

"Well," she said again, and the kettle popped. Outside the screen door a breeze swept through the dead, drying plants, rattling them, then subsided into a whisper. "Well," Rhea said again, in a different tone.

Selena said, "We've got a problem, Rhea. We came to talk to you about it."

"A problem," Rhea said, looking long and hard at Phoebe. She rose to turn off the burner and move the kettle. "I think in that case we need more than tea."

Watching her, her body taut with misery, Selena saw how Rhea, already an old woman, was growing truly old. Her lined and brown skin seemed to have faded over the past few weeks, and as she turned into the light, Selena saw a papery delicacy to it that had not been there before. There was a new absence in her eyes, too, a shutting off of depth, that had washed the colour from them.

They could hear Rhea moving around in the living room, opening a drawer, glass clinking against glass, and then she was back, a small Chinese brass tray in her hands, a decanter filled with a dark purple liquid and three small glasses on it. She set the tray in the centre of the table, took the stopper out of the decanter and filled each of the glasses while Selena and Phoebe watched.

"It's my chokecherry wine," she said, handing them each a glassful. She sat down in her place, taking the last one for herself. "Drink," she said, coaxing.

"It's sweet," Phoebe said, surprised.

"It's not really wine," Rhea said.

"It has a lovely flavour," Selena said.

"The chokecherries were good that year," Rhea said. "At least at the spot I know." She drained her glass, then reached for the decanter and filled it again.

"Now," she said. "What's this problem?"

Phoebe looked pleadingly at her mother. Selena slid her hands off the table onto her lap.

"It's Phoebe," she said, feeling tears welling up, fighting them down. She always felt so vulnerable in Rhea's presence. In this house, all her defenses vanished. "Phoebe is going to have a baby."

"I thought as much," Rhea said. "It's in her face." Surprised, Selena turned to stare at her daughter. While the two women studied her, Phoebe looked mutely from one to the other.

"The flesh," Rhea said. "The colouring." How could she not have seen it? Selena wondered. It was obvious now, that faintly fleshy look, the new volatility of her colouring.

Abruptly Selena put her hand over her eyes, then put it down again.

"It's worse than that," she said. "It's a real mess. I don't know what to do."

"What does she mean?" Rhea asked Phoebe. Colour rose into Phoebe's face, flushing her pale skin, mottling her rounded cheeks.

"I was raped." Rhea drew back, reached for her glass and Selena was startled to see that her hand trembled. She said nothing. Phoebe continued, gathering strength, "Brian raped me. But somehow or other, it's like it's my fault." She toyed with her glass, turning it so that the liquid rose and fell on the sides of the glass, the light catching it, turning it violet, then black. Selena reached out and put her hand over Phoebe's to stop that nervous turning.

Rhea said, "Some men are like that. Remember Mrs. Lucy Varga?" abruptly, to Selena. "She killed herself, finally."

"What . . ." Selena began, then stopped. She remembered the incident vaguely. Years ago, the wife of a homesteader drowned in a boating accident out by herself early one morning. She wanted to ask, how do you know all this?

"It's like this," Phoebe said, unexpectedly. "He didn't beat me, he didn't threaten me, not with a knife or a gun, or anything. And we were necking." She sighed softly. "And he was my boyfriend." She paused and Rhea could be seen to wait patiently till Phoebe was ready to continue. Selena, seeing this, held her tongue. Phoebe raised her head and looked intently at Rhea. "So, it turns out not to be rape if all I can say is that I didn't want to. I mean, he forced me . . ." this was a cry, "but Brian says that's not rape, and Dad says so too."

The kitchen was silent, the three women each deep in her own thoughts. Selena thought of how she had slept with Kent a long time ago. He had pressured her into it, it was true. But she had loved him, she had been afraid he would find another girlfriend if she didn't. Knowing what she knew now, it made her laugh to think of the silly things girls believed about boys' need for sex. She wondered if what had happened to her with Kent hadn't been a kind of rape, too. But that's ridiculous, she told herself. If that's true, then there's hardly anything that isn't rape. Look at all the times I've had sex with Kent when I didn't really feel like it. When I was dead tired or just not feeling sexy. Practically half the time, I think, and I just hid the fact that I didn't feel like it, even though sometimes I hated every second of it. I hated him for doing that to me. And other times, she thought, she had been the one to arouse Kent, when he had shown no interest. But look how careful I always have to be about it, she reminded herself, so he won't think I'm doing it on purpose. That always embarrassed and angered him, and in the end, had the opposite effect to the one she wanted.

Rhea sighed heavily. She looked so tired that Selena faltered.

"I shouldn't have brought her here. You've seen enough trouble in your day." Rhea's eyes seemed to bore into Selena's now, the colour returning to them, and Selena was aware of what a big woman Rhea was, nobody's idea of an old lady.

"And now I'm going to have this baby," Phoebe said.

"What does Kent say?" Rhea asked Selena.

"He says they have to get married," Selena said, "but I'll never allow that. And Phoebe won't, anyway."

"How do you plan to stop it?" Rhea asked. Before Selena could say anything, she went on. "In the end," she said sadly, "men don't know what to do with women. Not our men out here, anyway. All they know how to do is get women to work for them, and have their babies." Her words settled heavily in Selena's breast. She almost spoke out loud, don't say this, I don't want to hear this, I don't want Phoebe to hear this.

"There isn't a lot you can do," Rhea said, reflecting. "Have the baby without getting married. Have the baby and give it up. Have an abortion."

Selena remembered when one of Ruth's daughters had had an illegitimate baby, six or seven years before. None of them had seen the girl pregnant. She was living in Calgary, all they knew were the rumours that floated around the community. One afternoon Ruth had come to Selena in tears. I have to talk to somebody, she'd said, before I go crazy. I know I can trust you, Selena, not to tell anybody. You can't sneeze around here without everybody phoning to offer you a remedy. Jeannie isn't a bad girl, she's just kind of stupid—about men, you know. She wanted to have an abortion, but Buck raised hell, wouldn't let her. Some young social worker talked her into having it and giving it up for adoption. So she did that, a couple of months ago it was, and yesterday her roommate phoned us—and—she'd cut her wrists."

"I won't let her give the baby up," Selena said. She felt dizzy, and had to take a couple of slow, deep breaths.

"I won't marry him," Phoebe said.

Rhea looked at Phoebe, her eyes sharp again, glittering.

"That leaves one option," Rhea said, and waited. No one said anything. "All right," she said. "If that's what you want, I can manage it." Phoebe blinked several times. "Is that what you want?" Rhea asked. Phoebe shook her head, no, then shrugged, then lifted one hand to put it over her face. "Honestly," Rhea said, "you'd think the blessed world had come to an end."

"If he hadn't raped her," Selena said, "it would be different."

"I'll kill myself before I'll marry him," Phoebe said.

"Kent is making us go to Ross and Queenie's tonight, to tell them, make plans for the wedding, I suppose." Selena felt like crying again, but held back. Phoebe moved restlessly in her chair, and a flock of birds swept by the door with a rushing of wings. There were so many of them that they blocked the light for an instant and cast a dark, moving shadow across the room and the three women sitting in a silent circle.

Abruptly, in that shadow, Rhea raised her magnificent white head, and seemed to grow larger in front of them. Her eyes glittered, the room seemed to Selena to whirl inexplicably with the racing shadows and the sound of the wind. Rhea rose then, and put her hand on Phoebe's head, then simply stood there like that, beside Phoebe, looking out the window, her big hand resting heavily on Phoebe's head.

The Balfour ranch was a long way from theirs, up in the high, wooded country near Fort Walsh. The countryside was growing even emptier, if that was possible, as they drove, the sky still gloomy with banked-up grey clouds that contained no rain. All along the way they had passed short, thin crops, still standing in the fields, too poor to combine or even to cut and bale for the cattle. Even the grasshoppers were beginning to thin out with the approach of winter.

"Winter seems to be coming earlier this year," Selena said, more to herself than to Kent.

"Who'll go under this fall, I wonder," Kent said, looking at the uncut crop they were passing. People going broke right and left, losing their farms, disappearing into the cities. Look at Louise and Barclay, Selena thought, or for that matter, Diane and Tony, surely they were casualties of the same disaster. Gone from the community where they'd been born and lived all their lives. Gone to who knew what fate, trying to eke out an existence in a strange environment.

Balfours, for instance, had been ranching in this district as long as there had been ranchers. That made them aristocrats in the ranching community. If Phoebe married Brian she and Kent would be connected to them. She could imagine driving out to the Balfour ranch on a warm Sunday afternoon, staying for supper.

They drove down the winding, narrow trail that led through spruce trees, past the original log house and the decaying log barn. Several horses in the corral next to the new barn lifted their heads, pricked up their ears and whinnied at the approaching car. A couple of dogs leaped from the long grass along the corral and came running at them, barking. As Kent stopped the car, Ross came out of the house and stood in the doorway, and as they were getting out of the car, Queenie came out and stood on the steps too.

"Well, hello strangers!" she called. "What brings you here?"

And Ross said, grinning, "You folks lost?" When Kent did not smile and Selena merely opened the back door so Phoebe could get out, as if she weren't able to open it herself, the smiles on Queenie's and Ross's faces wavered. Selena noticed then that Brian's truck wasn't in the yard.

"Nice evening," Kent said, as they walked to the door.

"Not bad," Ross said. "Be a lot better if it'd rain."

"Hello, Phoebe," Queenie said, putting one hand on her shoulder as she entered. "It's nice to see you. Where are those big boys of yours?" to Selena, then, "Oh, this is roping club night, isn't it."

"That's right," Selena said. "They wouldn't miss that."

Ross led them into the living room, where they seated themselves. It was obvious that Brian hadn't told his parents.

"What brings you all this way over here?" Ross asked in his usual friendly way. He probably thought they were out looking for a horse to buy or maybe checking for stray cattle.

Ross was a tall man, stooping a little with age, his hair greying. He seemed puzzled as Kent, instead of answering him as easily as the question was asked, raised his hand to smooth his hair down for the second time.

Selena and Queenie looked at each other, then Queenie's glance shifted to Phoebe, who sat between her mother and father on the leather couch. Selena noticed that Phoebe was wearing the same white cotton dress with the pink belt that she had worn to the dance that night in July. Phoebe met Queenie's gaze briefly, then dropped her eyes and Selena realized that, in that instant, Queenie knew.

"I, ah, we got a problem here," Kent said, finally. Ross, who had been sitting in a rocking chair, tipping it slowly back and forth, stopped rocking and leaned forward.

"A problem?" he asked. Selena wondered again where Brian was.

"I sure do hate to be the one to break the news," Kent said, "but . . . Brian's not around, is he?" Phoebe kept her head lowered, as if she were studying the pattern of the brown and orange rug. Ross had turned to Queenie.

"Well, Mother, where is the boy tonight?" The light from the lamps on the wagonwheel light fixture hanging from the centre of the ceiling flashed on his glasses.

"He went to town right after supper," Queenie said. She dropped her head and her fingers fussed with her slacks. Both she and Ross looked at Phoebe.

Selena said, as gently as she could, "Phoebe's going to have a baby." For once Kent didn't interrupt or correct her. Maybe he was glad to have it said.

Ross pushed himself forward in his chair, as though to rise, and stared at Kent. Queenie watched Ross, her whole posture wary.

"That goddamn Brian." He turned to Queenie, who looked a little frightened. "And he beats it to town. He knew you were coming?"

"Yes, he knew," Kent said. "He was supposed to tell you before we got here."

"He never said nothing to me," Ross said, looking at Queenie.

"Me neither," she said. They could all see her blinking back tears. Brian was their youngest. The oldest three or four were long since married and gone, and there were only two girls older than Brian still at home.

Kent didn't seem to know how to proceed. He cleared his throat. "Did he tell you he'd marry you?" Ross said to Phoebe's bowed head. His voice was surprisingly gentle. She nodded without looking up.

"Sort of," she said. Ross studied her bent head for a moment, then shook his with an attitude half-sad, half-angry, almost as if he had expected something like this.

"Yeah," Kent said, and Selena silently willed him to tell Ross that Brian had forced Phoebe. Then, when she sensed that Kent wasn't going to, she thought, I'll tell Queenie, and lifted her head to look at Brian's mother. She was wiping her eyes with a tissue she had taken from her pocket. She was a short, stout woman, with the too-large hands of someone who had put in a lifetime of hard work. Her hair was short, unruly and grizzled in an unbecoming way. She would not even be allowed to grow old gracefully, Selena thought, and she was overcome with a pity for Queenie that silenced any words she had been about to say. What good would it do to tell them what kind of a son they had? Queenie must know, she hadn't even questioned Phoebe, and even Ross hadn't doubted them. They must know things about him that we don't, she thought. "We thought they'd get married as soon as the women can get a wedding pulled together, Kent said, but the conviction that had been in his voice the night before was gone.

Ross seemed surprised, as if it was too soon to be talking about weddings. "I guess," he said dubiously, "that's the thing to do." He looked to Queenie again. "Brian should be here. How can we talk about this without him?"

"He knew we were coming," Kent repeated. "He said last night it was his baby."

"Did he say he'd marry her?" Ross asked quietly. Queenie blew her nose. Selena said, "When I think about it now, he never did *say* he'd marry her." She gave a quick, surprised laugh.

"We must have took it for granted," Kent said.

Selena said hesitantly, "I'm not sure marriage is the right thing."

"Why is that?" Ross asked quickly. Queenie had lowered her tissue and looked with bright, surprised eyes at Selena.

Kent said, forcing ease into his voice, "Oh, you know kids. They think they know best, got to do everything their own way." Selena could feel some strong emotion coming from Phoebe, but she couldn't quite read it.

"She's . . . we're thinking about an . . . abortion," Selena said. All three of them turned to stare at her.

"Oh, no," Queenie said. "Don't even think of such a thing. Oh, no."

"Why tell us then? Why not just do it?" Ross sounded angry, and Selena was suddenly filled with confusion. Why hadn't they done that? Why had they come? She couldn't sort this out now, so she remained silent, looking from one to the other.

"This is crazy," Kent said, standing up. He was very angry. "We can't talk about this without Brian." Ross blinked several times behind his glasses, then stood.

"Was he wearing his roping club jacket?" he asked his wife.

"I never noticed," she said. She pulled herself out of her chair with difficulty. "I could look in his room."

"Do that, Mother," Ross said. She hurried out of the room. They could hear her puffing up the stairs. Almost as soon as she reached the top, she started back down again and they waited, listening. At the bottom of the stairs she stopped, and as they watched her through the doorway, she leaned against the newel post, one hand against her chest, and said, between breaths, "His things are gone."

In bed that night Selena said, "Kent, what if Brian doesn't come back?"

"Oh, he ain't coming back," Kent said sourly. He made a disgusted, angry sound and moved his long legs around under the blankets.

"What are we going to do then?" she asked, although her mind was made up.

"I could go after him," he said tentatively. She could tell this was the last thing he wanted to do. If I pressed it, he'd try though, she told herself.

"It's not worth it," she said. "You don't have any idea where to look, and what kind of a husband and father would he make if he got married with a gun to his head?"

"I don't know why he ran," Kent said. Far off in the purple felds a couple of coyotes were barking, and Blackie began to howl an answer. "They probably would have gotten married if this hadn't happened." They were silent, listening to the faint howling of the coyotes and to Blackie's voice growing softer as he ran out toward the fields to meet them. "Maybe he just got scared. Women don't realize how hard it is for a man. One day he's a boy with no responsibilities and then everything seems to happen at once. He's got to find a way to make a living, and then he gets married and he's got a wife, and first thing he knows he's got a family to feed, too. It's a wonder more men don't run away." He laughed, a faintly surprised sound in the dark.

"Well," Selena said, "She said she wouldn't marry him, so maybe this is for the best." She hesitated. "I think we should talk about an abortion."

"Don't be silly."

"Don't call me silly." She had never contradicted him so directly before, although he often said to her, don't be silly, and it always rankled. But now she was sick with anger. She had hissed the words, too angry even to shout.

"All right," he said, "you're not silly. But there'll be no abortion. You know I don't think they're right." She wanted to say, who cares what you think? You're not the one who has to carry it, or look after it, but she was still shocked by her own anger and by his mild response to it. She had expected a row like they'd never had before, and she had been so angry she was ready for it. Maybe I should talk back to him more often, she thought. "That's my grandchild she's carrying there, and there's no way I'm going to let her kill it," he said, as if he were the reasonable one, and she was not. He sighed. "I'll raise it, Selena," he said. "I gotta admit, I don't see what else we can do." She was afraid to move for fear he would take back what he had just said.

"You mean . . ."

"I'll keep her here," he said, a touch of irritation in his voice. "I'll feed 'em, keep a roof over their heads. And I won't ever say nothing." Instead of gratitude, she found herself thinking of all the things he would not say.

"But there was no rape," he said, his voice solid with conviction.

She was silent, knowing it was no use to speak, even her anger was washed away by the futility of trying to reach him. She closed her eyes, replacing the darkness in the bedroom with the larger, private darkness behind her eyelids. She stopped thinking about what he had just said, it was only a symptom, after all, of the way the men and women she knew lived their lives together—a way that over the last week or so, since Phoebe had told her story, that she was beginning to see differently.

So, this is how it is, she was thinking. All my life I've wondered how it really is between men and women. I thought for a long time that sex was what lay between us, then, when I had babies, I thought this must be it, each time he came into my hospital room, his eyes full of love, and he kissed me. After the kids were in school, I thought maybe it was sitting together in the audience at a Christmas concert with our kids on the stage, or I thought, even chasing cows together, or doctoring a sick steer. But now I see I was wrong. What lies between men and women is fear—fear and mistrust.

So bleak was this thought that Selena had to bite her lips to keep from crying out. All the things she had believed in, the rock bottom of security she had found in their marriage in the face of a bewildering, changing world, was dissolving, she could almost see it turning to liquid, and she held onto the bedclothes as if to keep from swirling away with it.

My life is broken now, Phoebe says, looking up at Rhea, who towers in front of her. The hem of her nightgown lifts gently, falls again with a sigh to cling to her calves. The grass prickles against her ankles, is stuff and dry under her bare feet.

It only seems broken, Rhea answers, because your mother raised you to believe that life is a long unbroken dream of safety and protection, when, in fact, it is a delving, a suffering, a rise and falling again, a long series of almost touching.

Phoebe lifts her face to the full white moon hanging suspended in the deep sky.

There is rape, Rhea says, looming black and shapeless before her, her face hidden in shadow. Her voice seems to be coming from somewhere else. Tell me what happened.

It was rape! Phoebe cries. I never thought that you would doubt me.

I don't doubt you. But we have to understand what it is that happens to us. We have to fold it into ourselves, make it a part of what we are. We cannot, ever, afford to reject our experiences.

He forced me. He held my legs apart with his hands and then his body. I was fighting to stop him, but he was too strong for me. And when he thought I might scream, he put his arm over my throat. He almost choked me. I couldn't breathe.

Had you been kissing? Had he been touching your body? Kissing it?

Yes.

And you allowed this. Welcomed it, even?

He tore my dress. He made me bleed.

You loved him, went everywhere with him? Thought perhaps you would marry him?

Yes. But what he did to me was still rape.

I agree. I would call it rape, too. But I want you to understand yourself. What Brian did is another matter.

It isn't right! Phoebe could hear herself shout, could hear the cry rise around her, lifted by the wind, up, up and around, into the glowing sky. Perhaps the moon heard it, with her white face bent so kindly toward them. Men and women, I know it, should come together only in mutual willingness, only, only, no other way.

Why did you change from wanting his caresses to fighting them?

Phoebe feels her passion, her certainty begin to crumble. The wind sweeps it up and whirls it away, leaving a hollow where it had been. Before her, Rhea's gown billows out with the wind, then drops silently to fold in around her.

We weren't married, she replies, *hearing herself mumble like a child. All the things I had ever been taught rose up before me, stronger than what I was feeling. You have to be the strong one, my mother said. So I tried to be.*

Keep going, Rhea says, her voice gentle, yet larger than the darkness, or even than the voice of the owl flying somewhere nearby, its voice sounding more human than Rhea's.

I was afraid.

Of what?

I don't know . . . of my life. Phoebe cannot say: of being a woman.

It is indeed frightening.

You're telling me I should have let him.

Welcomed him.

What about everything I was taught? What about the rules?

You have to take responsibility for your own life. That is the great lesson.

I can't bear this, Rhea. I can't bear this. I'll die if this is true. That is what men and women are. Animals. Only animals. Sweating and grunting. That is what love is.

You'll die anyway. The sooner you look that fact in the eye, the sooner you'll be able to live. I am trying to tell you to look beyond your girlish dreams. Illusion, sweet Phoebe, rid yourself of illusion.

He shouldn't have forced me.

No. He shouldn't have. But everything that happens to you is only a part of your life. Nothing is a mistake, or an accident. Everything that happens is your life. You must wipe away the feelings of shame, guilt, fear. Each time you do, you grow stronger and stronger.

Watch your Aunt Diana.

Long after Kent was asleep Selena lay awake beside him, thinking. How could we be married all these years without my understanding anything about our life together. Me, standing in the kichen day after day, peeling potatoes, washing dishes, cooking meals. For years standing at the kitchen counter working, lifting my head now and then to watch him working out in the corral with the cattle or horses, riding past my window on a greenbroke horse, or running a tractor by.

And as she thought of herself working in the kitchen, that pane of glass that stood between them, that had always seemed so ephemeral to her it was laughable really, took on a new hardness and impenetrability. She was struck by the soundlessness of the scene: his lips moving, but she, unable to hear his words even when he shouted; she standing on the other side of it, watching him rising and falling silently on a silent horse, his rope mutely whirling and falling.

This can't be, she thought, unable to lie still and bear such a view of their life together, and she got out of bed quietly, so as not to wake him, went downstairs and wandered into the living room. It was dark there, but she welcomed this and didn't turn on the light. Phoebe was sitting, wrapped in a thick white wool blanket, in her father's armchair.

"Can't you sleep?" Selena asked softly.

"No," Phoebe said. "You either?"

"No." Selena walked to the big front window and stood looking out of it, her back to Phoebe. In the ditch on this side of the road, two mule deer were grazing in the stubble, their backs shining white in the moonlight. Could you grow up in two, three days? Go from being a child to a woman in that short a time? Yes, she thought.

"Tell me again why you didn't scream," she asked. Phoebe moved, sighed, the blanket re-folded itself softly around her.

"Because everyone would have heard."

"It was in the parking lot at the dance?"

"Yes." And I was inside dancing, Selena thought. She remembered the strains of the waltz she had danced to with Kent, the violin lifting over the steady, muted beat of the drum and the guitar. She could see Phoebe struggling in the dark, Brian on top of her. The deer were beautiful in the moonlight, their silhouettes fluid and graceful. They began to move, first lifting their heads so their oversize ears stood high and alert, then moving slowly up the ditch, onto the road, crossing it and melting into the shadows on the other side. She was struggling to understand, to assimilate what had happened to Phoebe.

"He put his arm here?" she asked, turning, touching her throat with her own cool fingers, imagining Brian's arm on Phoebe's throat.

"Yes," Phoebe said, acquiescing to Selena's need. "Yes. There"

"What did he say?"

"He didn't say anything."

"You struggled?"

"I bit him on the wrist," Phoebe said, breaking into their litany. "I made him bleed, too."

"Good."

"I can still taste the blood," Phoebe said, a faint tinge of surprise in her voice.

"Why didn't you scream?" Selena asked again.

Phoebe repeated her answer carefully, gently.

"Because my skirt was up around my waist. My dress was . . . off my shoulders."

"I could kill him," Selena said, but even she could hear the lack of passion in her voice, the bewilderment.

They were both silent then, Phoebe a blurred egg-like shape floating in the shadows across from Selena. She wished she could see Phoebe's face. She thought of Diane now, somewhere in the city, wide awake in her brightly-lit doughnut shop, watching the people who came in: drug addicts, drunks, thieves, runaways.

"I've decided to have the baby," Phoebe said. "To have it and to keep it."

"Why?" Selena asked, after a moment.

"Because if I have it, people will have to look at me. They won't be able to forget what happened. They will have to see how the world is." How the world is? Selena thought. Is that what they will see?

"Your father has said he will take care of you and the baby."

Phoebe said, "Oh?"

"I know Diane would take you, if you'd rather go there."

"No," Phoebe said. "Let him see me every day." Let who see you? Selena wondered, since Brian was gone, then she realized that Phoebe meant Kent, and understood. Because he's a man—because he doesn't believe her, because . . . she was not sure what else. It seemed too hard to understand what else. It was all too hard.

"But," she began, hesitated, then went on, "what about you? What about your life?"

"*This* is my life," Phoebe said. Her voice was clear and strong. It was so different that for an instant Selena thought someone else had spoken. Then Phoebe said, "Now I'm not going to talk about it anymore."

OCTOBER

Selena and Ruth were in the hall kitchen mashing potatoes. Outside, in the hall itself, the noise was growing as people came streaming through the door in groups of three, four and five. Earlier in the day Selena had seen the first long, wobbling line of geese, its V uncertain, a big powerful gander breaking from the line to fly ahead and take the lead. Another fowl supper, another year gone around, and here we are again, Selena thought, as Ruth poured in the cream and dropped in a chunk of butter, then took the masher from Selena to take her turn whipping the potatoes. But everything is different now, Selena thought, nothing is the same.

"How's Phoebe?" Ruth asked in an undertone, pausing to rest. Women moved around them, intent on their tasks, filling the big serving bowls and setting them on the long buffet table.

"Two hundred people, already," Ella called over the racket, and there were murmurs of surprise and a few of concern.

They're still coming in. I hope we have enough," Helen said. "Somebody come and help me slice this turkey. We're going to need it right away." Enid hurried over.

"She's coming along all right. She never goes out though." Ruth nodded, pushing her glasses back up her nose. She went back to whipping while Selena went to the cupboard and took down two big serving bowls.

"Hurry up with those potatoes, Selena," Helen said into her ear, putting her hands on Selena's waist. "They're starting to line up." Selena nodded without turning around. Nobody had mentioned Phoebe, except for Ruth, which meant that they all knew everything there was to know—that she was at home, pregnant with Brian's child, that Brian had run away so as to avoid having to marry her. How they knew was a mystery, but they did, they always did. Maybe Brian had said something to somebody's son, and the son had told what he had heard. Or somebody who shouldn't have been was listening over a party line and heard a comment, a word dropped here or there, put two and two together, and now, everybody knew. But the rape, she thought to herself—the word still held power—they didn't know about that. She wished they did. But knew she would never say anything, although Phoebe would, if she were talking, if she were going out.

Selena had set Phoebe to work sewing maternity clothes for herself, and knitting and crocheting things for her baby. Keep her busy, Rhea had told her, and send her over here to me. I've got things to show her. So Phoebe went to Rhea's two or three times a week, and nowhere else. Selena knew she would never stop being grateful to Rhea. How would we ever get along without the older ones to take the lead, to show us how to do things, she wondered.

She and Ruth began to pile potatoes into the bowls and Joanne whisked Ruth's away while she was still piling the last spoonful into it. The noise in the hall rose, accompanied now by the clink of cutlery as people took knives and forks and filled their paper plates, then filed into the hall to find places to sit.

"Auntie Selena!" a small voice behind Selena called, and Selena thrust her bowl of potatoes toward Joanne—slim again, her baby a month old already and sleeping in its basket in the corner of the kitchen—and turned in surprise. Tammy was smiling half eagerly, half shyly up at her, decked out in a new blue and white checked dress with white eyelet trim on the shoulders and at the hem, her long hair carefully brushed and shining.

Selena bent at once and hugged her.

"Tammy! Where's your mom? Where's Cathy? And your dad?"

Phyllis passed, patted Tammy on the head, leaned swiftly down to say,

"What a pretty dress!" and then went on by. Tammy stepped back, delighted with her reception, and pointed out to the hall where the tables were rapidly filling.

"Mom didn't come," she said. "Just Daddy."

Selena left the other women to the work and let Tammy lead her to where Tony was sitting at one of the tables, talking to Kent. Coming up from behind, she put an arm across his shoulders and hugged him. He turned around, grinning, greeted her. "Hi, Selena. Tammy found you, eh?"

"You bet she did," Selena said, raising her voice to be heard over the noise. "Where's Diane?"

"She had to work this weekend, so I thought I'd give her a break, and bring the kids down here. It's good for the kids, too. I don't want them forgetting where home is." She lifted Cathy from the bench and squeezed in beside him, lifting Cathy onto her knee while Tammy pressed up against her on the other side.

"How long are you staying?"

"Just till tomorrow," he said. "I took a day off. We got here about noon and I took the kids over to Mom and Dad. Mom got them whipped into shape for tonight. Not that I couldn't have done it myself. You should see me tie sashes and hair ribbons." He laughed at this, but with genuine pride. "I want to get them back for tomorrow night so they have part of Sunday with Diane. They don't see enough of her these days." Kent sat on Tony's right, eating silently. Selena reached around Cathy to cut Tammy's turkey for her. Tony had returned to his meal, seeing Selena would look after the girls.

"Guess what, Auntie Selena," Tammy said, and began to tell Selena a long story about school and her new friend. Cathy struggled to get down and Selena had to let her go before she began to cry. She wanted to ask Tony if he had found a buyer for the farm yet, but he was turned away from her and was talking to Kent. Tammy left the table to bring Cathy back, then climbed back into her place.

Lana came rushing up the narrow aisle between the benches toward Tammy, bumping first into this back and then that one on her way. The two little girls looked at one another, smiling shyly. Lana spun around once, losing her balance, and Joanne's husband caught her by the arm and set her upright, laughing. Lana turned to run away and Tammy scrambled down again and vanished into the crowd, following her. Selena got up, picked up Cathy and went into the kitchen hugging Cathy and murmuring to her.

"How are you, sweetheart, how do you like your new house, is that a new dress?" It was meaningless, just a murmur of words into Cathy's ear, meant only to express her love, and Selena could tell by the way Cathy nestled against her and didn't even try to answer, that she wasn't getting enough attention.

"Who have you got there?" Ruth asked, as Selena set Cathy onto the counter beside her. She smiled at Cathy and patted her cheek. "She's such a little dear," she said, as Lola came over holding a filled plate.

"She's going to look like Tony, I think," Lola said. "Those big dark eyes." She set her plate on the counter and offered Cathy a bite of turkey covered with cranberry sauce, which Cathy accepted. Lola began to eat, too, standing up at the counter. Helen came over and leaned on the counter, watching the last of the crowd file by the buffet table.

"Aren't you eating?" Lola asked Helen. "There aren't any seats left out in the hall." Helen shook her head no.

"I'm not hungry yet," she said.

"You're not dieting, are you?" Margaret inquired, passing by with a pitcher of hot coffee, on her way to start filling cups.

"Margaret," Helen said, barely able to hide her exasperation. "You should let the young girls do that. Tracey!"

"Goodness," Margaret said, frowning. "They'll scald somebody," but she relinquished the pitcher to Tracey. Selena suddenly realized that she missed seeing Tracey jump off the school bus behind Phoebe, missed her staying for supper, the two girls giggling all night in Phoebe's room. Tracey avoided looking at Selena as she turned away from Margaret, steadying the hot pitcher, to make her way to the tables.

"You're getting too thin," Margaret said to Helen. "I don't think too much of this thin business. A little fat looks better on you." Helen's lips tightened. "That salad bowl's almost empty," Margaret said, and hurried away to fill it.

"That woman!" Helen said. Selena laughed, holding onto Cathy to keep her from falling off the counter. "The older she gets the bossier she gets."

"Don't pay any attention to her," Selena said. But Helen was thinner, and she hadn't been plump to begin with. Selena wondered if maybe there was something wrong with her. Helen was ten years older than Selena, at that age when things began to go wrong—breast cancer, cancer of the uterus.

"You have lost weight. Are you feeling all right?" Helen sighed, looked down at her body, and smoothed her skirt over her flat stomach.

"I feel okay," she said. "A hot flush now and then, but there's nothing wrong with me time won't take care of."

"You should see the doctor," Selena suggested.

"Hah!" Helen said. "When I sent Linda to see him because she was having painful periods and was sick the whole week she was premenstrual, he told her to drink a glass of orange juice every morning." They both laughed wryly at this. "No, if it gets really bad, I'll go, but not one second sooner." She flashed a quick smile at Selena, then, seeing a flurry of activity at the far end of the kitchen, hurried over to help out.

Tracey had returned with her pitcher empty. Cathy leaned against Selena's arm contentedly, and kicked her legs against the cupboard door so that her hard little heels in their good shoes drummed satisfyingly. Tracey came and stood beside her.

"Selena?" Tracey said softly so she wouldn't be overheard. "I just wanted to say how sorry I am." She seemed to be waiting for Selena's reaction.

"We're all pretty sorry," Selena said, tears dangerously near. She looked away from Tracey.

"Is there anything I can do?" Tracey asked.

"Come and see her," Selena said, hiding her face in Cathy's hair until the threatening tears receded.

"I phoned her, but I don't think she wants me to come."

"Come anyway," Selena said, lifting her face. "She feels bad, you know. She'd be glad if you came."

"Okay," Tracey said, and smiled. That light 'okay' and the trusting way she smiled made Selena's heart ache, because only a short month ago

Phoebe had been a girl like Tracey. And now she wasn't a girl anymore. Cathy was squirming, trying to get down off the counter. "I'll look after her," Tracey said.

"Could you take her to the toilet?" Selena asked.

Jason came up then, out of breath, his hair dishevelled, the remains of crushed weeds and grass stuck to the back of his jacket. She began automatically to brush him off.

"People are asking me where Phoebe is. What should I say?" He looked at her angrily, as if she were responsible for his embarrassment. His nose had started to run and she handed him a tissue from her apron pocket, noticing that he had grown since summer.

"You must have grown an inch!" she said. Pleased, he couldn't help but grin, but the grin quickly disappeared. "Tell them . . . she's sick." This didn't seem right, yet she couldn't think of anything else to say. Besides, they all knew where she was, she thought angrily. He must mean the kids are teasing him. "Tell them to mind their own business," she said. Jason turned to look out over the people through the wide doorway. "Did you get enough to eat?" she asked.

"Yup," he said. "Where's Mark?" She shrugged.

"I haven't seen him since we got here. Ask your dad." It occurred to her that she had always known where Phoebe was, that Phoebe had never gone anywhere without asking permission. It struck her that there was something not right about that, and she puzzled over it. Jason left her and went out into the hall. Lola, who had been talking to Margaret on her other side, turned back to Selena.

"I'm going to grab some pumpkin pie before it's all gone," she said. "Want a piece?"

"Okay," Selena said. In a minute Lola was back, carrying two plates with a slice of pie on each.

"I hope you don't mind if I ask about Phoebe. I just hope she's okay, that's all." Had Lola been pregnant when she got married? Selena tried to remember. They'd all counted backwards when the baby was born, she remembered that. She looked into Lola's wide brown eyes, and seeing real concern in them, smiled.

"She's okay. She just can't bring herself to go out in public." Lola nodded. "It must be hard for her. For all of you," she said. Selena didn't trust herself to answer. "That Brian!" Lola said. "I heard he got a girl from Swift Current into trouble." Selena turned, startled.

"What?"

"Didn't you know?" Lola flushed and put down her fork. "I thought everybody knew. Or maybe it's not true. I forget where I heard it."

"When?" Selena asked.

"Last year, I think. It's probably not true." Selena's heart had begun to pound. What possible difference can this make? she asked herself, and then answered, none. "Some men!" Lola said, angrily shaking her head. "I don't know what they think we are."

Much later, when they had finished the dishes, Selena went to find Kent. He and Tony and Kent's brother, Gus, were leaning against the wall in the corner of the hall by the stage. Tammy and some other little girls were nearby sitting on the edge of the stage, swinging their legs. Rhoda was leaning against the stage beside them, holding Cathy. The hall was almost empty. The few remaining husbands were collapsing tables and putting them and the chairs away. Kent went to help, and Selena went to Tony before he could go too.

"How are things going?" she asked. She looked up at him, determined that he wouldn't get away without telling her something.

"They're all right, Selena, honest," Tony said, smiling at her. "Diane's having the time of her life. She's taking night classes now, she's going to the first plays and concerts she's ever been to in her life, she's doing all the things she said she wanted to do."

"Has she got any time left for her kids?" Selena asked, angrily. Tony smiled at Tammy in her pretty dress, and then looked at Cathy in Rhoda's arms.

"Not much." He studied his boots, then lifted his eyes to Selena's again. "Give her a chance, Selena, eh? A year or so, then she'll settle down." He smiled at her, anxious to reassure her. "She's not like you and me," he said. "Stop worrying. I'll look after things, you can count on me." She found herself wanting to hug him, for his generosity, his reliability.

"What about your farm?" she asked.

"I got a nibble, an out-of-town buyer. We'll see," he said, and smiled faintly. She hesitated then, knowing she should tell Tony about Phoebe, but she couldn't find the words. He'd feel responsible for her, too, she thought, amused.

"Time to go, Tammy." Tony said. "Go get your coat." He turned back to Selena. "We're staying with Mom and Dad this weekend. I thought it was simpler than trying to set up camp in the old house for just a couple of nights. And Mom was dying to see the kids." Maybe it would be better if I write it in a letter to Diane, she thought.

Out of the corner of her eye she saw Mark come in from outside. Jason was already waiting for them, lounging on a chair by the door, and Mark leaned against the wall beside him. She felt a pang of loneliness for Phoebe, not coming out of the kitchen with her friends, not here with them.

On the way home in the car Kent said, "I heard something tonight I can hardly believe."

"What?" Selena said, thinking immediately it was about Brian and the girl in Swift Current.

"I heard Harry Halvorsen's bankrupt."

"Harry!" Selena said, astonished. "Where did you hear that?" And then, thinking back through the evening, "I bet it's true. Helen's as thin as a rail."

In the back seat Mark said, "No kidding! And they always take winter holidays in Florida and Hawaii and everywhere."

"That don't mean much," Kent said. "It's like Clarence Bradwell used to say: 'They can take back my land, but they can't take back my trip to Mexico.'"

"A lot of good that did him," Selena said disapprovingly. "He'd have been better to spend the money on fertilizer or paying his bills."

"Oh, I don't know," Kent said. "Maybe he's right. He lost the land in the end, and all that trip cost him, compared to what he owned, wasn't even a drop in the bucket." Selena was surprised to hear Kent say this. Wasn't he the one always trying to save money? To do without? God knows, she thought, we've never been to Hawaii. She changed the subject.

"When Doyle couldn't raise the money to buy Tony's place, I knew things were bad, but Harry's not like Doyle." Doyle was land-hungry, always buying. If land went up for sale he was crazy to have it, whether it was close to him or not. But Harry was third geneation, conservative in his habits, hadn't bought more land or a big new tractor. "I don't see how it could happen to him."

"He bought a new combine," Kent pointed out. "He must've spent some money helping Trevor get started on that Carlson place. It can happen. A few years like last year and this year, and the first thing you know, you're in trouble."

They could hear a flock of geese flying overhead, although they couldn't see them. Already there had been two snowstorms on the high plateau to the north of them, although both times the snow had immediately melted or blown away. Selena thought of all the fall work there was yet to be done: rounding up, weaning, selling calves, trailing cattle home from summer pasture. And winter crowding in on them, coming too soon, like it always did. All of them hating even to think about it.

NOVEMBER

It's cold here in the city. I find I feel it more here than I ever did at home, I don't know why. But I have a new winter coat. It's cherry red, long, with broad shoulders and I love it. I need something good and warm to wear while I'm waiting for the bus.

Selena was standing behind the old pole fence, watching the cows as they streamed out into the fields and hills behind the old corrals. They were leaving slowly, reluctantly, stopping occasionally to lift their heads and bawl plaintively, or to turn back to search for their calves. But the main gate had been closed, shutting them out. The calves were left milling in bewilderment in the big corral, bleating, wondering what had happened to their mothers.

You'll be selling calves soon, I suppose. I can see you out
there in the cold, in the hills, all day, chasing the darn things
around, then rushing home to cook a hot meal for everybody.
I always think "weaning" is such a strange word for it, when
all that happens is that you drive them all in and then bang,
like that, take all the calves from their mothers and they never
see each other again.

Was it snowing a little? Selena held up her palm, her fingers were cold
even inside her gloves, and a few small, dry flakes landed on the creased
yellow leather. They always waited to wean and sell their calves until the
last possible minute before winter struck.

Kent leaned over the fence from the main corral and called to her. She
had been watching the cows and didn't so much hear his words, lost in the
wind as they were, as recognize in the tone and then in his face, that he
wanted her. While she walked toward him and climbed the fence, he took
off his wool cap, pulled down the earflaps and put the cap back on, pulling
it down tightly so that it met the edges of his upturned jacket collar.

They had been up since well before daylight, had had breakfast, then
waited in their heavy clothes in the kitchen for the first rays of cloud-
dulled sun to provide enough light so they could begin the day's work.
Leaving Phoebe in the house, the rest of the family had gone out then,
silently crossing the bleak, frozen yard to the barn where their horses
were waiting, already fed and watered by Kent while Jason and Mark were
still climbing sleepily out of bed and Selena was cooking breakfast in the
kitchen. They had saddled the horses, loaded them into the stock trailer,
and with Kent driving the four-wheel drive, and Selena following in the
half-ton, headed out across the prairie toward their other corrals, which
sat in solitude in the basin of the hills fifteen miles west of their home
place. They had moved the cows and calves there in late summer, their
last pasture before winter set in.

They had arrived by nine o'clock, by ten had coaxed all the cows and
calves into the main corral, and by noon had separated the calves from
their cows.

"We better stop for dinner now," he said to her, "before we start separating the steer calves from the heifers."

"Okay," she said, and climbed the corral. Kent was already going to the big truck. He climbed in and began to back it around so that the long stock trailer acted as a buffer from the wind, while she took the box of lunch and the thermoses of coffee from the cab of the half-ton. He threw out a couple of hay bales from the stock trailer and using one as a table, she set the lunch out on it. The four of them sat down on the ground, their backs to the stock trailer, out of the wind, and ate the sandwiches she had made the night before. They ate quickly, and drank the coffee scalding hot, anxious to get to the next phase of the work.

"Cattle liners should be here about four," Kent remarked, looking up at the sky, and then out to the hills that receded slowly against it. "If we don't have no trouble, it should all work out just right." He couldn't seem to stay sitting down to eat, but kept standing up, holding his coffee in one hand and his sandwich in the other. Nervous, she knew, anxious, worried about what their calf crop would bring tomorrow morning in the sale ring. She ate silently and so did the boys, from experience, knowing it was best, to avoid sudden bursts of temper on such a day, for which he would be sorry the next day. She didn't really blame him, that sale represented their only income for the entire year, everything depended on it, it was no wonder his nerves were stretched taut.

When they had finished, the three men went to the corral while she gathered the remainder of the lunch as quickly as she could and set it back in the truck. Then she hurried over to the corral.

"You take the heifers," Kent shouted to her. "Jason can take the steer calves." He pointed to the pen he wanted her to use, then showed Jason where he was to work. Mark stood behind him, swinging his arms to keep warm while he waited. Selena nodded without trying to answer him against the wind and the bawling of the cows, went to the pen he had pointed out, and positioned herself behind the gate, which opened inward. Jason stood behind the gate in the pen next to her, bending to watch Kent and Mark from between the slabs that formed the gate.

She zipped her jacket up as high as the zipper would go, then, holding her gloves under her arm, fumbled with the knot of her silk scarf, tightening it. Pellets of snow hit her bare hands, stinging. It was not so bad when she was working, she usually got too hot, in fact, with the anxiety and the running around, but as soon as she stood still, she always got cold.

More than any other month she hated November, before the bare, hard ground had a covering of snow. It seemed to her the coldest month, the ground, the trees, were bare and frozen, nothing looked nice, even the cow pies in the corral were as hard as rocks, so that if you tripped on one you could break your leg or throw out your knee.

Kent was shouting instructions now to Mark as the two of them moved into position on foot among the calves.

"Call out what you've got," Selena heard him shout. Mark nodded, not taking his eyes off the calves milling around him, and Selena slid back the board that formed the latch on her gate. She turned to Jason, who was still leaning forward, watching.

"Jason" she was anxious he should be ready and not make any mistakes, so that neither Kent nor Mark would yell at him, "Watch!"

"I'm ready," he said, both hands on his gate, crouching to watch between the planks.

"Heifer!" Mark called, and Kent repeated the cry as he turned the calf Mark had started toward her. Quickly she swung her gate open wide to let the little calf trot through, and then shut it, quick, before any of the others following it could sneak in behind the first. She had to concentrate to hear Mark and Kent's shouts over the wind, the mooing of the cows in the fields around her, and the bleating of the calves in front of her.

"Heifers!"

"Steers!" The shouts went on, and she and Jason opened and shut their gates rapidly, trying not to let those they had already corralled escape out the open gate, carefully cutting back any calves that followed the one they were trying to corral, watching all the while to avoid being kicked. Selena had begun to sweat, and she let the zipper on her jacket down a few inches and took a crumbling tissue out of her pocket to blow her nose.

I'm selling records in a big record store now, working days again and trying to adjust to the change in hours, and with it, to the change in my visible world. It really is like night and day—that's a joke, Selena. I see some of the night people in here, the punkers with their turquoise and pink hair, and chains, and sometimes people I know must be musicians, but a lot of them are normal, ordinary city kids. All fashionable and trendy in their baggy, rumpled clothes, but just kids really, like we were, only richer, and not so grown up, I don't think. I had to lie to get the job. Did I know pop music? Who was this group and that? But I boned up ahead of time—you'd be surprised how smart I'm discovering I am, and I'm learning how to fake it, how to sort of bluff people out. It's a city pastime and I get a kick out of it. The trick is to know when you're doing it and to remember that you are. To remember the difference. Oh, I'm learning all sorts of things and it's wonderful.

In a lull when Kent mounted to ride to the far end of the corral to chase up a stubborn bunch of frightened little animals, Selena thought about the house, where a welcome stream of smoke would be rising into the grey, winter sky. She thought of Phoebe inside, the kitchen clean by now, a roast in the oven for their dinner, the house warm and comfortable, cozy even, in contrast to the harsh day outside.

But she had never been one of those women afraid of the outdoors, hating the work in the corrals and the yard, and neither had Phoebe been, at least not as far as she could tell. Selena had always welcomed the chance to be outside, loved that moment when she opened her kitchen door on the clean, strong outdoor air, was always glad to leave the stuffy house for the sense of freedom and power, yes, that's what it was, the sense of power to be found outside.

But now Phoebe would be learning how it was to stay inside, learning to draw in her expectations of the day, learning about that inward world bounded by the four walls, the roof, and the floor. How the smell and the texture of the house became a part of you—you knew the way the nap fell on the rug if you vacuumed it, or if you rubbed it with the palm of your hand, or if you stepped on it with your shoe or with your slipper; the feel of the kitchen floor under your hand when you washed it. She would be getting to know the minute scratches in the stainless steel of the kitchen sink, the patterns of the counter tops, like confetti, and of the tabletop's gold flecks, and the way the dust gathered in the corner by the door in the kitchen, nearly under the old, wide baseboards, and in the corners of the steps going upstairs, the smudges always coming at a certain spot on the polished door of the fridge, around the light switches, by the doorhandles.

She wondered what the house looked like to Kent. Vague, she supposed, shadowy. If you moved a chair that had always stood in one spot, he asked you if it was new. No wonder they didn't see eye to eye. They weren't even seeing the same things.

"Steer!" Mark shouted, and Kent's cutting horse swerved sharply, then swung its front legs back again, pivoting on its rear legs, to cut off a calf that was trying to double back. Jason swung open his gate and shut it again, fast, catching the last calf by one leg, and quickly releasing it. The calves in Selena's pen milled and cried, bleating for their lost mothers, and the cows in the field behind them bellowed frantically in reply, and ran along the fence nearest their calves, bumping it with their heavy bodies and making it shake.

It was better not to think about it. We have to eat, she reminded herself. We're cattle ranchers, we raise cattle, that's how we make our living. If we didn't do it, somebody else would. And at least here the cows are free to move around and graze on the open range. They aren't prisoners in those terrible feedlots, confined in a few square feet with dozens of other cows, standing knee-deep in their own shit all their lives. They don't even know what grazing is. She glanced down at the calves, then hastily opened her gate to let a bawling heifer through. But I suppose it really isn't right, she thought. None of it, but I mustn't think about that. Her cheeks were burning with the wind now, and she blew her nose again.

They were just finishing up when she happened to look out across the main corral and saw Tony. He was leaning on the railing, watching them.

Her first reaction was to look for Diane, but then she saw his empty half-ton parked along the fence. She knew by it, and by the farm clothes he was wearing, as well as by the casual way he leaned on the corral with his hands in his pockets, that Diane hadn't come. Whenever Diane was nearby there was a kind of tension in him, an eagerness that she had never exactly identified before, although she must have always known it was there. Wondering, she climbed the fence instead of opening the gate and risking the loss of a calf or two, and hurried across the corral toward him.

"Tony!" She hugged him, clumsy in her heavy clothes, and stepped back while he smiled down at her, then pointed out to the east toward the fireguard that served as a road. Puzzled, she followed his hand and saw the two big cattle liners, raising dust even though it was November, slowing on a curve coming down a distant hill, heading toward the corrals. Mark and Jason were coming now, and out of the corner of her eyes, Selena saw Kent leading his horse out of the corral.

"I'll help you load," Tony said, and hugged Jason roughly, slapping his shoulder, then putting his other arm out toward Mark, who stood grinning at him.

"Di not with you?" she asked, and when he didn't answer her, watching first the liners that were rolling heavily up the fireguard to the corrals, and then Kent, who was coming from the corner of the main corral toward him, she added, "I guess they won't need me to help load."

Then Kent had come up, was shaking hands with Tony, and all of them were moving aside and opening the main gate so that the first cattle liner could back in to take the first load at the loading chute on the other side of the corral.

Kent came up to her where she was leaning against the half-ton and said, "You might as well wait in the truck. There's six of us to load, we don't need you. After, I'm gonna run home and change my shirt and my hat before I follow the liners to town. You can get a ride back with me." She nodded, and climbed gratefully into the relative warmth of the truck cab. Her legs were aching from being on her feet since five-thirty that morning, and she was sleepy from the wind. She stretched them out and rested her head in the corner between the seat and the door, and for the first time that day, allowed herself to relax. Protected from the steady roar of the wind, the clamour of the cows and calves, the throbbing rumble of the cattle-liners' big motors, it seemed quiet in the cab, and she grew drowsy, and drifted off into a light sleep.

Before she knew it Kent was opening the door, waking her without even noticing it, and the two cattle liners were pulling out, roaring slowly down the trail. She sat up and moved over.

"What's going on?"

"I left the boys to load the stock trailer. They'll bring it home right away. And Tony's following in his truck." She and Kent and Tony would be in the yard in twenty minutes, but it would take the boys, going as slowly as they'd have to on that trail, about an hour to get home, and the cattle liners would have to travel even more slowly until they got onto a proper road. She'd have lots of time to get dinner on the table, and Kent could easily catch up to his calves before they arrived at the stockyards in town. Things had worked out all right—except for the price the calves would bring the next morning. Well, they couldn't do anything about that.

They arrived in the yard with Tony right behind them, and as soon as the truck rolled to a stop, Selena jumped out and hurried into the house. Phoebe stood at the sink peeling potatoes, wearing one of Mark's shirts that he had outgrown and the new maternity slacks Selena had helped her sew. If Phoebe wanted to, she had only to raise her head from the potatoes to see that they were finished with the cutting, that Tony had come, that the liners must have come and gone, that Selena had hurried across the yard to the kitchen. Tony and Kent would be having a conversation by the trucks. But she didn't, and Selena, watching her back as she methodically peeled potato after potato, paused, then unknotted her scarf with stiff, cold fingers, took it off, took off her jacket and sat down to pull off her boots.

"Tony's here," she said.

Phoebe said, "Mmmm."

The warm air in the kitchen was making Selena's nose run. She dug into her jeans pocket, found a tissue, and blew into it. The clock above the table ticked on, interrupted only by a gush of water from the tap as Phoebe turned it on to rinse a potato, then turned it off again. "He didn't bring Diane," she said.

Phoebe began to cut the potatoes and drop them into the pot. They thudded dully against each other and the sides of the pot.

Selena sat, sniffing, feeling herself not yet a part of the kitchen, her reddened hands resting on her knees, knowing she should rise, check the roast in the oven, start the salad, peel the carrots, set the table. Out in the yard the men would be leaning against the truck, talking, and far away the boys were inching the trailer and the horses slowly home. She was paralyzed, wanting neither the outdoors, nor the house, wanting suddenly, like Diane, to get in the car and drive away.

Away to where? To do what?

Phoebe was filling the pot with water. When it was full and she had set it on the stove and turned on the burner, she glanced over her shoulder at her mother. Selena shifted her gaze from the space where she had been looking at nothing, and met Phoebe's eyes unexpectedly.

Phoebe had all but stopped speaking. She nodded, she shook her head, she responded by doing or by walking away. Sometimes she murmured a 'yes' or a 'no,' or something that sounded like 'okay.' She did all this without a hint of shame n her manner, without a touch of humility, without anything resembling shyness. She would look directly at the person speaking to her. The intensity of her gaze would silence the questioner, make him drop his eyes, wonder at her. Selena couldn't understand this, she felt helpless against it, and yet somehow she found it reassuring. But in this instant, as Phoebe's eyes met hers in that disconcerting way, Selena dropped her eyes in confusion. It was almost as though there was some judgement there.

She jumped up and went to the stove, opening the oven door just as the kitchen door opened and Kent and Tony entered.

"Brr! It's cold out there!" Kent said, holding the door open to let Tony come in. The window above the sink rapidly steamed over with the rush of cold air that swept through the room. As Kent took off his cap and hung it up, she saw Tony look at Phoebe. Surprise crossed his face, then something that must have been embarrassment, followed by a quick side glance at Kent, who didn't seem to have noticed anything. "I gotta put on a clean shirt and follow the liners," Kent said. "I'll have to eat when I get back, or in town." Tony started to take off his cap and jacket.

"Are you going to stay? Or go with Kent?" Selena asked.

"Oh," he said, turning back to her, "I guess I'd better stay. I've got quite a bit to do today." He didn't meet her eyes. Kent had brushed past them and was taking the stairs two at a time. "How you doing, Phoebe?" Tony asked, pulling out a chair and sitting down.

"She's fine," Selena said. "Aren't you?"

Phoebe turned slowly from the sink and looked directly at Tony, her eyes seeking and meeting his. He looked back at her steadily, without flinching. After a second, she said, "I'm glad you're here," and then quietly left the room to go upstairs. Kent came back down again, still buttoning his clean shirt and reaching for his jacket and his good hat.

Sorry, I gotta run," he said to Tony. "I'll drop over tonight, if you're there."

"Sure," Tony said. "Maybe I'll see you at the calf sale in the morning." Kent put his hat on and hurried out. In a second they could hear the truck start and then roll out of the yard.

"The boys won't be here for another half hour or so," Selena said. The pots on the stove had begun to hiss softly. She sat down at the table in Kent's place.

"What brings you here?" she asked.

"Oh, business," he said.

"Have you got a buyer for the farm?"

"No," he said, "no buyer." He sighed, then said, "I decided not to sell." Selena was stunned by this, couldn't even think what to say. As if remembering something, Tony said, suddenly, "What happened . . . with Phoebe?" She was startled again. and he said, quickly, "I suppose it's Brian's?"

"He ran out on her," she said. Tony stared at her, his cheeks growing red. "Where is he?"

"Oklahoma," she replied. "He sent his mother a postcard."

"I could go after him," he offered suddenly. "I'm not too busy right now." Selena heard a touch of bitterness in his voice and her dread grew. The middle of the week, no Diane, no kids.

"No," she said, almost absent-mindedly. "Phoebe won't marry him anyway."

"Why not?" he asked, surprised. "Too much pride, after he ran out?" Selena hesitated.

"He forced her, she says," Selena said it slowly. Tony was after all, a man. He stared at her, puzzled, then something crept into his eyes, and the muscles of his face tensed. He swallowed, and she could see in the way his eyes shifted to the clock that he was trying to understand this. Selena found herself embarrassed. She had never spoken about such things with any man but Kent.

"How did Kent take it?" Tony asked.

"Not very well." She was surprised to find tears still so close. "But he knew when he was licked, he didn't even try to find Brian. But he wouldn't let her have an abortion, either." She threw her hands out, looking at him. "So here we are." Tony didn't say anything for a long time and neither did she.

At last he said, "I'm sorry to bring you more bad news." She forgot Phoebe and raised her head to look at him, hardly daring to breathe.

"Where is she?" she whispered.

"In the city." He took a deep breath, sat back from the table, and lifted his hands from beside the plate to place them on his lap. "She moved to an apartment last weekend. I quit my job. We're . . . we've separated."

Selena gasped, then thought, I knew it. I knew it all along.

"How will she manage without you," she said, not even asking a question. The expression on his face was puzzled, faintly surprised. He leaned forward and rested his elbows on the table.

"I couldn't stand it, Selena," he said, and she was surprised to hear him say her name. "When I thought of all the rest of my working years like that. I couldn't stand it. And she wouldn't come back with me."

Something has happened here. Something big. It feels like I've lost the bones that kept my brains packed tight inside my head. It feels like the world has changed, or that without those bones that made my head a prison, I'm freed to walk out in the world—this terrifying, wonderful world—for the

first time in my life. It feels like I'm walking out in it even
when my body is motionless, even when I'm in bed at night,
or sitting in the classroom, or feeding the kids breakfast.

"She wrote to me," Selena said. "Her letter scared me." Tony went on
talking as if she hadn't said anything.

"She changed to a day job. She's working as a clerk in a record store
now and still taking classes at night. I thought she might drop them when
she found out how hard it would be to work and run the house and
everything, but no. Cathy is in daycare and Tammy's in school and then
she goes to our neighbour's till one of us gets home from work."

"What can she be thinking of?" Selena cried, clasping her hands against
her chest. "You're a good husband! You love the kids! You love her!"

"Take it easy, Selena Tony said, alarmed.

"But to break up your home just to sell records! I'm sorry, Tony. I'm
so sorry." She had begun to cry. She lifted one hand and placed it over
her eyes, resting her elbow on the table by her plate.

"It isn't your fault," Tony said, surprised. "You did your best for her.
It's got nothing to do with you. She's grown-up." He pushed his plate
back angrily. "Something just got into her. I don't know what."

How can I tell you about this. How can I tell you that I see
my life now like a burgeoning bush, that's what it's like. For
the first time in my life I see that life is like a growing plant,
it just gets bigger and bushier, it blossoms, Selena, if you let
it, and there's no end to its richness and its beauty . . . or
maybe I'm talking about something else. Maybe I'm talking
about the human soul let out into the open . . .

"I'll go to her," Selena said, putting her hand down. "I'll talk to her."

"No," Tony said, gently. "It's no use, believe me, Selena, it's no use."

"But the kids . . ." Selena began. "I'll do whatever I can," Tony said,
his voice harsh, then more tenderly, "whatever she'll let me do."

I see now that we raise our children the wrong way, the girl children especially. We mother them too much, we try to protect them too much and in the end all we do is make them afraid of the world. We teach them to be slaves, Selena. That's what we do. I won't let that happen to my daughters. My daughters will grow up strong and fearless, not like you and me.

"Is she having a breakdown?" Selena asked. "Do you think she's maybe having a breakdown? Is that what's wrong?" Tony shrugged.

"The funny thing is," he said, "it seems to me that she's getting stronger, not weaker. She's sort of focused, like she's never been before. You know how she was always tense and reckless, bouncing around from one thing to another, never satisfied." He stared at the kitchen window, watching the small, hard flakes of snow whip past it. They were bigger now than they had been when she came inside, and they were coming down more thickly. It was beginning to look like the first blizzard of the season.

It seemed now to Selena, watching the wind-driven snow whirl past the window, that all the light was dying, that the snow would come and bury them all. Phoebe, pregnant, silent, piercing them each with that burning look of hers, as if the old Phoebe had died or gone away forever; Diane gone mad; the little girls sentenced to suffering because they were too young to speak; her own sons turning away from her as they grew up, as if she were the enemy.

"Hey," Tony said, touching her arm and then withdrawing his hand. "You take things too hard, Selena. I came to tell you—I had to do that— but it's not the end of the world. I'll visit them often. I'll bring the kids here whenever she'll let me. I'll keep a close eye on things."

Selena broke her gaze away from the snow whirling past the window. How handsome he is, she thought. How kind. A really kind man. No wonder Diane fell so hard in love with him. I could love him myself . . . and stopped herself, shocked. Since she had married Kent she had never looked at another man in that way. It hadn't even occurred to her that she might do that. Why would she want to? Tony looked steadily back at her and it was all she could do to stop herself from putting one hand gently on each side of his face, leaning forward slowly, putting her mouth on his . . . she pushed herself back against her chair, reached out and put her hand on his arm. "I'm so sorry," she said. They sat like that for a moment, before he pulled his arm away and patted her hand.

"I've got to go and open the old house," he said. "Get some heat on in it so I don't freeze to death tonight." He got up slowly, pushing his chair in to the table carefully.

"But, why don't you just stay there with her? Look after the kids? There's no farming to be done now, anyway." He was standing with his back to her, reaching for his jacket, putting it on. She could hardly hear his answer.

"Because she doesn't want me there. She doesn't want to be married." This, too, felt like a blow.

"But . . . you love her . . ." she cried again. He had turned toward her and pulled up the zipper on his jacket so rapidly that the hissing sound was louder than the pots on the stove.

"And she loves me," he said, and went outside into the cold and the snow, shutting the door quietly, but firmly, behind him.

> Although I know it doesn't sound like it, I think of you often, every day, in fact. I think of how you and Phoebe and Rhea and me, and Tamara and Catherine are the women of our family. I think about our lives. How you have chosen to go on in the old way, leading a life not much different than the one our ancestors led, all the way back to primitive people— raising children, looking after the food, and the needs of your man. How Phoebe will do the same. It doesn't seem wrong to me, either, just—incomplete, I guess, with the world so large and full, and paradoxical. I don't understand it.

Selena sat there, staring at the clean dishes on the table. She remembered now what she had deliberately forgotten. How when she had been waiting in the truck, before she fell asleep, she had been listening to the cows standing around the corrals in clusters, bawling their loss into the driving wind. After a while it seemed to her that she could hear one cow's voice over the others. The cow wailed again, a long, drawn-out cry. She had heard the anguish in its voice, as if it were a human voice, a human mother crying for its lost, dead child, and for the first time in all her years on the ranch, all the years that she had been listening to the animals, she had heard the sound. Horrified, she had raised her hands and covered her ears.

THE WINTER SOLSTICE

They set out at first light when there were still long blue shadows across the glistening, crusted snow and the distant hills were purple with shadows, the sky streaked with grey-mauve and a dull, sad pink. Selena drove the four-wheel drive loaded with square hay bales, while ahead of her, Mark, Kent and Jason each sat on horseback, trotting through the frost-filled, sparkling air.

Every year they walked the same tightrope—let the cattle graze as long as possible in the fall pasture in order to save as much as they could on their never adequate feed supply, but get them home to shelter before the winter storms would make it impossible to get feed to them. That critical moment had come; the snow cover was too deep for grazing, the grass was all gone anyway, and one more storm would prevent them from reaching them to bring them home. Ten below or not, they had no choice now but to start home with them in this lull between storms, before they starved or froze.

Ever since Kent had been granted a government lease on this section of grazing land, maybe fifteen years before, Selena had driven the truck when they trailed the cattle home. Every winter since Phoebe was born until Jason was seven or eight, she had had at least one child riding in the cab with her, and for a couple of years, she had had all three of them. The worst had been those years when Phoebe was five and six, too young to ride a horse that distance, Mark was two and three, and Jason an infant, and she had had to change diapers on two of them. They had climbed all over the cab, they had fought, and cried and slept and been sick, and begged to get out to play in the snow. She had driven like that through blizzards where she could barely see the hood of the truck and Kent had had to ride ahead of her to show her the way, through mud once, and more often, through the long, bright winter days when the snow-covered pastures and fields seemed to roll out forever, gleaming into dreams. It had not occurred to either of them to leave the children behind with a relative or a neighbour. This was the way things were done, they were a family, the ranch was a family ranch, the children included. If it was hard for Selena, it didn't occur to her to complain or to refuse. This was what it meant to be a rancher's wife, this was her lot. And one by one her children had gotten old enough to ride with their father, and had left her. She found she missed having someone riding beside her in the cab.

The terrain they were travelling through was a region of low, sloping hills, monotonously repeating themselves over and over again, some a little higher, some a little lower, with frequent rough, dry slough bottoms in the basins between them. There were no landmarks, no way to tell where you were except from a hilltop where black dots in the distance marked somebody's farm, or a faint fenceline could be used for orientation. And the sun. There was always the sun to keep them moving in roughly the right direction.

Nobody lived out here. For thirty miles west of the ranchhouse there was only mile after mile of grazing land, native grass or seeded grass, all of it belonging to the government, some leased out to individual ranchers, most of it forming a community grazing pasture. It would be easy to get lost out here, hard to find help, impossible to find shelter.

Occasionally Kent would turn in his saddle and point to a spot in the snow. She would drive the truck there, avoiding whatever he had seen that she couldn't see through the windshield—a snow-filled burnout maybe, or a rock hidden in the snow. She watched him slowly disappear from view down an incline till even his head was below her line of sight, and where he had been was only a grey melting-together of slope and hill. Jason followed him, and then Mark, till she was alone in the snow, inching forward, lurching over bumps, dipping into hollows and grinding slowly out again. She tried to follow the tracks of their horses, but the snow-covered earth blended into the grey, sunless sky making them hard to see. In a moment, having mistaken a shadow for their tracks, she found herself in deep snow, the truck roaring as she gassed it, but not pulling itself forward.

How many times over the years had this happened? Still, she couldn't quite control her panic. She pulled off her mitts, throwing them on the seat beside her, and using both hands and all her strength, managed to shift into reverse. She touched the gas gently, working the clutch, and the truck moved slowly backward a few inches before the wheels began to spin. She pressed a little harder on the gas, hoping it would take only a little more power to get her out, but no, she was only digging herself in deeper. She eased up on the gas, shifted into neutral, closed her eyes, took a deep breath then opened them again.

She would try rocking. If she got stuck too deeply, one of the boys or Kent would have to ride all the way back home for a tractor to pull her out. That would mean a delay of a couple of hours and Kent would be furious, although as usual, he wouldn't say much. She had to get herself out.

She put in the clutch again, feeding a little gas, and the truck rolled forward a couple of inches. Quickly she let it out, and the truck rolled back. Then she put it in again and gassed it so that it rolled forward. She repeated this several times, till, with rocking back and forth, it began to gain momentum, and at the right moment, rolling backward in reverse, she gassed it, and it gathered enough traction and power to roll right out of the depression it was stuck in.

Breathing deeply, working hard in her heavy clothes— the truck had neither power steering nor power brakes—she shifted back into low, cranked the steering wheel around, and moved forward to the right of where she had just been stuck, into the horses' trail.

Kent was riding uphill toward her as she pulled over the crest of the hill and started down. When he saw her coming, he turned his horse back again in the direction he had been going. Triumphant, but careful not to show it, although nobody was there to see, she inched her way down the slope. The riders moved on, often cutting cross-country where she couldn't follow in the truck, so that she had to loop around, finding her own way, to catch up with them.

Surprisingly, after such a dry summer, there had been an unusual amount of snow. She had made this trip many times when there was only the thinnest covering, barely enough, in fact, to provide moisture for the cows once the waterholes froze over, and no cover for the rabbits and other small animals. But this year it had begun to snow in November and had snowed day after day through the next five or six weeks, till now the banks were often knee-deep on the level and much deeper in the hollows. If a wind hadn't come up a few days before and swept away quite a bit of the snow, it would have been touch-and-go just to make it the fifteen miles out to the cattle.

Selena drove on, finding her way from experience, or sometimes with Kent's help, moving deeper and deeper into the hills. Sometimes she forgot where she was and what she was doing, the outer part of her mind watching the terrain and handling the truck, while the rest of her mind retreated into an inner world where she moved through the days of her life and the lives of her children.

Phoebe, five months pregnant now, her pretty, young girl's body turned bulky, slow and ugly, her plump child's face a jarring note over that woman's body. It hurt Selena just to look at her, but she made herself, she would be the last one to avoid looking at Phoebe. She drove on, peering out the windshield, which the heater was barely keeping free of ice, to the grey, freezing day outside, feeling it creep inside her, filling her with gloom.

It didn't seem possible that there would ever be an end to Phoebe's pregnancy. She couldn't even imagine such a time, and she knew that Phoebe couldn't either. Something in Phoebe's gaze spoke to Selena of a determination, a holding-on that did not dare to look beyond this time.

Phoebe had refused to marry Brian when that seemed a possibility, she had refused to have an abortion, she would not even listen to Kent when he suggested giving the baby up to be adopted. Selena thought, wondering even as she thought it, perhaps she has accepted her motherhood. She manoeuvered the heavy, unresponsive truck over the rough terrain, the distant hills growing closer, the three riders spread out, moving at a trot in front of her, dreaming on their horses, passing through the freezing day.

No, she replied to herself, it isn't that Phoebe has accepted her motherhood. Phoebe doesn't know anything about motherhood, doesn't really understand that what is growing inside her is a child, a human being. That will only come when she actually sees the baby.

No, what Phoebe was contemplating was something else. It was her womanhood, into which she had been dragged too soon, before she was ready. That was why her eyes had grown so dark, her gaze had become so penetrating. She was trying to understand what it meant to be a woman. Because, Selena suddenly thought, what did I teach her about being a woman? Dances and fowl suppers and showers and anniversary celebrations, making pickles, sewing a dress, combing out her long, bright hair.

She thought of Phoebe's first menstruation. She had told Phoebe, it's nothing, you'll never even notice it, just be careful you don't get blood on your clothes so nobody will know. And remember, you're a woman now, this means you can have babies. Phoebe had looked up at her, her eyes filled with questions, and when Selena had not known what else to say, she had simply looked away and they had not talked about it again.

How she wished she had said more. Her chest ached with all the unsaid words, with all the silences of womanhood, all the things she hadn't even the words for, nor had her mother, or, she supposed, her mother before that. You're a woman now, whatever that meant. Each of them left alone to brood over what it meant—having sex, the babies coming, the end of the bleeding, old age, and which of them knew, even then, what it meant to be a woman?

The truck lurched, the steering wheel pulling out of her grip to the right, the load swaying. For a second she was bewildered, then realized that she had driven over a rock buried in the snow, with the left front tire, and she struggled to turn the wheel to keep from going over it with the back tire too, where it would almost certainly loosen her load. When she was clear of it and on a level spot, she stopped the truck and clambered out, awkward in her parka and ski pants, and waded around the vehicle to see if any of the load of bales she was carrying, which were stacked higher than the truck cab and tied on with a couple of ropes, were loosening or falling off. Some of it they would feed to the cattle before they chased them home, and some she would need as a lure. It was important not to lose any of it. When she saw that it was all still secure, she got back in and drove on.

It was ten o'clock now, but instead of warming, the day was growing colder. Realizing this, she stepped on the gas, risking losing the load, and caught up with the riders. Rolling down the window, she called out to Kent, "Does anybody want to get in and warm up? I can ride for a bit." Kent drew his horse to a stop and looked steadily, first at Mark, and then at Jason, who had stopped too. In this cold, his eyes and the lines of his face had deepened. He said brusquely, "Jason, are you cold?" Jason promptly shook his head no, but they could see that his nose was dangerously white-tipped.

"You drive for a while," Kent said to him. Reluctantly Jason dismounted, handed his reins to Kent and put his hand on the driver's door to get into the truck. Selena reached for her scarf. "No," Kent said, "don't bother. I'll just lead him." Before she could reply, he had ridden away, leading Jason's horse. She slid over and let Jason get into the driver's seat. She wondered why Kent didn't want her to ride, and then realized that he was worried about the weather, and anxious to arrive at the lease so they could start back right away. He was too impatient to wait for her to put on her scarf and mount the horse.

"Are you cold?" she asked Jason, knowing whether he was or not, he would deny it. They all did, even if they were half-frozen.

"Nope," Jason said, sniffing, and throwing his mitts onto the seat between them. He had trouble shifting into low and she helped him, knowing that he didn't want her to, but doing it anyway. Both boys had to be better than she was at things she had been doing since before they were born. Sometimes it annoyed her, but mostly she accepted it. They had to do that to grow up, to be able to think of themselves as men. Phoebe she could teach. Phoebe expected her to be better at all the household tasks, Phoebe expected to learn from her. Boys seemed to be born with a sense of superiority. She wondered where it came from. Well, men are valuable out here, she thought; they can do all sorts of necessary things that women can't do, because they aren't strong enough. It's no wonder boys feel more important than the girls do, and that they grow up thinking they're better than women. She drove on, rocking across the prairie, lumbering up hills and down again.

Before noon they had arrived at the lease. As soon as the cattle, which had been scattered out all over the section searching for food, heard the truck motor, then came on the run, bellowing, their bags swinging, their backs crusted with snow. Selena hated to look at them, suffering as they were from the cold. At least we've brought them food, she thought, and they'll be home tonight, where there's shelter.

Kent and Mark dismounted and tied the three horses to the fence, scattering a little hay on the snow from a bale Kent broke, then came over to the truck.

"We'll throw 'em a little feed," Kent said through the open window, "then we'll eat while they're cleaning it up."

Jason rolled the window back up and began to watch in the rearview mirror. Watching in her mirror, Selena saw Kent climbing up on the load on her side and knew Mark would be climbing up on the other side. Jason put the truck into gear and began to inch it forward, watching carefully so as not to hit any rocks or holes that would rock the load and knock Kent or Mark off onto the ground. She had so much more experience, she wished she were driving, but she said nothing. Jason has to learn and there was only one way to do that. But, she couldn't help thinking, I like doing this, I'm good at it, and I never get a chance anymore. Somehow, that didn't seem right. She thought of all the outdoor work she had done for years. As her sons grew, they had taken over more and more of it as their birthright, so that she rarely got to do any of it anymore, and was increasingly—while hiding, not even acknowledging her resentment— being forced to stay inside. It isn't really right, she thought again, remembering the early days of her marriage, when she had worked alongside Kent each day, to shut women up in the house that way. Not when she loved being outside. But it was the same in most of the families, and she knew lots of the women preferred staying indoors, were glad when their sons grew up and could take over the outside jobs. And she wasn't one to hold her sons back.

Jason drove slowly down a curving stretch of fairly flat land while the two on the back tossed off chunks of bales onto the snow. The cattle came running, bawling, and ate it almost as fast as it landed.

When they were finished, all of them managed to squeeze into the cab to drink the first thermos of coffee and eat the sandwiches and cake she had packed. Kent took a flask of rye from under the seat and poured a small amount into each of their cups.

"Keeps you warm," he remarked, without looking at any of them, but Selena could feel Jason's pleasure since it was the first time he had been given any.

They ate without talking, squeezed in together, glad of the warmth, the truck windows fogging up from their breath so they couldn't see outside. They were packed in so tightly they could hardly lift their arms to eat.

"I thought they looked a little ganted up," Selena said.

"It's damn cold," Kent said. "I don't like the looks of that sky." He chewed his sandwich thoughtfully, peering out through the patch he had wiped clear on the windshield.

"Temperature's dropping," Mark said. "My toes are telling me that." He laughed in a boisterous way, a little embarrassed at this admission, but knowing that he was older and had proven himself and so could allow himself this, like a man could.

"I'll ride the minute anybody gets cold," Selena said. She added, "As long as the truck runs, nobody needs to freeze." Kent said nothing more, wiping the windshield again to check the cattle and the sky, then leaning back.

"No wind," he said. Nobody responded, chewing soberly, hearing this pronouncement both with gratitude and anxiety, knowing it could start to blow any minute. And that would mean a blizzard with all the new snow lying around. Selena prayed the weather wouldn't get worse.

Jason said, "I don't care if it storms," and Selena, irritated, wished he would get over his adolescent bravado, which she knew only masked fear.

When the cattle had cleaned up the half-load Kent and Mark had thrown to them and were bawling for more and beginning to tear at what was left on the truck, they hurriedly finished their coffee, and Jason, Mark and Kent got out, doing up zippers, flipping up parka hoods, pulling on mitts, and remounted.

"Now, remember," Selena called out the window, "if you get cold, trade with me." None of them replied, their horses turning, their hooves crunching in the snow.

It was her job now to lead the way back to the ranch. The idea was that the hungry cattle would follow her because they could see the hay on the back of the truck and would keep trying to catch up with her to steal some of it. She had to keep just ahead of the cattle so that they couldn't quite touch it, but if they got discouraged and slowed down, she had to stop the truck, break open a bale, and throw a little onto the snow to attract them back to her. In practice, although this worked to some extent, they always had a few old cows in the herd who inevitably took the lead, who knew the way back to the ranch and would have been there before the first storm struck, or shortly after, if there hadn't been fences and closed gates to stop them. They didn't need anybody to lead them. The riders rode behind to prod any slow or sick ones, and on the flanks to keep them together. Later, the cattle would string out and herding them was easier.

With the sky closing in and visibility so poor, she wasn't sure she would be able to find the way through each field. She would follow their tracks where she could see them, but the landmarks she normally used, like the elevators at Mallard ten miles away, had faded into the general gloom and couldn't be seen. If she couldn't tell which way to go anymore, Kent would ride up and give her local landmarks—two hills that made a peculiar silhouette, or a rock that lay along the outline of a distant hill—and if visibility got really bad, he would ride ahead of her and show her the way.

She didn't know why he should always be able to find the way while she couldn't. Maybe he had a better sense of direction, but maybe, too, it was that he felt the responsibility for not getting lost as his, while she had abdicated her responsibility to him, and that was why she could get lost.

She started the truck and drove away, watching through the rearview mirror, stopping, then starting again, till the cows were following her. She drove that way for half a mile or so till she had climbed the first hill and the lead cows were still plodding along toward the hill. At the top, she turned the truck around so that she was facing the herd and could see the riders fanned out at the back. That way she could tell if everything was all right, or if anybody needed her. She climbed out, stiff from sitting so long, and walked around the truck, checking the load and looking off into the blue and purple distance in each direction, as if she expected to see something useful out there. She waited, slapping her hands together for warmth, the motor idling roughly, till the lead cows had almost reached her. When neither Kent nor the boys tried to signal her, she got back in and drove on, picking her way carefully down the slope.

The wind was picking up. Occasionally the gusts were strong enough to pick up the fresh, soft snow on the surface and to blow it along as high as the knees of the horses. Once or twice in the next hour it blew up so high that she had to brake till the gust of snow passed, so that she could see where she was going. Most of the tracks she was trying to follow had already filled, and she had to guess at her direction for long stretches till she found an open place where a few of them had been swept clear by the wind, and she could reorient herself. At every hilltop she stopped, either turned the truck around, or got out and stood watching the herd and the riders spread out behind her. She wanted desperately not to get lost, to find her way on her own, and the fact that Kent hadn't ridden up to her to redirect her was proof she was still going in the right direction.

The cattle had finally begun to string out, settling in for the long, cold walk home, the old cows in the lead. From now on the herding would be easy. The hard part was enduring the cold.

At the top of one of the hills she saw Mark suddenly break away from his father, spurring his horse to a lope, coming toward her. She waited and in a minute he was beside her. Without speaking, he dismounted and handed her his reins. There were white spots along each cheekbone. She refrained from saying anything, knowing he knew they were there. Maybe now, she thought, he'll take a wool scarf when we trade back.

"You can ride for a bit, Mom," he said, as if he were doing her a favour. She almost laughed. Still, cold or not, it was good to get out of the stuffy confinement of the truck. She wrapped her scarf around her parka hood, tying it in the front, then mounted clumsily because Mark's horse was too tall for her and in her winter boots and heavy clothes she felt too weighted-down to spring up onto it. She waited as Mark drove away and the herd passed by her, their heads down, lumbering forward as if she weren't there.

It had gotten colder out, she felt it as soon as she was in the saddle and up higher. The herd moved slowly, heads down, one foot in front of the other, mile after mile. Their backs were humped up from the cold, their normally pink noses bluish, and their hooves cut and bleeding from sinking into the crusted snow. But she worried more now about her family. Cows could survive weather none of them could. When the herd had passed, she turned her horse and moved in to ride at the end of the mile-long line of cattle.

It was the shortest day of the year and already it was growing dark. She searched the heavy sky for the sun and found it, a paler smear behind the clouds, low in the southern sky. A strong gust of wind caught her and she turned her head and huddled down into her collar, blinking to hold back the water that a sudden blast of cold wind always brought to her eyes, and that would freeze on her face. When it had passed, she lifted her head again, then shoved her left hand, mitt and all, into her jacket pocket, holding the reins with her right hand. Only her face and hands were cold, her back was still warm inside her down-filled parka and she hadn't been out long enough for her feet to get cold, although, she thought with a measure of resignation, that would happen soon enough.

Kent rode up beside her and she freed her chin from her scarf to turn her head and smile at him.

"How far are we from home?" she called. He was shrugged down inside his parka, his hood and collar up, the earflaps of his cap down. She thought how he had been out for hours, since the first light, with only the noon break in the truck. She marvelled at his ability to endure the cold, and doubted if she would be able to stand it the way he could. Was he really stronger? she wondered, or was it only that he was more determined, had more at stake than she did. The ends of his silk neckscarf fluttered against his cheek and he brushed them down with his leather mitt. He turned to her and she was startled by the brightness in his eyes. It was his 'winter' look. It meant that things were hard, that he held out no hope for respite, that everything depended on his strength. Sometimes it made her angry.

"I figure maybe seven miles," he said. "It's hard going for them in this deep snow and they're weak from those goddamn storms." His horse swerved, sidestepping something that neither of them saw. "If we don't start making better time," he called, "we'll have to leave them in that coulee bottom on Albert's and go home ourselves. It must be damn near thirty below now."

Thirty below! She had been protected in the truck, had been thinking about other things, and hadn't realized how bad it had become. She had noticed that even with the heater on high she had barely been able to keep the windshield clear, and that the snow had hardened even more, so that the tires wouldn't grip going uphill and squeaked on the dry snow.

"Kent," Selena begged him, knowing it was futile, "trade off with Mark, won't you? He's warm enough to go back out for a while." He turned his head from her so that he was looking straight ahead down the long line of snow-covered, dark red cattle plodding through the crusted, glistening snow which had turned a deep mauve in the dying light, and to the old truck, lumbering along far ahead, a dark spot in the grey light.

"I'm okay," he said, then urged his horse into a slow lope and rode away to her left, toward Jason on the far side of the herd and ahead of them.

Men! she thought, wishing there was a woman there for her to say it to. They can't ever give themselves a break, but even those familiar words brought her little comfort. She changed hands again, this time pushing her right hand into her pocket and holding the reins with her left. She began to rhythmically flex her toes inside her boots, trying to get the circulation moving enough to stop the tingling that had begun in them.

Kent and Jason were riding at a trot now along the far side of the herd, which ignored them, towards the truck. Mark pulled the truck to a stop, and the old cows, which were not far behind, caught up and kept going, ignoring it, too. They wanted to get home, and knew they were almost there.

Selena was greatly relieved to see Jason dismount and climb into the cab. Unless the weather improved—fat chance of that—Jason had ridden as far as he was going to today. One less person to worry about. She only hoped he hadn't frozen his feet or hands. Kent was removing the bridle from Jason's horse, replacing it with the halter Mark handed him through the window. He clipped on the halter shank, mounted holding it, and rode back toward her, leading Jason's horse, while the truck speeded up and was soon in the lead again.

Kent had settled in to ride slowly on the left of the herd ahead of her. After a few minutes, her toes aching with the cold, she dismounted and began to walk in the path made by the cows, leading her horse. She had begun to shiver inside her heavy clothes, but she wasn't worried, knowing she would soon warm up with the effort of walking. The trick was to not start sweating, because then you'd never get warm.

It must be at least four o'clock, she thought, judging by the light. That meant at this time of year there was only about an hour of good light left. By six it would be pitch dark and they'd have only the headlights to help them find the way.

Walking like this on uneven ground, stumbling now and then, sinking in up to her knees when she missed the path the cows had made, the occasional gust of wind swirling snow up into her face, she was warming up rapidly. But even with her parka hood pulled up and as far forward as it would go, so that it blocked her side vision, her face was cold, her nose especially, and she didn't know how much more cold she could take. She didn't want to let Kent down, to make him feel that there was nobody he could count on, that he had no help. But, she thought, he thinks that anyway.

It seemed to her that he would never let her share, not really, that in the end, no matter how hard she worked and tried to understand his feelings, he pulled it all in to himself and thought of it as his own—the work, the worry, the ownership, the suffering. She felt helpless whenever she confronted this masculinity in him, and useless, and occasionally a little angry too. All right, she would think, turning bitterly away, when he got that look in his eyes and lifted them over her as if she were no longer there. Let him. When he needed help with a cow in the chute or one that was calving out in the field, or somebody to bale hay, he called on her soon enough.

Behind her, her horse paused, tugging on her arm, and she turned her head, sliding back her hood a little to see what was bothering him.

Nothing. She pulled on the reins till he started moving, then began to walk again.

She lifted her head and saw that Kent had ridden up to the truck again and that Mark had pulled it to one side of the line of cows and was waiting for something. Then Kent rode away and she realized that he had told Mark to spell her off. Mark's man enough to spell *me* off, she thought, but not man enough to take Kent's place. She had to laugh a little to herself, as she made her way to the truck, leading the horse. But she was grateful to get back in and drive. She handed Mark the reins without speaking. He would stay out there till he froze to death and nothing she said would make any difference. It would take Kent to chase him back inside.

Beside her, Jason was close to sleep. He had thrown back his hood and both cheeks were a bright, unnatural red. He kept sniffing.

"Want to drive?" she asked him. He shook his head.

"Naww." He kept moving his feet and she knew that his toes were hurting as the circulation came back. She said nothing. He would have to learn to take it like a man, like I do, she thought, and she laughed at herself again.

Peering through the frosted windshield, trying to find the trail, checking around for the right direction, worrying, she couldn't help but think that it would be nice to live a life where they didn't have to do things like this. Like in the city, she thought, people just catch the bus to work every day, stay inside warm buildings all the time, never really feel the cold, never really have to be afraid of the weather. People in the city have never known what it's like to have that thrill of fear that if you get careless, let your guard down, or have some bad luck like getting caught in an unexpected blizzard, you might actually die, right then and there.

She looked up at the sky again, leaning forward and scraping at the frost high up on the windshield. As high as she was able to see the sky was a deep blue, the indigo of a winter night. They were heading just about straight east. Behind them, she knew, the sky would be lighter toward the horizon. Far ahead of them in the dimness, sat their house and safety. Behind them were twenty or so miles of empty, open prairie, where nobody else lived, or even went very often.

A gust of wind swirled snow over the hood, blocking her vision. It could start to blizzard, she thought—right now—and we'd be caught out here, you can get lost in just minutes in a blizzard, there's nothing out here for landmarks, and it's so damn cold . . .

There it was. That thrill of fear, cutting down her backbone, for an instant stilling her heart, making her cold hands sweat against the steering wheel. She glanced at Jason. He was leaning forward, too.

"I sure hope it don't storm," he said, frowning, and he seemed like her child again, her youngest, her baby.

"It isn't going to storm," she said, her voice confident. "Anyway, we'll be home before we know it." She wondered how far they still had to go.

After a while Kent sent Mark back to the truck and she got out to let him get in. The tip of his nose looked too pale to her, and as he handed her the reins, she saw that he was shivering inside his heavy clothes.

"Quick, get in," she said, fumbling to pull her own mitts back on and to flip her parka hood back up. "Let Jason drive till you get warm." She said this firmly, into the open window, winding her scarf around her hood again. Mark didn't argue. Jason got out and came around to the driver's side while Mark slid over. Selena stood for a moment in the wind, feeling it reach like a knife inside her parka. She was studying Mark. He had bent over in the seat and was stamping his feet, shaking his bluish hands. "Take your boots off," she told him. "Put your feet under Jason, or sit on them. Get them warm."

She was afraid he had gotten too cold, that he wouldn't be able to warm up under these conditions—the drafty truck cab, the uncertain heat from the heater, a long distance to go yet—that he would be sick. Any concern for Jason left her, knowing that his cold was only the kind that strikes children, easily dispelled, leaing behind a pleasurable, sleepy warmth.

"Jason, there's an extra parka behind the seat. Get it out and put it over him." Mark was shaking uncontrollably now. Jason unfastened the latch, pulled the seat forward far enough so that he could reach behind it, and pulled out an old ragged parka of his father's. While Selena watched, beginning to shiver now herself from standing still too long, Jason threw it over Mark, then pulled it up so that it covered him from his knees to his shoulders. Selena was getting too cold to stand still any longer, and there was nothing more she could do anyway. Reluctantly, she struggled up onto Mark's horse.

And that was another thing. It was far too cold for the horses. They were restless, angry, hard to manage. Mark's horse kept stepping away from her as she tried to mount. She looked around for Kent, wanting to say, do something, it's too cold, things are happening, there's danger here. When she had finally settled into the saddle, she turned the horse— who kept tossing his head angrily, his ears back—and started back to the end of the herd. Kent was coming toward her, leading Jason's horse.

"It's only about a half-mile to that coulee of Albert's," he said to her before she could speak. "Can you hold out till then?" Fifteen, twenty minutes. She nodded. The rim of his parka hood was thick with frost and his collar, held tight around his face, had icicles hanging from it. His thin moustache and beard, which he had just begun to grow for protection during the winter, were both ice-covered. The lines in his cheeks and around his eyes had deepened so dramatically that he had taken on an eerie, frightening appearance. She was startled by this, for a second she couldn't find the man she knew, under this steely countenance.

"Are you all right?" she asked him, although these were only words. Their eyes met and then they turned their heads straight ahead again, and began to ride side by side through the gathering darkness, the cattle now only a line of dark spots in front of them, their outlines barely distinguishable from the shadows growing along the snow-covered slopes and valleys.

"I'll take your horse," he said. "You get into the truck." Surprised, she looked at him, pulling the edge of her parka hood back so she could see him.

"No," she said. What could he be thinking of? His hands would freeze, leading two horses. Jason's horse trotted up between them, blowing steamy air through its frosted muzzle. Icicles hung down from its halter and muzzle and she was tempted to lean forward and break them off, but refrained for fear of hurting him.

"Go on," Kent urged her, but she stubbornly shook her head no again. If he can hold out, so can I, she was thinking. I won't let him down.

A few minutes passed and he rode away, to the other side of the long, steadily plodding line of cows. She got down and began to walk again, leading the horse. If she walked on the lee side of him, he took the brunt of the wind and she got a little protection. Trudging along, her hood pulled well around her face, flexing her fingers inside her mitts, not looking up beyond the next footstep, she began to think of Diane. Or rather, she saw Diane in front of her, moving through the city with her brilliant eyes, her face flushed, trailing behind her an abandoned home, a lost husband. Not for Diane this kind of life. Struggling through the elements for a dubious cause. (But if we don't move them, they'll die.) Not for Diane a simple life like this, a life you could see and touch and hold onto. Who knows, Selena thought, pulling her scarf up over her nose, maybe she's right. For at this moment, it seemed to her that this was almost more than anybody ought to have to do.

Still, she had her family with her. This was a joint enterprise, not a fragmented, personal one like Diane's. She couldn't imagine Kent gone all day, doing things she wouldn't even know about, meeting people she would never know, involved in a life completely separate from her now.

No wonder there were so many divorces and broken homes in the city. At least things haven't come to that out here, she thought. At least out here families are still families.

The cold she felt had reached the point where it was merely pain, and it combined with a growing sense of urgency. It was nothing so trivial as a mere desire to run to the truck, get in and get warm. It was some underlying, barely controllable edge of emotion that she didn't dare examine, which she had to keep forcing back so as not to let it take over. She knew what it was: it was a life instinct, they all had it.

Mark had held out as long as he could against his, she admired him for that and was a little in awe of him for what she saw as that masculine thing, whatever it was, taking over in her child, making a man of him. In Kent that control was immovable. He would ride till he fell off his horse, a frozen block of ice, his expression wouldn't even change. Men are like that, she thought again, humbly.

She lifted her head from the footprints she was stumbling through, and looked ahead, surprised to find that she was climbing a hill. She made a mental adjustment, and the walking grew easier. Ten minutes. Five minutes. She wished she had a man's strength. She wished she lived in the city and had an easy life. No, she didn't wish that. At least here you know you are alive, she told herself, and was surprised at this, then, thinking about it, felt the utter, undeniable truth of it settle into her.

But wasn't that exactly what Diane had claimed for her new life in the city? Wasn't that what she had said was wrong with the way she and Kent and their neighbours lived? That it was mindless? Mindless . . . and dull . . . and disconnected from everything that matters. If she weren't so frighteningly cold, she would laugh.

She had been struggling forward, holding her head down like the cattle, watching her feet, when a shout brought her to a stop. She realized then that there had been more than one, and she looked up, startled. Ahead of her, the herd was bunching as it gathered and moved down into Albert's coulee bottom. The truck idled on the edge of the coulee beside them and there was Jason, on the back of the truck, helping his father break bales.

They had made it. They were still about three miles from home and it was almost fully dark, but they had made it to a place where the cattle would be safe for the night, and she could get into the truck. She started to back up to go around the end of the herd as it plodded toward the coulee, the more quickly to get to the truck's warmth, then changed her mind. Kent is still outside, she thought. If he can stay outside all day in this weather, I can stay out a little longer, till the job is done, and so she walked behind the last of the cows and hurried them up, so that they went faster down into the coulee bottom.

With the snow so hard and slippery from the extreme cold, it was impossible to drive the truck down into the coulee bottom to feed the cows in the usual way. They would never get it back up again. She gave the reins to Mark to hold through the open window—he wasn't shivering so hard anymore—and clambered up onto the back of the truck with Jason and Kent. There really wasn't room for the three of them, but it felt good up there, and she began to help them break the bales and throw the chunks over the edge of the coulee down to the starving cattle.

"They'll be only too glad to stay there till morning," Kent said, when they had finished and there was nothing but wisps of hay left on the truck deck. "We'll be back here at first light and bring them the rest of the way home." They got down gratefully out of the wind and Jason got into the truck while Selena stood looking up at Kent.

"You can't lead the horses home," she said. "It's too cold. Why don't you just chase them down into the coulee with the cattle and pick them up in the morning? Then you can ride home with us in the truck."

"No," he said. "They'll only disturb the cows and they need the shelter at home. I can make it home easy in another twenty, thirty minutes." She knew better than to argue with him. She got into the truck on the pasenger side, with Jason in the middle and Mark, who seemed all right now, driving, and waited while Kent unclipped Jason's horse's halter-shank and tied his own horse's tail through the halter and under the chin of Jason's horse, then changed the bridle of Mark's horse for a halter, and fastened the tail of Jason's horse in a knot in Mark's horse's halter, so that the three horses were tied in a string, tails to halters. Then he mounted his own horse, and kicking him hard to get him to go, set out at a lope, the other horses following closely behind.

"Should I go ahead home?" Mark asked her.

"No," she said. "Follow him. You never know."

All the way home in the dark, Kent and the horses throwing unwieldy black, jagged shadows across the headlights, she and the boys kept their eyes on Kent, as if at any moment he might ride out of the sweep of their lights into that awful, frozen blackness.

By the time they drove into the ranchyard, the wind had died, the sky had cleared and the moon risen, showing the familiar buildings in clear, sharp outlines against the sparkling, unbroken field of snow. The silhouette of Phoebe's head appeared at the kitchen window. So she had been worrying about them.

Silently they got out of the truck. The two boys went to the barn to help Kent with their horses and Selena gathered the remains of their lunch and the empty thermoses into her arms and started toward the house.

Her footsteps crackled on the packed snow of the path, and she could hear her own breathing in her ears, sounding ragged and forced in the silence of the winter night. She stopped in the middle of the path and turned slowly in a circle. The stars were brilliant, silver flames in the black night sky behind them. To the north the northern lights filled the sky, an eerie greenish colour waving, fading, growing brighter, dissolving, re-forming, spreading, shrinking.

The lights had gone on in the barn. She thought she could detect the faint smell of roast chicken coming from the house, and imagined the cheery warmth of her kitchen. Yet she felt totally detached from all these small, homely things. We live our little lives down here, she thought, while up there, some mystery that none of us understands, is going on.

Diane's inexplicable selfishness, her private vision that was so incom-prehensible, Phoebe's small tragedy and her struggle to understand what had happened to her, the strangling cosiness of her own family, her own failure to understand anything at all, stood in sharp relief. Yet under the dancing northern lights, the winter stars shining through them with a steady, flashing brilliance, all of this seemed trivial.

Behind her the barn door was being dragged open, screeching on its frozen iron runners. She turned and hurried to the house.

CHRISTMAS

When Tony had phoned yesterday to say that he was going to the city to pick up his family to bring them home for Christmas, Selena had felt a weight lifted from her. She had been worried, imagining her small nieces deprived of a family Christmas for the first time in their lives, imagining Tony spend-ing Christmas with them (since he had refused to go with his parents to his younger sister's in Edmonton), morose and lonely, imagining, with Diane not present, a confusion and sadness thrown over their own celebrations.

When she told Kent about Tony's call, he had laughed, a sort of snort, and said, "That's some separation—she gets to run around doing God-knows-what by herself, and then when she wants him, he comes running."

Selena had replied, "I know it looks that way, Kent, but I don't think that's really how it is." He had only snorted again and gone back to his paperwork. She hadn't even bothered to try to explain.

She knew he didn't want to know differently. He's so simple about things like that, she told herself, but without rancour, even with affection. He can't handle too many shades of meaning. Like he hasn't got the capacity for it. You have to keep things simple for him, so he can understand. And, of course, there were still those moments when she doubted that she was the one who was right.

Now she stood in the doorway to the living room, giving it one last check to make sure there wasn't a speck of dust on the windowsills or the television set, that the few pictures and the curtains were straight, the extra cushions on the couch plumped up and neatly arranged, the undeniably worn-out rug at least spotless and fresh. Mark and Jason were spread-eagled on the rug, their shoes off, propped on their elbows while they watched some loud Christmas special, and Kent, watching too, had stretched out on the couch, shoving all the extra cushions under his head. Phoebe, sitting across from them in the armchair, met Selena's despairing glance and smiled a little, the sight of which gladdened Selena. When the little kids arrive, the neatness won't last five minutes anyway, she thought, and was about to go back to the kitchen.

A commercial came on and Mark rolled onto his side, his long arm stretched out under his head, his hand flat on the floor. His sleeve slid up a fraction of an inch and she saw the fine, light-coloured hair growing on his forearm, and the unexpected width of his hand at the knuckles. His hand was shaped like Kent's, it was a hand she loved. Suddenly she thought, how would that hand, her son's hand, how would it touch a woman? She glanced at Phoebe, but Phoebe was still looking at the tv. She didn't want to think about it. She turned away and went to the kitchen.

She took the eggs and cream from the fridge, lifted her blender out from the cupboard, and set it on the counter. And when she had managed to get Diane on the phone to ask her where she wanted to stay, Diane had laughed that new, breathless, pealing laugh, and had said, your place, Selena dear. So the kids won't be disrupted so much, and they can have Christmas morning with your kids. But . . . Selena had said, dubiously, and Diane had interrupted. Yes, Tony and I will be sleeping together. Selena, embarrassed, hadn't known what to say. We still love each other, Diane had said, gently, into the silence, as if Selena were a child being initiated into adult mysteries.

She broke the eggs into the blender and reached for the sugar canister, hesitating, wondering if Kent had remembered to buy rum for the eggnog she was making, but there it was sitting on the counter in front of her. She had to laugh at herself and her distraction, pausing before she switched on the blender. What else do I need? Vanilla, salt.

She leaned against the counter, staring out the window above the sink, but it was dark outside, and the light from the ceiling cast a reflection against the glass so that instead of seeing the glistening indigo of the snowy yard spread out before her, and the inky, star-sprinkled sky above the silhouette of the old barn, she saw only her own face staring back at her.

Shadowy, vague, almost a silhouette, her long hair hanging loose on her shoulders for once instead of pulled back in a low pony-tail, and the puffed sleeves of the new dress she had made herself standing up pertly against the background of the brightly-lit kitchen. She saw her mouth, the lower lip full and curving, and the eagerness of her expression. I'm not old yet, she told her reflection, pleased, and smiled at herself. The woman in the glass smiled back, slowly, a puzzled look in her eyes, an innocence to the smooth curve of her eyebrowns. Selena frowned then, and looked back to the blender.

But still she didn't press the button. She was listening to the muffled laughter, both mechanical and human, coming from the living room. Had she heard Phoebe laugh too? Kent's deep rumble lay below Jason's childish giggle and Mark's higher-pitched hoot.

In this moment Phoebe's pregnancy no longer seemed a tragedy, a sorrow that they had to learn to bear. Tonight she could believe they would welcome her child among them, a baby, another member for their family. She sniffed, and all the Christmas scents rushed into her nostrils: the spice cookies she and Phoebe had baked, the chocolate in the candy they had made, the mandarin oranges, the mixed alcohol and fruit smell of the Christmas cake, the peppermint in the candy canes she had bought for her nieces, the buttery odour that came from the plate of shortbread sitting on the counter to her right, and who knew what the other smells were? The smell of other Christmases, of gifts and unopened surprises, affection and of hope.

She pushed the button on the blender, reaching with her left hand for the punch bowl that had been her mother's. I'd better use milk, she thought, that cream's too rich.

She felt a rush of cold air and somebody's arms in a scratchy wool coat go around her. She reached to shut off the blender, spun around, and there was Diane, her arms open, smelling of perfume and cosmetics, her long, dark hair gleaming, her red coat blazing with colour. Tony entered the kitchen and Tammy squeezed past him to run to Selena and hug her around the waist. Kent stood behind Tony, holding Cathy in his arms, and then Selena was hugging Diane, kissing Tammy, planting a kiss on Tony's cheek.

The boys squeezed past the men into the kitchen, shaking hands and accepting and giving embarrassed kisses, and there were cries of "Merry Christmas," all around.

"You'd think we'd been gone twenty years!" Diane said, laughing, pushing her hair back from her face. Kent gave Cathy to Selena, who kissed her, while he helped Diane take off her coat.

"Into the living room, boys," he said cheerfully. "There isn't room for everybody in here. I'll pour us some drinks," he said to Tony, who was following the boys.

"Where's Phoebe?" Tammy asked, as Phoebe, having stood aside for the males, came out of the living room and stopped just inside the kitchen doorway. Tammy ran to her, her arms out, and, striking her in the abdomen, bounced back. Diane turned away from Selena and went, without a second's hesitation, straight to Phoebe and put her arms around her. Of course, Selena thought, Tony told her. If only I could have brought myself to tell her.

"Have you eaten?" she asked.

Diane turned back to her, one arm still around Phoebe, and said, "Before we left the city Tony took us out for a meal."

"That was hours ago," Selena said. "You must be starved. Give me a hand here, Phoebe," she said over her shoulder, opening the fridge. She had gone over in her mind at least four times what she would serve them for lunch when they arrived, but found herself confused now anyway.

"Make way," Kent called, coming past Phoebe into the kitchen again. Then, in a rare, joking moment, "Us men are thirsty."

"But I'm making eggnog," Selena protested as he started to open the cupboard door where they kept the bottle of rye.

"Well, hurry up then, Mother," he said, and gave her a light pat on the bottom as he turned. Diane laughed.

"Here," she said, all efficiency, "I'll help Phoebe with the lunch and you finish the eggnog."

It was as if Diane had never left, as if Phoebe was still the innocent and faintly recalcitrant teenager she had been a few months before. While they worked, Selena and Diane talked, the words tumbling out, spilling over each other's voices, while Phoebe worked in silence.

"Where's Kent's mom and dad?"

"They went to Vancouver to spend Christmas with Janice and Bob and the kids. They'll be back for New Year's with us. How's your job?"

"Oh, it's okay. Where's Rhea?"

"She said, 'Spare me the racket, please,'"—they both laughed at this—"She'll be here for Christmas Day. Rhoda and Gus are coming too and bringing Sandy."

"Poor Sandy. Hand me the mustard." Poor Sandy was what everybody said whenever Sandy, Kent's retarded older sister, was mentioned. She lived in a spcial care home in the city, had for more than twenty years, and only came out for the occasional holiday.

"Eggnog's ready," Selena said. She lifted the bowl carefully and made her way slowly into the living room with Diane following with the cups. She set them on the coffee table in front of the men, as Selena, with Kent's help, lowered the big bowl of eggnog beside them. Diane went back to the kitchen and returned with the rum.

"Be sure to dip some out for the kids first," Selena warned Kent. She handed him the ladle. "We'll get the rest of the lunch." Together, she and Diane returned to the kitchen.

Phoebe had filled the last cake plate with Christmas cake, shortbread and candy, and had sat down in a chair that, in the commotion, had been pushed well away from the table. She looked up as they entered.

Diane paused in the doorway and looked at Phoebe as if she were finally seeing her. She looked for a long, searching moment, then moved silently past her and turned to face her, her eyes softening, a different light appearing in them. She went to Phoebe, touched her lightly on the shoulder, then stroked her hair gently back from her face. Selena saw that Diane was no longer wearing her wedding rings.

Phoebe was sitting very still, her plump, short-nailed hands folded quietly on her lap, her head tipped forward.

"Poor Phoebe," Diane said, smoothing Phoebe's fine, light-coloured hair. "I'm so sorry." Still Phoebe didn't speak, only sat without moving, while tears began to trickle down her cheeks. Diane stopped stroking her hair and stood motionless, one hand on Phoebe's shoulder, the other resting on the crown of her head. Selena went to them, put her hand out and rested it on Phoebe's warm, round cheek, feeling Phoebe's tears dampen her palm, feeling Phoebe's sorrow seep into her palm and move in a slow wave into her chest. Her breasts that had nursed three children suddenly began to ache. She thought briefly of Kent's touch on them, so remote from whatever it was she was feeling, thought of nursing each of her babies, how could she have known they would bring her such pain? She thought of the heads of all the people she had comforted, pressing them one by one against her breasts.

Something hung in the air, quivered around them, something powerful, perhaps it was the blending of the emotions each of them was feeling, their mutual sorrow and pain building and rising around them. It overrode the Christmas scents, the Christmas feelings, it overrode family and tradition, place and time, it connected with some current beyond all these things.

Diane lifted her hand from Phoebe's hair and put it around Selena's shoulders, and Phoebe, in an unusual gesture, lifted one of her hands from her lap and took in it her mother's hand that rested against her cheek. They remained this way, a silent circle of women, joined, each to the other.

In the morning as soon as the presents had been opened, the mess cleared away, breakfast cooked and eaten, Kent and Tony drove to Rhea's and brought her back to the house. Then they took all the children except Phoebe outside, where they hitched horses to an old sleigh Kent had restored, and took them for rides.

"Aren't you going to church?" Diane asked, as Selena and Phoebe finished the dishes. She and Rhea sat at opposite ends of the kitchen table.

"No," Selena said, fighting down the uneasy feeling that struck her whenever she thought about church. She hadn't been as faithful about going lately as she used to be. She could sense Diane waiting for an explanation. "Don't ask me to explain," she said finally. "I can't. I just don't like going as much as I used to."

As soon as they had finished tidying the kitchen, stuffed the turkey and put it into the oven, Selena went to the living room and gathered all of Rhea's presents from under the tree. She set them on the kitchen table in front of Rhea. With an air of bemused patience, Rhea unwrapped them one by one and remarked on them. While she sat quietly, they removed her shoes and put her new slippers onto her large, strong feet, they fastened the fine, gold chain around her wrinkled brown neck while they combed out her hair in order to place the shiny new combs in the thick, white tresses, and brushed her neck and wrists with her new cologne.

The three of them worked around her, brushing, arranging, bejewelling and scenting her as if they were her handmaidens. None of them resented this, and Rhea seemed to accept it as if this were the way things should be.

Rhea never brought gifts. This ought to have annoyed or hurt them, but it did not—not even the kids seemed to find this strange. Selena wondered why it should be that they all brought presents for Rhea, which she accepted, albeit with faint amusement rather than gratitude, yet seemed to feel no need to respond in kind. But when she thought about it, Selena realized that if Rhea ever entered the house on Christmas Day, her arms full of brightly-wrapped packages, the whole household would have been uncomfortable and puzzled, it wouldn't seem right at all. It was as if they all knew that Rhea's connection with them had nothing to do with that kind of giving and receiving.

It's because she's had such a hard life, Selena thought, that we treat her like this. It's because she's a pioneer, one of the last living ones, and she's old. But although this was true, it seemed to Selena an explanation that failed to touch on the heart of the matter, although what that might be, she had no idea.

"My goodness," Rhea remarked, her voice wry, "such splendour! I hardly know myself."

"Coffee's ready," Selena said. She poured four cups and they took them into the living room and arranged themselves lazily around the room.

"I don't hear them outside," Diane remarked.

"Kent probably drove them over to Simca's," Selena said. "It's only a couple of miles and it's not a bad day for a drive." Diane sighed.

"What luxury," she said, "not to have to rush around, not to have the kids in my hair."

"Honestly," Selena said, "I don't even know where to start." Diane looked amused.

"I know," she said. "Why did I leave Tony. What do I think I'm doing. Have I lost my mind?" She laughed and looked out past Rhea to the snow-filled front yard where a half-dozen partridges were ambling around on the crust of snow, searching for seeds. "Don't waste your breath, Selena."

"I wasn't going to ask you that," Selena said, hearing the hurt in her voice. But even as she spoke she knew it wasn't true. Of course she had been going to ask that. She had had little else on her mind for days. Some of her optimistic Christmas mood left her now, and her attention reverted to Phoebe sitting silently in Kent's armchair, smoothing her smock over her abdomen.

Instead of replying, Diane turned to Phoebe.

"When are you due?" Phoebe didn't say anything, merely dropped her head so that her neat, straight part revealed the startling whiteness of her scalp.

"She won't say anything," Selena said suddenly, surprising even herself. "I don't know why she won't." Phoebe didn't lift her head. "March," Selena said. "Late March." Diane looked at Rhea.

"Did you consider an abortion?"

Rhea said, "Phoebe knew what she wanted."

"But wouldn't she consider it?" Diane asked, looking again at Phoebe's bent head. At this, Phoebe raised her eyes to look at Diane. For a second it seemed as if she might speak, but instead, she looked away to the wall. Diane looked questioningly at Selena and then at Rhea.

Selena said, "She just wouldn't have it, in the end, although she thought for a while she would. She just . . . refused."

Diane was silent. Then to Phoebe's turned-away head, she asked, "Are you going to give it up?" Phoebe shook her head slowly no. Diane again looked questioningly at Selena, but Selena only shrugged, and sighed.

"We're going to have a grandchild in this house," she said, making her voice light, trying to sound pleased.

"You could come and live with me," Diane offered.

"You've got your hands full," Selena said. "And anyway, I want to look after her. I want her here with me."

Rhea sat, her body turned so that she could look out the window behind her into the front yard. The partridges had disappeared into the carragana hedge.

"Phoebe is trying to understand this in her own way," she said, without turning to look at them. A sparrow came and perched on the windowsill and pecked at the window frame, then flew away, knocking some of the fresh snow off onto the bank under the window.

Across the room from her, Phoebe moved abruptly so that Diane and Selena turned to her. She lifted her head.

"Things have to be complete," she said. "You have to accept what's given to you." Her voice was stronger than it had been months before, deeper, too. Selena's surprise at her speaking was overshadowed by what she was saying. "Rhea helped me." She paused, but before either Diane or Selena could say anything, if they had been going to, she went on. "When that happened to me, it wasn't just my body that changed. Everything changed. The world was different after that. Before, everything seemed bright and filled with hope. But afterward, it all became darker, there were shadows where I hadn't seen any before. I felt as if I had entered a dreamworld. But now I think that what I left behind, that bright world, was the dreamworld, and this one is the real one." She looked at them, one by one, meeting their eyes, but there was no certainty in hers, only that intensity and depth.

They didn't speak. Selena glanced tentatively at Diane. Surely Diane would understand, for wasn't she lost in some vision of her own, too? But Diane was only leaning forward attentively, watching Phoebe, apparently not intending to say anything. She looked then to Rhea.

"Why did you leave Tony?" Rhea asked, and all their eyes went to Diane. Unexpectedly, she blushed. "Was he such a bad husband?" Rhea went on, her voice filled with amusement. She laughed then, the sound girlish amidst the Christmas decorations, the crumpled paper that had been missed in the cleanup sticking out from under the couch, the open boxes turned this way and that under the Christmas tree, the smell of roasting turkey drifting in from the kitchen.

"No, he wasn't a bad husband," Diane said.

"He loves you," Selena said, accusing without really meaning to.

"I know that," Diane said.

"Well," Selena said indignantly. "Is love so easy to come by?" It hurt her to say this.

"Love," Diane said, gently, and gave a little laugh, dismissing it, then sobering slowly. Selena grasped her coffee cup more tightly with both hands, to stop them trembling.

"I haven't forgotten when you thought you couldn't live without him," she said.

"Ahhh," Diane said, remembering. "Well, it turns out that I can live without him after all." Her voice thickened, seemingly drawn from some deeper part of herself that was constant and strong. "I won't depend on anyone for my life."

"Your . . ." Selena began. She had been going to say 'life?' or maybe 'children?' Diane went on as though she hadn't spoken.

"Selena," she said, turning her dark, deep eyes on her sister. "Marriage is wrong. It has nothing to do with love. It's a fraud. It takes you and turns you into a fake, into a . . ."

"I suppose you're going to tell me I'm only a servant," Selena said. She was amazed at what she had said, amazed at the bitterness she could hear in her own voice. Anger swelled up inside her, she felt like she was choking, but she pushed the words down. The worst of it was that she was not angry with Diane now, but with things she didn't dare articulate. Rhea turned away from the window in a slow, dignified movement, till she was looking directly at Selena, her eyes piercing through the circle of shadow around her face. Selena felt herself caught in Rhea's gaze. She made a little noise, a tiny throat-clearing, or perhaps a whimper.

"Can't you even *imagine* yourself a single, free individual—a soul out there in the universe?" Diane asked. There was a silence as Selena tried to understand this.

"You're a mother!" she said, appalled.

"Men do," Diane said, evenly, ignoring Selena's accusatory tone.

"I don't know what you're talking about," Selena said. Emotions tumbled inside her—anger, sorrow, a desire to be left alone so she could think. Phoebe's eyes, as she looked at Diane, had a new, speculative look in them. Rhea was looking out the window again, at the blazing blue of the winter sky, at the brilliance of sun striking snow. How can she look at that brightness without shading her eyes? Selena wondered, and then remembered, her eyesight is fading, she's an old woman, she'll die soon. And then, Phoebe has spoken at last.

"Men," she said. "Men do a lot of things." Involuntarily her eyes sought out Phoebe's rounded stomach under her smock. Why did Phoebe persist in wearing white? As if she were a bride? A pregnant, virgin bride. She shook her head at this, confused. All of them were pregnant here, Diane with possibility, Phoebe with a child, Selena with the weight of her own unborn and incomprehensible life, Rhea with her death. A chill struck her, and she clasped her coffee cup more tightly to warm her hands—soon I'll die myself, before I know it—before I've lived.

"Oh, Diana, Diana," she whispered, returning to Diana's christened name, which they had abandoned long ago in childhood. "You're a woman. A woman, not a man. You can never be a man."

"Who'd want to be?" Diana asked, and Rhea chuckled. Diana looked at Phoebe again. Why did they all seem to be talking to Phoebe? "I like being a woman more and more," Diana said. "I am a woman."

"I don't know what you're talking about," Selena said helplessly. It was all too much for her, and she felt angry with herself because she could only respond to Diana like a child, she who was the older sister, who had raised Diana, been a mother to her. "Say something I can understand," she pleaded. "Tell me why you left Tony."

Diana swung her foot back and forth, looked down into her lap, then across the way to where Rhea sat in front of the window, a large, dark shape against the light.

"I'll tell you a story," she said, suddenly gay. "When I first went to the city, Tony and the kids and I used to go for walks along the riverbank when the weather was still nice. Sometimes we'd go into the downtown area and stroll along the streets and into that big downtown mall. Everywhere we looked, we saw people. All sizes, all shapes, all ages, all kinds. People in wheelchairs or on crutches or in baby carriages—or striding along with their heads held high, or running, or staggering. Once I saw a woman walking down the busy, main street of the city sobbing out loud, tears pouring down her cheeks. Another time I saw a Chinese man and a thin, dark-haired white woman walking down the street side by side. She was yelling at him, bawling him out and calling him names, telling the story of their lives toether. He didn't run away or even walk faster. He just kept walking, his expression flat, never saying a word to her. One time I saw a policeman arresting a teenage shoplifter in the mall. She was struggling to get away from him, screaming and cursing at him. Would you believe it? And I could tell she loved having everybody stare at her. You see all kinds of things in the mall. Women preening in front of plate-glass mirrors, a lost child crying, prostitutes fighting, small Asian immigrants strolling in clusters, looking lost and sad."

She paused, swinging her foot again, the one leg crossed over the other.

"At night I go to class at the university . . ." Selena wanted to say, and who looks after your children? but held her tongue. "One night I was walking to work from the bus stop. It was midnight, and I was so tired. My eyes were blurring, I couldn't even see right, and my mind wouldn't work, you know? I would look at things, but I couldn't see what they were. I mean, I could see the cars and the signs on the stores—the words—but I couldn't figure out what they meant. I was stumbling down this city street in the night, with all these . . . things . . . around me, and they didn't make any sense at all.

"I knew my kids were at home in bed, that my husband was with them, I could see them, but I couldn't understand what they were. I couldn't understand how they could be my children. I couldn't understand anything anymore."

Selena listened, fascinated, appalled, afraid to speak. Diana wasn't looking at any of them now. It was as though she were explaining to herself.

"Suddenly everything seemed different. I can't tell you how, but it was as if I could see the world the way it really is—without love and hate and all that wanting . . . I could see the people, just creatures, you know, just bodies that moved and were warm or cold, that laughed or cried . . ."

She uncrossed her legs and sat forward, her elbows resting on her red skirt, her chin resting on her fists.

"I thought of Mom, Selena, what I can remember of her dying. I remembered all of it. I remembered things I didn't even know I knew. Her lying in that bed, day after day, so thin, white-skinned, her eyes sinking deeper and deeper into herself, withdrawing from us slowly. I thought how . . . we all . . . die." Here she laughed a small embarrassed laugh and looked down to her lap. "You remember how she died."

"I remember," Selena said, although she never, never thought about it. Both Phoebe and Rhea were motionless.

"At night class I was studying Shakespeare—*Hamlet*—we took it in high school, but I never paid any attention. It didn't mean anything to me then. But this time I understood, really understood. Ophelia especially."

Selena couldn't remember who Ophelia was. Was she the one who drowned? Floating down the river singing that crazy song? The one all the boys had laughed at? Selena remembered blushing over that, as if she were the one floating down the stream singing that nutty song.

"So you see," Diana said, straightening, putting her arms down by her sides, looking across the room at her sister, "so you see I could hardly go on the same way I always had, after that, could I?"

Suddenly Rhea laughed, that long, ridiculous laugh, and abruptly Diana joined in with her, laughing and laughing.

They were thirteen for Christmas dinner, fewer than usual, but enough to support the weight of the occasion with noise and laughter. Kent sat at one end of the table, Selena at the other, with Rhea on her right. Diana, her children on each side of her and then Tony, Mark, Jason, and Phoebe, Gus, Rhoda, and Sandy, were spread down the sides. They had moved the table into the living room, where there was more room, put another, smaller one against it, then covered them both with a big tablecloth so that the join was barely visible. Then they had set it with Selena's best china and silver that had been Diana and Selena's grandmother's, decorated it with unlit candles in glass holders sitting inside plastic wreaths of holly, and laid a big, bright paper napkin with red poinsettias beside each place setting. A sprig of mistletoe hung in the doorway between the hall and the living room and everybody had been duly kissed and teased under it. Selena looked up and down each side of the table as Kent carved the turkey. It seemed to her that she had much to be grateful for, more than the quick grace Mark had mumbled could ever express.

After Rhea, the children were served first, from the youngest to the oldest. Diana bent to cut Cathy's turkey for her, and to spoon a little cranberry jelly onto it. When she had finished, Cathy reached for her glass of milk. Diana held it to Cathy's lips while Cathy got a firmer grip on the glass. Her hand remained around it as Cathy drank, she seemed oblivious to the loud conversations around her, to the passing of bowls and platters and the clink of cutlery against china. As Cathy drank, Diana's lips moved. In that second, she was pure, a mother.

Selena found herself thinking that her own children were grown now, that those moments were gone forever for her, and she regretted their loss. Something gone out of her life, something for which there was no substitute. Diana had turned away, to Tammy on her other side, and

Selena could no longer see her face as she bent, her lustrous hair falling forward over her shoulders.

Across the table, Sandy, a fifty-year-old woman who didn't look more than thirty-five, served herself from the bowl of carrots and peas that Selena had canned in the fall. Sandy, whose home was a big house in the city, full of people like herself who couldn't manage on their own in the world. Taken by her parents when she was fifteen to an institution and left there, then moved out of it into a group home. Allowed to go home only for the occasional holiday. She felt sorry for Sandy, who would never have her own house or children. She had been sterilized when she was a teenager. It's better that way, they had all agreed.

And there was Phoebe, next to her, pregnant, silent, but at this moment not seeming unhappy as she spooned a little gravy onto her potatoes, then passed the dish to Mark beside her. Her inexplicable words earlier that day. And across from Mark, Tony, whose beloved, beautiful wife had rejected him.

Here we are, a family, Selena thought. For the first time she saw them as something more than relatives who knew each other from birth. She saw that they were bound by invisible bonds of pain and sorrow and joy, not just by blood and accidents of birth. Rhoda, approaching menopause, Gus with what Selena privately thought of as a 'mean streak.' All families are like this, she thought. This is what a family is.

"God, before we know it, it'll be January calf sales," Kent remarked.

"Don't think about work," Selena said.

"Yeah, you're right," Kent said.

Gus said, "The way things are going, it's hard to think about anything else."

"I heard in town that Whitelaw had to sell all his two-year-old steers. He's back in the cow-calf business, like the rest of us," Kent said.

"And you're gonna keep your land," Gus said to Tony, shaking his head.

"Well, I see you and Kent are keeping yours," Tony pointed out, grinning.

"Have to," Kent said. "If I sell now by the time the bank got through with me, there wouldn't be anything left. I guess I'll stick it out to the bitter end."

"Have some more turkey," Selena said to Gus, who took the platter from her.

On her right, Rhea ate heartily. Rhea's appetite was a mystery to all of them, she could eat rings around any of them, a family of hearty eaters. Where does she put it all? Selena wondered for the hundredth time. Old people are supposed to have small appetites and all kinds of digestive troubles, but not Rhea. Thinking of this, she felt her mood lighten again, and she jumped up to refill the empty dressing bowl.

Late in the evening Gus, Rhoda and Sandy left, and Mark and Jason went upstairs to bed. Tony and Kent had retired to the living room and were dozing in front of the television set, and the little girls had long since fallen asleep on the rug and been put to bed. Selena, Phoebe, Diana and Rhea were sitting in the kitchen. It was almost midnight.

"Do you want me to drive you home, Rhea?" Selena asked. "I didn't realize how late it is."

"I'm staying here tonight," Rhea said. Irritated, Selena held her tongue. And where will she sleep? she wondered.

"I'll sleep on the couch," Rhea said, as if Selena had spoken aloud. Selena glanced up at Rhea, noticed that the skin of her plump cheeks and her neck looked white in the bright light, fragile, and was stricken with guilt because Rhea was an old woman after all, and would be alone in her own house.

"Good," she said. "You'll be here to say good-bye to Diana and kids tomorrow." Rhea, unexpectedly, sighed. A long sigh, filled with something like sadness. It made Selena wonder if she was all right.

Diana said, "I don't know if this is the best time to tell you or not." They stared at her. Apprehension grew in Selena.

"What?" she asked, her voice low and tense.

"What I have to do," Diana said, not looking at her. There was a silence around the table.

"Honestly, Diana," Selena said. "I don't know how much more of this I can take." Phoebe, who had been leaning sleepily in her chair, her head touching the wall, straightened, and put her arms on the table in front of her. In the living room, somebody was snoring.

"I've decided to leave the girls here," Diana said. For a moment, Selena couldn't understand what she meant.

"You mean, with us?" she asked slowly.

"No."

"What?" Selena asked, still calm. "You know I'd be glad to look after them till you get more settled."

"I'm leaving them with Tony," Diana said. Rhea stirred, lifting her head, as if her neck were stiff, then lowering it again. If she laughs, Selena thought, I'm going to hit her.

"For . . . how long?" Selena asked. She could hear the fear in her voice.

"Until they're grown," Diana said, lifting her eyes so that they met Selena's. Selena stared at her, aghast, hardly believing what she had heard.

"You don't mean it," Selena said, after a second. Diana's eyelids fluttered as if Selena had struck her. "You're going to abandon your own children? Have you gone cra—"

"I am not abandoning them," Diana said. Her voice was very quiet, yet firm. "I'm leaving them with their father." Selena opened her mouth to shout, but thought better of it and tried to control herself.

"Why?" she asked finally.

"Because . . ." Diana began, looking over Selena's head. "Because— it's too hard. I can't do it." Her voice wavered at this, ever so slightly.

"Do what?"

"I can't work out this thing I'm doing, and raise two children at the same time. It's too hard. I never get any sleep. I'm not there when they want me to be. I can't be there . . . and do this . . . thing, too. I . . ." She grew silent and drew in a long, quavering breath.

Selena sat and stared at her, pity, anger, horror, all churning inside her.

"Rhea?" she asked. The kitchen was so quiet, you could hear the air in the room. Selena began to feel her heart thumping in her chest. Squeeze, relax, squeeze, relax. She could actually feel her own heart. It frightened her. She could hardly breathe she was so frightened by the beating of her own heart.

"Rhea . . ." she gasped. Rhea was staring across the room . . . to the small frosted window at the top of the door leading outside, staring at that small, frozen square of night, while Selena sat and felt her heart squeeze, and relax, squeeze, and relax, inside her cage of bones. She thought she might faint.

"Ah, Selena," Rhea said, finally. Selena was startled because Rhea had chosen to speak to her and not to Diana. "What am I going to do with you?" Her voice was gentle; suddenly Selena heard echoes of her mother's voice in that sound. It seemed to her that her mother was speaking to her and she grew confused, looking rapidly from one woman to the other, for was she not Phoebe's mother? But Phoebe was a mother now. And was Diana not her sister? But she had mothered her—did that not make Diana her daughter? Who was mother here? Who was daughter? Who was sister?

She began to gasp, and Diana rose and went to her, stood behind her, and massaged Selena's shoulders and neck with her long, narrow hands.

"Calm down, Selena," she said. "Calm down. You're just . . . tired, worn out with all this Christmas work . . ." Slowly the panic that had swept over Selena began to dissipate under the gentle touch of her sister's hands.

"I don't understand," she said at last, putting up one hand to touch Diana's.

"I know," Diana said. "I know that. But my little girls will grow up anyway. With or without me. Tony will take care of them. He loves them. He *wants* to devote his life to them." All the while Phoebe watched Diana with wonder in her eyes.

"You'll come back sometimes and see them?" Selena asked.

"Of course," Diana said. "Often, and I'll take them now and then with me. They will always be my children." She said this gently, her voice breaking at the last. She took her hands away from Selena's shoulders and went back to where she had been sitting. She took a deep breath and said, "I'm going to go with Tony back to the old house tonight. I'm going to tell him." She looked at each of them as if she had nothing but questions. They stared back at her, each in her own way: wonder, despair, acceptance. Then Diana burst into tears.

She put her head on her hands, bending forward from her waist as she sat on the kitchen chair, her long hair falling around her hands, and sobbed as if her heart were breaking. She cried and cried and cried. While Phoebe, Selena, and Rhea watched her, not moving from their places.

Rhea is lying on the old sofa in the living room in the comfortable darkness. She is thinking about Diana, feeling pity for her. It is a long time since she has felt pity for any person. It irritates her, she rubs it away. Anyway, it isn't for me to judge, she thinks, even if I knew what the judgement should be . . . a single soul struggling in the universe, at least she knows that much. She's been shown something about life, she may not be strong enough, though, it may end in disaster.

It will end in her death, Rhea thinks, and can't suppress a quick snort of laughter.

Selena lies upstairs in her big bed beside her husband and thinks about Tamara and Catherine, Diana's children, not suspecting the terrible turn their world is about to take. But Tony will look after them as well as Diana has, she thinks, so what is this outrage I feel? What it amounts to is that once children are born, *someone* has to raise them, they can't raise themselves, so Diana's action, since she is their mother and the logical one to raise them, makes no sense, except for her, in a personal way. The world can hardly be run that way, can it? With each person caring only for her personal needs.

I remember, she thinks, that the teacher said *Hamlet* is a tragedy. Is it a tragedy because Hamlet dies? She can't remember if he died or not, she can only remember that Ophelia died. She sees Ophelia floating down the river, garlanded with flowers—brown-eyed susans, milkweed, wild primroses, bluebells, dandelions—singing. Is this a tragedy I'm living in?

A few miles down the road from her, Diana lies sleepless too. I won't pretend it's right, she decides. I feel like I'm above those kinds of rules, but I would never dare to say that aloud. I mustn't think about my babies, I mustn't think about them, because I have no choice about this. I have to do it. Men have always done this—neglected or abandoned their wives and children, driven by some vision, some obsession. They went off, over and over again, on some quest that made no sense to anybody else—that photographer at the turn of the century who disappeared for years at a time, taking pictures of the Indians. Nobody even knew where he was. Explorers, gone for years, scientists—buried in their work—might as well be in Antarctica—doctors devoting their lives to other people. Men have always done this, and always been forgiven. Well, I'm an explorer, too.

A free person in the universe? Selena thinks. Freedom? She wonders what freedom is, tries to imagine it. Is it getting up in the morning and not having to cook breakfast for anyone? Is it going to the city? Like Diana? But I hate the city, I hate the smell, it frightens me, everything happens too fast there. What is it, then?

Rhea is thinking about her death. She knows, she has always carried it as a dried and unsprung seed inside her. Tonight it is swelling, and she allows it all the room it wants, all the space it needs to grow and blossom in, so that she can, at last, take its measure.

She rises from the couch where she has been lying awake, opens the curtains and stares out into the motionless, cold, silver-blue night. A long time she's been waiting. And now, what is left? She sits down again, turning toward the warm comfort of the house, and she leans against the old couch and rests. I don't want any surprises, she thinks, I don't want anything left undone.

I wonder what they will say at my funeral: How hard I worked. All those miles of scrubbed floors, acres of washed clothes, mountains of kneaded dough. She sees her clean white sheets flapping in the wind. She sees herself stretching to hang them on the line Jasper built for her that the wind was forever tearing down, dragging the clean clothes in the dirt so that she had to wash them all over again. Her spotless kitchen, the loaves of bread sitting out on the table cooling, all the meals she cooked.

She allows herself to feel a second's satisfaction. But then thinks, whatever my life has been, it isn't quite that. Work was only the raw material out of which I fashioned my life, out of which I fashioned my soul.

All those children, they will say. This bothers her, she doesn't know what to think when it comes to her children. Woman, after all, she reminds herself, was made to give birth. That new life flowed through me, it is true. But that is only the way things are, I have been only an opening, a conduit, for the greater life to express itself.

So what are all those children to me? She lifts her large, once strong, farm woman's hands from her lap, then drops them helplessly. Still, they were my babies, she thinks, and I would have given my life for any one of them, even though now I can barely remember their names. The names I gave them belong to the babies, not to those gross, loud strangers who come sometimes to see me.

There'll be a minister at my funeral. Someone who never set eyes on me when I was alive. He'll say I was a pioneer, and he'll talk about the courage of the pioneers, about my courage. Courage! We did what we had to do, that's all. He'll talk about the hardship: the work, the doing-without, the loneliness.

All those years of loneliness. Never seeing another woman for weeks at a time, in the early days. Jasper up and out working before sunrise, not coming back till well after dark. Nobody to talk to but the kids and the animals and the air itself.

What it does to you, always being alone. People don't know how much they rely on other people to keep them from knowing what they are, to keep them from knowing about that other, that interior life everybody has. They're afraid of it, afraid it's nothing but a black hole into which their everyday selves will fall. People are afraid they will fall into that other world, into madness, and never be able to climb out again.

And they're right. It is a kind of madness into which I fell. I fell inside myself. Alone, day after day, with the wind and sky, the grass and the wild things.

They'll tell how someone came across me walking out on the prairie late at night, as they were riding home from a dance or from playing cards with the neighbours. How I frightened them, seeming to rise from the darkness up against the night sky, my hair wild, my feet and legs bare, how their horses reared or shied and wheeled. Or standing in the sun, my dress blowing around me, my arms raised to the sky, shouting something they couldn't understand. A crazy woman, a witch, they'll say.

Someone sleeping upstairs coughs once. She raises her eyes to the ceiling, sees only dark, bounded shadows. Sees them all lying in their beds. One of the boys, Jason. The house falls back into silence.

How it was when I was mad. How I wandered over the prairie, neglected my work, how Jasper, despairing, would send my children out to find me and bring me home again, how I could see nothing in those days but the insects scurrying over the earth, or the clouds in the sky. How they would lead me by the hand.

What a long time it was before I could see the grass as only grass again, the rocks as only rocks, the hills as hills. When at last I did return to the world as plain landscape again, I could never again see anything in the same way. I'd forgotten how everyone else sees this world. I'd forgotten what it is they think about. I'd forgotten how things seem to be to them.

Rhea yearns to feel that opening sweep through her again, that emptying of the little things, the erasing of memory, that left her with nothing but the clench and release of her heart, the hot rush of her blood. The gut knowledge that she belonged to the earth, was a part of it, an animal like the other animals. And that where she had carried her life, she had also always carried her death.

Death, too.

She moves her feet a little and they make small, sliding noises on the old carpet. Will the house seem emptier once I'm gone? Will I be missed? Oh, yes, she tells herself with certainty, because I'm a thread in the fabric of this community. They'll feel my passing. In those moments when they look out a window of their houses, over the long, undulating prairie, some deep part of them will whisper, the woman is gone from among us, but they won't hear the words. Only a piercing sadness, an edge of despair will overcome them, that they can't allow themselves to feel. No, no despair in this community.

It seems to Selena that she should ask someone what freedom is, but who? Diana says that men know what freedom is, but Selena doubts this. She turns her head to look at Kent, sleeping beside her. No, Kent doesn't know what freedom is any more than Selena does. She thinks of Phoebe and the child she is carrying. Once you have chilren, you never know what freedom is again.

The people I loved, Rhea thinks. Jasper. She tries to call to mind, the width of his shoulders under his faded blue denim workshirts, the smell of his breath, peppery and warm, and the way he walked across the yard to the barn, or handled a horse. Her children. She sees their faces, one by one, even the faces of the ones that died. How their blood and her blood mingled.

Serena thinks of Phoebe, the new life swelling, the child soon to burst out into the world. Selena sees the child taking its first steps, Phoebe hovering in the background, a blur, out of focus and only present from her mid-calves to her breasts, her hands out, palms forward, ready to catch the child if it should fall. Perhaps Selena is asleep now, she can't tell. It seems to her that this is important, this view of Phoebe. It is trying to tell her something. Out of focus, her head missing, and her feet. Selena begins to cry in her sleep.

Diana falls asleep and dreams. She dreams of walking alone over the world. She dreams of wisdom, she dreams of knowing. In countries hot or cold, far away or not so far, she watches women as they go about their lives: cooking, sewing, carrying wood and water, planting, tending the earth, bearing children, nursing them. She hears their cries—of love, of joy, of fear. She walks the earth with long strides, bending her head to them, her lucent eyes gaze upon them, the radiant curve of her smooth brow sends blessings on them, her tears baptize them. Diana walks among the women of the earth and where she passes the women slow, grow silent, and an arrow of loss for something valued, half-remembered, pierces their hearts with sorrow.

Diana moves restlessly in her sleep, turns over, moans, flings one arm up so that it rests on her thick hair spread out over her pillows. She turns again and dreams some more.

She is seated in a garden in Arabia. It is very hot and the garden is on the top of a hill. All around below the hill the green fronds of palms spread themselves offering shade. Cool fountains run thin, clear streams of fresh water over glazed tile decorated in shades of blue and white. A woman sits across from her at the table, and other figures, too, but in the manner of dreams, she can't quite make them out, nor can she tell if they are men or women. The other woman is dressed in long, flowing white robes of some opaque material and she wears a white headdress of the same material, rather like the headdress of an Arab woman or a nun.

Diana sees that she herself is wearing the same garment and headdress and this does not seem strange. The woman is olive-skinned, that much Diana knows, but whether she is pretty or plain, young or old, Diana cannot tell. She is a woman.

The table they are seated at is round and in the centre there is a round bowl filled with fruit. Seeing it, Diana reaches out, takes an orange, and without peeling it, bites into it and swallows. The woman across from her speaks then. In a voice devoid of fear or pleasure, distaste or anger, or even censure, she says that Diana should not have bitten into the fruit without washing it first. She points then, to small, rectangular buildings which Diana sees for the first time scattered below, beside the fountains, among the palm trees. There, she tells Diana, those are the washing houses. The fruit you ate without first washing will kill you. And Diana knows she will die.

Selena dreams she is walking in a garden. She recognizes the special warmth of a spring day when the sun is still gentle and life-giving, yet strong enough to warm her. She feels its glow, which seems to come from all around her at once, seeping through the skin between her fingers, probing its way between the strands of her hair to warm her scalp, spreading in a slow flood over her neck, shoulders, back, and legs. She feels it on her thighs and as it reaches her stomach, it spreads without resistance, through her very skin, inside her, warming and lightening her woman's organs.

There are green plants all around her, some taller than she is, some rustling about her shoulders and her knees or caressing her ankles as she passes. The tall ones bend and whisper to her, moving their curving leaves aside to let her pass. Sunlight is thrown like handsful of yellow topazes over the leaves and stems of the plants. The air is filled with the green, growing scent of the plants, of the olive pale leaves of the green and yellow beans, the tangy scent of the crisp, wine-dark leaves of the beets, the thicker, darker scent of the fernlike fronds of the carrots, and the honey-sharp scent of the tomato bushes. Plants she doesn't recognize, too, grow all around her as she walks. They bear fruit that hang in heavy, ripening clusters from their stems; speckled fruit the shape of lemons, or round, full fruit like plums. Their colours of rose and gold glow from within, and glistening drops of dew, like blue diamonds, drip from their variegated green leaves.

She kneels in the soil which is black and moist and newly tilled. She lifts a handful of it to her nostrils, it crumbles richly in her palms, its scent brings pictures of caverns and deep green valleys into her head. She is filled with the peace and content that radiate from the plants, from the earth itself.

All their faces vanish, evaporate like dew in the wind, and all that is left for Rhea is the wind sweeping across the prairie grass, the great round sky, the low curves of the hills. The beautiful earth, a pang of terrible loss sweeps through her, to lose the earth.

Rhea has stretched out on the couch again, pulled the quilt up to her chin and is lying with her arms across her belly, her hands flat, one above the other, on its rounded warmth. She closes her eyes. I have tried to understand my own nature, that's what I've tried to do. I have tried to find my self in myself.

One last spring, she says to herself. One last spring. And then she, too, sleeps.

FEBRUARY

I've changed jobs again. I'm writing copy at a radio station. They let me work from four to midnight and that way I'm free to take some half-classes during the day. I'm taking one in drama and one in art appreciation. It appalls me to see how ignorant I am, how I thought I was doing fine, and yet I knew nothing, nothing.

I take the classes with young kids. I think about my girls growing up to be like them: spoiled silly, selfish. But I know they won't be like that if only because I left them, made them different. Does that sound terribly cruel to you, Selena? Of course it does. I'm a monster. Your sister, the monster. Can I tell you how much I miss them? Or will you only say, it serves you right. What kind of woman abandons her children? What kind indeed? I wonder myself.

I wake up sometimes in the morning with a jerk, and the room looks strange, wrong, like I don't know where I am and I suddenly realize that my children are gone, that they won't come running to jump into bed with me, all warm and sticky and smelly, full of hugs and kisses. Can you imagine how I feel when I remember that? The temptation to come back to them and to Tony is so strong that sometimes I even get my suitcase half-packed before I can make myself stop.

It seems to me that none of us understands about motherhood. You think there's only one kind, and that kind is your kind, Selena. You have your children, then stay with them and worry over them, over every breath they take, until one day they up and leave you—they wrench themselves away from you and your motherhood.

So I'm trying a different kind of motherhood. Instead of trying to protect them, I'm trying to turn them loose in the world.

But I'm terrified, all the time, that I'm wrong, that I'm not doing it for them at all, but only for myself, that I am a selfish monster, an unnatural woman, like Lady Macbeth, because I want to live, and to heck with everybody else.

But I do know this: motherhood kills the life of a woman. It kills the woman's separate life, and I cannot, I will not believe that that is right. That any woman who becomes a mother has to die herself. Because if that is true, if that is the only way a woman can live, no better than a coyote out on the prairie, if women really are born to be slaves, then I will kill myself. I mean that, Selena. Because you have to see that life is bigger than mother-and-child. Woman's life is bigger. We betray our humanity if we think that our highest purpose is to carry and deliver a child.

Now do you see why Phoebe has been so silent?

Diana

Dear Diana,

I received your letter on Tuesday. They are closing the post office at Mallard so Kent has to drive to Chinook for the mail and he goes only every other day.

Mitchums have sold out. Their auction sale is next Saturday. Kent is going, and I will be selling lunch with the club. They didn't go broke, just got out ahead of the bank takeover. I can't imagine anybody being fool enough to buy the place. There's no way it can pay for itself, so I suppose the house will just sit empty. It seems to me that more and more houses are sitting empty around here. We just hope things will get better.

I know I don't have to tell you, but maybe it will help to relieve your mind a little to know that your girls look well and happy. Tony brought them over for supper Sunday night and I really don't see much change in them. A little maybe in Tammy, because she's older, but Tony takes the best care of them, even seems happy doing it.

Well, you know we don't see eye to eye on being a mother, and I don't want to fight with you, but when you get right inside motherhood, let it take over, it really is wonderful. It really does seem worth the sacrifices. At least, it always has to me. Although, I have to say that my boys have grown away from me. I feel them holding me away from them, and there's nothing I can do about it, but accept it, and it hurts. And it's true, too, that I'm afraid of the time that's coming soon, when all three of them will be gone and I will have to find a new way to live. It's hard for all the women around here, I guess, from what I hear.

Phoebe is in good health, but oh, Diana, I miss my dear little girl. It seems she went away suddenly, when I wasn't looking, she just vanished, and now it seems like she'll never come back again. I can't tell you how that breaks my heart. I think I'll never get used to it.

Look after yourself. Come home when you can.

All my love,
Selena

SPRING EQUINOX

"But I can't leave Phoebe alone," Selena said. They stood in the kitchen, Kent inching toward the hall where his coat was. "She's due any minute, and when I ask her to come into town with us and stay at Martin and Irene's place while we're at the hall, she just refuses. And Mark won't be back from that stupid basketball tournament till tomorrow."

"You're only going to be gone a little while," Kent said. "A few hours, that's all. You don't have to stay around for the parties afterward. I'll be here till eight or so, and you'll be home well before midnight. And if you're worried, you can phone every once in a while."

"She won't answer the phone," Selena reminded him.

"I'll make Jason stay with her," Kent said. "That way he can phone you at the hall if she goes into labour, or if you phone here, he'll answer the phone."

"I wish you'd stay home, Kent, just this once," Selena pleaded.

"Damn it," Kent said, without much rancour, but she flinched anyway, "you're being silly, Selena. A few hours, that's all, and she won't even be alone. I'll call and check on her myself if you want me to. Anyway, I've got to check on the calves, so I can't be away very long no matter what."

Selena gave up arguing. Phoebe, sitting in front of the television, had no doubt heard it all even though Selena had tried to keep her voice down. Absently, she smoothed her new green dress down over her hips, then fingered the frill that ran around the neckline and over her shoulders.

"You look nice tonight," Kent said, smiling at her from the doorway where he leaned against the frame. "That's a nice dress—something different."

"Do you really think so?" Selena asked anxiously. "I've never worn such a low neckline." She touched the single pearl that hung from a gold chain around her neck. Kent had given it to her for a wedding present. She hardly ever wore it. "It's pretty hard to compete with the town women and the big farmers' wives with their fancy wardrobes." She felt a little shy, he so rarely noticed how she looked.

"They won't have fancy wardrobes much longer," he said wryly. "You look damn good for a woman your age," he said, serious now. "Three kids—you haven't put on any extra weight. You look as good as any of them." Surprised into silence, Selena crossed the kitchen, put her arms around his neck, and kissed him lightly on the mouth. "You better get going," he said, not taking his hands out of his pockets. Selena stepped back, touching her hair carefully with her palms.

"Phoebe knows what to get for supper. You phone if there's the slightest sign of anything happening with her." She hesitated, then moved past him into the hall, looking for her coat, bending down to pull on her good winter boots, which she would leave in the car when she got to town.

"Have fun," he said. "Who's got the tickets?"

"Rhea," Selena answered from her crouched position, her voice muffled. "At least I sure hope she hasn't lost them or something." She went to the front door and put her hand on the doorknob to open it, then turned away and stood in the doorway into the living room.

"How do you feel, Phoebe?" she asked. Phoebe was sitting on the couch, leaning back, her eyes half-closed, cushions pushed in the small of her back, her abdomen huge in front of her.

Slowly she turned to Selena, her eyelids flickered a couple of times and she murmured, "Okay."

"Get Jason to phone the hall if you feel so much as a twinge," Selena said. "You hear?" Phoebe nodded her head yes, once. Selena waited a moment, thinking how she was like that each time too, in those last couple of weeks, sort of in a trance. "Your dad will be at Tony's. He can be here in five minutes." This time Phoebe didn't respond at all. Kent moved past the hanging coats in the hall to come and stand behind her.

"Will you stop worrying? Even if she starts you'll have lots of time. It's her first, after all. Jason and I will take care of her. Right, Jason?" Jason was sprawled full-length on the floor.

"Yeah," he said, without turning his head.

"You going to get Diane?" he asked, "or is she driving herself?"

"We thought we'd go together in one car," Selena said, turning reluctantly away, going to the door, opening it. "But I have to get Rhea first." Kent laughed.

"Well, go on," he said. "Diane came all the way from Saskatoon just to go to this shindig. Don't make her late."

"They say you can't get a decent table if you don't get there early," Selena said, as she stepped outside. "Kent . . ."

"Go," he said. "I'm on my way myself. You deserve a night out. Get!" In spite of herself, she had to laugh. She turned away, stepping carefully past the melting snowbank on her left, skirting a water-covered patch of ice on the cement, and went carefully around the car.

I know I shouldn't be going, she worried to herself as she got into the car, waved at Kent, and drove away. But I so want to, and she made a little face at herself. Ladies Night Out! How she had looked forward to it ever since Rhea had surprised her with the tickets, ever since Diana had phoned to say Rhea had called her, and she was coming home for it. Rhea ordered me to come, Diana had said. She didn't give me a choice, and she had laughed, as if this were a pleasure instead of an inconvenience. But when Selena asked her what Rhea had said, Diana had said, I don't remember. But I have a feeling she's going to die pretty soon. Nonsense, Selena had replied. She's healthy as a horse, she'll see a hundred if any of us do. But privately she thought how Rhea had lost weight and grown paler over the winter. She was all right at Christmas, she told herself, but now I'm sure she's thinner, and there's something funny about her eyes.

It was late afternoon and the sun hung round and red in the west, turning the few low clouds on the horizon golden and pink. She turned into the sun, going toward Rhea's. Here and there the road was muddy, and occasionally she drove across a patch of ice, but it was well-gravelled and she wasn't afraid of getting stuck. Besides, it's still freezing at night, by the time I have to drive back, the mud will have stiffened up.

"Tonight will be a full moon," Rhea said, as she climbed into the car beside Selena. She had been waiting at the door, coat and boots on, when Selena drove up.

"Should be easy driving home then," Selena said, pleased at how well everything was working out. A shiver of excitement passed down her spine and she turned to smile at Rhea. Rhea, however, was not smiling. She sat looking straight ahead, a solemn expression on her face, almost stern, her hands clasped formally and resting on her lap.

"I found a thousand crocuses today, on the south slope of that hill to the north. You know the one." Rhea spoke without turning her head. "Another year, another spring." She cleared her throat. Selena glanced at her, a little nervous. Not a bad mood, or a crazy one, she hoped. And then thought, what dignity Rhea has, she carries herself like a queen.

They drove past the turn-off to Selena and Kent's place and kept going down the grid till they came to the turn-off that led into Tony's.

"I imagine the girls will hate to see her leave again so soon when she just got home," Selena said as she pulled up in front of the house. The door opened before Selena could get out of the car, and Diana stepped carefully out, skirting mud puddles, her red shoes like bright birds against the muddy ground.

"No rubbers," Selena said.

"Hi," Diana said, as she climbed into the back seat. "Isn't it a great evening?"

"The spring equinox," Rhea said in a strange voice. She sat with her head tipped up a little, her mouth straight, her hands folded on her lap.

"Oh, yeah," Diana said, her voice bright, "isn't this some kind of ancient celebration—some rite or something?"

"A sacred time," Rhea said.

"It should be," Selena said with feeling. "The calves and colts coming, the grass starting to grow again, the crops being planted, the sun warming everything up."

The sky to the west had begun to fade and the old wet grass that showed in patches in the ditches had turned a deep gold in the twilight.

"It feels so good to be here, driving with the two of you to town again." Selena risked a quick look over her shoulder at Diana. She was looking to the north, out at the fields that were losing their cover of snow, turning black with the moisture, and at the low hills, purple now, in the distance. Her dark hair was loose and curled around her face and rested on the shoulders of her red coat.

"I swear you give off light," Selena said. "I don't know what it is, and red shoes, too."

"What colour's your dress?" Diana asked. She leaned forward and pulled back the collar of Selena's coat. "Bright green! Heavens! What's gotten into you!" She spoke in mock horror. "I never thought I'd see you in anything but those dresses you wear with pink and blue flowers or whatever on them."

"Oh, thanks a lot," Selena said.

They were approaching Chinook now. It was spread out ahead of them, the streetlights just switching on, lighting up the shadowed streets. To the east a full white moon hung suspended in the darkening sky.

"It's been a hard winter," Selena said, "what with Phoebe and everything."

"Meaning me," Diana said.

"When I got in that dress store, I felt like . . . things were different, or something. Not like they used to be. I don't know. But when I saw this dress, I knew it was the one I wanted. I just knew it. I held my breath till I saw the price tag . . . and the size." She laughed at herself, a little embarrassed. She had never cared much about clothes.

"And it's the perfect dress," Rhea said, still without looking at Selena. It was on the tip of Selena's tongue to point out that Rhea hadn't seen it yet, but she held back.

She parked the car a half a block from the hall. Women were walking by in pairs and groups of threes and fours, stepping carefully so as not to get mud on themselves, and cars passed by slowly, looking for parking places.

"Hey, there's Lola and Phyllis and Phyllis's mother," Diana said. Lola and Phyllis had been her closest friends.

"And Rena and Selma," Selena said. "Everybody's here."

"Phoebe should be here too," Rhea said, then grunted, as she wrestled her big body out of the car.

"Didn't you know who was coming?" Diana asked. Selena was bent over, struggling in the cramped space behind the wheel to get her overshoes off and to replace them with her new beige evening shoes.

"We started calving about three weeks ago, and you know how that is. I haven't had a minute to myself, much less to talk to anybody." Diana was already out of the car, checking her pantyhose, shaking out her long hair.

Selena got out too, slamming the door, and joined Rhea and Diana, who had moved together into the street. They walked side by side down the road, past the row of parked cars, falling in with the stream of women entering the hall, a bright procession of chattering, laughing women. Only Rhea was solemn. Inside, Rhea gave their tickets to the man at the door, they hung up their coats, helping each other, and checked, one by one, in the small mirror for imperfections in their makeup and their hair.

"Rhea, is that a new dress?" Selena asked. Rhea was wearing an old-fashioned black crepe dress with a rhinestone buckle in the centre of her full waist.

"I save it for occasions," Rhea replied. "It isn't new." Then Selena remembered that Rhea had worn it at Uncle Jasper's funeral, years before.

She was confused suddenly, for she understood now that Rhea saw something in this occasion that made it as important as her husband's funeral, and she was puzzled by this, and uneasy.

"It's perfect for you," Diana said, imitating Rhea's solemn voice, then burst out laughing.

Long tables were arranged at angles down the side of each wall, leaving an open space in the centre. Each table was covered with a long white cloth and the red plastic backs of the stacking chairs lent the room a festive air. Each table had a centrepiece of spring flowers, and coloured candles set in clear glass holders. There were men moving among the tables, lighting the candles, and the big room began to take on a cosy, intimate atmosphere. The guests moved among the tables, talking to one another, finding places to sit. The hall buzzed with their voices.

On the far side of the room, near the centre, someone was waving at them.

"It's Phyllis," Diana said. "Look, they've saved us a place." Pleased, the three of them made their way to the table where Phyllis, Lola, and Laverne, Phyllis's mother, sat. Selena sat down between Selma and Rena and Diana sat opposite her, flanked by Lola and Phyllis. Rhea and Laverne sat at the long opposite ends, Rhea, with her back to the women seated on the other side of the hall.

"Everybody's here!" Selena said. "Even the grandmothers. I wonder who's babysitting," and everybody laughed.

"Thank God for grandma," Lola said. "I'd go crazy if she didn't give me a break once in a while."

"Me, too," Phyllis said, smiling down the table at her mother, who smiled back.

One of the men who would be serving came to their table, carrying a long, open box piled high with corsages.

"Pick one," he said, faintly bored, and waited while Selena chose a yellow daisy tied with a green ribbon. He went to Diana then and waited while she chose hers. He turned away then and left without asking Rhea to choose one. Selena was about to say something when he suddenly returned, carrying a small white box, which he gave to Rhea.

He said, formally, as if he had rehearsed this, "As the oldest woman here, we have a special corsage for you."

Rhea showed no surprise. She simply waited with a regal air while he, somewhat nervously now, opened the box, extracted a corsage of five red roses and buds, and pinned it to the shoulder of her black crepe dress.

"That's beautiful, and "Isn't that nice!" came from around the table, while Rhea nodded her head in acknowledgement.

"Isn't that nice?" Selma said to Selena, looking around. "Is this your first time?"

"Yes," Selena said. "It's so expensive, and we're always calving and so darn busy in March."

"Rena and I came last year too. It's fun," Selma said. "I'd hate to miss it. There's something special about it. Just women, you know."

"I hear they're serving veal cordon bleu for supper this year," Rena said.

"What on earth is that?" Selena asked.

"Search me," Selma said. The same waiter had returned and took drink orders from each of them, then left again.

"It's veal with ham and cheese inside," Phyllis said. "It's good, but what a nuisance to make, and none of the men will eat it anyway." Selena was beginning to relax and enjoy herself. The same waiter returned, served their drinks, and left. It's so lovely, she thought, to be sitting at a table with real flowers on it, and a tablecloth, no kids arguing and spilling their milk, no grumpy husband, and me not jumping up and down every two minutes to get something. And all my friends around me.

Laverne asked, "Do the men do the cooking too?"

"No," Lola said. "The women do it first. Get everything planned and ready, and a couple of them stay in the kitchen all night to show the men what to do." She had to laugh at this.

"Men are such klutzes," Rena said. "Can you imagine them getting a meal ready for a hundred people?" They all laughed at this.

"John couldn't boil water if he had to," Laverne said.

"I keep Martin right out of the kitchen," Selma said. "I told him, I don't tell you how to run your ranch, and you can just stay out of my kitchen."

"There's Rhoda over there," Diana said, waving at a far table. "I don't see Ruth," Selena said.

"Ruth! Hah!" Rena said angrily. "Buck wouldn't let her out of the house, much less give her the money for a ticket."

"I'll never understand why some men have to be that way," Selma said, sighing. A hush fell around the table, a chill.

Diana said, matter-of-factly, "She shouldn't let him treat her like that." None of them said anything, thinking perhaps of Ruth, at home instead of with them. Rhea looked at each of them, one at a time, her eyes flashing. Selena felt herself blushing under Rhea's gaze, and didn't know why. Diana, Lola and Phyllis had their heads together, chattering to each other softly so the older women couldn't hear them. Selena took the moment to look up and down the long hall slowly, drinking in the atmosphere and the sights. She felt herself lifted somehow, felt lighter, out of herself in some strange way, unable to draw herself back in and down, into her own body. She felt a part of everything in the hall, all the women, and she rather liked the feeling, unfamiliar as it was.

The lights had been turned low so that the candles on the table seemed to glow more brightly, casting rounded, golden shadows, in the light of which all the women's hair gleamed. It caught their eyes too, and made them shine, and the many colours of their best dresses softened and blended into a muted rainbow of colour. Their jewellery sent flashes of light around the room, and in that soft light, even the plainest, most worn-out woman looked somehow pretty.

Feeling as though she had risen above the crowd, was seeing them all from a height, Selena was overcome by their beauty, by the way her friends and neighbours and relatives, all the women of her community had been transformed, as if by some magic she knew nothing about. As if femininity were a precious treasure that she was seeing in the abstract, for the first time. It took her breath away. She brought her eyes back to the table, to Rhea, sitting at its head. Women flanked Rhea on each side. Behind her, as she sat facing the women at her table, with her back to the rest of the celebrants, sat more women. She looked large, the largest woman in the room, seated as she was, at the head of their table in the centre of the hall, which was the centre of community life. Selena, surprised, studied her, trying to figure out why she looked bigger than all of them. It must be because she has on the only black dress in the room, she told herself.

The waiter was back again, bending, putting his face close to each woman's cheek as he took orders for drinks again. There was something faintly offensive, wrong, about the way he acted, his—was it fatherliness? No, more like seduction. As he put his face close to Diana's, Selena saw suddenly that her sister was beautiful. Had she always been beautiful? No, surely she hadn't been, or Selena would have seen it before. In the company of all these women, Selena thought Diana was the most beautiful woman she had ever seen. So tall, so richly-coloured, like a flower herself. Wasn't there a goddess named Diana? A huntress, wasn't she? You'd never know to look at her, that she's the mother of two children, a woman long used to the ways of the marriage bed. She looks like a . . . virgin.

Embarrassed by her own thoughts, she dropped her eyes. A virgin, she said to herself disdainfully. I must be getting drunk. But in that moment with her head down, a scent she had not smelled before crept into her nostrils. She tried to sniff discreetly and it rose, filling her head, a sweet, heavy smell, rich and beautiful. Puzzled, she turned to Selma, but Selma and Laverne were talking, apparently noticing nothing strange.

"I always thought I might have made a good nurse," Selma was saying. "I always liked looking after sick people, doing things for them. Mother said I was good at it." She sighed.

"Why didn't you go into nursing?" Laverne asked.

"You know how it is. I got married right after high school. Mother couldn't talk me out of it. First thing I knew, I had a baby, and then another one." She looked down at her place, touching the ends of her knife and fork, straightening them. Laverne sighed, too.

"I was raised in a time when you just got married, you didn't think about it. Just got your MRS and that was it. I used to play school when I was a kid, pretending I was a teacher." She laughed. "Yes," she said, sighing, "I wanted to be a teacher."

"Are you sorry?" Selma asked, watching Laverne with sympathetic eyes.

"Not really," Laverne said, after a minute during which she stared at the flame of the candle in front of her, her eyes having turned soft with sadness. "I raised my family. They all turned out okay, and now . . ." She shrugged. "John and I are ready to retire . . . And we had it a lot better than our grandmothers," she pointed out, her voice becoming brisker.

"Still, it seems a shame," Selma said, sounding as if she were speaking to herself. "There's a lot of thwarted hopes in this room," Selma said, glancing around.

Soft music had begun to play over the public address system.

"I don't suppose it's any easier for the men," Laverne said.

"It isn't the same for the men," Phyllis broke in. "They get to run things—the ranches and the farms and the businesses—none of us do." She sounded angry, and raised her drink to her mouth, holding it there for a second without drinking.

Rena said, "Look at Carmen Harris. She's been running that ranch of hers since her husband died, must be forty years ago."

"Yeah," Lola said, setting down her glass. "You'd think she was a man if it wasn't for her front. She dresses like one, cuts her hair like one." Selena laughed.

"She even talks like one. I heard her talking with Joe Ewan in the service station one day when I was buying camper fuel. I had to laugh she sounded so much like Kent."

"She's nothing!" Phyllis said. "I heard about that woman in Montana—my aunt knows her—she isn't even five feet tall, and the men came over one day and found her with a horse stretched out in the corral, cutting him."

"No kidding!" They were all surprised, and a little disapproving.

"That's not a word of a lie," Phyllis said. "She was all by herself and she had this stallion stretched out, ready to cut him."

"Is she married?" Rena asked.

"Yes, but he lets her do whatever she wants. She was raised on the place, rides, breaks the horses, everything. She told my aunt how when she was young on the big ranch next to theirs, they used to hire convicts from the state prison to work the place. One time she was out riding a long way from home and she saw this convict coming on horseback straight for her, just as fast as that horse would take him. And she saw right away that she was in big trouble, so she spurred her horse and rode maybe five miles as fast as her horse would go, with him right behind her. But she was better on a horse, and finally, he gave up and turned back. She told my aunt she still got scared, thinking about it."

"That reminds me of a story about my mother's cousin," Lola said. "They settled out here in the homesteading days, used to raise horses, blood horses, you probably heard about them. Anyway, Cousin Emma wasn't afraid of anything and she used to ride all over the place, even after she got married, even after she had kids. Sort of a wildness in her, I guess. Anyway, one time there was a horse sale maybe ten miles from where their place was and she rode over with her husband. But after a few hours, she decided to go home, so she started out by herself on her horse. Just as she was riding out from that sale, she looked back, and she saw this Indian, he'd been at the sale with some of his people, a young, good-looking guy, I guess; she saw him mounting his horse. It made her a little nervous, so she started out trotting, and when she looked back, he was trotting too. So she picked up speed, and when she looked back, he'd picked up speed too—well, they rode like that, him following her, most of the way home. When she got close to home, she just rode full out that last mile or two, and that Indian was right behind her. She said she rode into that yard so fast, she could hardly get the horse to stop, and when she looked back, that Indian was gone. Just disappeared."

"The things that happen to people," Laverne said, shaking her head.

"Funny, isn't it," Rena said. "Remember when you were young. Horses bucking all the time. You never thought anything of it. Just got on and did what had to be done, but now, if you knew a horse was going to buck, you'd sure think twice before you got on him."

"Getting old," Selma said. "It's sure no fun."

Lola said, "I leave all the cutting—calves, horses—up to Doug. I ride with him, but I sure don't cut things." She shuddered.

"It goes to show what you can do if you want to," Diana said.

"Who wants to?" Phyllis asked, her voice filled with loathing, so that everybody laughed, looked at each other, then laughed some more.

It occurred to Selena to think how different the evening would be if their men were with them. They wouldn't talk so loudly, they'd speak only to each other, not to the men, and the men would monopolize the conversation. And they would make jokes about the flowers on the table, and how they couldn't see without the lights on, and imply how silly the whole thing was. No, she was glad for once the men weren't with them.

Shrieks of laughter came from the table behind Diana and they all craned their necks to see what the cause of the commotion was. Diana leaned over to a young woman sitting directly behind her.

"What's so funny, Darlene?" she asked. The woman beside Darlene was laughing so hard tears were trickling down her cheeks. Darlene pointed to their waiter, who was walking away, his face red.

"It's that crazy Sheila," Darlene said. "She pinched him!"

"What did she say?" the others asked, unable to hear over the music and the laughter.

"My mascara's going to run if I don't stop laughing," Darlene said, wiping her eyes carefully with the edge of her hand. She was quite drunk. In fact, here and there around the hall, a number of women had had too much to drink.

While Diana explained about the cause of the laughter, the kitchen doors were propped open, the smell of cooking food rushed out into the hall, and the waiters began to carry out plates of food and to serve them.

Selena said, "It feels funny to be served by men."

"Doesn't it, though?" Rena agreed.

"I'm just going to enjoy it," Phyllis said, but she giggled nervously.

The noise in the hall was lessening now, dropping to a steady, low buzz, as everyone was served and began to eat. The waiter came again, carrying wine, and filled each glass. Selena's head was light, she could feel a warmth in her cheeks, it felt good, and she sighed happily. But someone at the next table was in tears. Too surprised to even point this out to anyone, she watched. It was Nadine Tomas, a woman a little older than she was, a farmer's wife, someone she hardly knew, although she had known of her all her life. The women on each side of her were comforting her, and gradually, dabbing at her eyes with a tissue, and sniffing, she got control of herself.

Somehow Selena wasn't surprised to see someone in tears. It was all too beautiful, it was all too different from the way things usually were for them, she could almost cry herself.

When dessert came, they all oohed and aahed over it, the first strawberries of the season to arrive in town. They rested on sponge cake and were smothered in whipped cream.

"The cake's a little dry," Laverne remarked, poking at it with her fork.

"Coarse, too," Rena said. "They must have bought it."

"Farm cream, though," Phyllis pointed out, and popped a forkful into her mouth.

"Yummy," they all said, and cleaned their plates, even the best cooks, who were disdainful of the efforts of others, ate everything, if only because someone else had cooked it.

One of the waiters had rolled down his sleeves and put on a sportscoat. He stood at the front now, tapping at his microphone to make sure it was working.

"It's time for a little entertainment, ladies," he said, standing too close to his microphone so that his t's popped and slurred.

Selena looked around the hall at all the faces turned toward him: at her sister in her scarlet dress, at Rhea, big and powerful-looking, the roses on her shoulder glowing and casting their scent down the table, at Phyllis and Lola, so young, and Laverne, stout and growing old, and at Selma and Rena, a few years older than her, and into the first stages of menopause.

Thinking that without meaning to, she was startled. Of course, that was what was coming next. She thought back to her first menstruation. She wasn't sure how old she had been, but she remembered the occasion of it, the sensation, the shock and awe as she stared at the blood staining her panties, followed by a surging sense of well-being, of things being right. And now it was almost over. All those years passed like so much breath, come and gone. One day she had been a shy virgin, and then she was a woman, one whose life was rich and full, and all that blood, years and years of monthly bleeding, had brought her her children, her husband, a house full of things that spoke of the moments of her life.

At the centre of the hall three men appeared, dressed like women. They wore ridiculous wigs—platinum blonde, carrot red, and black—and their faces were painted like rag dolls—exaggerated red lips, rouged cheeks, swaths of green and blue eyeshadow, and foundation cream that barely covered their five o'clock shadows. They wore shiny, sequined dresses that came to their knees, leaving their hairy legs exposed, and their big feet were stuffed into high-heeled shoes. Their bare, muscled arms and hairy chests looked ridiculous emerging from those flashing dresses, as did the big fake bosoms and fat fannies made out of pillows. They were pretending to sing, miming a recorded top forty song that all the young women in the hall seemed to know. Some of the women were laughing, swaying in time to the music, some had dropped their heads as if they were embarrassed by this display, and a few were watching, holding their faces very still.

How many times had she seen men dress up like women? At mock weddings, at Hallowe'en, during Christmas skits and in parades, and at private parties. It seemed for every occasion some of the men dressed up like women, and now, suddenly, she wondered why.

Is that how men see us? she wondered? All bodies? All wigs and paint, all phoniness and artificiality? Are they ridiculing us? No, she said to herself. No, that's not it. Maybe it's a kind of admission of our beauty, a tribute.

The three men were almost at the end of their song. They rocked back and forth in unison, did a few, careful, mincing steps forward, then turned, wagging their behinds, and finally stepped back and threw their arms out in each other's face to the last notes of the song. All the women began to clap and shout.

"Didn't you like it, Selena?" Diana asked, an amused smile on her face.

"I don't know," Selena said, staring back at her, wanting to say something, but not knowing what.

"I don't see what everybody thinks is so great," Laverne said.

"They really had to practice to get that right" Lola said, a trifle indignantly to Laverne.

"It's just a joke," Phyllis said, although she wasn't laughing.

"But if we dressed up like them," Laverne said, "they wouldn't think it was so funny."

"It wouldn't be funny," Rena said. "There's nothing funn about men. Ask Ruth."

"You could imitate their deep voices," Phyllis suggested, grinning. She was having trouble separating her words. Too much wine, Selena noticed. "And the way they walk. That would be funny. I've seen people do it."

"Maybe they envy us," Diana suggested. Everyone stopped talking and stared at her.

"Envy us!" Lola said. "Are you kidding?"

"Well," Diana pointed out, "they're always dressing up like women. At twenty-fifths, every time we put on a skit, at Hallowe'en, in the parades. I can't even remember all the times."

"They mean it as ridicule," Rhea said, but her voice lifted at the end of her sentence as though she wanted to hear what this would evoke from Diana.

"They may think they mean it as ridicule," Diana responded immediately, "but you only ridicule people if you secretly envy them, or if you're secretly afraid of them."

"Oh, who cares," Laverne said, lifting her wine glass and drinking. "This is a party, a celebration, it's for us women, and we shouldn't waste it talking about men."

The women laughed uneasily, their eyes thoughtful, and Diana murmured, "They're up to something, even if they don't know what it is themselves."

The fashion show was beginning, and everyone set their chairs in new positions to see it better. One of the women who had organized the evening took the microphone and began to talk about the dresses as the models paraded slowly by, pirouetting now and then so everyone could see all the details of each garment. The waiters, husbands of some of the models and guests, leaned against the bar, sipping drinks, watching quietly, their work done for the time being.

The models weren't wearing high fashion clothes, just dresses from a local women's clothing store, and the models were not beautiful, only attractive, slim local women, but the men watched silently, deferentially. Selena wondered what they were thinking. It touched her to see them like that, she thought suddenly, how good men are, how strong and honourable.

"Oh, I like that one," or, "That's too young for her," or "That would look great on you, Diana," the women remarked, and clapped as each dress passed by, enjoying all of it, even though most of them wouldn't think of buying, much less wearing one of the dresses.

When all the dresses had been shown, the woman took the microphone again and announced that they had managed to persuade a furrier from the city to bring a selection of coats and jackets to their Ladies Night Out celebration. Everyone began to clap. This was almost too much. Fur coats! The very best of the models had been selected to show the coats and they began to parade up and down the hall, twirling and holding the coats open to show the rich satin linings.

There were classic dark minks and light minks, foxes, fashionable wolf coats. "Looks like coyote to me," Laverne whispered, and coats made of two kinds of fur or trimmed with leather. The music was louder now, and the women were almost stunned into silence by the noise, the liquor they had drunk, and the riches they had seen. Finally the last coat was shown and the furrier announced that all the coats were available for trying on backstage immediately after the program was over.

"And that marks the end of the evening, ladies," the woman said, back at the microphone. "Thank you all for coming, and don't forget those coats are for sale, and you can try them on now." Everyone clapped, then began to stand and move around to talk to each other.

"Should we try them on, Lola?" Phyllis asked, grinning. Lola giggled. "There's no way I can afford one," she said, "but let's. Come on," she said to the others. Selma shook her head, no, and began to talk to a relative who had been sitting at another table. Rena had already left.

Rhea said, "I'll wait here," and Laverne said, "Me, too."

"Come on, Selena," Diana said. "We came all this way, we might as well get our money's worth." Selena rose and followed her to the stage door.

"I'll never in my life be able to own one," she said to Diana's back, "I can't imagine why I should bother to try one on."

"You've got the height to wear one," Diana said. "It'll be fun just to see how they feel."

In the crowded space backstage the furrier stood protectively by his rack of expensive coats.

"Gently, ladies, gently," he said, as one by one they were peeled off their hangers and women helped each other put them on. There were squeals of pleasure, and murmurs of awe.

"Here, Selena," Diana said, and before Selena could protest, Diana had taken the full-length dark mink off its hanger and was putting it on Selena. She began to protest, but as the cool satin slipped over her bare arms and the thick fur of the collar settled against her hair, neck and chin, her words slowly died, and she was left standing by herself, feeling the weight of the coat, its scent, the silkiness of the fur. She felt as though she had never known such softness, such luxury, or been so close to such a world of grace. For a second, all the things she would never have, would never even know about, all the spoils of the feminine world came flooding over her and she felt loss, and sorrow at that loss.

She felt poor, poverty-stricken, small and without significance in this larger world she had glimpsed. Almost in tears, her face still buried in the sleeve, she tried frantically to think of what she had.

What came to her were the faces of her children, and the prairie that she knew so well, that surrounded their small ranch. And she felt a little better.

"Here," she said to Diana, "you try it on," pulling if off as fast as she could. She wanted only to leave, go home. Diana slipped the coat on, but it was obvious that she had little interest in it.

"I forgot about Phoebe!" Selena said suddenly. "I have to phone, I have to . . ."

"Take it easy," Diana said, taking off the coat. "Jason or Kent would have phoned if she had gone in labour."

"You don't know how Jason can sleep," Selena said, as the two of them squeezed past the other women on their way out into the main hall. "And Kent's not all that reliable. If he and Tony get talking . . ."

"We'll be home in an hour, Selena," Diana said. She pushed open the door into the hall. It was half-empty now, the waiters clearing tables while women stood in groups here and there and talked.

The main doors at the far end of the hall opened and a man came through and stood looking around. His parka was covered with snow. He was joined by a second man, also snow-covered.

"Oh, no," Selena wailed.

The first man began to speak, then raised his voice to be heard. Everyone in the hall stopped talking.

"There's a bit of a spring blizzard out there," he called. "It's not too bad yet, but I wouldn't hang around if you've got far to go." He stopped, apparently not wanting to be seen as giving orders. The women's voices rose again in dismay or annoyance. It was nothing to the town women, and most of the country women had friends or relatives they could stay with if necessary. But Selena thought of Phoebe.

"I've got to get home!" she said, hurrying toward where Rhea was rising now from her place, where she had been waiting. They went together to the cloakroom, and searched for their coats.

"I've got a funny feeling," Selena said, as she found hers and put it on. "I had it before I left. I knew I shouldn't have come."

"What's gotten into you?" Diana asked, annoyed. "Kent'll be with her by now. I'm sure she's just fine." She shrugged into her coat, then reached under her collar to pull out her long hair. It fell in a shiny cascade onto her shoulders. Selena looked at Rhea, who was being helped into her coat by a woman who happened to be standing near her.

"Haven't you ever heard of women's intuition?" Rhea asked Diana, her tone half-amused, half-serious. Diana hesitated for a second, looked at Rhea, then Selena. She turned then, and led the way to the door, which she held open for them.

Swirling snow greeted them, whirling down the street past the power poles, over the banked-up snow on the sidewalks, whipping around their nylon-clad legs and up into their faces. They pulled up their collars and shivered.

"I'll go get the car!" Selena shouted, her words swept away in a gust of wind. She hurried down the steps, slipped in the fresh, wet snow and almost fell. It'll be bad out in the country, she thought, if it's this bad here, and that man said it wasn't bad yet!

She was already starting the car as Diana and Rhea climbed in, and she pulled out of the parking place against the curb as the first of the other women emerged from the brightly-lit hall into the storm. A blast of snow billowed up, glittering in front of the car, then was swept away like a ghost.

"I hope those women who drank too much don't try to drive home," Diana said.

"There's a time for drinking," Rhea said cryptically, and then was silent.

Already they were passing the last buildings in town, starting out down the snowswept grid toward home twenty-five miles away. As soon as they left the protection of the buildings snow began to whip across the hood, driven by the wind with such fury that sometimes she could see a few hundred feet ahead, and sometimes she could see nothing at all.

"Look at the ditches," she said. "They're almost full. It must have started to snow right after we went inside."

"At least it isn't cold," Rhea said. It was true, the temperature had barely dropped, but the snow was wet, hard to get through where it had drifted across the road.

"I didn't even bring slacks," Selena said. "The sky looked perfectly clear," and of course, Rhea laughed.

"Put your lights on dim," Diana suggested. Selena struck the button with her foot and found she could see a little better.

"Just go slow," Rhea said complacently, "and you'll be all right."

"This damn country!" Selena said, aware she was quoting Kent, and then went on in her own words. "Sometimes I hate it!"

"Now, now," Rhea said. "You don't mean that. It's spring moisture for the farmers."

"Fuck the farmers," Selena said, and Diana laughed. She laughed so hard she sounded as if she was choking and they could hear her rolling around in the back seat. Selena had to laugh, too.

"For heaven's sake, calm down," Rhea said. "It won't help any if you drive us into the ditch."

Diana stopped laughing and settled into silence.

"How did you like Ladies Night Out?" she asked, after a bit.

"I liked it fine," Selena replied, hunched over the steering wheel. "I've never in my life done anything like it, and I've begun to think, just now, as we're talking, that it's something I've always wanted to do, only I didn't know it. It was good. It felt good."

"Funny," Diana said. "It was so different from the things you do in the city."

"What?" Selena was torn between straining to see the road, and listening to what Diana was saying.

"It was all about . . . pretty things," Diana said. "About the things we women seem to yearn for, or need, maybe. Our kind of women, anyway, who don't have much more than the necessities."

"It was a celebration," Rhea said. Her tone gave the word some special meaning Selena couldn't divine. Diana was silent.

"Oh, God, I wish Kent was here," she moaned, braking again. They were ten miles from town and the storm was getting worse. "We could end up spending the night on the road."

"No," Rhea said. That was all, just *no*. The wind screamed against the car, plastering snow against the windshield and then blowing it off again.

"My turn-off should be coming up pretty soon," Diana said.

"You might have to get out and walk in front of the car to find it," Selena said. She hadn't taken her eyes off the road, or what she thought was the road, for miles now and her eyes were blurring from the strain. She blinked hard a few times and they cleared. A wall of white descended in front of her, she braked, then touched the gas carefully again when it passed.

"Never mind her turn-off," Rhea said. "You'll get us lost trying to find it. Just keep going." Selena expected Diana to protest, but she said nothing. They kept inching forward, finding, when the wind tore rents in the sheet of white, that sometimes they were on one side of the road, and sometimes on the other.

Phoebe, Selena thought. Her hands, gripping the steering wheel, were sweating, the muscles running up the palms to her wrists were aching. Her coat felt much too confining and bulky, as if she might be able to see the road better if she weren't wearing it.

"We're almost there," Rhea said.

"What?" Selena asked, surprised. "How can you tell? I haven't seen a fencepost or a crossroads or a stonepile in the last fifteen minutes."

"I can tell," Rhea said calmly. "There!" It was so sudden and so loud that Selena slammed on the brakes, throwing them all forward and then back.

"Jesus, Selena!" Diana said, more ruefully than angry.

"There what?" Selena asked Rhea, angry with her again.

"The turn-off to your place," Rhea said calmly. Selena stared through the windshield but couldn't see anything in the darkness and the blowing snow. "Just back up a little and you'll see it," Rhea said.

"What if I back up into the ditch?" Selena muttered, but shifted gears and backed the car as slowly as it would go.

"Eighty years I've lived in this country," Rhea said. "I guess I know your turn-off when I come to it."

Selena had stopped the car again and was peering, mystified, into the storm. But there it was, the new fencepost Kent had sunk in the corner of the field when one of the neighbours had run off the road in the mud and snapped the old one off.

"Well, holy cow," she said, and sat for a minute in surprise before she shifted back into low. They started down the side road toward the house at the other end which had been swallowed up by the night and the storm.

Now Selena knew. Phoebe was in labour, and she was alone.

"Phoebe's in labour," she said, her voice low, filled with apprehension.

"What?" Diana asked, startled.

"I know," Rhea said.

BIRTH

Phoebe was in the kitchen. She had apparently been trying to phone because the phone was off the hook. The chair that sat under the phone was on its side on the floor and Phoebe was lying next to it, on her side, her knees drawn up, her eyes closed, her arms over her belly. Selena was on her knees beside her at once, reaching for her pulse, one hand on her forehead. Phoebe's face and neck were slick with a fine film of sweat, but her body was not clammy to touch, only warm, as it should be. But her slacks were soaked down to the ankles, and Selena, frightened as she was, couldn't suppress irritation with Phoebe.

At her mother's touch, Phoebe opened her eyes.

"It's coming," she said, and gasped, stiffening, tossing her head from right to left and back again. Her face contorted and she let out a grunting cry. Selena looked up at Rhea, who stood at Phoebe's feet.

"Calm her down," Rhea said. "I think she can make it upstairs to bed."

Diana crouched beside Phoebe, opposite Selena, and began to stroke Phoebe's damp hair, to lift it from where it was plastered to her face and neck, and to murmur to her, "It's okay now, Phoebe dear. We're here. It's all right now."

"Phoebe," Selena said, her voice crisp, "we're going to get you upstairs to bed. Do you hear me?" Phoebe gasped, grimaced, then, as the contraction passed, relaxed a little.

"Okay," she said, lifting her head a little. "Just let me . . . rest a bit."

"You can rest upstairs," Selena said. "We don't want your baby born on the kitchen floor. Now get up." Phoebe rose on one elbow, the other arm still holding her abdomen. Selena lifted and pushed on her left while Diana did the same on her right. They managed to help Phoebe onto her feet and start her moving down the short hall to the stairs. The next contraction came before she had put her foot on the first step, and she hung onto the newel post and cried out.

"When we get you to bed," Selena said, "I want you to stop fighting it, you're only making it worse."

"It feels . . . like . . . my bones are being . . . pulled apart," Phoebe gasped.

Selena held to her more tightly, but Diana said, both wry and grim at the same time, "I guess nobody's told her that labour isn't pain," and Rhea snorted.

"She's just scared," Rhea said, behind them, and Selena was surprised, had forgotten she was there. They had almost reached the top of the stairs when the next one came, and Phoebe would have fallen if Rhea had not been behind her, and Selena and Diana on each side, lifting and holding her upright.

"Thank heavens we changed all the sheets this morning. Her bed is clean and ready." Rhea gave instructions while Diana threw back the covering on the bed and Selena helped Phoebe undress.

"We'll need some scissors and some boiling water to sterilize them in and I guess . . . some old sheets, if you have some, Selena. We'll put them under her so she doesn't ruin the mattress. And where are the baby clothes and the blankets?" She looked around the room. On the other side of the window the wind howled and whistled and plastered wet snow against the pane. "I can't think of anything else," she muttered, her hands on her hips.

Diana had already hurried out of the room to collect the things Rhea had asked for. They could hear her opening and closing closet doors. Phoebe, lying on the bed with pillows propping her into a half-reclining position, began to moan and gasp. She clutched at her mother, tears smearing her contorted face.

"Oh, God!" she gasped. "I can't . . . stand . . . it."

"Tsk! Tsk!" Rhea clucked disapprovingly. Phoebe fell back, letting go of her mother, and Selena finished pulling off her wet slacks and soaking panties. Gently Rhea bent the girl's knees and spread her feet. Another contraction seized Phoebe and she reached out blindly, thrashing, as if to strike someone. Selena took her daughter's arms and pulled them down to her sides, smoothing her forehead with her palm.

"Phoebe, you've got to stop this," she said, her voice unexpectedly sharp. "I'm disappointed in you. You're not a child anymore. You're a woman—a mother—now calm down. Stop this nonsense."

"Get her to come down the bed this way," Rhea said, her voice still calm, as though she hadn't noticed what was going on between Selena and Phoebe. "Take those pillows out from under her now."

Selena obeyed, carefully lowering Phoebe onto the cool sheet. Phoebe opened her eyes. That old, inward-turning look that had so disturbed Selena was gone. The old Phoebe was there again, alert and fully present, only her body was in the lead now, speaking to her with an urgency that would not allow retreat.

"Having a baby does have a way of getting your attention," Selena said, laughing, tears blurring her eyes because Phoebe was at last returned to her, but Phoebe paid no attention, probably didn't even hear.

"Concentrate on your breathing, Phoebe," Rhea said. "Take long breaths now, and when you have to push, don't fight it. Push hard, the harder you push, the faster the baby will come." Phoebe had begun to push again, her mother murmuring encouragement to her, and holding her hand. They could hear Diana coming up the stairs, two at a time. She deposited three of Selena's sheets, folded neatly, at the foot of the bed, and as Phoebe relaxed, panting, they lifted her just enough to slide them under her.

"You took that class," Selena said to Diana. "Isn't she supposed to puff or something, at some point?"

"Honestly, that was three years ago," Diana said. "I don't remember."

"I don't recall puffing when I had my children," Rhea remarked, and the other two had to laugh. Rhea had rolled the long sleeves of her dress up past her elbows and her arms still looked firm and strong.

Diana said, "I phoned Kent and Tony," but Phoebe had begun to push again and she didn't finish what she was going to say.

"A long, deep breath," Selena instructed Phoebe. "Now let it out, slowly, slowly."

When the contraction released, Selena went into the bathroom and put a facecloth under the cold tap. It was cold in there, it always was, and she shivered in the blast of cold air that found its way around the old, worn-out window frame, then turned to go back to the bedroom.

Jason had appeared in the doorway, squinting in the light, his pyjamas rumpled and his hair standing on end.

"What's going on?" he asked, his voice thick with sleep. Selena didn't know whether to laugh or be angry with him.

She was about to tell him, but overcome by irritation, snapped, "Nothing! Now go to bed!" He put one hand up, the palm forward, to shade his eyes, trying to see her, then gave it up, turned, and went. She was impatient with him because the two boys had been so resentful of Phoebe's condition, as if she had done it on purpose to embarrass them, and because he had let her down tonight. But they were her sons, after all, and Jason was still more child than adult. She hurried back to the bedroom and sponged Phoebe's face with the cloth.

"I can see the baby's head," Rhea said, suddenly, and there was a new note in her voice.

"Push, push, that's it." Phoebe was responding now, working with Selena, she was going to deliver this baby. "It'll be over in a few minutes now. That's the way. You're really working now. Good." She bent and kissed Phoebe's wet cheek.

Diana said, "The weather's letting up. The men said they'd come right over on the snowmobile. I know that thing, they're probably having trouble starting it. They'll take her to the hospital on that sleigh thing Tony bought for the kids."

"No need for that!" Rhea said, not raising her head. "She's doing fine right here."

Phoebe was pushing again and Selena and Diana urged her on, praising her and encouraging her.

"Where's that water?" Rhea suddenly demanded.

"Coming," Diana said. She hurried to the door and was gone, her feet tapping hard and rapidly down the stairs. In a minute they could hear her coming slowly back up.

"The head's coming," Rhea said, and couldn't hide a little delight.

"Now work," Selena said, "work!"

"It's out!" Rhea said, as a moan escaped Phoebe, the first one since Selena had scolded her, and Selena put one hand on each side of Phoebe's face, and held them there. "I've got it . . . only a little more, Phoebe, dear," Rhea said. That rich, powerful scent of flowers filled the room and this time, as Selena became aware of it, it no longer seemed strange, but instead, fitting and right.

"Aaaah," Rhea said, and lifted up a squirming, slick little bundle, setting it to rest on Phoebe's stomach. Diana, still holding the basin of hot water, quickly set it down on the chest of drawers, fished the scissors out of the basin, and handed them to Rhea, who cut the cord, as if it were something she did every day, knotted it and handed the scissors back to Diana.

"What is it?" Phoebe asked, lifting her head, reaching down with one hand to touch her baby.

"A girl," Rhea replied. "It's a girl, a female child." Then she lifted the baby, holding it in one big hand. "Get me a clean, wet cloth," she said. Diana turned to the bureau, did something, then turned back again, handing Rhea a small, wet cloth. Rhea took it and wiped the baby's tiny face with it. She cried then, a good, strong wail and Rhea reached out, dropped the cloth and pressed the baby against her bosom, murmuring to it. Then Selena gave her a baby's blanket that lay folded on the chair by Phoebe's bed and helped Rhea wrap the child in it, and then they set the baby in the crook of Phoebe's arm.

"I have to push again," Phoebe said, alarm in her voice.

"It's only the afterbirth," Rhea said matter-of-factly, and bent over Phoebe again. Diana had picked up the child and was holding it, touching its little face with her fingertips, smiling at it, while Rhea muttered at the end of the bed. "Go ahead, there, nothing to it." The afterbirth came, Phoebe groaned, this time with relief that came close to pleasure.

Rhea gathered the sheets they had placed under her and, with Selena's help, thrust them into a garbage bag Diana must have brought upstairs. This surprised Selena. She had never thought of Diana as competent, able to look after things, and this revelation pleased her immensely.

"What a team we are!" she said, laughing, and Diana laughed, too.

"It's twelve, no five after," she said. "She must have been born at midnight."

"We should bathe her," Selena suggested.

"Time enough for that," Rhea grunted, fussing around between Phoebe's knees. "Hand me that basin and another cloth." Selena hurried around the bed and gathered the things Rhea had asked for, brought them to the foot of the bed and set them down.

Rhea began to wash Phoebe, and Selena protested, "I'll do it." Rhea moved back then, and let Selena wash her daughter while she and Diana returned the pillows to the bed, propping Phoebe up a little so she could see her baby better. Then Rhea sat down in the chair in the corner, folded her hands on her lap, and closed her eyes.

Diana was searching through Phoebe's drawers, looking for a clean nightgown for her. When she found one, she set it on the bed, took another cloth, and helped Selena sponge Phoebe all over. Then, together, they put the fresh gown on her and covered her, tucking the blankets in around the baby.

Finished, Selena stood back.

"Oh, good," Phoebe said. "I feel really good," and she smiled. "I think she's asleep," she said, looking down at her child. "Isn't she?"

"What are you going to call her?" Diana asked.

Without taking her eyes from the child, Phoebe said, "I didn't think of names." Diana opened her mouth as if to offer a suggestion, but Phoebe went on. "But I kept thinking, just now, I mean, that I could smell flowers— roses, I think." She laughed, looking up at her mother. "I know it's silly, but I thought I could. So maybe her name should be Rose. No, Primrose, like those little yellow evening primroses that grow out there . . ."

"Or the big, pink, gumbo primroses," Selena offered. Those ones that spring up in the most awful places, where the soil is terrible and absolutely nothing else will grow."

"Yeah," Phoebe said. "Primrose. I like that. Her name is Primrose."

"She's so beautiful," Selena said, and began to cry.

"Poor Mom," Phoebe said, "it must have been awful for you." Selena was amazed to hear so little regret, so little sympathy in Phoebe's voice. She stopped crying and looked at her daughter, but Phoebe had eyes only for her child. She has no idea what it was like, Selena realized, and blinked, floundering in her effort to get a grip on this. She saw now that she had been expecting the baby's birth to change things. But why should it? she asked herself. Growing up, understanding other people, takes a lifetime. One labour won't do it. Sympathy for Phoebe, for all that lay ahead of her, flooded Selena.

The women rose, straightened the bedcovers, picked up the wet towels, the basin full of water, the cloths and the garbage bag and the scissors, and left the room. Behind them, Phoebe drowsed, her baby nestled against her.

In the kitchen Selena put the kettle on to boil. Rhea and Diana sat down at opposite ends of the table, and Selena sat between them.

"I'm exhausted," she said.

"I feel great," Diana said.

"I am very tired," Rhea said. "I never thought I'd help deliver another baby. I thought I'd seen my last. I didn't know this was what I was waiting for." Diana and Selena looked at her quizzically, but she said nothing more.

"I was surprised at Phoebe," Selena said. "I never thought she'd make a fuss like that."

"Well," Diana said, "you can't blame her for at least lodging a protest with the gods for what was happening to her. It's a bit much, after all."

"That's true," Selena said, "but still. In this country we don't carry on like that. We just do it. There's no use making a fuss about it."

"Maybe we should," Diana said. "In Europe women yell and scream and everybody expects them to. It makes sense to me."

"Never," Selena said. "I'd never do that."

"There've been a lot of changes since I had my children," Rhea said, "in the way we think about having babies, I mean. What with birth control pills, and overpopulation, and all."

"Honestly," Diana said. "I don't know which is worse: the old 'having a baby is suffering and torment and pain,' or the new 'having a baby is fun, something the whole family can do together.'" They laughed at that.

"There should be some middle way," Selena said. "It's a natural function, it happens a million times or more every year, and yet, there's no denying it, each time it's not natural at all, it's a little miracle. It's hard to figure out the right way to deal with that." They were silent then, each lost in her own thoughts.

"Still," Diana said, "this is a great way to have your baby. At home, surrounded by the people who care about you, instead of strangers. And sort of, not such a mystery, if you know what I mean."

"I think," Selena said slowly, "the worst thing that ever happened to me was when I had Phoebe. I had to go to the hospital in the city because she was early and old Dr. Sanderwell was away. When I was in the labour room they put my feet up in those horrible stirrups . . ."

"God, I hate them," Diana said, suddenly furious.

". . . and they had these handholds for my hands. When I tried to move my hand to scratch my nose, I realized that they had put straps around my wrists, and done them up, so that I couldn't . . ." she gasped, then got control of herself, ". . . and my ankles were strapped, too."

"They did that?" Diana said, not in disbelief, but in horror.

Behind her, the kettle had begun to hiss, but Selena ignored it.

"I remember I got panicky when I realized what they had done to me—I thought," she swallowed hard. "I thought, if I don't struggle, I won't know . . . I'm a prisoner."

Nobody spoke. Selena became aware of the clock that had been their parents' and their grandparents' ticking steadily above the table. She listened to it. Rhea sat at the end of the table, remote from them, her eyes closed. Diana sighed.

Upstairs Phoebe and her child slept on, dreaming who knew what, their dreams forever interwoven. The wind had died down, and they could hear faintly, in the distance, the roar of a snowmobile racing over the fresh-fallen snow, coming toward them.

Dear Selena,

Here in the Yucatan peninsula, I have been travelling through the villages. My Spanish is getting quite good and I can manage pretty well. You wouldn't believe it if you could hear me dickering for food and a place to sleep. I'm riding around on a motor scooter, staying out of the way of the tourists and the tourist centres.

The Indians have a hard life. They are such a small people, I tower over them. They are very poor, and most of them still live in the old ways, growing a little corn and so on, and living in *palapas*, which are thatch-roofed houses with no doors or windows, only openings and with no furniture inside. At night they just string hammocks and sleep in them. During the day they roll them up. They cut wood for their cooking fires and carry water, which is in short supply here, and grind their own corn as they need it each day. They work extremely hard for the most minimal existence.

But they too, like us at home, live among their ancestors. New little clusters of huts sometimes grow up around stone ruins that their ancestors built six or eight hundred years ago. I think of our women at home in Mallard and Chinook, cooking meals for their families, washing their clothes, nursing their babies and singing them to sleep. Just like their grandmothers did. So-called civilization is drawing closer though. There will soon be fast food stands outside Chichen Itza. And I shudder to think what will happen to the people then.

The women here are very dark-skinned, with black hair drawn tightly back from their faces. They don't smile much and they seem to do the hardest work. Their costume is a short, white cotton dress. It has about four inches of embroidery around the hem—always a flower pattern in very bright colours—and there are no proper sleeves in it, just a square yoke which extends over the upper arms. The yoke is also covered in brightly coloured embroidered flowers. And the material the dress is made out of isn't thick and heavy. It's light and almost sheer. For all I know it might be a polyester blend. They wear a slip under it, I guess because below the hem for another three or four inches, there is a white eyelet frill with a scalloped edge showing. It is a beautiful costume.

The amazing thing to me is that these women all wear this dress, and they wear it all the time. I have seen a woman less than five feet tall, standing in her white dress while her husband loads onto her back a big bundle of sticks (cut neatly in equal lengths) for firewood, so heavy that she bends over with it. And women carrying buckets of water so heavy they stagger, and big ceramic basins on their heads full of grain or corn to be ground, all of them wearing that white dress with the flowers embroidered around the hem and across the chest.

The first time I saw it, I couldn't believe it, couldn't imagine the spirit that would make them produce some beauty that they could live with every day, even in that hard, unbeautiful killing life that they lead. It told me something about women. In fact, it made me think about that argument we had about the community college—about all those classes in embroidery and sewing and different kinds of crafts, and I was so contemptuous of them and of the other women, too. And none of you knew quite how to defend them, or yourselves. I see now what they were for, what they mean. And my respect for the women I grew up with has grown. I may not have been entirely wrong, but I wasn't entirely right, either.

I think of the North Amerian native women doing all that beadwork with quills and sinew, and our own grandmothers turning the quilts, which they needed to survive the winter, into works of art. As if they didn't have enough to do.

Even when you turn women into packhorses and slaves, it seems their craving for beauty, which has given light and strength and meaning to humankind, can't be extinguished.

I am going further south from here, into the camps for the refugees from Guatemala, and after that I will move on south again. I am going further and further into the jungle.

Diana